THE HALLOQUEEN

QUAKER'S WHARF
BOOK ONE

EMELINE QUILL

e-book ISBN: 979-8-9864400-2-6

Paperback ISBN: 979-8-9864400-3-3

To the girls who leave skulls out as decor year round, and for the bad bitches that know Halloween isn't a holiday, it's a lifestyle.

You're stunning.

BEFORE WE BEGIN

Dear Readers,

I was doomscrolling on TikTok one night and saw a few posts that included the life changing text overlay of;

"TAKE ME DOWN TO HALLOWEEN CITY WHERE THE GIRLS ARE GOTH WITH PUMPKIN SIZE TITTIES."

Never before has something resonated so much with me. The idea then spiraled out of control and what was supposed to be a quick novella detailing a fat girl getting railed at a Halloween store, spun out into a full-length novel and series about the town Quaker's Wharf.

Quaker's Wharf is a fictional place, but in my head is located about 15 minutes from Salem and experienced much of the same history. The town is a hub to what this universe calls "Others" which include all manner of monsters, beasties and thing that go bump in the night. Because of the presence of Others, this is a paranormal romance series. Don't know what that is? Well... we're going to do some monster fucking and we're going to like it.

Monster fucking not your thing? That's okay, this book weans you in with a very humanoid vampire. Give it a shot if for nothing other than knowing Thomas doesn't need air when he's getting his face sat on.

In addition to monster fucking, I have the mouth of a sailor and the sex drive of a teenage boy, so there's going to be lots of cussing, and some explicitly written scenes.

Because of such, this book is intended only for readers over the age of 18 who are skilled in the art of single-handed reading while socializing with fully charged best friends.

This book also includes mentions of;

- rejection sensitive dysphoria
- mental health issues
- ghosting
- mention of flunitrazepam, commonly called a "roofie" (no one is drugged)
- extensive discussions of consent
- blood
- a fat chick who loves the body she lives in. (please note if this is a trigger for you, you've landed on the wrong side of booktok.)

This is book one in a series of standalone contemporary paranormal romances. Happy Endings and a Happily Ever After guaranteed. Please enjoy your first trip to Quaker's Wharf.

Love,
Emeline

ANNABEL LEE
AN EXCERPT

But our love it was stronger by far than the love
    Of those who were older than we—
    Of many far wiser than we—

And neither the angels in Heaven above
    Nor the demons down under the sea

Can ever dissever my soul from the soul
    Of the beautiful Annabel Lee;

— EDGAR ALLEN POE

PROLOGUE
ANNABEL

I have never seen a problem that could not be solved with skulls, plants, or glitter. Got an outfit that just seems kind of boring? Put a skull on it. Wondering why your living room is dull? Go buy a plant. Need to kick some ass? Buy the glittery combat boots. Skulls, plants, and glitter are able to fix any issue if you water them down enough. In fact, any bad day can be easily reset with a $7 iced coffee, and a trip to the hardware store to steal fallen pieces of succulents for propagating. After all, you'd just spent $7 on watered down bean juice...who would have money for the plant after that?

Thanks to the latest trends, plants were readily available for purchase at any store, and shiny, sparkly, glittery things were never in short supply when you knew where to look. The trickiest part of living your Bad Bitch happily ever after would always be finding the perfect skull for the occasion. Especially in March.

It was an issue I'd had more times than one would think. When I opened my online boutique, HalloQueens, a few years ago, I hadn't expected that finding spooky items for my flat lays would be the frustrating part. I could curate the exclusive pieces and stock the decor; I could even manage the backend of the website all on my own, but I couldn't manage to find the perfect mercury glass skull or realistic looking black roses at a reasonable price to really bring the look together in the middle of Spring. And that just couldn't fly since my aesthetic was my brand. No, I had to stock up for dark February days when the skull inventory was high, and that would always be the Fall.

I'd had aesthetic obsessions since my formative years when I realized that while my friends were going through their Emo phase at the chain stores at the mall, easily buying baggy black pants with lace, or pinafores with tiny mushrooms, my fat ass was stuck going into the old lady store. The business-casual mass-market potato sacks left me a depressed tweenager who needed to figure out how to make a purple polyester wrap dress scream, "I could kick your ass if I wanted to" (P:S, the answer was fishnets, bitchin' jewelry, and the sparkly combat boots mentioned above). Did these challenges give me creative problem solving skills? Absolutely. But moreover, they gave me a drive, a purpose. Goals. I wanted to grow up and make a one stop shop for all the girls, gays, and theys to purchase their gothic bohemian looks, and be the one to provide equal access to alternative fashion through size inclusivity and gender non-conforming staples.

To help achieve these goals, I stole my grandma's sewing machine and cactus when I was 13. I did it while I was wearing a men's xxl black cotton tee that I'd cut and tied up the sides and puff painted a skull with hearts for eyes on. I remember because my Grandmother asked why I was wearing the failed art experiment and *why* couldn't I just be happy with the clothes that were my size! She never had a shortage of insults or backhanded comments regarding my size or fashion sense, but that day, instead of listening to another one of her lectures, I found the dusty machine in the closet, and the sunburnt cactus on the kitchen's windowsill. They both came home with me that day.

The cactus still sits in my sewing room, thankful to be loved and kept company. Her sewing machine, unfortunately, met a sad death-by-frat-boy in college when Gregory James got wasted and tripped on the chord, slamming the ancient beast to the ground. I was able to buy my first commercial sewing machine by selling overpriced succulents in aesthetically pleasing containers to the boho girls (see: glitter decoupaged terra cotta), born from propagated pieces of cacti from my grandmother's plant, and embroidering skulls and flowers onto their clothes. Like I said, I hadn't met a problem I couldn't fix without skulls, plants, or glitter.

But the problem was finding the right skull, plant or glitter for the problem. Which is why when the seasons turned, I knew I'd be at the Halloween Store more times than any rational human being. Spooky Season was the time where I could buy a skull for five bucks, or purple twinkle lights that ran off a usb port in a discount bin. At the Halloween store, I could find gelly pieces of blood splatter, or bats that were cute instead of anatomically accurate. I needed to stock up on everything I'd need for the following year's designs, lest I get to March and have to pay $34.99 for a pink skull that would match the spring's latest pencil skirt.

I'd planned on chatting up the owner, Andrew, who was the spitting image of Comic Book Guy from The Simpsons, in hopes of creating a relationship with him that would allow me to purchase more at the end of the season at a steep discount before he closed up shop. That was the plan, until I found myself leaned over the counter locking eyes with the most beautiful stranger I'd ever met in my life. His French accent melted all of my hard parts and I bloomed under the desire that danced in his eyes as he stared at my cleavage.

I thought it was well in hand and that it would be easy to get that discount, and was extra happy that the experience wouldn't be nearly as unfortunate as having to flirt with the smelly guy from high school. That's all I'd wanted. I just wanted the discount. I had never walked in there with the intention of becoming the infatuation of a 400 year old french vampire on the rebound. That had never been on my radar. Although, perhaps it'd be okay. If I got in over my head, garlic was a plant, and plants, glitter, and skulls could fix anything.

1

ANNABEL

Fat Girl Fall was, by far, my most anticipated launch of the year. Autumn, being the most sacred season to the plus-size woman, as we gather around bonfires to celebrate the passing of uncontrollable boob sweat and the rebirth of the pumpkin spice latte. I'd know. After an insecure adolescence, I enjoyed adulthood at a voluptuous size 22, so any relief from the sweat of summer could bring a smile to my face. I'd worked hard to overcome the insecurities caused by being the fat friend as a teenager, and reinforced my body positivity daily thanks to my brand, HalloQueens. I'd created an online boutique where people like me could make our outsides match our insides, and allow us to present ourselves with the confidence that comes from feeling great in our own skin. I'm fat, and I *love* it. Even more, I want others to love their fat bodies too.

I love the way my ass fills out a pleated skirt, or how my large thighs stretch a pair of fishnets. I love the softness of my breasts and how the fullness of my hourglass creates a delectable waistline. I love my body so much that I turned it into a career. HalloQueens exists to ensure that any chubby teen goth girl can fit into a black cat hoodie and every thicc sex goddess can channel their inner Morticia, like I wish I'd been able to when my confidence had needed it. That was how I'd chosen to live my life - just a fat Morticia, raising hell through fashion while patiently waiting for my Gomez to blow my mind.

My spring collection had sold out almost instantaneously after I'd gone viral with a try-on video where my cat, Tim, had crashed through the frame and jumped into the curtains, ripping them down and landing the rod on my head. Was that how I wanted to become internet famous? Absolutely not. But by monetizing my content and feeding into the lusty comment section, I was easily able to put down a year's rent on a small office space and I no longer had to operate out of my dining room. It only takes a single viral moment to change someone's life if they can tackle the aftermath correctly, and I had, so for the first time since opening HalloQueens my senior year in college, I was able to leave my home daily to work.

No one talked about how lonely and isolating working from home was - sure, there were some perks, but at least by leaving the house I could drive through for a coffee without having to put pants on *specifically* to do it. Also, my collection of adorable skirts had skyrocketed because apparently, the hatred of pants was not exclusively a work-from-home problem. Having a designated work space and time had created more scheduled content and the popularity of my brand grew so much seemingly overnight that I'd even needed to hire a friend to act as my assistant to help keep an efficient shipping turnaround.

I knew I was one of the lucky ones whose boutique didn't crash and burn as soon as my five seconds of fame ended, but I attributed that to my desire for inclusivity that I highlighted on all of my social media accounts. That, or it was due to the array of spicy and chest accentuating transitions I'd perfected that had a tendency to blow up. Either way, between my influencer income and the boutique, I also was finally comfortable and able to live without four roommates for the first time by leaving the city and moving back to Quaker's Wharf. I will admit that my moms have compared my monetized thirst traps to sex work, but sales are sales. Also, everyone wants a shirt that they think will make their boobs look like *that*, and dammit, I'd gladly send it to them in three to five business days up to a 6XL to afford a private row house sanctuary for me and Tim. We'd earned it.

Thirst traps had become my most successful form of marketing. So much so that I turned one of the storage closets in my office suite into a filming studio. It lacked natural light, being a closet and all, but I was happy to abuse my ring lights to stop myself from purposely bouncing my boobs by the windows. People can see me shake my ass on the internet all they want, but the idea of one of my neighbors catching me doing fifty takes of the same stupid dance while half-dressed was so cringe. This wasn't a huge city - I was going to run into people at the grocery store. Try buying bananas while Mr. Smith stares and licks his lips. We'll file the complications of thirst trap marketing under things they don't tell you in business school. Pro: Influencer money. Con: Mr. Smith thinking that I would ever be remotely interested in his banana.

The thirst traps had not only boosted sales, but my self-confidence had solidified. Sure, there were always the "you're killing yourself and others by promoting obesity" or "ur fat" trolls in my feeds, chomping at the bit to cancel me the second that "thin is back in" but those were the idiots who weren't buying my stuff anyway. Neither was Mr. Smith, but at least he was paying me by the view.

I'd come to love coloring my hair obnoxiously to match a specific item I wanted to promote, or having an excuse to put on thigh-high boots and enjoy my ass jiggling in all the right ways. Teenage me was proud of adult Annabel. Adult Annabel had worked hard to get to this point, and adult Annabel had 650,000 followers on one app alone. *Thanks for watching me shake my ass, friends! Link to the corset is in my bio!*

All this to say, I'd been working around the clock for the last two months purchasing inventory, taking photos, and doing back-end website work to prepare for the drop of over two hundred styles and decor items for Fat Girl Fall. I did this while exclusively living off of some pumpkin spice latte menu hack I saw on social media. Because how was I supposed to sell Autumn if I didn't feel like it was Autumn? It didn't matter that it was only the beginning of September - spooky season waited for no woman.

My days ran together, ebbing and flowing in stress level depending on how far away from a launch I was, and with Fall coming, I was living at the office in a constant state of anxiety wondering if this was going to be the launch that somehow cancelled my brand. My eyes were probably going to fall out from staring at the computer screen so much trying to make contingency plans for my contingency plans and hundreds of social media posts.

I only looked up from editing one such video post to see my friend and assistant, Shannon, stumbling into the suite with her sunglasses on and her short white pixie cut hair looking more fucked than spiked. Her extremely pear shaped body was squeezed into a pair of black leggings that must have been blessed by a priest to remain opaque over the globes of her ass, and she accented her slender shoulders with a tank and a flannel tied at her waist. "Good Morning, Shan - have a good night?" I asked her a little louder than I needed to, just to test if she was hungover.

She cringed at the volume and brought the palm of her hand to her forehead, so the answer was clearly yes. "Morning, boss." She headed over to her desk, which was always meticulously organized compared to my system of piles, and even took a moment to sani-wipe her worktop before hanging up her black patent leather handbag and falling into her extra wide pink chair.

I'd been so excited to find pink office chairs with a higher weight capacity, only to get totally bummed when they arrived and the chairs were labeled by the brand with something stupid about being for a husky giant on the back, so that summer I'd used my new vinyl machine and added "you like my ____" to cover that shit up. Shannon's chair says "you like my giant thighs." and mine says, "you like my giant tits." I felt it was a nicer addition to the workplace than sitting in a chair with *made with herculean strength* tattooed on my lumbar support. Bonus, the labeling helped us from accidentally taking the other's chair and messing with all the settings, thus making it an entirely functional addition to the furniture, and not at all about making us laugh. But if it was, I'm the boss, so whatever.

"I need to run to the store," I said to her as I loudly dropped my keys three or four times while gathering my things, trying not to laugh at her obvious discomfort, "I don't think all of the marketing props survived the move." Fat Girl Fall's launch was creeping up on us and I felt way behind on taking marketing images because of how many things got destroyed in the move from Chicago to my Moms' garage and then to the office.

Shannon nodded, wincing and holding her forehead with her stiletto-tipped red nails, "Oh I know, I found multiple broken styrofoam skulls and a whole lot of chipped spray paint."

"And that, my friend, is why we are no longer spray painting the same skull forty times a season for pictures."

In the early days of my boutique, every penny meant the difference between groceries or begging my moms to Cash App me, so to save a buck I'd spray paint cheap props before every photoshoot. It slowed my process down, but I always felt like the aesthetic of the brand was more important than my time. Once I reached the point that Hallo-Queens got hundreds of orders a week, I realized that my time was also money if I could have been working on influencer stuff instead of painting a foam skull. So adult Annabel needed to go buy an array of skulls and props from the Halloween pop-up shop and store them properly to stand the test of time.

The Halloween store opening was to me like what I assume the lighting of the town Christmas tree is to people who weren't raised by two pagan lesbians. And, thanks to millennial elder emos and gen-z witches, almost every store now carried spooky stuff in the fall, which has allowed me to hone the aesthetic of the brand even further.

"Do you need anything while I'm out?" I asked standing by her station.

A groan escaped her, clearly trying to alleviate the pressure in her skull, and she shook her head, causing the little white blonde spikes in her hair to dance like a porcupine.

"Are you sure? I'm happy to get you some greasy food or coffee. You're no use to me hungover."

"Oh god, Bels, I'm sorry. I didn't know when I went out last night that I'd be this hungover. It was karaoke night and my date was a little extra. Shots were had. Bad decisions were made. Journey was sung."

"Mmmmhmmm, and does that explain the hair too? Did you at least make the poor boy breakfast before you kicked him out?"

Shannon snorted and shook her head, her round face blushing to a shade of strawberry, "Of course not. I was at his house. *He* fed *me*."

I cackled and headed to the door, "alright, I'm heading out. I left a list for you of what I need done today. Drink some coffee, shake it off and get at it."

"Yes, boss. Love you!"

I headed towards my black jeep, admiring her freshly washed shine, and noticed Shannon closing the window blinds behind me. I'd known Shannon for about ten years, having met in a sewing class at the local fabric store the summer before I started college and we'd become quick friends. Now, at 29, I found myself back in my home-town to help care for my moms, and Shannon found herself a single mom of two in need of a flexible job. We reconnected over pastries and since she's the only adult I see regularly, so I supposed that made her my best friend. And by a regular basis, I meant at all. Since moving back to Quaker's Wharf, schedules, families, and traveling had made it near impossible to reconnect with anyone I'd known from before I moved to Chicago. My phone was full of thread after thread of canceled, rescheduled, and forgotten meet-ups. Being an adult was busy for anyone, but owning your own boutique and posting your ass on the internet four times a day was more time consuming than anyone would think.

I started my car and inhaled the scent of pennyroyal and sage emanating from the small herb bundle hanging from my rearview mirror and headed toward the shopping district. Our small Boston suburb has very segmented districts due to the historical sites around town. After all, it wasn't like the town would allow a developer to rip out a colonizer graveyard to put up a burger joint. Ergo, all the burger joints were on the outside of town, along with all of the shopping, which left the historic parts of the city to cater to the witch trial tourists and gave the locals a workaround so we could avoid said witch trial tourists. Cause, no, Deborah, I don't want to take a picture of you with your head on a chopping block while your husband "ironically" cheers in the background, I want to go buy toilet paper.

The layout of the town worked well enough. My office was in the in-between, not quite in the shopping district where the rent is astronomical and not quite in the city center where you have to have a retail front for the tourists to paw through your shit. Maybe someday I'd be able to manage a brick-and-mortar for Deborah to wander through, but for now, I was happy in my office suite spending my days shaking my ass on the internet to hawk pleated skirts.

I pulled into the abandoned big box building and avoided ocean-sized potholes, trying to find a safe place to park so I could go into the pop-up store, already fearing that my credit card was going to catch on fire. I was in desperate need of almost everything - fabric, skulls, flowers, bones, bats, netting... I couldn't even wrap my head around how much replacing all of it would cost, but thanks to Tim and the curtain rod, I was now firmly in the "spend money to make money" phase of my little boutique. There was nothing worse than finding an influencer who said they had an online boutique and then you clicked on their bio only to find a sloppy cash app site with grainy phone pictures - or worse, online stock photos. It made me want to shudder just thinking about it, and I refused for someone to think that about me.

It didn't help my credit card that I was just genuinely excited to head into the store for the first time this year. Adult Annabel in a Halloween store was about as bad as kid Annabel in a candy store. I tried to remind myself to stay focused and not go into a manic shopping spree with stars in my eyes and a crazy grin glued to my face, and to stick to list I'd planned. I was there on a mission. Buy the props, reintroduce myself to Andrew, flirt with him a bit, and mention the possibility of being able to order wholesale from him or purchase things at a discount at the end of the season. Get out of there and get back to work. I needed to keep my eye on the prize, and my lists were the easiest way to eliminate the distractions and keep my anxiety in check. I was easily distracted by shiny things.

I smoothed out my black skirtall dress and off-the-shoulder black and white striped crop top, pausing to make sure my leatherette choker with a black cat charm was centered, and triple checking I had business cards in my wallet. A spooky business boss should never walk into a Halloween store unprepared to borrow their customers. I snapped my knee-high socks to make sure there was enough of my fishnets peeking out between them and my skirt, and opened my car door. It was time to shop.

2

THOMAS

Opening day. How the fuck had I fallen so far from grace? How did I go from ⅓ owner of the Herses' Haunts, the number one walking ghost tour company in all of Boston, to commandeering a gods damned seasonal shop in Quaker's Wharf? I leaned against the counter and scratched my scalp, rustling the chin-length espresso strands out of their natural wave pattern, and sighed.

My hair was annoyingly shiny and kept catching my attention in my periphery, almost like my body somehow knew that mortals would be surrounding me for the next two months so I must be in peak predator mode. *Oh, look at the scary demon - he's so beautiful.* What I would give to look like hell for just a minute! I yearned to be able to look like the abandoned piece of shit I was. It was my first season alone in 230 years and I didn't want to be hunting for sources. I merely wanted to wallow in my heartbreak a little bit more. I wanted stained sweatpants and a beer belly. I wanted my outsides to match my insides. The magic that made me appear as a perfect lure all of the time was making me extraordinarily cranky lately, and that was saying something since I was never a particularly un-cranky kind of man.

I used a remote to turn on the LED open sign in the window and got myself comfortable for the ten-hour shift ahead. I took a moment to spin my fingers full of silver and turquoise rings and to scratch the disgustingly beautiful dusting of facial hair that was forever frozen in a perfect five o'clock shadow. I didn't want to be sitting on a wobbly stool in an abandoned shell of a store. All I wanted was to go read a book, have a drink and forget about my ex-partners, but *non*, I needed money, so I had to sell superhero costumes and slutty animal accessories to the insipid mortals of Quaker's Wharf. All. Damnsed. Day.

I didn't bother to look up when the bell rang, signaling the arrival of the first stupid human of the morning. I'd been open five minutes - who the fuck spent their days waiting for the Halloween store to open? Like that was possibly the best way to spend their time.

"*Bonjour*," I called out, picking up my worn copy of Edgar Allen Poe poems. Stereotypical, I know, but forgive me for missing the broody bastard.

"Good Morning," a woman's voice called back and I heard the carts rustle and clang as she removed one from the queue. The smell of sage slightly burned my nostrils, having wafted in with the woman, so I turned on my oil diffuser without even looking at it. I was always prepared. Some mortals smelled intoxicatingly delicious, but most? Most seem to have forgotten basic hygiene. The number of times I'd been assaulted by revolting body odors and garlic breath could be counted as cruel and unusual punishment. The fact that I was created to appear as a perfectly beautiful man, designed as a quintessential predator, and yet the gods expected me to hunt unwashed, greasy snails was almost insulting.

I didn't understand the need for my appearance to stand out in any room, it only drew unwanted attention to myself, especially when I prefer to be alone, but I also didn't understand the need for such a drastic gap in aesthetic between us. I hadn't even fed from a mortal in fifty years as I'd lost the taste for their unwashed flesh - hospital bags only for this guy - so why must I stick out like a fucking boy band member all the time?

Modern times were simpler for us and I appreciated the ease of ordering a set amount of blood and having it delivered in unmarked crates to whatever shop I was running at the time. We'd been doing it since the invention of the modern security system in Boston when it became dangerous to hunt. Blood delivery was safe and easy and kept us out of harm's way. Sure, there had been that one night when I'd been drunk off a bad bag and I scoured the streets of Boston to find a mortal to cure the burning thirst, but bad bags were rare, and that was the only one I'd personally come across. The experience only validated the expense of delivery when I was revolted by the salty tang of the mortal's sweat that mixed with the acrid droplets of his bottom shelf body spray. I'd never gone back to the hunt for a meal after that, but sometimes I did have to get my hands dirty as I did in my acquisition of this establishment. Murders were few and far between for me in 2022. I'd learned a lot of lessons over my time as a vampire. One certainly being the lack of mortal hygiene, and the oil diffuser worked for both stinky and alluring kinds of mortals and helped me stay level-headed.

"Hey, I'm so sorry to bother you, but can you point me towards the decor section? I wasn't expecting this place to be so big!" The woman stopped at the counter and her voice sent a snake sliding down my back creating a line of chill. From under my book, I could see the toes of black boots.

"There is a sign over there," I said, pointing without putting my book down at the eight-by-four banner hanging from the ceiling. I appreciated that when I acquired the franchise the man had already ordered everything from the shelves to the signage, and my only task had been to hire a crew to assemble it, a team to help run the store, and set up a cash register. I'd created many businesses in Boston, so the basic tasks were not new to me, but in our many years I'd always been the man behind the curtain. Monique had been the one to lead the mortals in dumbstruck awe at her beauty through the streets of the city, or the woman behind the counter to seduce them into spending more money. Yusuf handled whatever slack needed to be picked up. I handled the business. She was the face, he was the filler,

I was the fixer. It worked beautifully for us and yet, here I was, alone, sitting on this fucking stool, huffing essential oils and pointing at clearly marked signs while they were gods-only-knew where.

"Thanks," She drew out the word like I'd offended her, which, fuck off if I had, go buy your coffin-shaped glue-on nails and leave me in peace. "Hey," she spoke again, placing her hand atop the spine of my book causing me to release a small growl.

"What?" I snapped, before looking up and freezing at the lush ivy green eyes of the woman. She was of medium height and had obvious rolls and mounds under her fitted black dress. Overalls? Dress overalls? Whatever they were, they were fantastic on her supple form. Her clavicles were pronounced above her huge bust and she had a black metal outline of a cat's head sitting directly on her jugular.

"Hi, good morning, are you the owner?" She asked, assessing me quickly, at least I'm sure she thought it was quickly. Her evaluation from my hair to belt probably only lasted a moment, but I saw the entire judgment pass over her face, first curious, then attracted, then confused, and finally accepting.

"*Oui*," I said, dropping some of the bite from my tone. Her curled purple hair was half up on the top of her head and held in place with a black scrunchie. Were scrunchies back? She had distinctive black eyebrows that, along with her eyes, seemed to have a line drawn around them to accentuate them. Monique no longer had to apply makeup, which had overjoyed me when she was able to stop powdering that thick lead shit all over her skin and subsequently getting it all over me. "How can I help?" I asked, giving one more glance down to her enormous bust. *Merde.*

"I just wanted to introduce myself since I will probably be in here a lot." The woman said, extending her hand, "I'm Annabel Williams. I own an online boutique that specializes in alternative fashion and I use a lot of Halloween decor as props. I have no doubt I'll be in here a million times to try and get everything I need for the season."

Her hand was warm, and she flinched slightly at my cool skin when I placed mine in hers. "*Bonjour*, Annabel, I am Thomas Corbin. Welcome to my shop."

She arched one of those black brows slightly and gave me a closed-mouth smile, "You're not Andrew. He's been running the Halloween store here for years - you run him out of town or something?"

I smirked, remembering how his end had felt like crushing an ant, "or something."

She laughed sweetly and reached behind her to pull her hair to one shoulder, exposing a tantalizing neck that somehow didn't smell of the sage she brought in with her. A new scent of ginger and citrus wafted from her skin and my cock immediately twitched in my pants. Well. That was unexpected. I hadn't come to attention in a very long time.

"You'll let me know if you should require any assistance, Annabel?"

She nodded and a slight flush spread across her pale cheeks, "Yeah, absolutely."

I tilted my head slightly, following her gaze to my jaw, and released a smile, allowing my two faint dimples to indent my cheeks, wondering if I could work out a different kind of frustration with her. "Forgive me, Miss Annabel, but you are quite beautiful. I am having a hard time not staring."

Her eyes widened in shock and she took half a step back, laughing, "well, it appears they don't lie about French men being flirts, huh?"

"Depends, who is *they?*" I leaned forward, placing my tattered book face down between us, which she glanced at.

"You like Edgar Allen Poe?"

"He knew how to set the mood, *non?* The man understood the importance of ambiance."

She smirked again, "that's very true. Well, nice to meet you, Thomas. I'll be right back with far too many goodies."

"Looking forward to it, Annabel." I tracked her as she disappeared into the stacks, heading toward the back of the store, and by the stars above, that peach of an ass looked juicy enough to bite. I tried to go back to my book, as boring as it was, seeing as I was with the bastard when he wrote most of it, but the girl. The scent. The ginger and citrus attacked my senses like a dinner bell, causing my fangs to elongate and my mouth to salivate.

I jumped up and quickly moved behind the wall of curtains that separated the Halloween area from the giant shell of the department store, and took a quick selfie. Sure enough, my eyes had darkened and my teeth were visibly sharper. *Merde.* I couldn't remember the last time that my body reacted to a mortal. I hadn't even met anyone that aroused me other than Monique and Yusuf, and they...well, they certainly kept me busy enough to hold my attention for two centuries. Since they disappeared eleven months ago I hadn't had any desire for companionship, let alone the desire to slake the needs of the flesh.

I took a few deep breaths, hoping to soothe the urge to go slam the woman, Annabel, into the stacks and ravage her body and blood, but her scent continued to fill my lungs despite knowing she had to have been at the other end of the store by then. Her fragrance was pushing my senses to go into overdrive and for the first time in hundreds of years, I felt the beast vibrating within me, pulling my body in her direction, causing my feet to move on their own. What he wanted with her, I could only hope was manageable during these daylight hours when I had a part to play, but he did tend to have a mind of his own. The ginger and citrus had woken that feral piece of me like smelling salts, and he'd made it clear that we needed to talk to Annabel.

3
ANNABEL

Holy fucking shit-on-a-stick. Frenchie was hot. Slimmer than what tended to draw my attention, but defined muscles were apparent on his trim figure and his hair was so shiny. Like, ridiculously shiny. Would it be weird to ask a hot guy what conditioner he used? Dear God.

I walked to the back of the store, making sure to sway my ass a little more than usual. My initial plan had simply been to flirt with Andrew as I had in the years before I moved. Andrew had been awkward around women, mean around men, and impatient with children. His wonderful attitude was accompanied by him frequently glistening with sweat and having very poor teeth and thinning hair. I'd gone to high school with the guy, so I knew I could seal the deal with a couple of boob shirts and slight touches to his arm since he had zero game. Now I needed a new plan. No way was a Frenchman going to be seduced by a glimpse of decolletage. I came to the wall of skulls and stared absentmindedly. What was a guy that looked like that doing running a Halloween pop-up store? Even sitting I could tell he was tall and his inhumanly shiny brown hair had subtle waves that framed his chiseled face. That very distracting face housed piercing brown eyes so

19

deep they were almost black, perfectly thick and groomed brows, and a delectable dusting of stubble along his jawline. He should be a model, or an actor, not...replacing Andrew.

What in the absolute fuck?

I picked up each skull, feeling its weight for quality, and assessing the textures. For photos, it was important not to just have coordinating colors, but the texture of it mattered as well. I didn't want to spend hours editing out reflections and smudges in photos, but I also didn't want them to get covered in lint. The amount of time I spent thinking of these things was truly exhausting and slightly ridiculous considering it was hotter than hell in the stuffy store, and my overactive mind was assessing the merits of velour skeletons. Shopping for skulls with boob sweat was not for the faint of heart.

I grabbed one covered in spikes and held it at different angles to see if they would even be noticeable in photos or if it would just look like a shiny silver ball, before putting it back and grabbing a black rhinestone one.

"You take your skull shopping very seriously, *mon coeur*."

I jumped and turn to see Thomas leaning against a rack of fake candles and squeaked, "Jesus, you scared me. I didn't hear you coming."

He moved his long arms to put his hands in his pockets and gave me a sly smile with a small shrug, "I'm sorry. I didn't mean to frighten you, I just...why are you fondling my inventory?"

A laugh erupted from me, "I'm not fondling them, I'm...assessing them."

He raised a single brow, "is that what the kids are calling it nowadays? Your hands are all over them, *non?*"

I put the black sparkly skull in my cart along with several solid-colored ones in various sizes. "At least I'm taking them home with me?"

"It is the least one should do when they fondle someone. As long as it is consensual fondling, that is."

I blushed, "I look at them so closely because I use them in photos to sell clothes. I don't want them to be cracked or chipped and then spend the rest of my life photoshopping a sliver of black porcelain back into place."

"Ah, that makes sense. Though, I don't know if I should be insulted that you believe I'd stock subpar skulls during their busiest season."

I leaned down to grab a pink to purple gradient skull with silver glitter eyes from the bottom shelf and squealed, "Eeee! This is perfect! Look at her, she's gorgeous."

"Not as beautiful as you, *mon coeur.*"

Scoffing, I gently placed it into my cart, "you went from angrily telling me to read the signs to calling me beautiful real quick, didn't you, Thomas?" I took a few steps into the next aisle to grab various netting and confetti and he leaned over the chest-high shelves to continue flirting.

"Yes, well, I hadn't looked at you yet," His bright smile was the most playful one I'd ever seen, creasing two dimples into his cheeks and making his eyes sparkle.

"Mmmm," I hummed, "So you admit that you're only nice to pretty people? Is that supposed to make me feel special?"

"*Oui.* Most customers are...shall we say...a little ripe around the edges. You, *mon coeur*, are perfection."

"You are shameless!" I laughed and walked back to my cart to place the items inside.

"*Non*, just French, *mon amour.*"

I stopped a couple of feet away from him and took a few obvious sniffs, finding that I couldn't quite smell him. He didn't smell bad, but I couldn't figure out what his scent was either. As he was the one pushing the line, I decided to play into it. Maybe my Andrew plan would work just as well on Thomas? "Thankfully, you aren't ripe around the edges either."

"If you wish to smell me, amour, come closer so you can get the full affect," I caught him looking me up and down and I popped my hip, placing my hand on it to accentuate my waist.

"Thomas, I've known you for about four minutes. I don't know if we are ready to start huffing each other."

"And yet, you're blatantly smelling me like I'm your favorite tea. I am not just a piece of ass for, what is the word.... oggling! Unless you're into mutual oggling, then by all means continue so I can enjoy oggling you as well."

I snorted and headed back towards the front of the store with my cart, grabbing random goodies as I went, "Come on, I need to get back to work."

"And where is work? Here in Quaker's Wharf?" he asked as he walked behind his makeshift desk.

"Yes, are you from around here?"

He raised his shoulders in a slight shrug, "I am from lots of places, but yes, currently I find myself here." He scanned a few of my items and then asked, "where do you go for fun around here?"

"Fun?" I asked "Like a bar or something? I know a lot of people -"

"*Non*, Annabel, I wasn't asking about other people, I was asking about you. Where do you go for fun?"

I fumbled a bit in response, "who said I have time for anything fun?" Thomas finished ringing up my items and I couldn't help but cringe at the total - I knew I could afford it, but it still hurt after years and years of scrimping to barely make it through. To spend hundreds of dollars on decor was just...terrifying. "Eww..."

"What is wrong?" Thomas asked, furrowing his brows, "Did I come on too strong?"

A blush burned through my skin and I nervously shook my head, "oh no, no. It's a me problem. Don't worry about it."

"*Bonne*. So where can I take you tonight?"

I laughed again, swiping my card, "Who said I'm going out with you, Thomas?"

"I thought we were heading that direction, what with the huffing each other, as you called it. I thought I'd risk coming on strongly, before you walk out of here and I spend my day worried that I'll never see you again." He pushed his long charcoal sleeves up over his forearms and my blood heated. I could never help myself around a nice set of forearms, and I was hardly subtle as I stared at his defined muscles with a thin covering of dark hair and corded veins on them.

"Uh..." I shook my head, trying to snap out of it, "Thomas..."

"Give me your number at least, *amour*, if you need longer to get to know me before braving the real world together that is fine, but at least let me text you until you can no longer resist my intense french charm," He handed me my bags and I hesitated.

I hadn't dated since coming back to Quaker's Wharf, having tried in Chicago and found that it distracted me too much from my work, and with Fat Girl Fall coming up there was no way I'd have time to pursue anything. ...But, then again, this was probably his busiest time of the year too. What was the harm in a little text flirting to get under his skin? *Do it for the discount, Annabel. Sink your claws in.*

"What the hell," I shrugged and extended my hand, "give me your phone."

Thomas glowed with victory and handed over his beaten-up phone that was at least four years old. I typed in my number and hit call, waiting for the intro of Steve Miller Band's *"Abracadabra"* to begin playing from my purse before hanging up and handing it back to him.

"Don't make me regret that, Thomas."

He gave me a perfectly mischievous lopsided grin, *"Moi?* Never, Annabel. I shall talk to you soon."

"Yeah... talk to you soon," I grabbed my bags and headed toward my car, feeling intensely like I'd forgotten something, but I knew I had everything I came in with. It was like my body didn't want to leave the store, but I carried on, getting back to my Jeep and climbing in, putting the bags next to me in the passenger seat. I shook out my hands and took a cleansing breath. Why was that so intense? That shouldn't have felt that crazy, I was just buying things from his store and flirting a little. That's all it was. It shouldn't have felt like a defining moment.

———

When I returned to the office, Shannon still had it darker than the Bat Cave and I found her hiding under her desk doing work on her phone, which was set to dark mode.

"What the hell, Shannon, how much did you drink last night?" I asked, "It's like two in the afternoon and you're still a zombie."

"I'm not *still* a zombie," She groaned as she stuck her head out to look at me, "I'm just...pregaming the fact that I'm going to absolutely be a zombie tomorrow."

I plopped into her chair, 'What are you talking about?"

She beamed, and if there was any light in the room, I thought that I'd see her blushing like a schoolgirl, "he asked me to go out again tonight. The girls are with their dad, so I think I'm going to do it."

"Two nights in a row? Doesn't that send the wrong message?" I opened her desk drawer to her stash of chocolate bars and handed her one and opened my own, "Besides, I thought you said the guy was extra."

She shrugged and opened the chocolate, releasing a small moan as it melted in her mouth, "he was, but the cringy karaoke was before I saw his enormous dick."

I cackled, "Okay, but how can you trust your judgment? If you were so drunk that a cringe guy became a hookup, how do you know that it wasn't just a jumbo crayon down there?"

She ate another piece of chocolate, "If it was, he knew how to use it and that's what matters."

"Again, how do you know you weren't just so drunk you *thought* he knew how to use it?"

"Fine, bossy, if you want to screen him for me, come out with us tonight. If he doesn't pass your test I'll drop him and continue fucking my way through town."

Laughing was natural and easy with Shannon. She had no filter and no shits left to give when her daughters weren't around, and I loved when she was able to turn off mom mode and turn back into a young professional, and since she'd entered her ho phase, I enjoyed her even more. I'd had several serious boyfriends, and I dated and hooked up with my fair share of men and women in college, but I'd never had the balls to do it with someone in Quaker's Wharf as an adult. Something was unsettling to me about fucking where you ate. I didn't want to hook up with some horrible lay from 7th grade and then run into them at the gas station for all eternity. Quaker's Wharf had more than enough tourists if I ever got brave enough and needed a fix, but townies were not my typical fare.

"I can't, Shan, you know I have to get everything ready for the launch. I feel like I could work around the clock for the next week and I still wouldn't finish."

"You do know that there's such a thing as overworking right? Come blow off some steam and then on Monday you'll be able to come in and kick some ass. Take the weekend off. Your list will still be here on Monday."

"Oh please, you've been hiding under your desk for your entire work day, I've got to do my work and everything you weren't able to do today," I scoffed.

"Bels, come on. Come out with me. I only get six weekend days a month to let my hair down, let's go have some fun." I skeptically grimaced and she pushed on, "the kids are at their dad's two weekends a month. You can come let your hair down for those and work yourself to death the other 24 days. It's balance. When was the last time you even went out for a drink?"

I shrugged, "I don't know. I'm still settling from the move."

"Yeah, but you grew up here, it's not like you don't know where to go or who's going to be there. Come on. Go with me. Please? Please? Please?" She gave me a perfect impression of her oldest daughter, Annie's whine.

"Ugh, where are you going and when?"

"Witchcraft."

"The club downtown? It's tourist season, are you insane?"

"Hey, the drink specials are good and it's easy to get lost if you need to bail on someone." She grinned, "Please come, Bels?"

"Fine. But I'm not paying for parking so you're paying for my rideshare."

"Of course! I'm getting ready at your place anyway."

"Oh, are you?" I raised my brow at her.

"Obviously. You have shorter skirts than I do."

I laughed, "If you need something to wear, go to the storeroom and pick something out. You know all you have to do is leave me a list of what you take."

"We should wear stuff for the new launch to get some attention. Couldn't hurt, right? A drunk girl stumbles up and is all 'Oh Em Gee, I love your dress' and we can be like, 'thanks! It's from HalloQueens, here's a card' and then BAM - tax deductible drinks. It's a foolproof plan."

"That's not how it works."

"Shut the fuck up. Let's go shopping." She crawled out from under the desk on her hands and knees, stood awkwardly, and headed toward the inventory boxes with a little spring in her step. "Also, let's go home early. I'm meeting him at five, so I'd rather go get freshened up and stuff."

"Shannon, you got here late!" I scolded her, not actually caring if we ducked out a little early on a Friday.

"Come on, boss!"

"Fine, but I get to wear the black skater skirt and the sheer and solid dotted tights."

"Lame! Fine." She started looking at the pictures on the boxes trying to find different styles to try on.

"You shop, I'm going to go film a few more posts and schedule them so if I'm hungover it doesn't kill my algorithm."

"Seriously? You can't just exist without thinking about work? It's Friday night, no one is looking at their feeds."

I gasped loudly in mock outrage, "HalloQueens is my baby! I can't even take a shit without worrying about it. Give me half an hour to film and then we will get out of here to go get ready. I'd rather have too many posts than not enough. Deal?"

"Fine, fine... your ring light is by my desk."

I stopped and slowly turned to her, "and why is my ring light by your desk?"

She froze and gave me a coy smile, "don't ask questions that you don't want answered, boss."

"God help me."

4
THOMAS

I'd lost my mind. I'd positively lost my mind. Since Annabel left the store that morning, I had talked myself out of texting her half a dozen times. The thirst she ignited within me was all-consuming and the ridiculous teenagers coming in and out of the store trying to steal eyelashes and plastic fangs had burnt my fuse to nothing. If I wasn't careful, I would end up hurting someone. Not that I'd eat them - let's not forget the body spray incident, but if someone pushed me too far I would snap, and subsequently snap them in half.

I'd finally called uncle at six, closing the store an hour early, and retired to the curtained area where I'd blown up a double high air bed to crash. I had everything I needed, my game console, tv, a fridge full of blood bags, and a place to sleep, but it was a far cry from the luxurious row house in Boston that Yusuf, Monique, and I had shared for many years. We'd each had our own room as well as a shared primary suite with a custom-made bed for the nights where we all wished to lay together. I remembered that Monique had commissioned it specifically to feel like you were sleeping on a cloud, but firm enough that you could fuck as hard as you wanted without sinking into the foam. Memories.

Contrary to popular young adult fiction, we could sleep. A lot of us had adapted over the years to stay up overnight since it was easier to hunt in the dark, but we certainly didn't explode in daylight. Well, not my kind anyway. The Dracula type, called the Undead, existed and could only come out at night, turning into a bat to sleep in dark hidden spaces during the day and was repelled by spiritual items, but we weren't locked into the same rules as them. An Undead was merely a vampire that had lost its balance and was deteriorating into dust. A vampire could be born from an Undead and become Undead themselves, or they could become an Undead from a lack of harvesting. Monique, Yusuf, and I were known commonly as Vampires, and our lives were entirely dependent on harvesting a delicate balance of blood and energy to refrain from turning Undead. The energy of mortals, either emotional or physical, needed to be harvested to maintain balance, and to be able to remain in the daylight. It also made us a little more indestructible than our decrepit counterparts. Falling to the Undead had been on my mind a lot since my partners had left, often fearing that they'd met that fate, or that without them back, it would be me that did.

Just like the movies, if bitten, a mortal could turn into an energy vampire, but anything was able to fall down the path to the Undead. Unfortunately, Undead vampires could bite mortals or Other creatures and turn them immediately into another Undead, making Others unwilling to mix company. For now, the store was a perfect front for energy harvesting as I could transfix patrons long enough to drain them and send them on their way without having to hunt.

I never killed on an energy harvest, but I would take enough to make someone tired or depressed through light touches, like handing someone their credit card. Monique always preferred sexual energy, harvesting lust, and fear during the haunted walking tours or by going clubbing with Yusuf where they could get blood and lust simultaneously. They always wanted me to join them, but as comfortable I was in our triad, harvesting random lust always felt uncouth to me. It made me feel dirty, like I was inviting any mortal into our bed.

I laid on the air mattress, drinking a bag through a straw, and remembered how Monique would stumble into the house, reeking of booze and dark lust. I'd never been able to sleep next to her on those nights. The number of times she came home high on lust that had spurred from bad intentions made me uncomfortable. Sure, they probably prevented something bad from happening, and Yus always claimed that the nights they'd harvested dark lust resulted in the most mind-blowing sex for the two of them, but I couldn't. I wouldn't. I didn't want that energy in my body.

Between the curiosity eating me alive in desperation to know more about Annabel, and remembering her ginger and citrus scent, as well as the potent perfume of young and dark lust on Monique, my cock was aching. I hadn't enjoyed bodily pleasures in a year, since before they left, and I'd had no desire to touch myself apart from a few angry instances in the shower where I imagined myself fucking Monique's deceptive throat so hard she was crushed against the tile, but the release never felt good - it just left me hungry and in need of more energy.

My mind wandered and my usual image of Monique melted away to one of Annabel on her knees. I quickly opened my phone and searched the internet for Annabel Williams. The page rendered the HalloQueens boutique website she'd mentioned as well as multiple social media platforms and news articles praising the inclusivity of the brand. I clicked on her most active social media channel and, by the moon, if my heart could beat, it would have stopped. There, on the internet, for everyone to see, was Annabel's delicious body.

Hundreds of videos scrolled across my feed showing her dancing, lip-syncing over sounds, and doing mini fashion shows. She must have been wearing her boutique's clothes in them all since it was the official HalloQueens page, but fuck. A mortal woman had no reason to look that tantalizing. A notification popped up, showing that she had just posted a new video and I clicked on it to see her dancing in a loud bar. The text laying over the clip stated that the HalloQueens were at Witchcraft in downtown Quaker's Wharf wearing some of the new fall line, and if you found them, you'd get a code to a pre-sale of their autumn line's launch.

I had no interest in a coupon code for women's clothes, but when I tapped to the next video, I was greeted by Annabel's plump behind. I could feel my dick straining against my zipper, suddenly desperate for attention, and feeling as if the last year of missed ejaculations had to be remedied in the next few moments or I would explode. I watched clip after clip of her ass in pairs of cheeky panties with her thumbs pulling them higher onto her hips and looking over her shoulder while biting her lip. I devoured every dimple and stretchmark over her luscious cheeks and curves, feeling the beast in me rattle his cage again as if I was no better than a newborn, ravenous for energy and blood while giving fuck-all about the consequences. Sliding to the next video, my fangs elongated watching Annabel spin in a skirt so short that you could see the bottom curve of her ass. I couldn't contain the possessive growl that emerged from me when I paused the image to get a better look at the giant tattoo on her meaty thigh. My girl. *Mon coeur*. She had a fucking raven tattoo. I was literally branded onto her skin and she didn't even know it. My ears roared and the beast slammed against his cage with desperate snarls. I couldn't stop the word from tumbling out of me, for I knew it was true down to my very bones.

Mine.

5
ANNABEL

"I can't believe he stood you up!" I shouted at Shannon, "You must be a shitty lay!"

She threw her head back in a laugh, "He did not stand me up, he's running late, there's a difference!"

We had been at Witchcraft for over two hours and were already well on our way to being hammered. We had filmed a couple videos for our feeds stating where we were and had multiple people come up to us for coupons and to buy us drinks. Who were we to turn down their generosity, especially if they were buying top shelf?

"Who is this guy anyway to blow you off on a Friday night?" I yelled into her ear as we danced against each other in the middle of the crowd of tourists.

"He isn't standing me up, Bels! Don't be such a pessimist." I scoffed and turned around to grind my ass into her so I could finish my margarita and she was so comfortable with my body that she rested her hands on my plump ass and gave me a playful squeeze. "You should get laid tonight Bels!" She hollered.

"Mmmm, pass," I replied, spinning back around and wrapping my arms around her neck, "If you're not getting laid, why should I?"

"Because he is not standing me up! I am getting laid!" She groaned and grabbed her phone from the pocket of her skirt, "Ha! He's here! Told you! Now go find some ass while I go get mine." We both wove our way out of the pit and up to the bar so she could stand on the rungs of a stool to try and see through the crowd better, "Ah! There he is! I'll be right back."

I smiled and shook my head. Who makes the mistake of hooking up with someone you don't want a relationship with two nights in a row? *Hello, red flag, my name is desperation, what's yours?* I flagged the bartender my way and crossed my arms over my bust, pushing my breasts up inside the sheer spider web crop top I'd thrown on over a purple bralette. I looked smoking hot and it only made me more excited for the launch. Everyone deserved to feel this good when they went out.

"Hello, Beautiful, what can I get for you?" The bartender was cute in that preppy beach guy way, but not my type. It seemed like every Harvard prep fuckboy had a fantasy of hooking up with the goth girl, so I was constantly being hit on by Michael Paul Georgerson Fartface III and had zero desire to reciprocate.

"I'd like a pineapple upside-down shot please," I grinned at him.

"Coming right up."

"You can put it on my tab." I turned to see who offered and was shocked by the guy from the Halloween store coming up next to me and placing his hand on the small of my back, "*Bonsoir, mon coeur.* Fancy meeting you here."

"Thomas! What are you doing here?"

"I was just dropping off fliers when I noticed you ordering a drink. I figured now I ought to stay for a few myself." I assessed him and noticed that his hair was still perfectly voluminous and shiny. So fucking unfair. I'd already had to dry shampoo twice to combat the heat and humidity. He was wearing a button-down with the sleeves rolled up and the first three buttons undone, showing a glimpse of his sculpted chest.

The bartender slid me the shot, complete with a cherry, and I quickly downed it before turning back to him, "I'm here with one of my friends. She just went off over-"

"Bels! Fuck, I've missed you, gorgeous!" I was suddenly swept up into a giant's arms and for a moment my booze-idled brain wondered if somehow Thomas had lifted me, but when I blinked, I saw that he was still in front of me, but his eyes had darkened and he was wearing a fierce scowl. I pulled back from the warm body and couldn't keep the shock off my face.

"Trae! Oh my god. What are you-"

"Gosh, sorry, someone stepped on my shoe and broke the fucking heel," Shannon limped up next to Trae and leaned against him, "Did Trae introduce himself yet?"

Trae. Of course, it was Trae. Trae held the distinctive honor of having taken my virginity with fumbling hands and the aid of the cheapest bottle of vodka we could get the college kids in Salem to buy us on Dead Horse Beach. Cause nothing quite says romance like equine spirits! We'd been fifteen, I thought we were in love, but then when the rest of the lacrosse team found out that Trae had slept with the fat chick, he had quickly declared it a joke.

Unfortunately for Trae, I was armed with the knowledge that the whole encounter lasted about 63 seconds and he was so panicked after, and that he thought I'd know whether or not I was pregnant the next day. He was shocked to discover that the female reproductive system didn't work that way - yay for public schools! He had cried next to me while I put my clothes back on about how there was no way he was ready to be a father. It was...embarassing.

As soon as I slammed him into a wall of lockers and hissed that I'd be willing to tell my side of the story if he wanted to start rumors about me, the whole thing got buried pretty quickly. It didn't hurt either that I'd told him that if he ever told anyone about us again that I'd pay someone to hex his nutsack.

I'm a sucker for a beautiful man though, and when he came out the other side of puberty like a marble statue we'd hooked up a few more times over the years. Now we were friendly enough with each other, occasionally liking and posting stuff on each other's social media, me enjoying his photos from his new job as a basketball coach and him enjoying my thirst traps, but we hadn't seen each other since we fucked last Christmas when I visited my Moms and had left it kind of open-ended with a 'fuck ya later' farewell.

"Oh, Trae, you're here with Shannon?" I gave him a wide-eyed expression, hopefully conveying that Shannon had no idea that we'd slept together and to please keep it that way. "Shan, Trae and I went to high school together."

I looked behind Trae's immense 6'4'' stature and saw that Thomas was leaning nonchalantly against the bar while staring at a woman across the room intently. I saw Shannon deflate slightly looking between Trae and me. She'd always had an inferiority complex with me and always assumed that any guy would pick me over her because she has kids, which was complete bullshit. I quickly reached around Trae and took Thomas' cold hand, pulling him to me and nuzzling into his black cotton shirt, to assure her that I was not stealing Trae from her. "Guys, this is Thomas. Thomas, these are my friends Shannon and Trae."

Thomas seemed to shake himself out of some kind of trance and came back to our conversation, "Nice to meet you both." His french accent was smooth and subtle and I felt the definition of his body beneath my hand when he pulled me closer to him, wrapping his long arm around my waist.

"Thomas," Shannon almost sang his name out slowly, "Uh, where did you come from, Thomas?"

"Thomas and I have been seeing each other casually for a while when I visited my Moms, but I didn't know he was back in town so I was surprised when I saw him here. That's why I didn't tell you he was coming," I said hurriedly before Thomas could add anything, giving him a gentle poke in the back hoping that he'd play along.

"Where have you been then, Thomas, and why have I never heard of you?" She raised her brow at him and I noted that Trae was assessing him from top to bottom.

"I just got back from France. I've been there for most of the year."

"Really?" Shannon wasn't buying it. I didn't tell her everything, but I did tell her enough that me not talking about fucking a French model would be odd, even if I was her boss.

"*Oui*. Now, if you'll excuse us, it's been far too long since I've had my hands on this beautiful woman," he gave them the briefest of nods before he dragged me to the dance floor, turned me swiftly, and placed my hand behind his neck before moving my other up as well. He then placed his hands firmly on my hips and pulled me into him.

"Do you have any idea how lovely you smell, Annabel?"

I laughed, confused, "I don't think I told you that I'd dance with you."

He gave me an inconsequential wave of his hand and a smirk, "But we've been dating for a while, and I thought you wanted me to get you out of there."

"I did. God, I wasn't expecting him to be here..."

"Yes, I didn't get the feeling that you wanted to explain to your friend that you'd fucked her boyfriend."

My eyes widened, "what?! How do you-"

He shrugged, "I have a unique ability that allows me to understand the connection between people and the ability to differentiate between complicated emotions. Not to mention the shock on your face, and the way he was undressing you with his eyes made it kind of obvious. I didn't think you wanted Shannon to notice."

"Shit," I hissed, "Thank you for the out. But for the record, when I fucked him he definitely wasn't her boyfriend," I justified, peeking around him to find her leaning against Trae with her broken heel in her hand. "How did you know I was here?" I asked and looked into his eyes again, feeling inexplicably drawn to look at him instead of turning around and dancing back to front like most of the other people in the brewery's club.

"I didn't. Remember? I was dropping off fliers. Or I've just returned from France and we stumbled into each other and are now desperate to head into a weekend of devouring each other to reconnect. Which-ever story lets me keep my hands on you like this."

I shook my head, blinking longly, entirely captivated by his eyes and took a full breath, "What? Jesus. Of course, you had said you were dropping off shit. Sorry, I spaced for a minute."

"I'll try harder to keep your attention." He dug his fingers into the rolls that sat just above my apron, barely long enough to sting, and then rubbed the spot softly to soothe it.

Pulling back so I could look into his dark eyes, I smiled, "You're not very subtle, are you?"

"Would you prefer I was? It's been a long time since I've done this."

The song changed and the tempo slowed down, allowing us to shift closer together, "how long?"

"Pardon?"

I rolled my eyes, "how long has it been since you've fondled a strange woman on a dance floor?"

"Ah, that. Never."

"Never?" I laughed, "I find that hard to believe."

"*Non*, my last relationship..." He paused, seemingly to check his wording, "we started long enough ago that we weren't going out to places like this. She enjoyed it, but I never joined in."

"Hmmm..." I took a moment to weigh his words, "And how long ago did you break up?"

"She left last Christmas. I've mostly been in Paris since."

"Oh, so that wasn't a lie?"

"*Non, mon coeur*, the best lies are the ones laced with truth, yes?"

"Is your family still there? How long ago did you move to Boston?"

"Non, my family isn't there but I still have business dealings in the area. I also thought I might be able to find her if I went to France."

"And you didn't?"

"*Non*, but France is a very big place."

"Do you still want to find her?"

He looked down at me and ran a thumb down my neck, "shouldn't we be talking about you and me, not me and her?"

My brow arched, "Is there a me and you?"

He shifted slightly, moving his hands, and pulled me even closer to him, "remember, we've been casually dating for a while. Those were your words, not mine."

"You come on really strong, Tommy."

It was his turn to raise his brow at me, moving both hands to my neck, holding me firmly but sensually, "Tommy?"

"Too soon? I thought we'd been dating for a while."

He laughed brightly, "I do not think anyone has ever called me Tommy before. Though, it doesn't quite go with the french pronunciation, non?"

I shrugged, "You're Tommy now."

He laughed again, "As you wish, Annabel. I can be your Tommy. Are they kissing yet?" He spun me slowly so I was able to see Shannon and Trae better.

"Ugh, no. They're drinking."

"So we get another dance?"

"Looks that way," I sighed.

"Why did you say we were dating? Was it just to not tell her that you and he had?"

"Oh, he and I never dated, we just..."

"Ah."

I bristled, ready to defend myself if he was going to judge me for the things I'd done with my body, especially when he was seemingly trying to reach the same goal, "Shannon is my friend and she has low self-esteem. When she realized Trae knew me, I knew she was going to drop him, but she deserves to be happy. You were the closest victim. I knew that if I found myself otherwise occupied tonight that she would let herself keep him."

"So you're telling me if I'd been," he paused and looked around the dance floor and locked his gaze on a guy that looked like he just sauntered off his daddy's sailboat, gesturing to him with his chin, "If he'd been next to you instead of me, you'd be on this dance floor with him?"

"Probably."

"I don't think I like that answer, beauti-"

"Oh my god! It's you!" two women charged toward us and practically pushed Thomas off me, "can we have the presale code? We love your store."

I laughed, "For sure, Queens! Want to take a quick clip for our page?"

Thomas looked at me curiously and crossed his arms with amused patience.

"Oh my god, really?! Yes!"

"Of course! Here," I handed them their business cards with the code printed on the back that would let them shop before launch day. "Could you guys shake your asses for me when you show me your cards?" they laughed and blushed like I asked the impossible, and after they wiggled a little I stopped them, "No, bitches! I said SHAKE YOUR ASS!" I yelled and they burst into laughter and gave me the footage I wanted. "Thanks, ladies!" I waved at them as they walked away. "Sorry," I grimaced at Thomas and held my hand out to him, "buy me another drink?"

A slow smile crept over his face and I yawned, "gosh, sorry, I didn't think I was tired."

He appeared to shake himself, "*Non*, I'm sorry. Of course, I'll buy you a drink."

I took his hand and wove through the crowd to the opposite side of the bar from Shannon and Trae and climbed into a stool, "So, you come and go from France a lot? How did you end up with the Halloween store?"

He flicked something off the bar, "It's a fast way to make some cash this time of year. You'd be surprised how much comes through that place."

"No, I bet it's a cash cow, but what are your plans for after the holiday? Are you suddenly going to turn into Santa and sell Christmas trees?"

"You know, I've heard some of the teenagers say things like, 'that's a future me problem' and I think for now that will be my mantra."

I waved over the bartender and we ordered another round of drinks, "so you have no plan?"

"Like I said, I just got out of a long relationship, I'm not sure what the future holds right now. How long were you and tall boy together?"

I snorted, "Uh, it was just a casual thing."

"You do a lot of casual things?" He clenched his jaw as he swallowed down some scotch.

"I find there's a time and place to blow off steam, plus it allows me to focus on my work without having to build in time to nurture a relationship," I lied. I hadn't done this in over a year either.

"Are you not interested in a relationship then?"

I smirked, "What are you asking me, Tommy?"

"Nothing," his dark eyes sparkled, "I'm just pleased to be in the court of the HalloQueen." He gave me an exaggerated bowing motion with his hands and I laughed.

"Tommy?"

"Yes, *mon coeur*."

I looked over his shoulder and saw Trae looking directly at me, "Would you be opposed to kissing me?"

He barked out a shocked laugh, "*Quoi?*"

I leaned against my hand and subtly nodded toward Shannon and Trae, "They're looking at us. Would you mind horribly if I kissed you? It doesn't have to mean anything."

"Oh, I'm not worried about that, belle, if anything, I'm worried we won't be able to get enough of each other and you were just here breaking my heart by saying things like you only do casual."

I grinned, "I didn't say I only do casual, I just mostly do casual."

He returned my smile and put his hand on his cheek to block his mouth from Shannon and Trae, "Are they still looking?"

I took a sip of my cider and nodded, "mmmhmmm."

Thomas reached over and grabbed my stool, pulling it towards him with alarming ease and I turned my body to face him while he sandwiched my thick legs between his muscular ones. For someone so lean he apparently had a lot of hidden muscle. I saw the corded veins in his forearms twitching as he ran his hands up and down my thighs, reaching precariously close to the hem of my short skirt.

"Come here, *ma* chère."

"You don't have to if you don't want to, you won't hurt my feelings."

He laughed once again, eyes sparkling, "*Ma chérie,* at this point if you choose to not kiss me, you will hurt mine."

I blushed. Who was this guy? "That was charming," I said softly and he leaned into me, holding the side of my neck with his large hand.

He shrugged and smiled again, "I'm French, remember?"

"How could I forget when you keep calling me..." I spaced, looking into his dark eyes, "Uh..."

"*Mon coeur.*"

I tilted my head, "and what does that mean exactly?" I reached over and placed one of my hands on his leg.

"You can't tell?" He was close enough that I could feel my body being pulled into the energy of him.

"Maybe I just want you to say it?"

His smile turned sensual and against my lips, he whispered, "my heart."

I hummed when he finally pressed his luscious lips against mine, and I reached up to scratch his stubble, loving the way the coarse hair felt under my nails. He kissed me softly, but passionately enough that I felt like my soul was being pulled away from my body. I could feel him from my toes to my space buns, and goosebumps erupted all over me. I felt his essence inside of me from one kiss - that wasn't normal.

I pulled back, breathless, "Your heart?"

He nodded and pulled me off my stool so I was standing between his legs and I could easily grab his torso, "*Oui,* Annabel. Mine." He wrapped his arm around my back, pulling me flush against him and I couldn't resist the urge to dig my fingers into his sides. He was about my height on the barstool with me standing, and with his forehead against mine, I swore I heard him growl like I was in some kind of fucking romantacy book or something.

He took my lips with his again and the world around us turned into static. It was as though there was white noise everywhere and the bar faded away to nothing. There was nothing on earth except for me, Tommy, and this kiss as we floated in a place devoid of space and time. He kissed me over and over again, making me wholly melt against him, feeling as though my bones were leaving my body and my brain was short-circuiting. I pressed my hand flat to his chest and hummed. His chest rumbled beneath it and heat spiked in my core. I was about to climb him like a fucking tree, drowning in a lust I hadn't experienced in years. That was why after god knows how long when I felt a hand on my shoulder, I was shocked to see Shannon standing there bringing the bar came back to life around us. It took me a moment to register that we were still even at Witchcraft at all.

"Oh shit, sorry Shan, you scared me."

"Yeah....well... I need to pee, come with me?"

I shook myself back into my body, "Yeah. Yes. Yes." I scratched at my chest, which I could feel was flushed and heavy, begging for attention, "Um, I'll be right back. Are you staying?"

"*Oui, mon coeur.* I'll be right here. You want another drink?"

"Uh, no, I'm alright. I'll be right back." I moved out from between his legs and instantly the bar felt far too loud, too hot, too much. It was like with Thomas I had been in a bubble that dampened everything around us. Shannon and I got into the ladies' room and she spun around, causing me to crash into her.

"Ouch, Shan, what the fuck?"

"Who the hell is that guy?" She demanded from me.

"I told you, that's Thomas."

"Bels, I've known you for a decade and I have never once heard you talk about a Thomas and you looked like you were about to let him fuck you in the middle of the bar."

I shrugged, "I don't tell you about everyone I hook up with."

"You're a liar."

"How are things going with Trae?" I asked, hoping to deflect the conversation back to her and away from the fact that I was two seconds from dry-humping the guy I met that afternoon.

A blush spread across her cheeks, "We were actually about to get out of here, but I wanted to make sure that you didn't need me to pull you out from whatever the hell that was before I left." She gestured towards the hall. "It looked, uh...intense."

I nodded and dragged my teeth over my bottom lip, "Oh yeah. It was intense."

"Are you sure you're okay?" I saw the maternal fear in her eyes, scanning me to ensure that I hadn't been drugged or manipulated.

"Yes, I'm fine, now let me get mine while you get yours. This was your idea after all!"

She gave a small nod, "Okay, well, text me tomorrow morning? Brunch?"

I shrugged, "We'll see what happens. I'll see you later though, don't worry."

"Don't forget to take detailed notes, I expect a full report about the Frenchman - no more hiding hot foreign guys!"

I shook my head and headed to the sink to check my makeup and wash my hands, "get the fuck out of here. Go have some fun."

She blew me a kiss before spinning and walking out of the bathroom. I looked at myself and noticed that my flush was more contrasting to my skin than usual as if I had gone pale, and my lips were swollen from Thomas' scruff. Was I doing this? I hadn't had anyone to my rental since getting back to Quaker's Wharf, but no one else had literally taken my breath away with a kiss.

I shook out my jitters once more, danced a bit on my tiptoes, and rolled my neck. It's girl law that you're allowed to get all the anxiety out in the bathroom and no one can judge you, and I needed that minute to get my shit together. When I walked back out to the bar, my senses were overstimulated again and I found myself suddenly desperate to get out of there. I walked back to the bar and saw Thomas chatting with some guy who seemed incredibly close to him and I examined them skeptically. The guy reached out and rubbed Thomas' shoulder and looked at him like he hung the moon, and I felt a stab of jealousy, making me unable to help but strut in his direction like he was my property.

"Hey, sorry about that. They're heading out, she just wanted to say goodbye."

Thomas looked at me and the man he was speaking with seemed to realize Thomas hadn't come alone and snatched his hand back like he wasn't sure how it had ended up on Thomas in the first place.

"Uh, are you otherwise occupied?" I asked, nodding towards the man.

"*Non, cher*, he was just telling me about this restaurant down the road."

"It's okay if you want to go with him..." I'd never been with a man who liked men, but obviously, I swung both ways and I was raised by east coast liberal lesbians so there wasn't much about sexuality that could shock me.

"*Non.*" His face slightly hardened and he put his hand around my waist and held my chin, bringing my eyes to him, "tonight is for you."

I leaned in and whispered in his ear, "do you want to get his number? You don't owe me anything, it's okay." I felt his grip on my waist tighten and he pulled me closer.

"I said *non, ma chérie.* Look," He turned me and I saw that the guy he'd been talking with had disappeared into the crowd, "I was just talking to him. It was nothing."

"Do you like men?" I asked bluntly.

"*Oui.*"

"Do you like women?"

He lowered his brow and gave me a condescending look.

I held my hands up in surrender, "Just making sure we were on the same page."

He stood from his stool and dropped a fifty on the counter, "want to go for a walk? It's very loud here. We could go down by the water."

I bit my bottom lip again in thought but became distracted when he dragged his thumb over my mouth, pulling it free and caressing my cheek. He pulled me to him and pressed his lips to mine, coaxing me to melt against him again. Thomas' kisses should be illegal, or at least come with an alcohol content warning because they were fucking intoxicating.

I nodded, "Yeah. That would be nice. I do feel like it's gotten louder in here in the last half hour. Let's go."

"*Mon coeur?*" He took my hand and stopped me from walking forward.

"Yeah, Tommy?"

He gave me a lopsided smirk at the moniker and pulled me into him, going to my ear and whispering, "I may like men, and I may like women, but you, *ma chérie*, you are something entirely different than anyone I've ever found before. You are in a league of your own."

"So what you're saying is that you think I'm a nice lady?" I grinned.

He grabbed a handful of my ass and exasperatedly shook his head, "come on, *ma chérie*, let's go for that walk."

6

THOMAS

This woman was incredible. The citrus and ginger scent swirled around her and I was as desperate to claim her as a fish to a shiny lure. Her energy was delectable- bright and genuine. I'm able to lure mortals to me and soothe them through eye contact, but I needed physical touch to harvest their energy. I was hoping that pulling her aura would soothe the primitive beast in me, but once I'd tasted her on the dance floor I immediately knew that it wasn't enough.

I needed to taste her, kiss her, fuck her. She had the most powerful aura I'd ever harvested - it was as if someone took an energy drink and plopped it into a red eye, while somehow also wrapping you in lavender so your heart felt soothed instead of like it was going to explode out of your chest... it was indescribable. She fueled me more in those few touches and kisses than the entire store of mortals today. I needed more.

We walked along the water, talking about her business and the launch of her new line she had coming up. I could feel the stress radiating off of her and, while my typical tastes leaned toward happiness and passion, I couldn't help but take her hand in an effort to take that anxiety away.

She sighed and squeezed my hand, "You're a good listener."

I tapped slightly at the wall of her mind and took some of the anxiety out. "I've had many years of practice. I've found that other people are far more interesting than myself."

Annabel scoffed, "That can't be true, you've traveled the world and owned businesses and immigrated for crying out loud. I can't imagine leaving everything I know behind to start over like that."

"You said you moved from Chicago back to here, didn't you?" I pulled her closer to me so I could release her hand and wrapped my arm around her waist. The more of her I touched, the quicker I could remove her negative feelings.

"Well yeah," she wiggled closer to me and the feeling of her soft body contouring to mine made me want to purr, "but I didn't have to learn a new language or anything. Besides, I grew up in Quaker's Wharf, so when I moved from Chicago back to here it was just like coming home. Not like leaving the French Countryside and moving to Boston."

"I had to leave France. Things there were not going well politically and it seemed more worth the risk to make the journey here than to stay there and potentially lose our lives."

She looked up at me, "ours?"

"*Oui*. I told you I was in a long relationship, right?"

"Yeah," I felt her tense slightly and I pulled harder at her energy until she relaxed, "what happened with that?"

I shrugged and felt the desire to place a kiss on the top of her head, surprising myself at the casual intimacy I craved with her. "I actually don't know. I woke up one morning and they were gone."

She tensed again, "They? Like your wife and kids?"

"*Non*, I don't have any children. Never got around to it."

A laugh bubbled out of her and it warmed me, "you say that like you're a million years old. You're what, in your thirties? Men can have kids when they're like eighty; you've got time."

47

"*Non*, I don't think so. That ship has sailed for me."

I felt Annabel's hand slip into the back pocket of my jeans, "so what did you mean 'they' left?"

"It was not a relationship of only two people."

She paused our walk and turned to look at me, "Wow. You had a triad that worked for that long?"

I nodded, "the three of us balanced each other very well and when we came to Boston our relationship was fairly new. The drastic change probably linked us together more than if we'd stayed in France since we needed each other."

"How long were the three of you together? You said they left at Christmas?"

"*Oui*. We were together too long for me to dump all that on you on the first night. Tell me more about you?"

She shook her head and pulled herself into my body, "Can I say something absolutely insane?"

"More insane than telling me to kiss you in a room full of people?"

A delicious blush crept across her cheeks, "Sorry about that."

I leaned down and pressed my lips to hers again. She had wonderfully soft lips. The bottom was deliciously plush and I wanted to allow my fangs to drop so I could drag them across it until she was panting. Her hips were so wide, wider than anyone I'd ever held against my body like this, and the feeling of my cock against her luscious body was decadent. Hard and soft. Life and death. The girl and the raven. Balance. She moaned slightly against my mouth and I gripped her ass to hold her against me.

"I will never accept an apology for any reason that allows your body to touch mine. If I could take the feeling of the warmth of your skin and carry it within me all day, I would in a heartbeat."

"You're intense." She looked up at me with embers crackling in her green eyes.

"And you're perfect. You can't blame me for wanting to make sure you are aware of it."

She scoffed and shook her head in disbelief, "I've never met a guy that just...says shit like that. I feel like I should be concerned that you're some kind of insane man whore and you're playing me like a fiddle-"

"*Non*, Annabel."

She gave me a soft smile, "but, the insane thing I was going to say before is that for some reason I feel so," she paused to search for the word, "calm, and safe with you. My instincts aren't typically wrong when it comes to people, and something feels right when I touch you."

I felt the energy circling through our embrace, me pulling her anxiety out and putting peace back in. Part of me felt bad about manipulating her feelings, but I'd never felt energy like hers before. It also didn't seem to be draining her like it typically would. I'd taken and channeled more energy from her in one day than I ever do and yet she was still standing there, kissing me when she should have probably passed out somewhere. I knew I was funneling energy back into her, but I was positive that I was taking more than I was giving. There was the moment earlier when she yawned like I'd pulled too much, but since we kissed she'd been able to give and give and give. She was like a bottomless well of delicious fuel.

"You say I say too much, but I can already feel myself becoming addicted to you, Annabel. You are," I hesitated, but it came out of me anyway, "sunlight and stars. You feel like a soft breeze on a hot day. Your spirit sounds like the ocean caressing the sand. You fill me up."

She arched a brow, "You can hear my spirit?"

I froze, thinking maybe that was time I'd said too much, but I quickly gave her a nonchalant laugh and responded, "French, remember?"

She laughed back, "I didn't know that being French meant that you could feel souls and energy."

I shrugged and raised one of my hands to hold her neck again, loving the softness of her skin, and the extra waft of her scent that came when I moved her hair away from her pulse point, "I'm just special I guess. Annabel-"

"Do you want to come to my place to watch a movie or something?

It's a little cold down here by the water," She interrupted me, and the beast inside of me froze. She was inviting me into her home. She was *inviting* me.

"Are you sure? Your home is your safe place." I couldn't help but give her the subtle warning, "I do not want to impose on your hospitality."

She shook her head and went up on her tiptoes to kiss me again, "I said you feel safe to me. Unless you're planning on murdering me, I would love to have you come over."

I softened to her embrace and the truth poured from me, " I don't think I could hurt you if I wanted to."

7
ANNABEL

I could come to regret it. I'd only intended to flirt, maybe give a few gentle caresses, because at the end of the day it was supposed to be a business relationship. I didn't intend for sex to be on the table, but that was also when the man on the other side of the counter was going to be Andrew, not Thomas.

Any hookups I'd had in Chicago began with frenzied kisses in a cab, but the peacefulness that Thomas exuded left us simply cuddled up to each other in the ride share. Who cuddles their hookup? It was only a hookup, right? I didn't have time for anything else... the launch needed to be my priority. My to-do list was miles long. I needed my head on straight to prep the website and shipping shit, shake my ass, and hopefully manage to go viral a few more times before it drops...

"You're thinking very loudly, *mon coeur*," Thomas whispered into my ear and I shivered at his stubble scratching against my jaw.

"It's nothing," I give him a fake smile, "What kind of movies do you like?"

"Whatever you'd like, Annabel."

I elbowed him in the side, "That's a lie. Everyone hates some kind of movie. What do you like?"

"I don't watch a lot of movies, I'm mostly a TV show kind of guy. I don't have the attention span for full movies, usually."

"So what tv shows do you watch?"

He smirked, "Don't worry about it."

"Thomas."

"Why can't I lie to you?"

"Because I'm incredibly good looking." I grinned and he sighed.

"I like cooking shows, okay? I think they're soothing."

The defeat in his voice made me laugh, "Cooking shows? Like the old lady in her Martha's Vineyard mansion or the cutthroat ones where they're cooking on a time limit and stuff?"

"All of it, especially the competition ones. I love those."

"I wouldn't have pegged you for a cooking show guy..."

"I hope I haven't disappointed you with my domesticity."

I laughed again and the ride share pulled up outside of my rented row house, "this is it." I leaned forward, "thank you for the ride."

"No problem, you guys have fun now," The driver was a man probably in his mid-twenties and he flashed us a knowing smile that quickly dropped when he looked at Thomas.

I turned around to see what Thomas was doing but he looked perfectly normal to me, patting the guy on the arm.

We headed up the four steps to my front door and I unlocked it and stepped inside. Thomas hovered awkwardly at the threshold.

"Are you okay?" I asked, feeling a weird tension coming off of him for the first time that night.

"Are you sure you want this?" He asked me sincerely, and if anything, it only solidified my decision to fuck the Frenchie.

"Tommy, shut up and get inside." He hesitated again as if assessing what I'd said so I reiterated, "Thomas, please come in, I don't bite on the first date."

He nodded and stepped inside, seeming to relax once I closed and locked the door. "How long have you lived here?" he asked me, toeing off his shoes and I sat on the steps leading upstairs to unzip my boots.

"Not long, I crashed with my moms for a while when I got back, so excuse the mess, it's only been a few months and I loathe unpacking," I laughed nervously, "Do you want a drink?" I led the way to the kitchen and exhaled raggedly into the fridge as I grabbed a bottle of wine. My nerves were seemingly cranking up by the minute. There was a guy in my house. In my space. I typically went to their places but for some reason, I hadn't even suggested it.

I stepped to the kitchen island, a beautiful antique butcher block, and put the wine down, then turned to get a few glasses out of the rack, "do you like red?" I asked.

He nodded, "anything is fine."

My hands were shaking by the time I got the corkscrew inside the bottle. It was like all the peace I'd felt had evaporated and my to-do list was choosing the worst possible time to come crashing back down onto me. I had my stress managed when Shannon and I went out earlier, but now it felt like I would have to play catch up for the few hours of fun we'd had, making me worry twice as much as I would have if I'd just stayed home and worked.

Thomas leaned against the island about a foot from me and ducked so he was in my line of sight, "Annabel, do you want me to leave?"

"No!" I said hurriedly, "No, I'm sorry, I just suddenly got really stressed out about my to-do list. You own a shop, I'm sure you know how the little things haunt you at all hours of the day."

He took the bottle from me and steadily poured it into our two glasses, "I have a store, yes, but I am positive that my stress level owning a costume shop is substantially less than yours when you're trying to build a brand."

I sighed and turned around, placing my butt against the counter, "I feel like there's not enough hours in the day and that I never get to turn off. Someone's always watching me and it feels like someone is always waiting for me to fail. I get home and tend to just...crash"

He took a sip of wine, "why do you say that?"

I shrugged and felt myself shrink a little under the weight of my emotional exhaustion, "there's always another beautiful girl in the wings waiting to go viral; there's always another small boutique trying to make it big. There's enough room for all of us at the table, but a lot of people feel like they need a monopoly on something for it to be special."

"Do you go viral often? You good at those lip-syncing videos or something?" he asked.

"Umm...no... if I go viral it is usually because I'm half naked and dancing." I blushed, feeling unusually embarrassed about my work. I never felt ashamed of what I did - I used what I had to make my living, there was nothing wrong with that, but for some reason telling Thomas that I monetized my appearance felt dirty. I hadn't felt a connection with someone in so long that being the sexy girl online was just a part of who I was, if anything it was a confidence booster, but now I found myself nervous about his reaction.

He laughed, "Well look at you, *ma chérie*. Of course, everyone wants to see that. In fact, I might have some internet stalking to do when I get home."

I smiled and put my wine glass down, stepping to my sink to poke at the dirt in a couple of my plants to make sure they weren't thirsty.

"You like plants?"

Shrugging, I poured a little water into one of the pots, "I find them peaceful. I'm not very good at it, but my mom has a green thumb. Though you do get to put them in cute shit and they make the air cleaner, so I feel like tending to them is worth a try." I picked up my desert rose and showed him the black glitter skull that it currently inhabited and he chuckled.

"Where on earth did you find that monstrosity?"

I feigned offense, "Hey! Shannon and I made a lot of them. Why should they live in boring terra cotta? I know I wouldn't enjoy that." I gestured around the room. I hadn't had a lot of time to decorate, but the few things I have put up clearly showed that I leaned towards Dark Edwardian Maximalism. I wanted all the cool photos in gilded oval frames and the overstuffed velour wingback chairs and the piles and piles of books that I may or may not ever have time to read.

He turned to lean against the counter across from me so we were facing each other, "Annabel, why are you so stressed all of a sudden? We don't need to do anything. I'm not going to force you. We really can just watch a movie."

"No," I sighed, "it's not that. I'm just a worry wart around launch times. I'm sorry, I get home and I deflate a little bit, I totally get it if you'd rather hang out with the exuberant girl from the bar. We can try again another night when I'm not so frazzled?"

He smiled and gestured for me to come into his arms, "come here." I happily followed his direction and almost immediately felt some of the worry melting away at his touch.

"How do you do that?" I asked amazed.

"Do what?" He leaned his head atop mine and tightened his grip around me

"I was like two seconds from an existential crisis and you just... poofed it."

A small snort and contemplative noise reverberated through his chest, "I poof it?"

"Poofed."

"I don't..."

"You made it disappear. Poof." I said, snuggling in deeper, "Jesus, I'm sorry, I probably sound like a fucking crazy woman. Should we make some popcorn and watch someone bake a cake or something?" I pulled back and tried to make light of the sudden stress that almost crippled me, but he didn't loosen his embrace.

"You don't sound crazy. I'm glad I can make the bad feelings poofed."

"You'd use poof there."

He rolled his eyes and his french accent got exaggeratedly thicker, "well excuse-moi for not knowing the conjugation of your silly 'poof' word."

I couldn't help but laugh and snuggled back into his chest. The rumbling from it was hypnotic.

"You mentioned watching someone bake a cake. I don't need

popcorn, but watching a cooking show with you sounds like a wonderful way to end our night."

It felt warm and natural to be holding him in my kitchen. It certainly didn't feel like I introduced myself to him only twelve hours ago. I took his hand and pulled him toward my living room to curl up on the couch, stopping to give Tim a scratch behind his huge black ears. "Hi Tim, did you have a good day, baby?"

"Tim?" Thomas asked, looking at the overweight creature on one of my armchairs.

"Yeah, it seemed very fitting for him."

"So now you have a Tim and a Tom?"

"Maybe I'm making a collection," I smirked and lifted Tim off my black fluffy blanket before I pulled my projection screen down above my fireplace and curled up on the couch.

"A projector?" Thomas asked before sitting next to me and pulling my feet onto his lap, covering them back up with the blanket.

I shrugged, "I'm nothing if not a whore for aesthetics. I like being able to put it away when I'm not using it so I'm not just staring at a giant black box on my wall." I pointed to my bookshelf to turn the projector on before setting it to a streaming cooking show. "This one okay?"

"Of course, Annabel, whatever you want."

I burrowed down a bit into the couch, "so what is your favorite thing to cook?"

Thomas turned incredibly bashful, "would you believe me if I said that I don't cook? I just like to watch other people do it. Especially French cooking. I miss French food."

I laughed, "I can believe that. A mug of coffee is about the extent of my cooking most days. I get groceries delivered here but it's not like I'm ever itching to be in the kitchen at the end of an insane work day. Most of my dinners include a sugary cereal and a glass of wine."

"So what do you do to relax at the end of the day?" He rubbed my legs through my tights.

"I like to design clothes, I'd like to have my own line someday instead of just curating pieces."

"Ah, so you leave your clothing business to come home and think about more clothes." The way he delivered his comments so dryly was funny to me.

"I...." I looked around, "I read too."

"Do you really?" He raised his dark brow at me, "Anything besides our dear Poe?"

I laughed "Okay, I read a lot of romance books. They're a nice escape when I'm too fried to even watch tv."

"That makes sense."

"What do you like to read?" The chefs on the projector were panicking over how to turn a pickle into a dessert and I cringed at the one trying to make it into a funnel cake corndog type thing.

"I've read a little bit of everything. I enjoy meeting authors too and picking their brains. They have a different energy than most people do, I think it has something to do with the fact that they can create something out of nothing. I find it very intriguing."

"There you are mentioning energy again, are you totally woo woo or something? Like crystal alters and all that?"

He lifted one shoulder, "we live in Quaker's Wharf, everyone here is a little woo woo, are we not? All the fun of Salem and none of the insane housing market?"

"I don't know about that. Though I know we monetize it here. Everyone wants to think magic is real."

"You don't think it is?" He asked and chuckled when I groaned at the corn dog pickle thing falling apart as soon as it got out of the fryer.

"I don't know," I answered honestly, "I think there's got to be more out there than just us, whether that's aliens or sasquatches or gods or whatever; it would be very self-absorbed to think that all this is just for us, but I don't know if that is actually magic or if it's just a part of life that I don't understand."

"That was very deep."

"What about you?" I asked, stress floating away the longer he rubbed on my legs and feet.

"There are definitely more than mortals here."

"Mortals? That's an interesting choice of words."

"Humans? People? Walking blood banks?" He laughed awkwardly, "what should I call mortals?"

I shrugged, "You say that like you're separated from it. I don't know, 'mortal' certainly isn't the word that comes to my mind first when thinking about other people."

"Blame my woo woo," He gave me a toothy smile and waved his hands as if cleansing his aura.

I sat up and leaned toward him so I was sitting sideways on the couch. I wanted to look at him, "You're a very beautiful man. Is that a French thing too? If I move to France is everyone going to look like you?"

"*Non, mon coeur*, I am a special case. I guess you're stuck with me."

I absentmindedly chewed on my bottom lip again, trying to decide what I wanted to do. He was peaceful. Did I want to fuck that up with sex? Did I want him to be my best friend? Did I want to lean into and rely on what I was sure was an insanely passionate man?

"You're thinking loudly again, Annabel." He said, fidgeting with the bell jar that housed an upside down faux bat skeleton on my side table.

"I'm just wondering if kissing you again is a bad idea. I like the way you make me feel."

"If you like the way I make you feel, why would kissing me be a bad idea? Besides, haven't we crossed that line already?"

"I..." I hesitated. How could I possibly put the absence of human connection in my life into words? How did I say that while I'd like to ride him six ways to Sunday that it'd been a long time since I'd felt comfortable around someone?

He turned to me and ran the back of his hand up my arm, "what if I kiss you instead then, *ma chérie*?"

"I'm overthinking again."

"That's okay. We don't have to do anything you don't want to. Or I can think for both of us if you'd like."

"No, kiss me," I leaned and pulled him by his shirt to me. I felt myself loosen again when his lips met mine and his hands gripped me around my waist. I felt nothing but heat and desire and lust. I teased his lips with my tongue to enter his mouth and he happily let me, pulling me up and onto his lap easily so I was straddling him. He pulled back to say something to me but I was suddenly drowning in desire and I moved so I could kiss his neck while grinding down onto him. He groaned when I began to trail open mouth kisses down him and he hardened beneath me, tightening his hold around my waist. The heat cranked up by the second igniting a blazing inferno of desire and I could suddenly think of nothing *but* kissing Thomas. Of devouring him. There was no way I wasn't going to go through with it.

So why did everything go dark?

8
THOMAS

Dear Gods, this woman would have killed me if I were a mere man. The delicious weight of her on my lap grinding into me, combined with her lustful energy coursing through her embrace and into me was more intoxicating than the purest bag of blood I'd ever purchased. Her energy was so strong that I wanted to bottle it up and save it for a rainy day. I pulled and pulled at it, growling and clawing at it, reveling in how her energy could mix with mine.

Usually, when I pulled someone's emotions I felt refreshed like I'd gotten a good night's sleep or experienced what I remember eating a good meal felt like. When I feed, it leaves the mortal feeling the opposite of what they had been since they then only feel the absence of it. If I harvest their happiness, they feel sorrow, if I harvest their excitement, they feel bored, etc. I'd been feeding off of Annabel's anxiety, which usually leaves someone peaceful, but Annabel's energy had steadily veered from anxiety into very unpeaceful uncontrollable lust.

I tasted her lust, wanting to see what her need would feel like inside of me and the first dose exploded like a perfect, juicy orange, making something inside of me combust. I became one with my beast and we yanked on her energy, fueling my desire for the gorgeous woman. Instead of slowing down, she kept cranking up like she'd passed her boiling point and there was no way I'd be able to pull it out of her fast enough for her to calm down enough to stop. I was amazed by her ability to release so much energy and I wondered just how much of her I was going to get to taste.

But then suddenly she went limp against me.

Merde.

"Annabel?" I asked, holding her neck and pulling her away from me, "Annabel, *mon coeur*, are you okay?"

She was wearing a stupified closed mouth smile and was easily breathing in long drawn-out breaths.

Shit. Shit. Shit.

I sighed and looked on the bright side, at least I only cock blocked myself and didn't kill the poor woman. I considered my options, wondering if I took her up to her room if she'd be okay with that or if it would feel like an invasion of privacy, but part of me needed her to sleep against me for a few more minutes.

The cooking show had moved into the last round of the competition and I rubbed my hand up and down Annabel's back, lying to myself that I was only staying to make sure she was okay. I knew she was fine. She'd sleep like the dead and when she woke up she would be back to her usual spitfire self. And yet, feeling her steady peaceful breathing against my neck and having her body pressed into mine made me feel like a love-sick puppy.

The show ended quickly, and shocker, the funnel cake pickle dog lost horrifically. I decided to leave Annabel there in her living room. Maybe she'd think the whole thing was some drunken wet dream, but I didn't want there to be some proof I'd been here. I'd want her to remember me. I twisted her so I could lift her like a bride off of my lap and stood up.

"Don't look at me like that," I hissed at her black cat, Tim, who was eyeing me suspiciously, "I'm not going to hurt her."

I turned and gently set her back down on the couch and tucked her into her soft blanket. I wrapped it under her feet and then wondered if she was the kind of mortal that needed to have their feet covered to sleep or if she was the kind who felt suffocated if her feet weren't in the open air. I decided I'd rather her be covered and she could uncover herself later if she wanted or got hot.

Tim immediately jumped on her and curled up in the little hole that formed between her bent knees and the back of the couch and began purring as if the evening had turned out exactly how he wanted it to.

"Yeah, well, that makes one of us, Tim." I watched her for a few moments more and when she wiggled into the couch further and sighed, I knew I could leave. "You're on guard duty," I said to the cat, "Don't let me down."

I left out the front door, unhappy that I couldn't lock the deadbolt from the outside, and settled for pressing the lock on the doorknob before closing it. I had to hope that would be enough for one night. I could've stayed and stood guard, but honestly, after overindulging in her energy, I was feeling a little drunk myself and I wasn't sure that I would've been any help if, gods forbid, something did happen to her. Knowing instinctually that I should find a bag of blood and my bed to call it a day, I began to run back towards the shopping district.

It only took a few minutes to run the several miles thanks to all the energy coursing through my system and I was hardly fatigued when I reached the shop. I unlocked the door and stepped in, locking it behind me. Being a vampire, you'd think not a lot would creep me out, but something was unsettling about being the only one in the mall with the light of the moon casting strange shadows on the Halloween decor. Logically, I knew I'd be able to smell if anything or anyone was here, and if they were, they'd be dead before they even realized I was, but a shadowy grim reaper statue is enough to give anyone the creeps.

The shop was inside of an abandoned department store so there were huge expanses of space that weren't being used. The Halloween section was made of faux walls of stretched fabric and PVC pipe, and behind the curtain by the cash register was what most people considered to be the stock room. Which, I guessed it was, but it also led to where I slept. I'd gotten back from Paris looking for Monique and Yusuf to find someone else living in the row house that we'd owned for years and years. I hadn't quite been willing to accept that I needed a new place to live on my own, and with them having squandered or stolen most of our money I had the proud distinction of being a homeless vampire. Yes, I could cash out some of my private assets and settle somewhere, but settling alone sounded...horrible. I couldn't commit to a place unless there was a reason to, so, there I was, sleeping in the empty half-lit skeleton of a home textile area on an air mattress, with a mini fridge full of blood.

It was enough for me. I'd hung up my clothes on the abandoned racks and the store had its own bathroom. I'd end my nights by going to the 24-hour gym located in another old department store to shower and burn off some energy, and then I'd watch cooking shows on my tablet until I passed out. It was September so I could run the Halloween store halfway through November, and then if I wanted to stay I could turn it into a Christmas shop - toys and ornaments or some shit, or I could move on. The option of being able to do either appealed to me, but it meant that I needed a more concrete plan or destination come Mid-January.

The plan had been to go back to France to look for Monique and Yus again, but when I'd spoken with the Coalition in Paris a few weeks before, they'd said they were still checking in and paying their dues, so they had no reason to divulge where they were. The only way the Coalition would violate the privacy of a member was if that vampire was becoming a danger to the mortals or not being subtle enough to keep us hidden. I'd hesitated staying in the Coalition when we'd left Paris and came to Boston, but now I was thankful that Yusuf had insisted we stay above board; at least I knew they were alive. Thanks to Yusuf keeping us up to date on our dues and that I'd proven that Monique and Yusuf took off and left me in the lurch, I was able to collect the stipend that everyone paid into.

It was an idea they'd stolen from the American idea of Social Security or Unemployment Insurance, we all paid dues to the Coalition to keep us safe and informed, and in turn, they managed assets and accounts that would help house injured vamps, the ancients trying to pass into the Undead, and the abandoned. Which was now me. Because that wasn't a blow to my ego.

Sometimes I wondered if being Undead would be easier than the bureaucracy of being Other. As a vampire, I wasn't mortal and therefore couldn't live a "normal" life, but because I wasn't Undead, I had to follow all the rules laid out by mortal society and ours. It could be stifling at times.

So, I was homeless, unsure of what the future held, and at almost 500 years old I was watching cooking competitions alone while drinking blood from an insulated water bottle. Living. The. Life. But now there was Annabel. *Is* Annabel. Could I turn this misery into something that would be worth staying around for? The Coalition frowned upon dating mortals, but if I claimed her, if I never hurt her, they wouldn't have a reason to separate us, right?

The way she smelled. The way she felt. The way her energy poured out of her as if it was from a bottomless cup... *merde*. That was how I took so much she fell asleep - I got so lost in her that I hadn't considered where she'd bottom out. I cringed just thinking about how confused she was going to be when she woke up. I had left her dressed and on the couch in hopes she'd realized we hadn't slept together and that she was safe, but mortal women weren't exactly known for their level-headedness.

Fuck, the way she had ground into my cock and the softness of the skin on her neck. The way my fingers could dig into her hips...the way she molded against my chest. I was powerless against her. I lay on the air mattress and imagined her in enough detail that the scent of ginger and citrus began to waft over me and my body started to quake. I needed to fly.

Sometimes I could burn through the energy while in my body by fucking or running, but I'd taken too much from her and the other mortals at the bar and the magic was vibrating within me trying to escape. I removed my clothes and lay them on the bed before stretching tall above my head. With a crack and a shudder, I took flight, my raven's wings booming with each flap in the cavernous space. When my magic gets to be too much, the only way I can expel it is to use it. I found that using my raven could burn through substantially more energy than anything else.

While the Undead were stuck as annoying little bats, only a few inches across - hardly big enough to eat a bug, vampires could turn into any kind of winged creature. While I was a raven, Monique had been a barn owl and Yusuf was a hawk. Some vampires only hunted for blood in their animal form, but you typically had to kill multiple creatures to slake your thirst, whereas you only needed a little from a mortal and it wouldn't kill them, but neither sat well with me. I found that a nice delivery from the blood bank where a mortal was given a cookie and sent on their way sat better on my already questionable conscious.

As I soared around the empty space I felt my head begin to clear. If there was one thing I'd learned in my many, many years, it was that magic and immortality were about balance. Because we leave an imbalance in the world by not passing on, our existence is delicate. We must take energy, but not so much that it is wasted. We must take blood, but not so much that we need to take life. We must use magic, but not so much that it damages ourselves or the world around us. When a vampire begins to throw off the balance, the process of becoming Undead begins. It can be that they aren't feeding at all, or that they're feeding too much. Same with magic, or energy, or a number of other things. It was all about balance. The start of the transformation could be stopped with the right help, but typically no one realized they were falling until it was too late. To be a vampire was a far greater gift than to be Undead.

We got to live fairly normal lives as long as we helped maintain said balance, whereas the Undead were sick. They could never see the sun. They could never feel. They could never love. They were dark, sad creatures who were ill with bloodlust and fear. An Ancient once told me that an Undead drinks so much blood because some part of them thinks that if they absorb enough humanity they can come back as one of us, but to be Undead is irreversible. True Ancients are rare, as eventually, the will to survive falters, and vampires either transition or ask to die. I'd assisted one Ancient in his passing, and I hoped to never have to do it again. To see someone who doesn't need air cease to exist is a heady thing. It isn't like what you see in movies where their chest stops moving and their eyes glaze over and the mortal passes to the other side. No, the Ancient just...ceases to exist. As Annabel would say, they poof.

I pushed myself harder, soaring, flapping, weaving through pillars and up and down the unused escalators while lost in thought. Lost in the existential crisis of my own half-life. Just the idea of becoming Undead was enough to terrify me, despite sometimes being depressed enough to think it would be easier. To lose what little I had left of myself... I'd already lost so much.

After my energy settled, I flew back to my bed and shook myself back into my body, suddenly overcome with exhaustion. I would need to be careful with my beautiful Annabel. I couldn't lose what little I had left because of overindulging in her intoxicating energy. It was with the troubling debate swimming through my mind of what I could do with her energy, versus what it could do to me, that I collapsed into the mattress and fell asleep.

9
ANNABEL

I woke up with a start. The sun was shining on my face through the windows whose curtains had never been closed. Stretching, I saw that Tim had made quite the nest beside me and I scratched his ear. "What the hell happened last night, Tim?"

I sat up and immediately laid down again. Oh, that's what happened. My head was pounding like a full colonial fife and drum corp was trapped inside of it. I covered my eyes with the heels of my palms and waited for the world to stop spinning. Then I cracked one eye open and reached into the pocket of my skirt hoping that my phone was still there, but I discovered that it had fallen on the floor beside me. The battery was dead. Awesome. I didn't even know what fucking time it was. I slowly sat up again and saw that I was, indeed, still fully dressed, complete with stockings. The projection screen was down and I could see my boots by the front stairs. Did I just come home wasted and fall asleep watching TV?

The last thing I remembered was that I'd left the bar and gotten into a ride share with...Thomas - the guy from the Halloween store. I stood and hobbled toward my front door and saw that it wasn't locked so I slammed the deadbolt over with a flinch. My space buns were still half on my head and the rubber bands were killing me. Did he just bring me home and then see I was wasted and escorted me inside before he left?

I went to the kitchen to look for toast and saw all the evidence I needed. There were two half-drunk glasses of wine on the counter. He had been in my house. But I was dressed. But...god I'm such an idiot! Anything could have happened to me! I never got drunk enough to blackout, it'd never happened once in my entire life, not even in college. Someone must have slipped me something. Someone must have - Oh. No.

I ran to the half bath located under my stairs and emptied the contents of my stomach into the toilet. I gasped for breath, but heave after heave tortured me. I didn't typically drink enough to even end up sick. Especially on nights like last night where Shannon and I were technically "working".

Once I thought I could stand without ruining the carpets, I flushed the toilet and grabbed my phone, beginning the arduous journey of slowly heading upstairs to plug it in. I walked into my bedroom and was relieved to see that nothing was out of place there. My bed was still made, complete with my squishy ghost stuffy proudly in the center. It looked exactly the same as it did when Shannon and I got ready last night. I removed my soiled clothes and dropped them in the hamper, noting that there wasn't so much as a rip in any of them, and threw my tights into the lingerie bag before I plugged my phone in and headed to the bathroom.

"Jesus Christ," I said to no one when I saw my reflection in the mirror. My hair was in such a state that I thought I'd have to cut the bands off, and my previously smokey eyeshadow looked like I had two sparkly-purple black eyes. I reached into a drawer and grabbed an envelope opener, a trick I'd learned from my moms, and wove it under the rubber band, pulling it away from my head to slice it. I had to unwind the rest of it by hand and I groaned when the bun finally fell flat. I repeated the process on the other side and then massaged my scalp with my fingers.

"Oh holy shit, that's good." The feeling of loosening the tension against my scalp was almost orgasmic, and I finger combed through it and climbed into the clawfoot tub so I could take a shower.

When I rented this house I was so excited to have a real clawfoot tub. Like, hello cottage core life, but when I quickly realized it was also the only shower kit in the house I discovered that clawfoot tubs are actually the worst. I had to have two curtain liners inside the tub to wrap around the circumference and the plastic constantly stuck to my skin. A thin woman may not have a problem with it, but I take up the entirety of the space available and the feeling of the soap-covered curtain liners touching me freaks me out. I also hadn't managed to take the time to have a bath in the damn thing yet. Who has the time to sit in their own body-filth soup for an hour?

I took extra time with my hair, masking it before adding my color depositing conditioner to refresh my purple. I could hear my phone blowing up in the bedroom, seemingly having charged enough to turn on, but I decided to enjoy washing off the scuz of the night before - well as much as I could with the plastic fondling me. I made sure to flip every roll and pull my body in every direction to make sure that I wasn't injured in any way, but the only thing I could find were perfectly shaped finger bruises on my love handles, and for some reason that didn't upset me at all. We must have done something, but what happened? Did he rob me? If he didn't assault me then why can't I remember anything?

Once I was dry and in a pair of black lounge pants and my favorite crop top (it had the sweetest little bats on it), I sat on my bed to begin going through my phone. Holy hell. It was 11:45 in the morning.

Nothing was making sense.

I opened a text thread from Shannon, but they were all her gushing about her fuck fest with Trae last night and didn't provide any clues about Thomas and me. I made the conscious decision to not tell her something might have happened until I spoke to Thomas because I was going to speak to him and quickly texted her that I was okay but not feeling the best for brunch. Besides, it was September.

Brunch in Quaker's Wharf on a Saturday in the fall? Yeah, good luck with that.

I thought about simply texting Thomas to ask him what happened, but realized that I wanted to see his face. I wanted him to look me in the eyes and tell me how we spent our night. Unfortunately for him, I didn't know where he lived, so he was going to have to be okay with me crashing his shift at work. I didn't even know if he worked at the store on the weekends, but I did know that I was going to find out. I braided my long hair down the side of my head and went to go find my sandals.

With the power of ginormous sunglasses, I was able to walk the block to my car and headed toward the fast food place for something greasy and an orange juice in hopes of releasing some of the cramping in my stomach. Sadly, the queasiness was replaced with nerves. I had genuinely liked Thomas; I hoped down to my toes that I was wrong and assuming the worst.

I psyched myself up in the parking lot and was amazed at the number of people already swarming the store. Part of me wanted to be meek and come back at closing, but the other part of me wanted to go embarrass him in front of everyone if he had the balls to try to hurt me. I finished my orange juice with a gulp and burped up a clump of acid that made me want to die all over again. I flipped open my glove box and sifted through the small sewing kit, condoms, and medicine bottles until I found the antacids. Always be prepared.

Using the slippery fabric of my lounge pants, I slid out of my tall Jeep and locked it behind me. My anxiety climbed with each step toward the store and I felt my throat closing. I may be a strong, independent woman, but I was horrible at confrontation. Any time I mask into a boss bitch who is all party and confidence, I can sell more clothes and do a better job, but I have textbook rejection sensitive dysphoria. Just ask any of my grade school teachers; they'd all made me cry while they tried to give me constructive feedback on my assignments. It is by far one of the biggest things I hated about myself. It was embarrassing to burst into sweat and tears because I have to lay the hammer down or defend myself, and the fear of criticism does prevent me from putting myself out there a lot; if I didn't put myself in criticism's way, there'd no criticism to give me. That was the reason I worked for myself - if I'm the boss, I'm never wrong.

I took off my sunglasses and went inside, the store was darker than most for ambiance's sake and my hangover was delighted about it. I looked around for a minute and saw him talking to a teenager in a purple polo with a neon pumpkin on the back. God, I did not miss having to wear uniforms - it's like companies pick the most unflattering thing they can find on purpose. I had only been hiding behind a shelf for like two seconds before Thomas seemed to sense me and glanced up from his conversation and began looking around. He patted the acne-ridden boy's shoulder and mimed that he'd be gone for one minute and he began to walk toward where I was hiding.

I knew I'd be found whether I wanted to be or not, so I stepped out, immediately seeing his eyes light up and then a deep frown etch down his face.

"Annabel, what's-"

"I need to talk to you. Alone."

He looked around as if he was assessing if the teenagers could manage to burn the building down in ten minutes before he nodded and went to take my hand. I crossed my arms instead, despite desperately wanting to feel him against me - to feel his calming, smooth touch, but if the dude had fucking roofied me there was no way I was ever letting him touch me again.

He walked behind the cash register and opened a curtain, and waved his hand to welcome me through.

"To the left," he said when I came to a split in the maze made of black fabric, and then he stepped ahead of me to open another fake door.

I stopped short when I entered his...place? Clothes were hanging on metal retail racks and an air mattress with disheveled bedding - there was even a little tv and fridge. I spun to look at him, "Do you live here?" I hissed, quietly enough for no one to hear us in the front of the store.

He shrugged, passively putting his hands in his pockets, *"mon coeur,* why are you looking at me like that?"

"Like what?" I snapped.

He tilted his head to the side and studied me, "I...you're angry with me? Why are you angry with me? I thought we had a great time last night."

"Did we have a great time last night?" I didn't know why I was poking him, it wasn't like anyone would volunteer the information that they drugged their date.

"I thought so... but you are...very, very angry, *ma chérie.*" He extended his arms to me for an embrace, "come here."

I stared at his arms longingly, feeling my anger dissolving into anxiety and fear, but shook my head, "I have a urine sample in my car."

He scrunched his face like the idea was disgusting, "ehhh.... Why?"

"This is your only chance to tell me the truth, and I know you didn't rape me."

He released a loud anxious laugh, "What? *Merde, amour,* what, why-"

"Did you slip anything into my drink last night? Did you roofie me or help anyone else do it? Tell me the truth before I drop the urine off at the lab and I will not press charges. If you lie to me, your ass is going to jail."

He blinked awkwardly fast for a moment and then pushed his shiny brown hair back with his slender hand, "I...No. No, I didn't 'roofie' you. We went back to your place and were watching tv and kissing and you passed out. I assumed you were drunk so I tucked you in on the couch and I left. That's all that happened."

"So if I check the security cam-"

He scoffed angrily and began to pace back and forth in front of me, radiating tension, "check whatever the fuck you want, Annabel, you will not find a damn thing from me."

"Then why are you looking at me like you're sorry!" I said slightly louder than intended, "why are you pacing with your arms crossed like you're not willing to talk to me, or curling your shoulders in or getting defensive? I've watched enough crime shows to know those are all signs of regret and lying."

"Oh yes, Annabel, your binge-watching history is clearly enough to determine the value of my honor."

I slammed my hands onto my hips and raised my brows, "Then why are you acting like this?"

"Maybe because you're accusing me of hurting you?!" He took a few alarmingly fast paces my way as if he was going to grab me by the shoulders and though I tried not to, I flinched, causing him to freeze and shake out his hands.

"*Mon coeur*, I didn't touch your drinks. I didn't poison any food or hire anyone to do it for me. I would never do that to you."

"Then why are you looking at me like that?"

"Christ, Annabel, you don't like it when I don't look at you, you don't like when I walk around, you don't like when I-"

"If I drop off that urine, are you going to jail?"

"*Non!*" He leaned into me with the words, "I did nothing to hurt you."

I hesitated, "did you do anything to me that may not have hurt me but still violated me in some way? Cop a feel on your way out? Make me fall asleep so you could rob me? Doing a test run on me before you do the real thing on someone else?"

"I did not! Like I needed to fondle your unconscious body."

"Then why for the first time in the ten years I've been drinking do I have a gap in my memory and why do I feel like I got hit by a bus?!" My heartbeat picked up and my breathing became shallow, cracking my voice, "why do I feel like you took something from me?" Thomas visibly deflated and my heart broke a little, "you did, didn't you? You did something."

He extended his toned arms out to me as if offering an embrace and I cringed.

"Why would I let you hold me when you clearly did something to me?!" I took a step back instinctively.

"Let me show you," He said quietly and waved his hands asking for a hug again.

"Tell me what the fuck is going on. What if I go to hug you and you like...stab me in the neck or something? I know there are arteries in there that if you hit them I'll bleed out in a matter of minutes. I've seen it -"

"Yes, you've seen it in the media many, many times. I understand. Please let me touch you and I will show you what happened last night."

I hesitated. I shouldn't. If I thought he had the ability to do something awful to me I definitely shouldn't let him near me again, but I could feel calmness radiating from him and I began to wonder if I was overreacting. His eyes calmed me and it was like they implored me to listen to him.

I stepped into his arms stiffly, and he delicately cupped one hand under my chin while the other wrapped around to the small of my back, pulling me to him. He leaned in and placed his lips on mine.

The feeling was instant. It was like I was drunk. The anger and fear quickly dissipated and was being replaced by peace and lust. It wasn't like getting a kiss that made you swoon, it was like getting kissed while a movie witch was sucking the soul out of a child with big, straw-like sucking breaths. I broke my lips from his, pushing him away and stepping back fast enough that I bumped into the air mattress and fell onto it. "What the fuck was that, Thomas?"

10

THOMAS

I smelled her before I saw her. The delicious citrus and ginger seeped through the disgusting tang of the high-school-gym-locker stinking teenager named Jonah that was next to me. To keep up appearances, I'd hired a crew of teens to work alongside me on weekends. They were easy harvests and if I worked all day, every day people would get suspicious. I had no doubt that I could run the place by myself, but mortals could be annoyingly observant sometimes.

I hadn't so much as needed a sip of their energy, still satiated from my night with Annabel, but the hunger grew to desperate levels the minute I saw she was angry with me as if my body knew it needed to subdue her. My mind spun with everything from, "she's back for more," to "she just wants to shop," to "she regrets kissing me," though if she regretted kissing me, she would need to get over that very quickly. She was mine. I couldn't imagine going back to harvesting a stranger's punitive amounts of energy after tasting Annabel's power-fully course through me while we kissed. I imagined that it probably felt similar to the difference between smoking a joint versus doing heroin. After all, they say it only takes one hit to become addicted, and I *was* addicted.

I was pacing the room as my beast slammed against his cage inside me, desperate to taste her. She accused me of trying to assault her and the need to force her to apologize for the insult was as potent as the desire to lay at her feet and beg her to realize I did no such thing. I settled for going to grab her shoulders but thought better of it when my beautiful girl flinched at the thought of my touch. Last night our touches had become so casual that I didn't need to harvest throughout the night, only taking what she threw at me. There were actually times when we were just able to exist together. It was amazing. Magical. We kissed - a lot, and now, now the woman flinched from me.

"*Mon coeur*, I didn't touch your drinks. I didn't poison any food or hire anyone to do it for me. I would never do that to you."

She was wearing a mask that was intended to make her appear strong, but I could see and smell the fear she held that she was alone with someone who might hurt her. If she thought I would hurt her, why would she possibly choose to be alone with me? If she pulled this shit with someone who really meant her harm I would have her delicious ass over my knee in an instant. "Then why are you looking at me like that?" She bit the words, clearly thinking she had the upper hand.

"Christ, Annabel, you don't like it when I don't look at you, you don't like when I walk around, you don't like when I-"

"If I drop off that urine, are you going to jail?"

Rage and hurt coated what I imagined was left of my soul, "*Non!*" I leaned into her, practically begging her to push me one way or the other. Who did she want to take control of this? "I did nothing to hurt you."

She hesitated, assessing my words and taking inventory of herself, "Did you do anything to me that may not have hurt me but still violated me in some way? Cop a feel on your way out? Make me fall asleep so you could rob me? Doing a test run on me before you do the real thing on someone else?"

This was getting absurd, "I did not! Like I needed to fondle your unconscious body." I could have gone home with any woman in that bar last night, fucked them until the sun came up, and then never spoke to them again, but no, I picked her because she was everything I needed in this world wrapped up in a curvy purple package.

"Then why for the first time in the ten years I've been drinking do I have a gap in my memory and why do I feel like I got hit by a bus? Why do I feel like you took something from me?"

Oh, merde. Fuck.

She somehow figured it out. She knew. She knew something different happened but she couldn't find any explanation for it except that I meant to hurt her. It had to be something black and white like that to her, unfortunately, my life was a never ending gradient of grays.

"You did, didn't you? You did something," her voice cracked and I could see her facade failing. Her eyes glistened as though she was going to cry, though nothing had been said yet that should hurt her feelings, and she was practically trembling.

The anxiety was coming off of her in blinding waves and I knew that it wouldn't go well if I just went straight to, *"Oh yeah, I'm an energy vampire, no bigs though. By the way, every paranormal creature you've ever thought of is some variation of the truth, but I'd still like to claim you and live happily ever after because you smell freakishly good. And let's not forget that some primal part of me wants to cuff you to a bed and fuck you until we both die. Sounds great, right?"*

Her feelings were already strong enough that I could taste them without even touching her. It made me wonder if she was any more emotional if I'd have the ability to harvest from her without touching her directly.

Touching her. I should just touch her. I could soothe her. I could fix this and explain it to her in a way that wouldn't scare her more if her anxiety wasn't so elevated. I just needed her to let me touch her, that was it. I extended my arms, hoping I wouldn't need to convince her.

"Why would I let you hold me when you clearly did something to me?!" She pulled back from me and the beast within me snarled. *Mon coeur* does not get to be afraid of me.

"Let me show you," I spoke softly as if she was a scared dog, backed into an alley corner and I only wanted to help her get to food and safety.

"Tell me what the fuck is going on. What if I go to hug you and you like...stab me in the neck or something. I know there are arteries in there that if you hit them I'd bleed out in a matter of minutes. I've seen it -"

I wanted to scoff. I wanted to throw something, though I owned nothing to throw. What a stubborn woman. "Yes, you've seen it in the media many, many times. I understand. Please let me touch you and I will show you what happened last night."

She hesitated again and I was about to say fuck it and throw her over my shoulder when I shook my head and reminded myself to remain calm and lure her in. I'd always been able to lure people in with my eyes, I could at least encourage her to trust me, so I locked eyes with her, imploring her to give in. I saw the minute she made the decision and came to me. The moment I touched her skin it was as if the clouds had parted and the angels sang, I felt so right and warm against her lush body. I moved a hand behind her back, spreading my fingers and pulling her against me, wanting to groan at the delicious way her body contoured into mine. I placed my other hand under her chin, tilting her head slightly up to me so I could place a kiss on her lips.

I didn't have to jump over any shields to get into her energy; it was as if the second I touched her she sent a tsunami wave of them in my direction and I was slammed with every negative feeling that had plagued her in the past twelve hours. They crashed over and over me, and almost drowned me since I wasn't expecting to take anywhere near that much of her energy. I'd intended to simply take the edge off and make her peaceful enough that we could have a conversation, but it felt almost as if her spirit found a willing vessel for her anxiety and was thrusting as much of it as she could away from her. It was almost too much for me with how much of her was still in my system from last night. I could feel her old and new energies swirling together within me like brackish water. She was fucking magnificent. I went to kiss her again when she yanked herself from my grip and stumbled back with terror in her eyes, falling into the air mattress.

"What the fuck was that Thomas?" her voice was shaking.

"I might ask you the same question, *amour*." I leaned down, placing my hands on my knees and I closed my eyes, trying to give my body a moment to process everything she had chucked in my direction.

"Me? What did I do?!" Her eyes widened, anger reigniting within them and acting more like the Annabel I'd met yesterday. This poor woman's anxiety was crushing her bit by bit.

"Why were you so anxious that it would have killed a lesser woman?"

"What?" She snapped the word as if I'd invaded her privacy, when, yes, obviously, that was my goal, but she had willingly shoved those emotions at me. "How could you possibly know-"

"*Amour*, I told you last night that I can read people's emotions."

"Reading my emotions and changing them are two entirely different things. How did you do that? What the fuck happened last night? Who the fuck are you?" Her voice was becoming progressively more shrill.

I heard a sudden quiet come from the store. "Annabel," I said her name firmly, snapping her to attention, "you will draw too much attention to us. I am going to sit with you and I will help you stay calm by holding your hand while I explain, yes?"

"What? No."

A growl began to rumble in my chest involuntarily, "Annabel, this is my place of business. You will either let me help you remain calm or you will leave now and not come back until the store is closed. I will give you answers either way, but you must choose how you will behave while we discuss it."

"Don't speak to me like I'm some petulant child when you-"

I raised my brow, "Do you wish to speak to me now, or do you wish to leave?"

She glared at me with those fierce green eyes for a few more moments before she sighed and stuck her hand out.

"I think I might hate you," she muttered with a pout on her lips.

I laughed, "My love, you do no such thing." sitting next to her on the air mattress, I watched her bob up and down as the air leveled out and she begrudgingly took my hand. I pulled slightly on her energy, trying to discover how to filter through her cascade and her shoulders relieved some of the tension they'd been carrying.

She sighed, "Okay, tell me what the fuck is going on? This isn't normal." I could tell she wanted to say it with force and power, she wanted to put me in my place, but she was for all intents and purposes, stoned at the moment.

I thought for a second, debating how to approach it, "I am not like you."

"No shit, Sherlock, tell me something I don't know."

Against my better judgment, I chuckled slightly, "Annabel-"

"Don't call me that." Her eyes were closed and her breathing was steady. I released the tether I'd been pulling on and continued to hold her hand, hoping to keep her in this place of lucidity but complacency.

"Why not? It is your name?"

"It's not my name to you, Tommy. You always call me *mon coeur*."

A crooked smile formed on my face and I decided to go for it, "*Mon coeur*, I am an energy harvester, I am not mortal."

"What is an energy harvester? Like a dementor or something?"

"*Non, ma belle.*"

"Bels."

"What?"

"My friends, some of them call me Bels for short. You might as well just call me Bels too."

"Ah," I said, surprised that she'd detoured away from the whole, I ate your soul's energy thing. I paused and assessed her relaxed face, "You're the most beautiful woman I've ever met, Annabel. When you looked at me with that anger and fear in your eyes I think it could have destroyed me if I'd stared too long."

"Because you're a...mood farmer?"

I chuckled again, "energy harvester, smartass, though most mortals simply call us Vampires."

It wasn't until I said that word that her hand yanked away from mine and her eyes shot open like I'd admitted I was carrying the plague. I could tell she was slow on the draw with how languid I made her, which was exactly what I wanted - I didn't want her to run from the conversation, but her anxiety immediately ratcheted up again.

I grabbed her hand to try to subdue it, "calm down, *ma chérie*, calm down."

She ripped it from me again and leaned away, hissing, "You're a vampire? Like *I've come to suck your blood*, vampire?"

"*Oui, mon coeur*, but you have nothing to fear from me. Mortals have long since mixed up vampires and our sick brothers."

"You're a vampire."

"*Oui.*"

"Oh my god. I've died. I've hit my head somewhere, I must have fallen out of the Jeep or drunkenly fallen down the stairs. Shit, what if I'm still in the shower and I'm slowly drowning..."

"Annabel-"

"No! You don't just get to say that like I've stepped into a fucking Twilight movie and expect me to be totally chill with it! What happened to me last night? If I have nothing to worry about, why can't I remember? Did you wipe my memory or something? Did you hurt me?" She pushed herself up making me sink closer to the floor. She began to pace with her hands on her head and I could hear her heartbeat steadily increasing, "Jesus, are you an Edward? Have you been breaking into my house and watching me sleep? Are you 120 years old and obsessed with a teenager? Are you a total pervert? Do you have a creepy cloaked army of Dakota Fannings about to attack me!?"

"You're spiraling, Bels."

"Do you kill animals?!" She stopped and stared at me wide-eyed, "Do you go out at night and hunt black bears?!"

"Annabel, if you'd stop moving I'd be able to explain what

happened, but if you need to continue to compare me to a teenage romance book I can come back later."

She turned and scowled at me, "Tommy." She said my name almost pleadingly like she wanted me to say that she'd been pranked.

"You have the most intense emotional pool that I've ever encountered. It's fascinating."

"What the fuck is that supposed to mean? Yesterday my emotional pool was just fine thank you very much; you're the one that's fucked it all up."

"*Non*, Bels, I barely touched it."

"Then explain why I woke up thinking I got roofied?!"

"My love, I have a store full of customers. I have staff out there-"

"Jesus Christ, if you're going to eat those kids-"

I was so offended that I laughed out loud, "You think I would risk exposure for some zitty teens?"

"You're the vampire here, not me."

I jumped up and flashed to her side, pressing my index finger to her lips and her eyes flew wide in disbelief, "I need you to be quiet, *mon coeur*. I am trying to live here, just like everyone else. I am not suddenly going to kill a store full of people when I need their money to move on." I sighed when the overhead intercom called for a manager to the register knowing damn well that I was the only manager.

"I'll meet you tonight and explain everything, okay?"

"But, I, Tommy-" She was flustered and turning a wonderful shade of pink, clearly wanting more information that very moment.

"Go drop off your 'sample' if you don't want to believe me - there will be no drugs in your system, and if I was a vampire interested in killing you I would have done it by now."

Her eyes widened further, and I caressed her soft cheek with the back of my hand, calming her enough that she whispered, "But - I... I have so many questions."

I nodded, "I'll answer all of them. I'll see you tonight." I leaned forward and pressed a kiss to the top of her head and took her hand to guide her back out to the front of the store. My insides churned, frustrated that mortal teenagers were so useless that some sort of pirate or black cat-related emergency couldn't possibly be solved without me during one of the most important conversations of my life.

"I promise. I'll come by tonight."

"But-"

"I promise you, Bels."

11
ANNABEL

Okay, I didn't know what I was expecting, but an energy-sucking vampire wasn't it. I was hoping he'd say I'd just fallen asleep and I was out of my mind, and then I'd go to the urgent care and prove him right, but when he touched me I felt my emotions drain out of me. It was like I was an extra thick milkshake and I was trying to ease my stress through a coffee stirrer, and then Thomas blasted through all of my defenses with a boba straw. I felt in control of my body like I could have pushed him away from me if I'd tried, but I wasn't scared of him, if anything, it was a relief to get the anxiety out of my system so fast.

I climbed into my Jeep and pulled the bottom elastic on my crop top to blow some air conditioning on my boob sweat to help dry it out. I didn't know if it was boob sweat from heat or nerves, but regardless, I needed a second to air them out while I got my head back on straight.

A vampire was a vampire, right? I mean, folklore doesn't exist out of nothing. Stories, tales, and warnings that came down verbally over centuries didn't just poof into someone's head.

"Well excuse-moi for not knowing the conjugation of your silly 'poof' word."

I laughed, hearing his words in my head so clearly, it was as if he was yelling them into my ear. Oh my god. Could he read my mind? Please let me be a Bella.

I panicked and grabbed a stack of sticky notes out of my purse, and quickly scribbled, "can you read my mind?" on it before peeling it off and sticking it to my dash with a nod. Then I scribbled out, "are you going to accidentally or purposely kill me at any time?" and slapped that on my dash as well.

I needed a fucking coffee. I pulled out onto the road outside the shopping center and drove the three blocks to the coffee place with a drive-through and ordered myself a Roasted Marshmallow. It was my drink of the summer while I waited for PSL to return. It was a white chocolate and marshmallow syrup latte with an extra shot of espresso. It tasted like camping. Not that I'd know, or camp, really - these boots were made for walking, not hiking.

My car's phone system rang and I picked it up when I saw it was Shannon.

"You get laid?" I asked instead of saying hello.

"*I was calling to ask you the same thing!*" her cheery voice echoed through my car and I immediately turned the volume down. If he was such an energy sucker, why couldn't he have found a way to remove the stupid hangover symptoms?

"Uh, no, I apparently passed out on the couch and he left," I answered honestly.

"*Well, I guess it's a good thing you've been fucking him for years then, right? At least you didn't fall asleep in a vulnerable position with someone you just met yesterday.*"

Even I heard how awkward my laugh was, "oh my god, I know right?"

"*What are you doing? Want to go get brunch?*"

"I actually already grabbed something to try and help with my headache. I'm sorry, I forgot we'd talked about that."

"*Wait, you got hungover?*"

On autopilot, I turned toward my office, "I know, I was surprised too."

"You can drink me under the table any night of the week and still wake up fine. You got a hangover? How much did you drink after I left?"

"Shannon, you're asking me questions like a mom again."

She sighed, *"Sorry. Force of habit."*

"Well, I'm an adult, and I'm your boss so..."

"Oh, you want to play the boss card? Fire me then."

"Yeah, yeah. I'm headed in to work on the launch for a bit. I'll text you when I'm hungry - maybe we can grab something later."

She was quiet for a moment and then covered her phone and said something jumbled to the person she was with. *"Is it okay if Trae comes with? If you're busy I think we are going to go do something."*

Internally I cringed. The more times we are together, the more opportunities I had to fuck it up for her. She never got this attached.

"That's like 72 hours straight now, Shan."

A girlish giggle escaped her, *"Yeah, well, it is what it is."* I could hear her squealing mentally and knew she was only pretending to appear nonchalant about the whole thing.

"I'm at the office. You kids have fun."

"See you later, Bels!" I heard Trae holler over the line and I disconnected it and shut off the car.

I loved working on Saturdays. It was especially great for online marketing since the building was always empty except for me. I could play my music as loud as I needed to and do take after take of a clip without making the people next door want to get me evicted. When I got into the office, I went to the filming area and plopped into the giant furry beanbag I kept in there so I could scroll through the trending videos while I drank my coffee. I wasn't trying to invent the wheel, I just wanted to piggyback off of something someone already made popular by making it about my ass.

Ironically, or maybe not, some of the music from popular vampire movies were starting to trend, which was fitting for my life and my new line. I quickly saved the sounds and kept scrolling, hoping to be able to bank a bunch of drafts for the week. I frequently had to jump on a sudden viral trend during the middle of the week, but I liked my filler content to be sitting around. I used to make it whenever the mood struck me and found that the constant interruptions made for horrifically unproductive days.

With my coffee finished and 16 sounds in my files, I headed into the storeroom to pull and steam outfits. Over the years I'd learned to streamline the process by steaming, styling, photographing, and filming an outfit all at once, but it still takes way more time than the regular person would think. People are like, oh you own a boutique, you just take pictures, post them and then have some company ship everything out for you? Wouldn't that be the dream? No, I spent each and every day curating, purchasing, shipping, marketing and even doing my own damn web development. Before Shannon, HalloQueens was entirely a one-woman show.

I pulled out multiple bat and spiderweb outfits as well as some bell-sleeve blouses and large statement jewelry. I hadn't put makeup on before confronting Thomas so I would be able to film a 'get ready with me' before I started. I'd take some additional clips to make a 'day in the life' one too. I knew it sounded overwhelming, but it was thinking like this that saved me time and made me successful, unfortunately, it also made it so this was eight full-time jobs all sitting squarely on my shoulders.

I spent the morning making video after video, banking them in my drafts, while also feeling my stress level begin to climb simply from being in the building full of future work. I was angry at how much better I felt around Thomas - what gave him the right to make me enjoy his energy milking kink? This launch was too important for me to fuck it up. Even though my last two launches had sold out almost instantly because of our viral videos, I knew all it would take to close me down was one failed season. That was the curse of internet fame; the same crowd that could make you go viral could also shit post and get you canceled faster than you can say hot potato. All it would take is someone's shipping taking too long, or not having any product for size exchanges or god-forbid, actually having a life outside of the boutique. There'd been people that messaged me at midnight with questions and when I didn't answer until the next morning I would get scathing replies about how poor my customer service was so they'd gone somewhere else for the item. Like, excuse me for sleeping, Ashley.

I was in the middle of flipping myself onto a doorframe, which trust me, was not easy, and I would have bruises on my calves from it, but the pose made my tits look great in lingerie so I continued to use it, when my phone stopped recording and a text came in, "son of a bitch," I cursed, falling to grab it. I swore I had it on airplane mode so I wouldn't get cut off, but there was a text from Thomas that paused the filming and ruined my handstand.

TOMMY: I AM THINKING OF YOU. I AM SORRY ABOUT THIS MORNING.

I scowled at it for a moment before texting back, wanting answers, yet not knowing how to discuss it with him.

ANNABEL: ARE CHUPUCABRAS REAL?

Almost immediately the three little dots popped up

TOMMY: IN A SENSE.

ANNABEL: WTF DOES THAT MEAN? AREN'T THEY JUST LIKE FREAKED OUT WERE-VAMPIRES?

TOMMY: WE CAN DISCUSS THE INNER WORKINGS OF OTHERS SOCIETAL STRUCTURES LATER.

ANNABEL: Mermaids.

TOMMY: What?

ANNABEL: Mermaids. Are they real?

TOMMY: Sirens are real. Though they certainly aren't wearing seashell bras and trying to work through their daddy issues.

ANNABEL: So sirens, like, ancient Greece, lure you to your death.

TOMMY: Oui. Nasty beasts.

ANNABEL: They might say the same about you, you know.

TOMMY: I have no doubt they do. We don't tend to enjoy sharing the same waters.

I plopped down into the beanbag, prepared to word dump all over him.

ANNABEL: Unicorns?

TOMMY: Non.

ANNABEL: Fae?

TOMMY: We don't talk about them.

ANNABEL: Leprechauns?

TOMMY: Annoying little bastards.

ANNABEL: Werewolves?

TOMMY: Oui. Lived with one for a while, great guy, but I couldn't get past the wet dog smell.

That made me laugh out loud.

ANNABEL: What do I smell like?
TOMMY: You smell divine.

I considered that for a moment and decided to accept the compliment and circle back.

ANNABEL: Loch Ness Monster?

That one took him a few more moments to reply, and I burst into laughter at what I saw pop up on my screen.

TOMMY: I'm not at liberty to say.

Another text came through before I could reply.

TOMMY: I can't spill all our secrets via text. You're going to have to work for some of the answers.

I gnawed on my bottom lip absentmindedly.

ANNABEL: And how would one earn answers?

TOMMY: We can discuss tonight over dinner if you'd like.

ANNABEL: Am I on the menu?

TOMMY: Non, amour, I thought I could cook for you.

ANNABEL: You cook?

TOMMY: I watch enough cooking shows that I presume I can, but I can't taste it so I'll need you to tell me what you think.

ANNABEL: You can't taste food?

TOMMY: Non, everything tastes the same to me.

ANNABEL: I bet we could monetize that and go around to bars having people place bets on your ability to handle a ghost pepper and then you just...obliterate it and take their money.

TOMMY: Maybe another night. Tonight I want to make chicken marsala because I've always thought it looks delicious.

ANNABEL: Sounds yummy to me.

I waited a moment.

ANNABEL: I'M STILL ANXIOUS ABOUT BEING AROUND YOU, TOMMY. I DON'T KNOW IF THIS IS THE BEST IDEA.

TOMMY: I KNOW.

ANNABEL: THAT WAS COMFORTING.

TOMMY: I CAN'T EASE YOUR ANXIETY FROM ACROSS TOWN, AMOUR. I'LL SEE YOU LATER.

I sighed, switching on airplane mode and putting my phone back on the tripod. The internet never slept and my tits weren't going to bounce themselves.

A few hours later, I felt confident that I'd captured the energy of the lingerie collection and decided to go home to take a nap. The movement and coffee helped the hangover a little bit, but it honestly felt like something was wrong with me. I had to force movements and think harder to achieve results that should have come easily to me. I felt as useless as a sedan trying to haul a travel trailer up a hill. The more incapacitated I felt, the more my anxiety rose, and the more my anxiety rose, the angrier I got with myself because my first stupid thought was, "if I was with Thomas I could just chuck these feelings at him and move on."

Only, I couldn't trust my feelings anymore, could I? If he was able to take them from me, how did I know he wasn't manipulating me into wanting to give them to him? He hadn't even explained how this worked yet - would this kill me? So far, he claimed he'd only taken depression and anxiety from me, but could he steal my happiness? Could he manipulate my lust? It was as if the harder I thought about it, the more gray any level of consent with him would be. Could I believe that any of my thoughts and desires toward him were genuine? Would there be a way for there to be clear and enthusiastic consent?

But fuck, two seconds with him was better for my soul than a freaking Xanax. If there was a way to keep it mutually beneficial for us... what was I saying!? He was a vampire! VAMPIRE. I wasn't some 16-year-old damsel in distress singing Evanescense in my beater car smoking stolen cigarettes, well, not anymore. This was my real fucking life. Decisions with this would impact my entire world - also, Tommy worked at a Halloween store and was sleeping on an air mattress, so I didn't think I'd won the sugar daddy lottery like all the books on my e-reader claimed I would if I found a monster.

I headed out to my car, determined to sleep and recharge my battery before whatever terrifying revelations were going to be dropped on me, and drove back to my row house, finding parking two blocks down. I loved my neighborhood, but things like street parking were not something I was looking forward to doing in winter again. My place in Chicago had a bus station directly in front of it so I hadn't bothered with keeping a car there. I could only imagine what a snow plow could do to a parked car.

Checking my watch, I saw that it was only 4:45, so I headed upstairs, took off my lounge pants, and crawled into my big delicious bed in only my crop top and undies. I could never sleep with pants on, something about the fabric on my legs always had made me feel tangled. My bedroom was the only room in the house that I'd managed to fully unpack, and that was solely out of the need to have the place where I slept be as soothing as possible. I'd found an online vision board that was a dark academia mixed with boho plants and had immediately become obsessed. I'd filled the tall bay window facing the street with hanging plants in macrame and a ridiculously soft chair and a half, which was perfect for reading in on rainy days, and I'd bought all of my bedroom furniture second-hand to give it an eclectic vibe. I'd found a big iron bed that looked stunning against the mercury glass moon phases I'd gotten online and hung on the wall. My bedding was made up of moss, whites, and blacks in varying textures, my favorites being the faux fur and velour ones, and my nightstands were made with brass snake pulls and mercury glass mirrored tops. This room also housed my beautiful and extensive smut collection. My life had been changed when exclusive reprints with discrete covers had become popular. How I could suddenly get all of my favorite book boyfriends inside of leatherette covers with gilded pages? Sold. Sold every single time.

I leaned over to turn off my vintage fringed lamp and it was only a matter of moments before my eyes fluttered shut, taking me away to dreamland.

When I awoke, my house smelled divine. I was confused for a moment, laying under the piles of blankets with my eyes closed, since I knew I hadn't put anything in the slow cooker that morning, but when I heard, "Annabel," I screamed and jumped from the bed clutching my chest.

"Jesus fucking Christ how did you get in here?!" I placed my hands on my knees and bent over, resting my ass against my wall, and tried to slow my heart. A freaking vampire was sitting nonchalantly on my bed like he had every right in the world to be there.

He smiled, "When I got here you were asleep so I thought I'd let you rest while I cooked you that dinner, *amour*."

I gasped through a swallow and waved my hand at him, "no, like, I knew you were coming over, but how the fuck did you get in my house?"

He blinked at me confused a few times before answering, "you invited me."

My eyes closed to slits and I glared at him, "yes, I know, smartass, but how did you get into my house while I was dead asleep and manage to cook an entire meal without me waking up or knowing that you were here. I could have died!"

Tommy shrugged as if it was nothing consequential, "you were tired, you weren't answering my texts and I figured you needed the rest. Are you ready for dinner? I'm desperate to know what it tastes like, *amour*."

"Aw, shit," I grumbled, grabbing my phone from my purse and turning off airplane mode. As a slew of texts came through, I heard a deep rumble come from across the room so I turned to look at him, "What now, bat boy?"

His eyes were glued to my legs and ass. I had strong thick legs which made my german ancestors proud since this bitch could haul her own plow when the horse went lame, but genetics had softened up a bit on my rump making it freaking huge and covered in dimples from years of cellulite and weight fluctuation. He seemed to be stuck on my tattoo, which covered the majority of the side of my thigh, and was a large grayscale raven, sitting on a stack of books.

"Please insert cash or select payment type," I said dryly and his eyes blinked before meeting mine.

"Pardon?"

A laugh escaped me, "you going to oggle me all night? It's not free."

"Right," he swallowed loudly and wiped his hands on the canvas gray material of his pants, "dinner? Let's," he stood and then hesitated again, tilting his head just slightly and growled again, "you have the most beautiful ass I have ever seen, *mon coeur*."

"Good enough to eat?" I teased.

"You have no idea."

I groaned, "get out so I can find some pants, please?"

"If I stay will the pants remain off?"

I leveled a glare at him and he put his hands up in defeat before walking to the stairs. Once he was gone, I sighed and gave a small chuckle before pulling my lounge pants back on and stuffing my phone in my pocket. I quickly brushed my hair and redid my space buns, then sighed and followed Thomas down the stairs.

"You never said how you got in my house?" I hollered as I came into the foyer, turning to head toward the kitchen. Quickly assessing and running inventory of the space, I could see that he hadn't stolen anything obvious while I'd been asleep, and I didn't feel horrifically drained again, so I don't think he ate me either...harvested? No, that sounded extra creepy. He didn't answer me but I gasped and froze in my tracks when I entered the kitchen, seeing that he'd cleaned the entire space, lit candles, and was wearing the frilly french maid apron I'd used for a Halloween costume a few years ago. He looked far too comfortable in my space while stirring the most delicious-smelling sauce on the stove. My eyes drifted downward and noticed the hand towel stuck into his back pocket and I admired the curvature of his ass that it accentuated.

"Insert cash or select payment type," he mimicked me without turning around.

I scoffed, leaning my elbows against the island and resting my chin on my hands, "so should I just swipe a credit card down your asscheeks, or what's your preferred payment method?"

That comment caused him to throw his head back in a loud laugh and he shook his head, turning back to his sauce, "oh, *non, non, non.*"

"Was that a no on the ass register then?"

"An ass register? Really, Annabel?" He chuckled and turned to my iPad which he'd somehow unlocked and synced up to a streaming service where an old woman was making chicken marsala. He'd clearly been following it to a T and was moving the dot back and forth along the video progress bar, rewinding, freezing, and restarting specific parts. "Would you like to taste this and tell me what you think? I think I've done everything they said."

Without hesitating, I stepped up to the stove and leaned over it to lick the sauce off of the wooden spoon. I relaxed into Thomas' touch at the small of my back and moaned at the mixture of fresh herbs and wine. "Mmmm, it's good!" I say, happily, "You should try it."

He shrugged, "I won't be able to taste it. Do you think it needs anything?"

"A little salt, maybe, but no, it's really good."

"Wonderful," he smiled at me brightly and got down a wide pasta bowl, ladling in some noodles and sauce with a full chicken breast, garnishing it with parsley, and presenting it to me like he was a barn cat that was pleased as punch with the vole that it'd dropped at its owner's feet.

I returned his enthusiasm and took the food, sitting at the island and enjoying a big bite as he poured me a glass of wine, "I don't know if I should just enjoy the service or be mildly bothered that you seem to know where everything is in my kitchen."

"You were asleep a while."

I arched a brow and took another bite, "and you just made yourself at home?"

"Like I said," he grinned, "you invited me in."

"So what would it taste like to you?" I ask when I notice that he'd already turned and begun to clean up his mess.

He gave a contemplative noise and turned the sink on, pouring some soap into it, "have you ever thought about what a library smells like? How it's kind of musty and stale?"

"Yes, it's hands down the best smell on the planet."

"*Oui*, but it isn't the best taste," He said with a grimace.

I considered it, bringing another forkful of pasta to my mouth and he began to wash the dishes, "Hey, the dishes can wait, come, sit with me. We have a lot to talk about."

He shrugged, "it only makes sense that because I can't eat that I get it all cleaned up while you do."

"Sure, but you're not Cinderella, Tommy, stop avoiding the conversation and sit down. Besides, from the looks of it, you already helped with like three days' worth of dishes before you started cooking anyway."

He sighed, drying his hands on the towel from his back pocket, and walked around the island to where I was sitting on a stool, pulling one out to sit on himself, "What do you want to know?"

"We can start with how you got into my house?"

Thomas chuckled, repeating, "You invited me in."

"But I didn't answer the door, and I know it was locked."

"Ah. Well, once a mortal invites one of us into their home, no lock can keep us out. We can kind of come and go as we please."

I cried in outrage, "Well that's not fair!"

"Says the woman who woke up to a clean kitchen and a good meal?"

"Says the woman who had a vampire staring at her ass when she was half asleep."

He nodded at that, "valid."

The stool allowed me to spin slightly to face him, "Can you kill me?"

"Easily."

Groaning in exasperation, I rolled my eyes at his blasé, "Thomas."

He smirked, gesturing to my bowl to indicate I should continue eating, "You're going to have to be more specific in your questions, *amour*."

"Alright... are you going to kill me? Can taking energy kill someone?"

"I suppose it could. I personally have never killed anyone that way, but I'm sure when there's a will there's a way."

"Hmmm... are there blood vampires?"

"Of course. I need to eat blood too."

I froze, "What?"

"No, I do not intend to eat you, Annabel, I've been having medical-grade blood delivered for years. I have no interest in hunting a mortal down."

"Okay," I nod, "So, you don't like to hunt for blood, and you can't kill someone by harvesting energy?"

"*Oui.*"

"What makes you so scary then?"

"Every monster is different. There are many a vampire who enjoy the hunt. They harvest the terror from the individual they've taken the blood from - more like a one-stop shop. Some vampires are very dark. However, at our core, our job is to maintain balance. If I were to go off the deep end and Jack the Ripper half of Quaker's Wharf, it would kill me."

My brows shot up, "what do you mean by that?"

"That's a story for another day."

"Okay, but what about last night? What happened to me?"

He grimaced, "I'm sorry about that."

"No, don't apologize, just explain," I gave him as cold of a look as I could muster, "I deserve to know what you did. I felt so safe and happy with you and to know that it was all manufactured-"

He spoke quickly, "it was not all manufactured, *ma chérie*. I have never had that happen before."

"You've never made a woman pass out and left her to god-only-knows what fate?"

Thomas sighed and dragged his hand through his hair, "*Non, oui - ugh.* Typically when I harvest I need to touch someone and it's just a pull - a taste. I never take enough for them to notice much of a difference, other than maybe they'll be a little sad or tired, but it quickly wears off and they just feel like they've had a fleeting emotional thought. On the contrary, if I harvest sad or anxious energy, it leaves the person feeling happier and more refreshed, though I usually end up feeling their anxiety as it works through my system, so I tend to ignore that. It is usually very much a one-way street when I harvest energy."

"And with me?"

He blew an exaggerated breath from his lips, "with you it is...like a circuit? I feel like I can pour energy into you just as much as I can take it away. Like you're some kind of conduit." I took a large bite of my dinner while he explained, "You seemed almost bottomless, not to mention you were practically throwing your emotions at me. I never risk taking more than a little from a person because they can drain so quickly that I don't want it to ruin their day so to speak, but with you, it was like because I was able to funnel energy back into you, you were a never ending chalice. It was incredible."

"Until it wasn't?"

"Until it wasn't. I think when we began to be intimate that I-," a naughty smile spread from his lips, "- stopped channeling back into you and it...caught up with you. It felt like you were creating more and more and I didn't think to give any back. I think you bottomed out and

99

that's why you fell asleep. I assure you that you were perfectly safe and fine when I left."

I considered that. "And what would have happened if you'd kept conducting the energy through us both?"

He gave me a pathetic grimace, "I don't know, *amour*, I've never experienced this before."

"Never?"

"Never."

I needed a minute to process that, so I moved on to my next thought, "You said you can just come and go as you please; if I'm mad at you, how do I keep you out of my house and out of my energy?"

"You talk to me?" He answered incredulously like it was the most ridiculous question I could have asked.

"Says the vampire! I am clearly at the disadvantage here!" I grabbed a slice of bread and mopped it through my sauce.

"You are not at the disadvantage, *mon coeur*, I think you will find that I am quite susceptible to your whims."

I clicked my nails against the island's butcher block, "I don't like that you're eating those kids you hired. It's violating."

He furrowed his brows, "Bels, I'm not eating them. They're still fully intact at the end of their shift, I assure you. Most people never notice when they've had their energy tapped. The most it ever does it makes someone feel like they need a nap." He went to fill my wine glass, but I shook my head.

"Thomas, you fed from me and it cost me my whole day - and I'm a grown ass woman! I don't like the idea of you violating children like that."

"Violating?"

"Do you have their consent to harvest their energy?"

He went quiet, trying to sort through his various answers, clearly stumped.

"I...don't... but - that's not how it works."

"It's not? And why not?" I firmed up my tone, leaving no room for bullshit.

"Have you ever seen a vampire movie where they pause to ask for permission?"

"And that means that you shouldn't?"

"I just... it's like a lion asking a gazelle for its dinner. It's odd." His face was scrunched up, deep in thought, his thick dark brows were drawn and twitching in distress.

"Would you rape me?" I asked bluntly.

"What?! Annabel-"

"Would you rape me?" Each word I spoke was stunted, emphasized to prove my point. "After all, I'm just a gazelle, right?"

"I would never."

"Because it'd be against my consent?"

"I would never take from you that way. I wouldn't-"

"Do something to someone without their permission?"

He froze and glared at me, "Annabel, I can't *not* eat, and frankly it isn't like I can ask for volunteers. It doesn't hurt anyone and they don't even know. You asking me not to harvest is you asking me to take on a fate that I'm unwilling to accept."

"Because it'd kill you?"

He shook his head solemnly, "I can assure you that it's worse than that. I would cease to exist and I would become a black hole on this earth."

"But-" I started and he shook his head.

"I don't want to talk about that with you Annabel, not yet."

I turned and tucked my legs between his. It was my turn to furrow my brow, "okay, but what if I had a proposition for you?"

He gave me a sad smirk, "then, of course, I would be happy to listen."

12

THOMAS

Annabel turned in her stool so her legs were sandwiched between mine. The warmth of her skin was intoxicating and her energy thrummed through the fabric of our trousers. Her steady vibrations made me want to wrap my arms around her and get one more taste. If she was about to give me the "bite me and then get out of town" speech, I might consider ending this existence willingly at the thought of never tasting her again.

"Okay, but what if I had a proposition for you?" Those were her words, and I knew that it couldn't be a good thing. It felt like one of those awful nights toward the end when Yusuf would come in after work and sit in front of the fire, releasing a deep sigh and announcing, *"we need to talk."*

I tried to steady my nerves, but I knew I was already fucked when it came to Annabel. I'd be haunted by ginger and citrus for the rest of my existence. I feigned confidence and answered, "Then, of course, I would be happy to listen." She bounced her legs for a moment and I placed my hand over her knee. She glared at me and I quickly reassured her, "I have to be touching your bare skin, amour. This is just because I want to."

She worried her bottom lip, as if the courage she was trying to summon was at the bottom of the Mariana Trench, and opened and closed her mouth several times, unsure of how to start her train of thought.

"Bels, *mon coeur*, you can ask me anything. You can *tell* me anything."

She muttered, "says the vampire," again and I chuckled.

"You know, you'll have to watch yourself in public, that seems to be becoming one of your favorite arguments and it won't hold up in mixed company."

Annabel nodded again, "Okay. Proposition time."

"*Oui...*" I couldn't hide my smirk when her legs started bouncing again.

"Fuck, I can't believe I'm doing this."

"What, Bels?"

"When you harvest energy from me...share energy with me...mix our mojos?" She grimaced, "when whatever it is happens, I feel safe and calm and comfortable with you. Though I do feel like any lust I feel when I'm with you could be a gray area of consent because I don't know if you're-"

"I can't force an attraction between us, Bels, I'm fairly certain that the chemistry between us is *au naturel*."

She grunted at that thought, "I feel like I need to take control of this a little bit."

"Okay..."

"What if we agree that if I let you harvest my anxiety from me so I can get through this stupid fall launch without wanting to die, that you don't harvest from anyone else in town? No kids, no tourists, nothing."

I arched a brow at her, "you want me to be exclusively feeding from you?"

"Is that a thing?" She asked with an uncertainty that bordered on adorable.

"Uh...it can be, but usually there's a...precedent for it."

"What kind of precedent?"

I hesitated, how did I want the conversation to play out? How did I tell her that I wanted nothing more than to claim her as my own and tell everyone else to keep away from her? How I wanted her to be mine? How I wanted that raven on her thigh to mean nothing to her other than my name?

"Usually a mortal that is an exclusive-" I swallow hard, cringing at the next words, " source..." She grimaced and I gave her an apologetic look, "is called a Claimed Mortal. That mortal belongs specifically to a member of the...lions."

"And why is that?"

"It's a fairly serious thing," I shrugged, I had never claimed a mortal. Yusuf, Monique, and I had bonded together after leaving France while the mortals were busy chopping each other's heads off and got the hell out of there and never separated. "But, it's also a safety concern. If you were my only source of energy, that means that my entire existence would depend on you. It would be needed to make you untouchable to other...lions... because what if they fed from you? You'd have nothing left for me and I could..."

"Oh."

"Yes, but it also protects you from any random were-whatevers or beasties coming after you. Unless they're looking for a whooping, that is. Untouchables are a very serious thing among any of the 'Others'."

"Untouchables..."

"Another term for Claimed Mortals," I clarified, "There is a cere-mony called a Handfeasting which solidifies the bond magically. It can only be broken by the Coalition and is...quite painful to terminate. The ceremony is simple enough to perform, basically a mortal Handfasting, stating commitments and intentions, but instead of only tying a knot between the parties, we feed from each other's wrists."

"Jesus, I'm not like...marrying you with this am I?"

I shrugged, "if you want your proposal to stand, it is as good as a mortal marriage." *Be mine, my beast roared.*

"But like, 50% of marriages end in divorce." Her eyes were as wide as saucers and she seemed paler than usual. I couldn't help but grin at her discomfort.

"By that logic Bels, 50% live happily ever after. Who's to decide we'd fail other than us?"

"You're a vampire!"

"*Oui.*"

"There's no happily ever after for vampires. You're not alive!"

I shrugged again, "you were the one who brought up that insipid movie. It took four books and a creepy CGI baby, but they got there. Also, I am very much alive."

"I met you yesterday." She bit out, "I'm not marrying you."

"Then I suppose I will 'eat' however many teenagers I please while I serve out eternity in my vampy 'No Happily Ever After'."

She groaned and stood from her stool to take her dishes to the sink, rinsing them and loading them into the dishwasher, "You're not actually going to eat anyone are you?"

I scoffed, "I told you, I get blood delivered."

"Right. Like some kind of meal subscription box from hell," She leaned against her sink and looked out the window into her backyard, "and there's no like...energy drink subscription? Some horrific caffeinated coffee shot that can do the same thing?"

I shook my head with a faint smile, "*Non, belle.*"

"I'm just saying this seems like it can be a mutually beneficial situation," she said after a moment, "I don't think we need to complicate it. You keep me level-headed enough to get through the launch, I keep you fed through Halloween. I think that's decent enough of a setup, don't you? No need for wedding bells."

I got up from my stool and went to her, wrapping my arms around her waist, and nuzzling into her neck, not failing to notice that she leaned into me instead of pulling away, "may I submit a counter proposal?"

"I suppose that's only fair."

"You pair with me until Halloween, unofficially, but come the first week of November when the shop closes, you will either commit to me and we will bond, or I will leave town, free to raid and pillage villages along the eastern seaboard as I see fit and you agree to never tell anyone that I was here. I will also need you to help me pay to move."

"What?" She turned around, "You want me to pay you to leave town? That's absurd, I don't have money like that."

"Fine, then make me a shareholder in HalloQueens and commit to depositing a percentage of profits into an account that I can access from anywhere in the world."

She growled, "So pay you a ton of money I don't have now, or commit to paying you off forever? Are you insane?"

"There's gotta be something in this for me that makes it worth me packing up and leaving you behind." I smiled internally, knowing that I'd already been trying to figure out what my next step was. If I could benefit from this arrangement, be it with an Untouchable or regaining some of my financial security, then all the better.

"And what if I just flat out say no, never mind?" Her eyes narrowed like she was shooting daggers at me. I moved to cup her cheek and she flinched, swatting my hand away, "you're not touching my skin until this conversation is over. Free milk and the cow and all that."

"You are not a cow, *mon coeur*."

"Shut up. What if I say we drop the whole thing?"

"Then we go our separate ways. You panic your way through your launch and I keep plundering the emotional wells of every hormonal teenager in the Halloween store. Oh, and you make the unbreakable vow stating you'll tell no one I exist under penalty of death."

"DEATH?!" She screeched.

"If I don't have to worry about you exposing me then you should have no problem making the vow."

"But what if it's relevant information to like a police investigation or something?! I'm just supposed to live knowing a murderer lives in our town?"

I grinned, "your town is no different now than it was last night or the night before."

"Yeah, but then I didn't know! I can't be an accomplice to murder for the rest of my life."

"I don't kill people, Annabel."

"But others do."

"I'm not them."

She groaned and knocked my hands off her waist and began pacing the kitchen. "And we can't just...casually let you calm me down or something? Open eating relationship or something? Feeding with benefits?"

I lost my patience and played dirty, "Annabel, like calls to like. Now that you know that Others exist, they will find you. If you want my protection, I will not share you."

"Oh good, so now I have a death vow and the creature from the black lagoon will be joining me for tea?"

"I wouldn't worry about Frasier. He's a nice guy."

"Jesus Christ."

"Now, *he* was before my time," I grinned and she groaned, sliding down onto the floor with her fingers in her hair.

"Fuck." She exaggerated the 'F' and the stress came off her in waves palpable enough to make me shiver. I squatted in front of her and extended my hands, palms up, to her.

"Touch me, Bels."

A tear slid down her cheek, "I thought I was so clever, coming up with a plan and you had like four others."

I shrugged one shoulder, "they were good plans. Take my hands. Let me help." She eyed me suspiciously and I sighed, fully sitting on the floor, "no vow required. Let me help you."

She extended a shaky hand and I took it, breathing deep as another enormous wave of her feelings tried to drown me, "fuck, Bels, breathe."

It felt as though I was caught in a riptide, quickly trying to sort through the onslaught of her feelings, siphoning out the bad and pushing back the good through the hand I'd placed on her hip.

"Annabel, I promise you that I will not hurt you. I promise you that I will never force you to do anything. If you want to move forward with any of the proposals, yours or mine, it will be your decision. I am already addicted to you, and I hope you know I'm open to alternate plans too. I have never met someone like you before, and gods be damned, I want to keep you, but I will not steal you from your life. I will not be the monster in your nightmares or the villain that locks you in a tower. You are the only one capable of making the decision that works best for you."

She released a shaky exhale and the waves lessened, softening into a gentle roll as her heartbeat steadied.

"You promise you can't manipulate me into wanting you?"

"I promise, and even if I could, I wouldn't want to. If you decide to want to be mine, I want it to be because you want to, not because I made you."

She nodded once and pulled me toward her until her lips touched mine, the feelings coursing through her changing so rapidly that it felt like we were moving from water into fire, so I pushed feelings of calm back into her. I couldn't compete with how strongly she feels things, but I would not have her pass out on her kitchen floor either. Who was this woman with feelings deep enough to drown an immortal?

"Please tell me if we do the Twilight thing that you won't make me wait until marriage?"

I laughed against her lips and pulled back, "God no, *amour*, I'm European and far too old for such nonsense."

She laughed with me and my insides heated while her hands drifted under my shirt, "I also like my headboard."

"You know that I haven't seen that monstrosity in its entirety, right?"

"Oh, we are fixing that. We are having a full marathon. I'm putting it in the contract."

I grinned, "whatever you'd like, *mon coeur*."

She kissed me again, "I'm not willing to marry someone without knowing if we have...compatibility."

I glanced down, bringing her attention to the erection straining almost painfully against my pants, "I can confidently say there's compatibility."

Her breath hitched, "Can vampires and mortals..." She bit her lip and hesitated, "I mean, they mention it in Dracula movies and stuff but it seems we are way off script of anything I've seen."

"Do you want to? A minute ago you were freaking out at the idea of Frasier coming over for tea."

She laughed again, "Yes, I want to. I won't lie, I'm...morbidly curious as to how this whole...energy transfer thing will work in a... heightened state." Annabel grinned and quickly added, "but please god, if you make me pass out, will you leave me be? I'm not into that."

I couldn't contain the snort and I shook my head, "I promise not to have sex with your lifeless body, amour."

"Oh good, I'm glad we both have standards. Um, what about..."

"I can't make you pregnant and I can't carry diseases."

"Hmm...how handy that you just have that information at your disposal."

"Well," I kissed her again, " you're the one that is going to have to navigate how to maneuver a two-pronged penis, so I like to come to the table with all my cards."

Her eyes widened and her voice jumped an octave, "a what?!"

"I'm kidding, Bels. All equipment is...how you say...factory standard."

"You're not funny."

"Yes, I am," I grinned and she moved to stand, pulling against my hand to stabilize her and she groaned as she came up off the floor. Once she was up, I pulled her into me, relishing the fact that her soft body was against mine again, "I'm not going to force you into anything."

She nodded, "Okay. But...I want to try. No strings attached for this round, okay?"

I didn't answer, hoping to attach as many strings to this as possible before the evening was over, "did you get enough to eat?"

She nodded again, taking my hand and leading me toward the stairs, "Don't break my headboard."

"Wouldn't dream of it, *mon coeur*."

13
ANNABEL

I was nervous. Every movie I'd ever seen said that vampire sex would be awesome, but that there was a high likelihood that it would end in my death. However, it seemed as though multiple scenarios Thomas had presented had either resulted in my bankruptcy or death, so what was a little hot sex between friends?

When we walked up the stairs, I could feel his eyes on my ass and I couldn't resist sashaying my hips a little more than usual. He growled and pinched me, making me squeal and run up the rest of the steps, crashing into my room where the dim glow of the street lamps softly illuminated the space. I moved to turn on the light, but Thomas spun me and pushed me into the wall. I gasped, thrown off by how much smaller than me he was although he was taller and infinitely stronger. He shouldn't have been able to move me at all, let alone be able to toss me around like a rag doll, but his apparent strength made my stomach flip and my heart pound.

He pinned me against the wall with his hips, pressing his erection into my soft stomach, and began kissing up and down my neck. The idea that he could go off the deep end at any moment and sink his fangs into me added an element of danger and adrenaline to the encounter like really hot BDSM on steroids, unfortunately, it also caused my anxiety to spike.

"Thomas," my voice surprised me, breathless with desire and yet and full of fear.

"*Oui,*" he continued his way down my neck and onto my clavicles, lavishing me with his mouth, grinding his length against me.

"Thomas," I said again, confused at the heat pooling within me while simultaneously wanting to hyperventilate in panic, and he froze, pulling back to look at me. In the dark, his eyes were no longer a luscious brown but had become ominously black.

"What is it?"

I took another shaky breath, embarrassed that at almost thirty he had me as nervous as I was in seventh grade for my first kiss. And that wasn't even a good kiss. It was with Derek Kurtz and he was literally the worst and I just wanted to tell my friends I got kissed before them. I laughed apprehensively, "I'm nervous."

"Do you want to stop? I thought you-"

"I do," I said confidently, in fact, if he stopped touching me I thought the cocktail of hormones, anxiety and adrenaline coursing through my veins would kill me.

His shining onyx eyes were predatory, but his touch was gentle, "do you want me to make it go away?" Considering, I bit my lip, but he pulled it free using his thumb, "I won't do anything unless you want me to. I promised I'd never hurt you, Bels."

All I'd wanted that afternoon was for him to take away my stress, and at that moment, with an orgasm on the line, somehow I was so off-kilter that I wasn't sure if I'd be able to go through with it and let Thomas take me.

"What does it feel like for you when you take anxiety?" I whispered, wrapping my fingers into the fabric of his shirt.

He paused and ran the back of his hand up and down my arm, "With most people, I absorb the anxiety and become anxious myself." I shrunk, not wanting to have him feel the awful things that coursed through my body at all hours of the day. The never ending to-do lists, the fear of failure, the fear of an unknown future, it was enough to paralyze me and make me dissociate the minute I got home each evening. Thomas placed his fingers beneath my chin, lifting it to look into his eyes, "But with you? Anything you have to give me feels amazing. Harvesting has never felt like this before."

"It won't hurt you?"

A soft smile eased across his lips and he looked at me nothing short of adoring, "*Non, amour.* You won't hurt me." I hesitated again and he leaned his forehead against mine, "Can I calm you, Bels?"

We were already there. The fire had already been lit. We were already being physical, so I consented, relying on the knowledge that I had made up my mind that afternoon and I was determined to not let my nerves get the best of me. I was about to fuck a vampire, after all, it was every emo teenager's dream. When I nodded shakily, he feathered his lips across mine and smoothed his hands over my head, taming my hair and cupping my cheeks. He closed his eyes and took a deep breath, and I felt that pull from him in my mind, like a fishing line being reeled in. It didn't scare me; it was as if my mind knew it was him inside of it easing my anxiety as softly as a caress from a lover.

The relief was almost instantaneous. My heart rate slowed and my anxiety dissipated, allowing my lungs to open and me to breathe easier. The boulder of my responsibilities that had been crushing me all afternoon was breaking apart piece by piece and turning to dust that could simply blow away in the wind.

"That doesn't feel fair," I whispered.

He shuddered as if my feelings coursing through him gave him goosebumps. "I disagree. I've never been so thankful to be able to do it."

I chuckled, "because it might get you laid?"

Thomas rubbed his nose softly against mine, "*Non, amour.* Because I can feel it helping you."

With my heart lighter, I kissed him deeper, lust replacing nervousness and I wove my fingers through his luscious coffee-colored hair. Then fiction popped back into my head, and the question slipped out of me between breaths, "wait, how old are you? Are you like...my grandfather or my great-great-great-great-great grandfather?"

He laughed, warming me and making my stomach flip, "I think all you need to worry about is the great-great-great-great-great sex you're about to have *ma fille*."

"Oh yeah, Frenchie? You gonna rock my world?"

"That's what Tommys do, isn't it?"

I laughed at his Mötley Crüe reference and he grinned, reaching beneath my thighs and lifting me. I squealed in shock and slapped at his rock-hard shoulders.

"Oh my god! Put me down!"

"Why would I do that?" He asked devilishly, turning us toward my bed. He was carrying me like I was lighter than air, meanwhile, I was grasping his neck like I was going to fall to my death instead of simply landing on the floor three feet beneath me if his strength gave out.

"I don't want to hurt you!"

He scoffed in a horrifically French fashion and threw me onto my bed where I landed with a bounce. "Don't insult me, *mon coeur*, even more, don't use that insulting tone on yourself. Everything I will do with you is because I want to, and you will accept every look, compliment, touch, and orgasm with a smile on your face and the knowledge that you are utter perfection." Thomas stood on the side of the bed like a predator, "Strip, Bels, let me see you."

"You don't want to..." I gestured to the space next to me and he shook his head slowly.

"*Non.* Off."

I watched him as I tucked my fingers into the elastic waistband of my lounge pants and slowly pulled them down. He'd already seen me in my underwear before dinner, but he still devoured every inch of skin I revealed with starving eyes. Once my pants were off, I pulled my crop top up over my head, exposing the tantalizing sheer spiderweb bra I pulled from inventory that afternoon to model. It matched the cheeky hipsters that Thomas was drooling over with wide eyes while a deep rumbling tone emanated from his chest.

"Are you growling at me, or purring?" I sat up, fantastically relaxed and not caring that my stomach folded over on itself or that my apron of weight was causing the beautiful panties to roll down. I loved my body, and he clearly loved what he saw. Folding my legs, I quickly pulled at my skin to stop it from pinching on my knees out of habit.

"Yes," He spoke softly but with enough power that it ignited my blood.

"And are you going to make me do everything or are you going to be an active participant?" I teased and mischief flashed over his features.

"You know, you were much more easygoing when you were anxious." He removed his leather belt with deft fingers, pulling it out of the loops before he unbuttoned and pushed his jeans down, stepping out of them and exposing muscular thighs and tightly stretched black boxer briefs. Dark hair dusted his legs and when I drew my eyes up his body, he pulled off his threadbare shirt with one hand, exposing god-like muscles on a lean torso.

"How are you so ripped but you don't look like a gym rat?" I asked, cocking my head to the side.

"I don't need to hunt with strength, only speed."

"So you're not a bear...you're a... praying mantis or something?"

He grinned again, "I'm going to pretend you didn't just compare me to an insect." Prowling onto the bed, he grabbed my crossed ankle, and pulled, making me fall back into the mattress. He swiftly flipped me with my one leg, making me yelp and my ass jiggle as I landed on my stomach.

"It really is good enough to eat." He slapped both hands down on my cheeks, sending a rush of electricity straight to my pussy. His amazed tone held reverence and I found myself slightly disappointed that I didn't see the look on his face. He settled between my legs, running his trimmed nails up my legs, making my heart pound, and he paused to grip my thick thighs with another growl, clearly enjoying the extra padding where other girls had a thigh gap.

"You're lucky I don't eat fresh blood, *mon coeur* because you are positively appetizing."

"Thank you," I responded quietly, following his orders to accept his compliments.

"There's the good girl." He placed a gentle kiss on the back of my knee and began trailing his lips to the apex of my thighs, his nose leaving a trail of gooseflesh. I'd never had someone start out with me on my stomach and the unfamiliar territory made my pulse thrum. Thomas reached the round of my bottom and gave it a playful bite.

"Thomas! No teeth!"

He chuckled, and his laugh resonated through me, "It will take more than me giving you a love bite on your beautiful ass to change you, *mon coeur*. Relax." He nudged my legs with his shoulders, "on your knees, Bels."

I hesitated, "Uh...I haven't done a lot of...I don't know if we should start with..."

Thomas shushed me, sucking on the globe of my ass and I felt that pull again, calming me enough that going up on my knees seemed like a silly thing to be worried about. I worked with him to remove my panties and put my naked behind in the air. I felt so exposed, possibly too exposed, presenting myself like one of the omegas in my books, desperate for the pounding of a lifetime. I whined and wiggled my hips for him, making him he growl and immediately lean in to press his tongue against my slit. I gushed instantly at the sensation. Omega indeed.

Between brushes of his tongue, he soothed me, "Breathe, *mon amour*. Let me take care of you. I will not take your rose yet, but I will make you come."

His tongue felt so normal while somehow being far too skilled to belong to any ordinary man. It was wet and warm and the jolts of pleasure made my fingers dig at my bedding. He worked on licking my clit from behind, digging his face between my ass cheeks, circling it confidently and I shook with pleasure, whimpering each time I felt his nose brush past either of my entrances. His eagerness intensified, groaning at the taste of my wetness, which seemed to be pouring out of me, while he picked up speed, devouring me with each lap of his tongue.

"So fucking wet, Bels. You're so wet for me." He wrapped his arms under my thighs, pulling me tighter to him, digging his fingers into my ass, practically sealing us together with his face was burrowed between my cheeks. I attempted to roll my hips, to grind his jaw into me and ride the wave, but his strength kept me stationary, and my desire was twinged with helplessness. I was stuck with my ass in the air at his mercy until he deemed me satisfied enough for him, and it was exquisite.

The dirtiness and foreign sensation of discovering unknown nerves and pleasure points in my ass made me groan and cling to my bedding. I was lost in trying to comprehend the sensations where I'd never felt them before, wanting to figure out how to piece them together to reach orgasm as fast as I could instead of this slow boil he was relishing. It was taboo the way he took long, glutinous swipes with his tongue, sliding from my clit up to my ass that made my empty core clench in desperation, needing to add more, more, more.

Blood rushed to my head and my forearms collapsed and I turned my head to see him over my shoulder. He was watching me over the curve of my ass and he arched his brow in question, checking in with me, and I fucking begged for it.

"Thomas," I breathed his name, my mind adrift from being held so firmly while he did something so forbidden, "God, please, Tommy."

He paused his delicious torture to give another soft bite on my cheek, "there's no god here, my sweet, only us." He kneaded my flesh and withdrew one hand, landing it back against me with a smack. I groaned, shoving my ass at him, flattening my chest into the mattress, making him chuckle and smack me again.

"Fuck. I need to come," I gasped.

"You will, Bels." He plunged one of his fingers into me, thick and strong. "So tight. So fucking wet. You're positively dripping for me aren't you, *mon coeur?*"

"Yes, Tommy. Please, I need your cock inside of me."

"Come, first." He curved his finger inside of me, making me moan and curl my toes at the tightening coil of pleasure inside me while he pressed against the spongey tissue of my gspot. He jiggled his hand back and forth instead of in and out, never giving me a moment to lose the sensation and curled me tighter and tighter until I snapped. I screamed, gushing out spend for him as my pleasure raked through my body, leaving me boneless.

"*Très bien.* Do you want me like this, Bels?" His free hand flexed against my hip and I nodded, desperate to know what he felt like taking me from behind; wanting the pleasure of him hitting the back wall of my pussy.

He paused. "Do you need any help old man?" I asked on a delirious giggle, my channel fluttering tiredly around his fingers. He growled and smacked my ass again, the spark of pain leaving a delicious bite and tingle on my skin which I was sure had perfectly pink Thomas shaped handprints on it.

"What do you like, sweet girl? What do you need? I do not want to hurt you by going too hard on you."

I laughed at the idea of it ever being "too hard". In my experience, I'd never found anyone able to give it to me hard enough, there were never hard enough thrusts from a woman, and no cock was hard enough long enough to send me through the ceiling. "There's no such thing."

Thomas withdrew his finger. "*Très bien.*"

I heard him shove his boxers down, and his heat pressed into me in one fluid movement and behind my closed eyes, I saw all of heaven and hell before me.

"*Merde*, Bels. I think you could kill me all over again."

14
THOMAS

Annabel was Other. There was no alternative explanation for the way her body made me feel. Her skin was smoother than silk, her body softer than down, her lips were too luscious and her core was amazingly snug. There was no way this goddess was mortal.

"*Merde*, Bels. I think you could kill me all over again," I groaned as I pushed myself into her, wanting to get as much of me inside of her as I could.

"Holy shit," My beautiful girl, my sweetheart, *mon coeur,* rocked back against me until my pelvis pressed into the plushness of her delicious ass. That delicious, scrumptious ass which I had just spent a minimal amount of time getting acquainted with. I could spend days worshipping it. This was not enough. This wasn't going to be enough. An immortal had no true concept of time, but as someone who'd lived for hundreds of years, I could say immediately in earnest that there would never be enough time in my existence to touch Annabel. Never enough time to feel this body against mine.

"Thomas that feels so good," she groaned into her mattress, her body shifting slightly with each thrust of my hips. Looking down at her form made me want to glue my eyes open. The downward slope of her back emphasized her small waist and the roundness of her hips. I dug my fingers deeper into her, careful not to lose control and hurt her. I had to hold back. She said there was no such thing as too hard, but she obviously didn't realize that I could snap her in half if I wanted to as if she was no more than a pencil in my hands.

"More, Thomas, I know you won't hurt me. I'm not glass."

Her words rattled my beast's cage, roaring to own her, and I couldn't resist plunging into her hard enough that I bottomed out, pressing against her back wall.

"Holy fucking hell," she groaned. The flesh on her bottom bounced and compressed beneath me and the sight was worthy of a painting. Moving my hands up to her waist, I pulled her up flush against me wrapping one arm around her and bringing my other to her throat, pulling her hair over her shoulder so I could kiss and nibble at the pulse point in her neck making my beast delirious at the flutter of her heart against my lips.

"Annabel," I chased the feeling tightening inside of me, the blood being brought to a boiling point. I nipped at her ear and rumbled, "fuck, Bels you're so slick and tight."

Her body quaked and her walls began to flutter faster against me, so I continued my constant, brutal rhythm, keeping perfect pace with her as her breaths came shorter and small noises escaped with each resounding connection of our bodies. It took everything in me to hold on and not lose myself in her heat and fill her with my seed too quickly.

I dragged my teeth down the length of her neck, making her release sweet whimpers and took my hand from her waist to slide it down her body. I caressed her luscious skin and slid under her stomach from the delectable dip in her side to reach for her clit. The small bundle of nerve endings was engorged and begging for attention, so I pressed into it for the first time since entering her. With a squeal, her hand slammed behind us, grabbing onto my ass, determined to keep herself upright so she could enjoy her tortuous climb to ecstasy.

Incomprehensible moaning was pouring from Annabel, seeking salvation from any entity her brain could conjure up, but my poor girl would never find help in our bed. I tapped into her energy, feeling her navigating a suffocating labyrinth of pleasure in which she was desperately hunting her way to release. I thrust my feelings back into her, pounding her flesh while filling her soul with the indescribable way she was consuming me. I sent in my lust, my sudden devotion, my carnal need to keep her forever, to make her *mine*, and I felt her bloom with the added emotions flowing within her. I brought out my fangs and nipped her shoulder, not hard enough to break the skin, but enough that it made her concentration slip enough to relinquish control. She came with a scream.

15
ANNABEL

I went hurtling off a cliff, screaming and praying that he would catch me on the other side. I didn't know this man, and yet the emotions that filled me were ones of permanence, of commitment, and something that felt scarily like love. You can't love someone you just met - especially when they're a fucking vampire and you're a "mortal".

"Oh my god," I squealed, trying to curl up into myself and he growled, pulling my hips back to his.

"Annabel, you feel so fucking good," his words were each defined with powerful thrusts into me and the sound of our bodies clapping together.

I whimpered at the orgasm that raged on and on, refusing to allow me to rest like my typical experiences, and I was almost in tears when I realized that I was feeling *him*. I was feeling his passion and lust for me and the climb to his orgasm, while I was exploding in mine. The culmination of our two desires had me falling and falling, screaming into a bottomless pit of pleasure, begging him to come for me.

"*Non, mon coeur,*" I heard him in the darkness when he withdrew and flipped me onto my back, seamlessly moving back inside of me, licking my breasts and scooping his hips up into me to hit my gspot.

Everywhere his fingers touched me, my skin zapped with tiny sparks. I could feel that fishing line within my mind pulling out my negativity and being replaced by his thoughts, his clear obsession. I realized I was able to breathe just in time to feel the tightening of another climax begin within me again.

"Shit. I'm going to come again if you keep doing that, Thomas. Fucking hell." I was losing the ability to make feminine, or hell, even human moans as I took flight once more. I made guttural, animalistic noises while feeling myself contract more than I ever had before, honestly shocked my vagina hadn't somehow amputated his cock to keep inside of me forever as a trophy.

Thomas was kissing up my neck, lavishing me with attention while I uselessly writhed beneath him. I felt momentarily like I was a shitty lay because I was putting no effort into this interaction at all, but then he rumbled against my ear, his chest vibrating, and rasped, "again, give me one more, *amour*."

"Fuck!" I screamed and slammed my eyes shut. I fucking screamed. I didn't even know I was a screamer before this and now my neighbors were definitely going to call the police. Tears filled behind my closed lids, and one slid slowly down my cheek and Thomas gently removed it with the pad of his thumb. He slowed his pace, beginning to move more tenderly inside of me, and leaned down to kiss me.

His kiss wasn't hungry or desperate that time, it was savoring, it was worshipping, and it held enough behind it to make a rational woman panic. His hand caressed the tattoo on my thigh, stroking the ink reverently.

"Bels, I'm going to cum," he whispered into my lips.

"Come in my mouth." The demand surprised me, but it was out there and floating around us before I realized what I'd told him to do.

He moaned gruffly and pulled out, grabbing and placing me in front of him to take in his length, and upon meeting the beast for the first time, the word *perfect* flashed through my mind in neon. Every neuron inside of me fired off demanding that I memorize the shape, taste, and feel of his beautiful cock.

I pulled him into my mouth, relaxing my jaw, and ran my nails up the back of his legs, pressing him into me. It matched his body exquisitely, long and strong without being overly intimidating or ostentatious. Thomas was beautiful.

"Shit, Annabel...*mon coeur*..." He began losing control of his movements, thrusting irregularly into my mouth, clearly fighting the desire to throw his head back while also not wanting to miss a moment of my lips being sealed over his length. I looked up at him through my lashes and he lost it. A low, deep groan was the last warning I got before ropes of cum shot down my throat that I was swallowing on reflex.

He shuddered, holding my head in place through his climax, and then his grip let up and he smoothed my hair again, leaning down to kiss my forehead while removing his softening length.

"Bels..."

I fell back onto my bed with him taking deep, desperate breaths while trying to slow my heart, and stared at the black ceiling fan spinning slowly above us. The quiet of my home returned and only amplified the fact that we had been so loud.

"Holy shit," I laughed in disbelief.

He tilted his head, his chin-length hair flipping over his scalp, "I... wow." Thomas shook his head as if he couldn't believe it either.

"That was intense."

"*Oui.*"

"Is vampire sex always that intense?"

"*Non.*"

I pushed up on my elbows, "hey, if you're dead why does your cum taste normal?"

He stared at me for a moment and narrowed his brows, laughter erupting from him, "we just had the most mind-blowing sex of my existence and you're asking about my ejaculate?"

"Ew, not if you're going to use words like ejaculate," I giggled and reached for the soft throw blanket at the bottom of my bed to pull over my body, trying to soothe the goosebumps that were creeping over my skin in a confusing mixture of blazing heat and freezing cold. I laid back down onto my far-too-expensive pillows, delighting in the sound of the feathers compressing under me and smiled when Thomas' face filled the pillow next to mine. "I haven't had anyone in this bed yet. You're the first."

His mischievous smirk creased his cheeks, placing his large hand over mine, bringing them to his lips for a kiss. "I'm honored. It is a very nice bed."

I shrugged, "I have no boyfriend and no kids. I buy myself all the nice shit I want when I want it. I don't have to answer to anyone and I like it that way."

He tightened a bit, "You won't have to answer to me, Bels. I just want to be with you."

Shit, I hadn't meant to make the conversation take such a heavy turn, so I removed my hand from his and lightly ran my fingers through the smattering of hair on his chest. "That was amazing."

"I wasn't lying, Annabel, it was the best sex of my life."

"How is that possible? You're like 2000 years old."

He barked a laugh, "I am not."

"Well you didn't answer me when I asked which of my grandparents would have been your peers, so..." I thought for a moment, "how did you die?"

He snuggled down into the bed and I opened the blanket for him which he accepted and moved closer to me. "I don't remember."

I arched my brow, "you don't remember, or you don't want to tell me?"

"I don't remember," he reached up to fiddle with a lock of my hair, "I think I'm in my late twenties, maybe early thirties, but people lived much shorter lives then - we aged differently."

"When?"

"Well, I remember that my entire life that a monarch lived at Versailles. I remember being in Paris and it being positively disgusting."

I laughed at that description of the City of Love.

"There wasn't plumbing so everyone stunk of perfume and shit. It was horrible." He paused, "I remember the revolution being after I changed, and I know America had already rebelled and was independent since that event is much clearer." With a shrug he twirled the piece of hair, "I remember very very little of my life before. I do not remember my parents, my family, friends... I used to, but it all blurred together at some point and now I don't. Things from before are almost behind a sheer curtain, I know they're there but they're distorted just enough that I can't decipher one thing from another. Facts and fiction are blurry."

"Does that bother you?" I couldn't imagine not knowing my mothers. The thought alone made my heart hurt.

"*Oui*. I wish I remembered my mother. I know that she was very special to me. I feel like she died badly, as if we were attacked or something, but things were just so different then." He shrugged easily, "who knows, maybe that's how I died too."

"So you're like...400 years old?"

"Around that, maybe 500? I think Monique once said I was born in 1584 - but I don't know how she came about that number, and I don't remember if she thought that was when I was born or if that was when I changed."

"Is Monique one of your partners that left?" I asked.

"Yes. She was incredibly important to me. I loved her very much."

"Do you think she's dead?"

He pressed his lips against my forehead and shrugged, "I do not know where she went or what she's doing. As I said before, she and our partner Yusuf left together and I have been alone since. But last I'd heard they're alive."

"So, basically what you're saying is that I'm such a beast in the sack that sex with me was better than sex with two people at the same time who had a gajillion years of practice?" I teased, hoping to lighten the sadness radiating off him.

That got a smile, "don't let it go to your head."

"How long were you guys a family?"

"Since before the revolution."

"American or French?"

"French." He laid on his back and sighed, "it was all a very long time ago."

"If you were together since before the French Revolution that means you were together like 200 years, Tommy."

"Oui. As I said, I loved them very much."

"And they just left."

He nodded slowly, "*Oui.*"

"That's awful," Feeling him wilt like an abandoned puppy left at the pound, I asked, "have you been with anyone since they left?"

"Not like this. Not like that."

I grunted in acknowledgment and laid my cheek against his chest and my leg over his, "I'm sorry they're gone."

"I am too, but they never told me why - that's what bothers me most. I can't fix something if I don't know what the problem is."

I felt him graze at my emotions again, almost in asking, and I nodded, letting him in. I showed him my genuine sadness for him, my elation over the mind-melting orgasm, and the comfort I felt in his arms. I didn't know what attribute he had that could make somebody snap badly enough to leave after 200 years, but I did know that at that moment, I was happy.

"Thank you," he said softly, "your emotions are so...interesting."

"It didn't help you with them?"

"No, we can't harvest emotions from someone who also harvests emotional energy, and even if you could, who is to say if it would be their feelings or whoever they just fed from." He said it so nonchalantly that I huffed a small laugh.

"You talk about eating people so...easily."

"It's my life, *amour*, it's no different to me than you ordering a pizza."

"Except I don't kill the pizza man."

"Neither do I, but I will often steal his high - you know how many delivery guys are stoned out of their minds?"

I laughed loudly and he rubbed his hand up and down my back, "why don't you rest, Bels? You had a long day - do you want me to go?"

I shook my head, "No. I don't want you to go. Do you need to?"

"No. I didn't want to either, I was just trying to be gentlemanly."

"Well, stop it."

He snorted, "There's something about you that makes me want to stay right here forever. You're going to have to tell me to leave."

Nodding, I pulled myself closer to him and he kissed my head. I did some mental math while I drifted off, still floating from bliss.

I didn't understand it, and I didn't know how it happened or where he came from, but somehow I had to wrap my mind around the fact that I had just slept with a 400-something-year-old vampire less than one year out of a relationship, and he had given me the most intense orgasm of my life.

16

THOMAS

She was beautiful while she slept. Her eyes would flutter and she'd release small moans or humming noises as if escaping into her dreams was the relief she'd needed her whole day. I laid there contentedly as she snuggled against my chest, her long hair freed from the buns she'd had them knotted in on either side of her head. Purple hair splayed across her pillows and the scent of ginger and citrus intoxicated me and make my mind drift into a trance like state.

I should have slept. I should have given in to the bone-deep exhaustion that I'd earned from the emotionally and physically arduous day I'd had, especially after it had taken me years to reteach my body to sleep like a mortal. I'd experienced the never ending day of immortality when I'd been turned and I'd hated it. If our lives were bound to balance, then our days should be balanced with nights, and wakefulness with sleep.

I twirled a lock of her hair around my index finger and thought about how entirely different she was from Monique or Yusuf. Not that that mattered, but Monique had radiated sexuality from her lithe form. Her straight white blonde hair and predatory beauty could stop a man in the middle of the road, fascinated by the creature in front of them and she basked in it. She fed on it. Her sexuality was intense enough that I often wondered if she was left unsatisfied by Yusuf and me and if she needed more. But *merde,* when she looked at me with claiming and love, it stopped *me* in the middle of the road. Her beauty was unparalleled and she knew it. Her kindness and logic were sometimes lacking, but she had been through so much that we never held it against her; she knew that Yusuf and I would have destroyed ourselves to bring her joy.

Yusuf was a handsome Persian, with bushy and coarse dark hair and brows and delicious smooth olive colored skin. He was toned, yet soft, and his short stature often left people feeling more comfortable than they should have around him. He was a filler. He knew how to fill any void, any where. He was a chameleon, shifting to fit the needs of others, or to blend into the crowd. He took control of situations that needed to be handled on the regular - like taking care of Monique's whims or leading the tours when she simply couldn't bother with them.

The woman next to me didn't project the cruelty and sex that Monique did, or the deceptive stealth and persona of Yusuf. She didn't feel like the self-obsession or entitlement. Yes, she held confidence and love for herself, but her kindness covered the hole that she guarded inside of her that needed to be filled with love from another, *for* another. I could feel it in her mind- the need to love, to give instead of take. I could feel her need for *more* not to come from exclusively physical connections from others like Monique craved, but from a desire to simply coexist with another in mutual affection.

She was a woman who wanted someone to eat breakfast with, someone to hold her hand as they walked along the ocean dreaming of their future. Her desire for a partner was so potent in her emotions that I couldn't ignore it. And yet, this was a woman who lived alone, worked alone, did everything alone. It was confusing. Why should such a magnificent creature live without a companion when she so desperately wanted one?

I'd finally managed to close my eyes as the sky began to lighten with the dawn, but even then, I woke quickly and pulled myself from her bed with a need to please her. This woman wanted someone to eat breakfast with and while I may not be able to eat it, I knew I could cook it.

I put on my jeans and slunk to her kitchen, quietly switching on the overhead lights and rummaging around her cabinets to look for breakfast ingredients. This woman, my beautiful creature had almost no food in her home. I'd wanted to make simple crepes for her, knowing that she'd find the stereotype delightful in her strange way, but Annabel didn't even have eggs. I'd made myself comfortable with the layout of the space and knew where to find utensils and such, but as I'd brought everything for dinner last night with me, I hadn't bothered to look in her fridge. It appeared I should have brought things for breakfast as well, though that likely would have been presumptuous of me.

I considered going to the store quickly to grab a few things, but then I thought about how much it would hurt Annabel to wake up alone, with me nowhere in sight. I immediately marched back up the stairs, undoing my pants as I went and climbed back into her bed.

I wasn't going to let her wake up alone, and mortals had created grocery delivery apps for a reason. I downloaded one, created an account, and immediately piled in everything I'd wanted to eat for years. Strawberries and hazelnut spread, lemons and sugar, blueberries and mascarpone...*mon coeur* would have everything I couldn't, I'd give it all to her. The need for her to be in my life and to be happy in it had only multiplied overnight.

Annabel rolled and shimmied her bottom against my hip while releasing one of her small sleep-filled moans. I couldn't resist the urge to run my hand down her smooth side as I sat beside her, enjoying the dip of her waist and the feel of the small indents of stretch marks across her hips. Her tattoo filled most of her thigh and I ran my fingers over the details, leaning over to place a kiss on her shoulder and she moaned again.

"Good morning," she yawned, scooting even closer to me.

"*Bonjour ma chérie*, you should not be awake yet, the sun is still rising."

She stretched her legs out, extending them fully and I heard her back crack with the movement, "then why are you awake?" her nose wrinkled, "oh god, do you sleep? You haven't just been sitting in my bed staring at me all night have you?"

I scoffed a laugh, "*non, mon coeur*, I wanted to make you breakfast, but it seems to be the end of your shopping week - you didn't have so much as a glass of milk in your fridge."

She flushed in embarrassment, "yeah, I don't cook much. It sucks to put in all the effort for one person."

"Well, fear not, far too much food is on its way." I waved my phone at her, "it appears that Judy is shopping for us now."

"You know how to grocery shop?"

I shrugged, "sure, I clicked a couple buttons and delicious things will appear at your door like magic."

Arching a brow, she asked skeptically, "would you even know how to pick out a ripe piece of fruit if there was a bowl of it in front of you?"

"*Non*, but I'm sure Judy can and will."

She chuckled, "okay, but you really don't need to cook for me again, I can just grab a bagel while I drive through for some coffee."

"Absolutely not. This morning I am making crepes, and I noticed you had a very shiny-looking coffee maker in the kitchen."

"Yeah, but that doesn't make pumpkin spice lattes," she rubbed her nose against my chest, like she was itching it and her arm tightened around my torso.

"Hey," I spoke softly, wanting only to have her look at me with those intense green eyes.

She looked up, not moving her head from my chest, "hey."

I placed my pointer finger beneath her chin and tilted her head so I could lean down and kiss her. I touched my lips to hers, feeling a shudder flow through her. I didn't tap into her feelings - I didn't need to, and I just wanted to feel her against me, not everything that was inside of her mind.

She kissed me back, pulling herself into my body and smiling against my mouth.

"You're a good kisser," she said with a sleepy smile.

"Thank you. I could kiss you for hours."

She stretched again, "while that would be lovely, I have a million things to do today. Just gotta find my list."

I felt it then. She instantly went from a languid, sex-happy, snuggly, warm body to a stressed and managed creature, creating lists in her mind and preparing for her day. The change in her was startling and all-consuming. It wasn't just internally, it was like she had woken up for the day and picked up a mask from her side table and slapped it on, ready to take on whoever or whatever challenged her with enough bravado to survive until she could come back home and put it back on the nightstand. Her features sharpened, brows dropping, worry lines forming between her eyes and a slight frown marring her perfect mouth.

"It's Sunday," I kissed her again, trying to bring back the placid woman who'd been kicked to the curb by the boss, "stay with me today."

She scratched her head and swept her fingers under her eyes, "don't you have to work today?"

"I'd rather be with you."

Scoffing, she untangled herself from my arms, "oh come on, you can't miss one of eight Sundays before Halloween because you want to lay in bed and fuck all day."

I grinned, "sure I can, I'm the boss."

"Thomas."

"Annabel," I mimicked her tone, pulling her back so we were laying her back to my front. I laid kiss after kiss across her shoulders and down her spine.

"Thom-mas," she whined, but snuggled further into my embrace, wiggling her ass into my hips.

"I am going to eat you, and then you're going to eat breakfast," I growled, nipping at her ear.

"You said-"

"Don't take it so literally," I kissed across her shoulders again, and rotated away from her so she could lay down on her back. I moved my attention to her neck, her collarbones, and then lavished the mounds of her breasts. Her breathing quickened, and I could tell that she was torn between continuing to wear that boss mask or if she could put it down and play with me for a few moments more.

If she wanted to be the boss, I'd let her be take control. I stopped my ministrations and laid down, "sit, Bels."

She easily moved to sit over my hips and I grinned, feeling my erection press into her slit as if she was a homing beacon, "not what I meant, *amour.*"

She arched her brow and then her eyes widened in realization, "what?"

I grabbed her hips and pulled them up towards my face and she slammed her hands against the headboard, locking her elbows, "what? No way!"

"You've never done this before either?"

"God, you make me feel like a fucking nun."

"I can assure you that you are not a nun."

"What, do you, Frasier and the Nuns get together for card games? How would you fucking know?"

I laughed, "don't deflect. Get up here so I can taste you."

"You said everything tastes like nasty books anyway."

I pulled at her hips again, "I said food tastes like books. You taste like the fountain of youth."

"That makes no sense," she huffed in exasperation.

"Bels. Come here."

"Listen, I've seen porn, I know what you want me to do and I'm telling you that my stomach is going to suffocate you. I'm not saying that to be self-deprecating, I'm saying it because literally, I carry all my weight here-" she grabbed the apron of flesh hanging over her mound, "it will, like, cover your whole head and you'll die. I'm not being mean to myself, I'm being logical."

"Vampire," I quipped back.

"Thomas-"

"Annabel, I haven't needed to breathe in 400 years, I'm stronger than you and I want to." She hesitated still. "Are you saying no because you don't want me to taste you again or are you saying no because you're worried about me not being a thousand percent obsessed with every inch of you?"

She gripped her stomach, nerves cracking through the mask, "you could just-"

"Sit on my fucking face, Bels, before I put you there." Her eyes widened, "Just try, *mon coeur*, if you don't enjoy it, we can stop, but I can promise that you will."

A glint of mischief shone in her eyes, "and if I don't?"

"If I make you come while sitting that delicious pussy on my face, you put away your responsibilities for the day and stay with me. If you hate it and want to stop, we will kiss, eat some crepes and go to work. Deal?"

"You're on, Frenchie."

17
ANNABEL

Thomas used his otherworldly strength to pull me up his body, placing his mouth directly under my most sensitive parts. I nervously held onto the headboard, hovering slightly and disliking the feeling of my stomach covering his head - I couldn't see a thing!

"Tommy, isn't part of what makes this hot supposed to be that I'm able to watch you? All I see is me and your scrawny little legs sticking out behind me - it's not very hot."

"Shush, Bels," His hot breath cascaded over my body and contrasting chills skittered up my back, "Sit," he growled.

"I am sitting," I huffed, feeling his tongue stroke gently over my clit and I tilted my head, focusing on the sensation. His light touches were delicious, but I didn't see how this was any better than me on my back.

"Sit," he growled again, wrapping his arms around my legs and pulling my hips down onto him, thoroughly crushing the poor man - creature...Thomas.

"Holy hell," I gasped. The force of his strokes was amplified by the weight of my body pushing against his face. His firm nose teased my clitoris and his tongue swept inside of me, reaching places I'd never imagined a tongue could. "Shit, Thomas."

"Mmmhmmm," he hummed against me, sending vibrations through me and I arched.

I slapped the headboard and began to fall over. My abs were already killing me from trying to hold myself up on him while feeling my insides melt so I leaned myself into the metal, wrapping my hands around the bars. The new angle was even more intense, it was like I was permanently ground into his face, which I normally wouldn't do with my partners until I was so close to orgasm that I'd lose control. Being able to start with that intensity that was usually the end made my brain explode. I subconsciously began to rock myself, fucking his face, and moaning into my forearms. He tightened his grip on my hips more, allowing me to chase my high with rocking, but not allowing me to remove the pressure of his mouth on me.

He sucked and licked, and inch by inch he helped me grow wings.

"Thomas, what - shit." I groaned, grinding my pelvis into his face, delighting in the vacuum he'd created around my clitoris which was making me go from a three to a ten in seconds. In the fastest recorded time of my life, my thighs clamped around his head and I lost control, bucking and moaning against him, not once experiencing the frustration of almost being there and him losing his breath and having to stop. I got to soar from beginning to end in one swift movement and my body quaked with the force of it.

He continued to slide his tongue around my entire core, licking up every last drop of my cum, and groaned himself, making me tremble from overstimulation.

I slapped his hands away from my hips and pushed them into the air, sliding down his body to collapse on top of him. Thomas gently ran his fingers up and down my spine while I struggled to catch my breath. He grinned, "Am I allowed to say that I told you so?"

I shook my head, eyes still fused shut, "gloating isn't a good look."

He chuckled and kissed my temple, "You're not looking at me at all."

Cracking open one eye, I glared at him, "There. Now," I checked to make sure he was looking at me, "Thomas, gloating isn't a good look."

A deep laugh rumbled from him and he shook his head, "How should we spend our day, *mon amour*?"

I sighed, "You're really not going to let me go to work? I have so much to do."

"You agreed to the terms, *ma chérie*," he shrugged his slim shoulders.

I huffed and snuggled closer into him, "Well, in my defense, how was I supposed to know *that* was going to happen?"

"Because I told you it would," His grin widened and he sighed, tightening his arms around me.

"I thought you said you didn't need to breathe?"

"I don't," he arched a brow.

"So why did you just sigh?"

"Ah, well...there are certain mannerisms that we have to teach ourselves to help blend into modern society. Someone would notice if I never breathed, or sighed, or gasped. It takes years for a newborn to be able to act well enough to pass for mortal in public."

I slid off to his side, lightly running my fingers through his chest hair, "it sounds hard to be different."

He shrugged, "To be Other is just to be. We are no more unusual to you than you are to us. Especially for those of us who don't remember our mortal existence." His phone dinged and he grinned, "Now, it appears as though Judy has arrived with our order. Would you like some crepes or a shower first?"

I stretched, my spine cracking loudly and grimaced at the unlady-like sound, "I could use a shower. And some mouthwash."

"You go hop in, I'll get the groceries inside."

With a loud smack on my ass and a squeal, I darted to the bathroom, turning on the shower, and before I'd even stepped in, Thomas was back, wrapping his arms around my waist.

"I thought you were getting the groceries?" I asked, leaning into him.

"I did."

I turned my head and gave him a confused scowl, to which he answered with a dramatic eye roll, "Repeat after me, vamp - ire."

"Repeat after me, Fuck-you," I laughed, climbing into the clawfoot, him close behind me, "dude, this is already very tight quarters."

"Let me take care of you."

"I am perfectly capable of washing my own hair."

"*Oui*, but I want to do it." He spun my body easily, bringing my back to his front, and comfortably lathered and massaged my scalp with my grapefruit shampoo.

"So, you're not a *vampire*, but you're a vampire?" I asked quietly, running my nails up his muscular thigh.

"I am a vampire, but not how mortals think of them. I'm assuming you think I'm about to fly away as a bat, or turn into dust in the sun, or begin maniacally laughing at and counting everything?"

"Or sparkling."

He snorted lightly, "right. Sparkly vampires. *Non, ma chérie*, those are called the Undead. I am not Undead."

I scrunched my face in confusion and tilted my head back under the spray, pausing to kick the plastic curtain off my leg, "wait, but you're not dead, but you still exist so you're Undead."

"*Non*, I'm Other."

"That's confusing."

He turned me and began to smooth in my color depositing conditioner, chuckling at the purple cream in his hand, "*non*, because many things are Others."

"Like Frasier."

I felt his grin behind me, "Like Frasier."

He rinsed my hair again and settled his head down into my shoulder, holding me, "thank you, *amour*."

I turned in his grasp, "for what?"

He shrugged as if he was embarrassed, looking like a model with his wet chocolate hair slicked back and dripping onto his shoulders, "I have been alone a very long time. I have missed having someone to talk to, to take care of."

"A year isn't so bad. Especially not to an immortal, right? Like, the time they've been gone is probably a drop in the bucket isn't it?" I say casually.

Thomas smiled sadly, *"non,* it feels like the hundreds of years we were together flew by in an instant and this past year has been slower than a melting icecap."

I leaned into his chest, loving the combination of his hard body and the hot water sluicing over us, "well, at least mortals have sped that up for you."

His chest shook and slapped my ass playfully, "just accept my thanks, and let's go get some food in you."

"I promise I'm not hungry, you didn't need to order groceries and stuff. I usually don't eat until after lunchtime other than some coffee. We can just watch some more tv or whatever?"

"Well, I can't eat, so you will."

"That seems bossy of you."

He arched his perfectly defined brow.

"Yeah, yeah, vampire. Come on, Frenchie." I reached to turn the faucet off and pushed the valve back down with my foot before opening the eggplant-colored brocade curtain.

I grabbed a fluffy towel from the hook and began drying myself and noticed that he was still standing, dripping in the tub with a stupid smile on his face, resting his forearms against the round pipe holding the curtain. I furrowed my brow and reached behind me, handing him another towel, "what?"

"You're a goddess. Positively perfect."

I blushed, noting his delicious lean muscles and tapered waist, trying to make sure not to stare at his junk with him watching me so intently. I knew it'd just been inside of me, but manners existed for a reason. "I'm going to go get dressed." I scurried off towards my room and grabbed a pair of black bike shorts, a basic soft t-shirt, and a wireless bra.

Thomas came in, towel drying his long hair as I was leaning over the bed to grab the bralette. "You don't need to wear that today, you are taking the day off. Fuck, you can just remain naked and stay in bed and I'll bring you whatever you desire."

Shrugging, I answered, "it hurts my back if I don't wear anything. They need some kind of support."

He gave me that lopsided grin of his again, "I have hands, *mon coeur*. I will take on the burden of supporting them all day if I must."

I laughed loudly, "while I appreciate the offer, I am fine, thank you."

He jumped into his low-slung jeans, shaking his hips slightly to adjust the fit, and shrugged back, "I'm just going to take it off you. I have plans."

I dropped the bra and placed my hands on my hips, "Plans, huh?"

"*Oui*." He closed the distance between us and cupped my heavy breasts, lifting them and relaxing my back, before leaning down and pulling each nipple into his mouth in turn. "Leave it off," he growled against my skin.

Pushing playfully at his shoulders, I gave an exasperated sigh and put it back in my drawer before pulling my shirt quickly over my head, noticing immediately how his eyes tracked the bounce of my unrestrained breasts. "Happy now?"

Thomas grinned and I noted that he didn't have any vampy-like teeth, "very."

I cocked my head and opened my mouth, using my fingers to mimic fangs, "where's the weaponry?"

"*Quoi?*"

"You don't have fangs. How do you drink blood without fangs?"

"Usually in a foam cup with a straw."

"Thomas."

He smiled, "they're there, Bels. I just don't need to risk slicing my lips open all the time. They show when I need them." He grabbed my hand and led me back towards the stairs, allowing me a moment to check out every single muscle in his swimmers' shaped back.

Tim meowed from his resting place on the stairs and swatted out his paw playfully at Thomas, making him jump, "shit, I forgot about him."

In feigned outrage, I shook my hand free and leaned over to grab him, "You forgot my Timmy?

He grumbled something incomprehensible and turned the bottom of the stairs to head back to the kitchen and I followed, snuggling into Tim's soft fur, "I won't forget about you, baby, don't let the scary vampire bother you." After walking into the kitchen, I froze at the sheer amount of grocery bags on the counter. "Oh my god, Thomas. Who the hell is going to eat all this food!?"

"You are, *ma chérie*." He began sorting through things, putting delicious-looking berries and cheese into my fridge. "You're getting three five-star meals today."

"This is enough food for a small army, I'm only one person - I think your eyes were bigger than your stomach."

"Humor me, Bels."

I laughed and shook my head, heading to grab my coffee pot and fill it with water. I went through the motions of making my coffee, feeling my to-do list build with each step.

Pour the water in.

Finish photographing the lingerie.

Close the lid.

Make marketing images for social media.

Grab the grounds.

Prepare old inventory for clearance.

Measure out the coffee.

Create ads.

My mind spun and my foot began tapping so I grabbed sticky pads out of the drawer and began listing everything out and chewing on my nails while it brewed. The room faded around me, filling with a visual static as I hyperfocused on the launch for a moment. God, there was just so much to do, how could I possibly spend a day at home?

Suddenly, hands grasped my hips and lips brushed against my

neck, "Bels?" he whispered and I shivered, returning slightly to the present, but quickly scribbling down a few more things on my mind.

"Bels," he said again, more firmly.

"Just a sec," I tapped the pen quickly against the countertop, I knew I was forgetting something.

"Bels," He growled, "Come back to me."

"I just know I'm -"

His hands tightened on my hips, "let me help."

"I -"

He growled again, running his hands under the hem of my shirt, pressing against the flesh of my stomach and my heart rate slowed with the gentle pull from his power.

"Annabel. Come back."

I sighed, relaxing back into him, as if someone had laid a heavy blanket over me, soothing my worries and comforting me. The list was still there, it was all still waiting for me, but I was able to breathe around it.

"You're allowed to take a day off. You're allowed to be here with me." He said, smoothing my damp hair and pressing his hips into mine. "I promise, the launch will not fail because you are taking a day to orgasm into oblivion and eat well. I'm going to take care of you so you can go back tomorrow and do even more. If you burn yourself from both ends you'll fail before you get started."

I furrowed my brows, "I thought you weren't going to feed from me unless I gave you permission."

"Oh please, that was but a nibble, *amour*." He kissed my neck and turned back to the grocery bags, continuing to put things away so I poured my coffee and leaned against the butcher block, fingering the leaves of my succulents and wishing them a good morning. It was a strange scene of domesticity playing out in my home - one that I'd never expected. A handsome man preparing to cook breakfast, a shiny black cat sunning on the faux brick floors, and the smell of coffee and freshly washed bodies permeating the space.

"What was it like when you, Yusuf, and Monique lived together?" I asked, unable to help myself.

He paused, then returned to slicing the berries, "I'd assume it was... normal, I suppose. I didn't have anything to compare it to."

"Normal is relative." I said plainly, sticking my nail into a container holding a string of pearls plant, "What was your role? What was theirs? What did you guys contribute to each other's lives? What was the dynamic? Were you the housewife or something?"

He paused mid-slice, considering, and then shook his head and continued, "okay, maybe it wasn't entirely normal." He grabbed a perfectly plump strawberry and brought it to me, "Open," he said before quickly popping it in my mouth and I hummed in approval. "Does Judy deserve a good rating?"

I nodded, chewing, "oh yeah, top-notch produce selection."

He smiled and went to his station, preparing a large mixing bowl with ingredients listed on the tablet in front of him, "The three of us were together so long that a lot of things happened without needing communication. Where one of us was failing, the others, Yusuf more often than not, picked up the slack automatically. We kind of delegated tasks to whoever understood them the fastest because things have changed so much since we turned. I did a lot of the back-end business stuff, as well as maintaining our home, Monique tended to the money and tours, and Yusuf did anything he could to make our lives easier. He was a good male."

I took a sip from my mug, "and they really just left?"

He shrugged and poured the runny batter into a pan, "*Oui*, they poofed," he paused and smirked before continuing, "I think when you're together so long that you don't *need* to communicate that it evolves into you *not* communicating at all. We coexisted wonderfully, but I had no idea they were unhappy. I would give anything to just have a chance to talk to them and know what happened."

I moved so I could see his face, "Would you get back with them if they came back?"

He furrowed his brow, considering, "*Non.* I wouldn't want to open myself up to the hurt again. I'd just want to talk to them."

"But you want to open yourself up to me hurting you?"

He flipped the crepe onto a plate and poured another, "I'm higher in the food chain." he grinned, deflecting, and quickly flipped another crepe out, pouring lemon juice and sugar over them before putting some strawberries on top.

I growled, "errrr I'm bigger than you and I'm higher in the food chain! Roar!" I grabbed the plate from him and suppressed the happy hungry noises trying to escape from me. "We are equals here, Frenchie. You don't get to pull that shit with me or I'll cut you off my delicious... aura vibe thing." I waved my hand over my body, "and my boobs. No aura, no boobies, no nothing. Equals."

He smiled and came to me, enveloping me in his arms, and kissed my shoulder, "*Oui.* Equals. Just keep talking to me."

"Even if I'm bothering you?"

"*Especially* if you're bothering me. You're cute when you're feisty." I bucked him with my shoulder and he laughed, hugging me closer, "are you still anxious, *ma chérie*?"

I considered, "No. I'm not." I took a bite of my crepe and unconsciously wiggled my hips in delight, "this is yummy."

"*Bonne,*" he kissed my shoulder again and smiled, "Now where is Tim's food? He's touching me and I can only assume that means he's decided I need to feed him too."

I giggled and looked behind me, sure enough, Tim was wrapping himself around Thomas' ankles, purring loudly while strutting in figure eights. "It's under the sink," I said with my mouth full, and he went to open it, grabbing a large scoop out of the container and Tim gave a meow of joy.

I watched Thomas squat down, dumping Tim's kibble into his little bat-shaped bowl and scratching his head, quietly speaking to the animal in French about something. I popped another strawberry in my mouth and wiggled my hips again, "Thank you for breakfast, Thomas."

He turned, still squatting and scratching Tim, and a piece of his brown hair flopped into his eyes. He smiled and it was as if his face lit up at the sight of me, "anytime, *mon coeur*. Even if you deny my access to your aura and boobies."

I grinned, "*Especially*. The phrase you're looking for is especially if."

"Whatever you say, *ma chérie*."

18

THOMAS

We spent the day laying on the couch, touching each other and watching an entire season of some glass-blowing show that Annabel was obsessed with. And, despite her constant grumbling, I was able to get multiple meals in her, loving the way that her body wiggled when she thought something tasted good.

It was as if when the good taste reached her stomach her whole body had to dance with joy that it was delicious. She'd make this small closed-lip smile and begin wiggling from her hips all the way up to her head to a beat only she heard, and then she'd hum in delight and then beam at me.

"Have you ever made glass before?" She asked, bouncing her ankle against my thigh and I reached down to rub it.

"*Non*, it looks hot."

She arched a brow, "can you even feel heat?"

"Of -" I stopped, "Well, I know I'm supposed to feel hot so my body acts like it's feeling the heat."

"That doesn't make any sense."

"There's a lot about me that doesn't make any sense," I smirked, massaging her calf.

"We should try it sometime. I think there's a studio in Boston where you can take classes. Maybe after the launch?"

My chest warmed, not wanting to spook her for mentioning us doing anything after this probationary period she had put us in, "Absolutely. Whatever you'd like."

She popped another piece of cheese into her mouth, "I'm going to go on a mission to find all the stuff you haven't done."

"Why is that?"

She shrugged, "It would be fun to experience stuff together for the first time. It's not going to be any fun if you're bored with everything."

"I don't think I could be bored doing anything with you, Annabel."

She scoffed loudly, taking her foot from my lap and sitting up to sit cross-legged, "Oh come on, you're 400 years old. I'm 29 - that's quite the experience gap. I can't imagine you'll enjoy everything I suggest we do. You've probably done everything before."

"But I don't think that's mutually exclusive to the fact that I'm immortal and you're not. The world has changed a lot in my life. There's always something new to try. You can visit the same mountain range twice and it isn't the same."

"Ugh, you're trying to be deep when I'm suggesting making you go on a hayride and take awful pictures with Santa at the mall. Wait, can you be photographed?"

"Yes, I can be photographed. I just prefer not to be," I answered.

"Why?"

"Call it a paper trail. It would look suspicious to have photos spanning twenty years and I don't look different in any of them."

"Can you change your appearance at all? Like does your hair grow and stuff?"

"To a point. I am cursed with good looks -" I grin at the groan she releases as she rolls her eyes, "like I can't grow my beard or hair past a certain point or gain or lose weight."

"Can you get hurt?"

"*Oui*," I answered, remembering the time Yusuf broke his leg when we were on the run and we couldn't take him to the hospital. After all, heart monitors are a little concerning to nurses when you don't have a pulse. It was a painful night for all of us as we waited for the physician to come, who then had to rebreak his leg to set it since it had already begun to heal wrong.

"What's your favorite place you've been?" She was so full of questions, I loved talking to someone who didn't have the answers to everything - it was fresh and new.

"The Redwoods. Those trees are incredible."

She thought about it, "Trees? You've been alive for over 400 years and your favorite place on earth is somewhere with really tall trees?"

"Have you ever seen them?"

"No," she answered instantly, "I'm not...outdoorsy."

"Then don't question me. They're incredible, and some are easily accessible by car for the indoorsy." I grasped the flesh of her thigh, squeezing it lightly. "Do you want to travel?"

"Yeah, I mean who doesn't?" She grabbed another piece of cheese and popped it in her mouth, "but I need to be here for my moms. They are having a harder time each winter but refuse to leave Quaker's Wharf. I offered to move them to Chicago to be with me and they flat out refused. They've been here longer than I've been alive and I think they're just set in their ways, but they're almost 70 and getting forgetful."

"That must be hard to see."

"Yeah, they were older when they had me anyway and I didn't have a Dad - they're both very.... secretarial?" she laughed, "They weren't 'fun' moms, I wasn't their kid, I was a member of the family, so I was the child who spent my time reading and learning to crochet and brew tea. They didn't stop living their lives so I got to see some pretty cool shit, but I definitely wasn't running for student council or playing pee-wee soccer on the weekends. I think it's easier watching them age knowing they've always been my old tea-drinking buddies rather than like...seeing someone who ran marathons suddenly be unable to walk. It's not quite a jarring change to come home and see Mama under a blanket reading a book when that's how she spent most of my childhood. She just doesn't always remember to turn the page now."

"So you're here to turn their pages?"

She gave me a soft smile, sweeping her hair from her face, "they said I needed to come home to learn about the family before it was too late. I've been here for several months and so far have made no progress on that front so who knows what they actually need from me."

"What about your grandparents? Are they still alive?"

Bels shook her head, "no, I only ever met my granny, and she was... awful," She laughed hesitantly, "She was a fatphobic, judgey, angry old woman. I don't miss her."

"And your other grandparents?"

"Never met them."

I hummed, "so it's just you and your moms?"

"Yep." She emphasized the P and then stretched her arms up high, arching her back and groaning. I pounced, knocking her back onto the couch, and pushed my face into her amazing breasts.

"Hey!" she squealed, wrapping her arms around my neck and I lifted my head, placing a kiss on her lips. She melted into the couch again, wrapping one of her legs around my torso and running her fingers through my hair. "It's getting late," she spoke softly.

"*Oui.*"

"Shouldn't you go home?"

"*Non.*" Like there was any way I was going to leave this beautiful woman in this empty beautiful house to go back to the store and sleep on an air mattress alone. I couldn't think of anything less appealing than a night with my fist after spending an amazing afternoon with her. I kissed her again, asking her lips permission for more before moving my tongue into her mouth and grinding my pelvis into her. The give of her body against mine made me insatiable. All I could think about was getting the soft warmth of Annabel under me when everything in my world was so hard and cold. "I want to be here with you," I murmured into her mouth between kisses.

"No tricks tomorrow, Thomas. I have to go to work. I can't miss another day." Her anxiety immediately clicked on and I felt her tense.

I shushed her, kissing her again, "and you will. We will both work tomorrow, and then you'll come home, I'll feed you something delicious and you'll tell me everything you accomplished after having a day to shut off and relax."

She hummed and smiled, "oh yeah? That's the plan? Do I get a say?"

I smiled back, "*Non*."

Annabel laughed, pushing playfully on my shoulder, and then grimaced and shook out her hand, "Um, ouch."

"Vam-"

"Yeah, yeah, shut up."

"Want to go to bed?"

She sighed again, checking the time, and frowned, "yeah, I probably should. I just need to feed Tim and then we can head up."

"I've got it." Tim and I had spent the day in each other's company and if I could take something as simple as feeding her cat off her plate then I'd do it. I stood from the couch and offered her a hand.

"You guys besties now?" She asked, accepting it and pulling against it so she could easily stand.

"Obvi." I mimicked the horrible voice that the teens in the store use, all nasally and entitled and she giggled. My body warmed knowing that I'd succeeded in my mission of making her happy, even if it was just for a moment. "Go settle in and I'll be up in a minute." I wrapped my hand around her hip and pulled her into me, kissing her soundly, joining our mouths together.

"Okay," She scratched my jaw then bent to scratch Tim and headed to the stairs, smiling at me as she ascended them. I moved about the lower level turning off lamps, folding blankets, and replacing pillows.

I went into the kitchen, puttering about, feeding Tim, loading the dishwasher, and resetting her coffee pot for the morning. If I only had until the first week of November to convince her to Handfeast, I was going to make it impossible for her to say no.

19
ANNABEL

"You're late again! That's twice this week - is everything okay?" Shannon was sitting at her desk, rotating in her chair absentmindedly and editing the photos that I'd taken on Saturday for the website.

"Yeah, totally fine, I've just got a case of the Mondays." I grumbled, hanging up my purse and moving to look over her shoulder, "those look good."

"It's Thursday, Bels. Also, thank you." She straightened and smiled before scrolling through the ones she'd already finished editing. "I'm hoping to have these loaded in by the end of the day for the launch."

"That would be great." I pushed off her desk and moved to mine, sitting down and wiggling my finger over the trackpad, "I can't believe the launch is next week. I feel like we're behind."

"You always think we are behind," she clicked around on her computer, "I think, all things considered, we are in fairly good shape. I'm nervous about the impending shipping nightmares, but back-end wise I think we will be done by tomorrow. I assume it's going to be worse after the launch than this. I'm assuming you want my extra help tonight and tomorrow right?"

I grimaced, "Is that okay? I've got a...complication that's put me behind and I could use the hand."

She crossed her thick legs and spun toward me, "is the complication of the skinny French variety?"

"He's not skinny..."

"I didn't say he wasn't fucking ripped, I just said skinny. Is that a yes?"

I sighed, placing my phone down and leaning against my hand, pushing my fingers into my hair, "he's uh... I guess unofficially staying with me?"

"What?!" She screeched so loud that the short white blond spikes on her head seemed to stick up even straighter.

"Well, he hasn't left yet other than to work."

"So you've just been shacking up since Friday?"

"Kinda?"

"Babes. You just gave me shit for seeing Trae multiple times in a row and you're like...living with this guy?"

Scoffing and rolling my eyes, I turned away, "it doesn't count as living together if it's only a few nights."

"So you're going to ask him to leave?"

Ask him to leave? This weird, delightfully funny man who makes me delicious food and cleans my house, and fucks me senseless? Who holds me all night and snuggles my cat and eases my anxiety? Who's face I can sit on as much as I fucking want? No way. It had been an amazing few days.

"Listen, this is a completely different situation than you and Trae. Besides, now that I know it's Trae, I'm happy you're happy. I said that before I knew it was him. And I don't have kids to think about."

"I don't care if you've known Thomas for years," *I haven't*, "it still seems like unusual behavior for you right before a launch."

"What's wrong with blowing off some steam while I'm stressed?"

"Well, you've been late twice this week. Are the orgasms worth it?"

I cackled, "they are *absolutely* worth it. Have you ever sat on someone's face?"

She screamed with laughter and waved her hands at me, "oh my god, stop. I can't-"

"It's a 10/10 babe. Do it." I laughed again and opened my email and shop interface, "Man, there's a ton of orders today considering there's new stuff coming out next week. I'd have thought people would be waiting for this stuff to go on clearance."

"Don't look a gift horse in the mouth. Just click accept and go pack it up."

"Isn't packing boxes your job?"

"You want me to stop working on the launch photos?" She arched her dark brow at me. I was always jealous of how she could pull off having such light hair and dark statement brows.

I sighed, "Right. Okay, I'm going to film a little too so don't knock."

"You got it, boss." She gave me a thumbs up and I zapped all the orders to my phone so I could easily print the shipping labels and I sent the packing slips to our main printer, which spit out each order on a light orange sheet with a watermark of our logo in the background. I loved my logo. The heart-eyed skull and crossbones wearing a crown made me smile every time I saw it in an unboxing video or ad. It was one of the many things that made me feel like I'd actually started my own business. Also, packing tape. Who knew that black packing tape covered in my logo would make me feel like an adult?

The storeroom was overflowing with boxes waiting to be fully inventoried, sorted, and tagged, and while that was the easiest kind of job to hire out, they were also the simple kinds of tasks that I enjoyed getting lost in. I loved feeling every item that came through my store and the repetitive motion of stabbing them with the tagging gun and sealing the bags.

After setting up my phone for a timelapse, I went about grabbing order items from the shelves and assembling the black packing boxes, double-checking my work, and humming along to a song in my head. As I worked, I thought about the past few days with Thomas. They were almost a blur. When I came home late at night he would be in my kitchen, petting my cat and watering my plants, cooking me a lovely dinner, or doing dishes. I didn't understand it at all. If he wanted me anxious so he could feed, he was definitely shooting himself in the foot by making my life easier. We'd turn on a cooking competition and he'd hold my feet and tell me about his day at the shop and I'd feel him massage every ounce of tension out of my body and replace it with contentedness. It'd been like this the last five nights. In the morning I'd wake up to him kissing my shoulders and neck, we'd have slow, tender, delicious morning sex and then he'd leave for work and I'd scramble to get my life together enough to do the same.

He was distracting and I couldn't decide if that was a problem or not. Yes, it had been a great week, but I also had done nothing but work and Thomas. Considering this was supposed to be a business relationship, it was getting a little habitual. When I was with him it was like I couldn't imagine not having him there, but once we both went to work my mind would race. It was supposed to be that he got to eat and I got to not panic - that was the arrangement, not him whispering stories to me in the dark while he caressed my sides, not him kissing my shoulder and wishing me a good day at work while I brushed my teeth. It wasn't the first day that week that I'd tried to separate myself from whatever was going on with him as soon as we were apart. It was moving fast, and together that felt natural, but apart it felt terrifying. I moved about my morning, and once I'd finished the original orders, I started opening the boxes of new inventory, stopping to flash a few pieces at the camera and make an exaggerated excited face. I pulled a few pieces to take home, as I was the best advertisement I had and turned my face to the phone when I heard the telltale beep saying that the recording had stopped.

TOMMY: How do you feel about Bouillabaisse?

I couldn't hide the smile that swept across my face that I quickly tried to school.

ANNABEL: WTF IS BOUILLABAISSE, FRENCHIE?

TOMMY: FISH STEW. I'M GOING TO HEAD TO THE MARKET IN A BIT AND I THOUGHT IT LOOKED INTERESTING.

ANNABEL: I CAN LITERALLY EAT CEREAL, YOU DON'T HAVE TO TRY SO HARD.

TOMMY: BELS.

ANNABEL: TOMMY.

TOMMY: SEE YOU AT HOME FOR SOME SUPPOSEDLY DELICIOUS FRENCH FISH STEW.

I laughed and shook my head and then reread his last message. See me at home? Home. Like our home? It was *my* home, not *our* home. It was little things like that that as soon as we were separated for the day caused my anxiety to spike and I began to feel insecure about our arrangement. I furrowed my brow and answered.

ANNABEL: SURE, I'LL MEET YOU BACK AT MY PLACE.

I stepped back out into the lobby, "Are you and Trae serious?" I asked Shannon with no warning.

Her head shot up from her phone, "Uh, what?"

I nodded at her phone, "The dude you're sexting on the clock - are you guys serious? How long are you with someone before you start deciding things are serious?"

She looked at me bewilderedly, "What the fuck are you talking about, Bels?" Her phone dinged again in her head, "Also, this is my ex bitching about the girls' quantity and quality of socks, as if he is incapable of purchasing socks on his own, so I'm definitely not experiencing any sexual pleasure from this exchange. But I can totally let Trae know you're cool with it if you want?"

I sighed, leaning against the door jam, "How long after you and Jake got together did you guys move in together?"

"I mean, we were in college. I basically moved into his room the first night we had sex."

"Okay, so it's not totally weird-"

"I didn't say that," she spoke slowly, navigating the minefield of a conversation, "we were 18, not 30. We were not making any decisions past 'Human pretty. Sex good. Bang bang long time. It was entirely a caveman kind of thing. There was some obvious lack of frontal cortex development happening."

I grunted and nodded, "Okay. Good talk."

"What did Thomas do? Two hours ago you were all 'this is fine!'" She yelled after me.

"Nothing. Everything's fine." I shot her a smug grin and headed into the filming room with another lingerie set.

"What are you doing?" She jumped up and came towards the filming room where I was already removing my clothing to slip on the rich purple body suit.

"I'm filming, what's it look like?"

"And you making a thirst trap right now, in this very moment, with zero relation at all to the French man we were previously discussing?"

Shrugging, I lifted my breasts into place in the cups, making sure the snake heads were over my nipples, "It's my body. It's not like he owns it. We aren't in a relationship of any kind."

She crossed her arms, "are you proving a point about something or trying to sabotage a good thing?"

I shook out my hair, "I can't suddenly stop posting thirst traps. It's part of my brand. Big is sexy. I am sexy. Buy my clothes and you can be sexy too. It's a whole thing. Confidence!"

"Mmmhmmm, and while I usually support that 100%, you don't typically interrupt Jake yelling at me about socks to question my relationship experience looking like you've seen the Ghost of Christmases Yet to Come."

"Dude, how often are you and Jake fighting about socks?" She and her ex had been divorced for a long time and he seemed to become more of a pain in her ass instead of less as time went on.

Shannon snarled, "that man could fight about anything."

I moved to zip up the black pleated mini skirt and attached a snake chain at the hip. "Thigh highs?" I asked.

"The answer to that is always yes. Do you want solid or fishnet?"

"Um, the sheer and solid striped, I think."

"Nice choice," she disappeared into the closet where I kept my collection of tights and other multi-use things and tossed a pair at me.

"And the long black chain necklace - the one that joins at the clavicle and then hangs straight down."

She grabbed it as well and came over to put it on me while I darkened my eyeliner.

"Don't shoot happiness in the foot, Bels."

"Don't give me contradicting advice on the same day, Shan."

"Is he going to be upset about you shaking your ass on the internet?"

"It's the same ass that was on the internet yesterday, and the day before that, and the day before that. I'm not changing myself for anyone. I can be an awesome fucking adult and eat cereal for dinner and not consume anything but coffee until 2:00 and I can shake my ass on the internet as much as I want."

"Uh huh..."

"Get back to work."

"I'm going to tell Thomas he isn't doing a good enough job if you've been banging since Saturday and you're still this cranky."

I filmed three transitions to splice into the basic looks I'd filmed the day before and posted one, choosing the one where my thighs jiggled a little more than the others when I kicked my leg over my head and dropped it to the floor. So help me god, I was going to make thigh jiggles a goal for women everywhere. I'd never met a person who didn't love squeezing a soft thigh. Whoever started the smear campaign against thunder thighs did the world a disservice.

After posting, I moved to my desk and pulled my makeup wipes out of my drawer and began to wipe off the dark shadow, still wearing the singlet and Shannon whistled next to me while watching the clip, "Damn girl, you are a certified level ten hottie."

"I'm telling you, Shan, one of these days I'm going to get you in there to film. There's something incredibly liberating about owning your body like that."

"You seem a little less on edge than you were before you filmed, that's for sure. You wanna talk about what that was all about?"

I tossed the wipes in the trash, "I don't know, I'm just...he called my place home and I think I just...independent woman'd for a second."

"Maybe you need a break from him? Come out tonight with Trae and me. It's Thirsty Thursday at the Cauldron and we were going to go right after work."

I scrunched my lips, "that sounds really nice but Tommy said he was going to make this French stew and he seemed excited about it."

"So come out after dinner. Go home, eat with him and then send him home and come out with us. He can spend a night at his place while you hang out with your friends - if he can't, that's a huge red flag that you shouldn't ignore."

"Yeah," I hesitated, "No, yeah, you're right. There's nothing wrong with us going out for the night." I reached for my phone.

ANNABEL: I'M GOING OUT TONIGHT APPARENTLY. IS THE STEW ALREADY GOING OR CAN WE RAIN CHECK IT UNTIL TOMORROW?

My phone almost immediately went off.

TOMMY: Non, I'm still at the shop. I can make it tomorrow. Everything okay, amour?

ANNABEL: Yep, just going out with friends. I'll see you tomorrow after work?

TOMMY: Okay...do you want me to come out with you?

ANNABEL: Nah, it's okay. I'll be fine. Enjoy a night to yourself.

TOMMY: Be safe. Remember, like calls to like. Don't go for walks with strange men.

ANNABEL: Me? I'd never pick up a stray like that.

TOMMY: Of course not. Have fun.

I shrugged, "It seems like he doesn't care. He said to have fun."

"Awesome. Then let's finish up and head out. Don't change, you look amazing."

I grumbled, "Okay, but then I have to redo my makeup again."

"Boohoo. The boss is definitely going to fire you."

Shannon's phone rang and she put it on speakerphone, "Hey Trae, you're on speaker, Bels is coming out with us tonight."

"Oh yeah? Awesome!"

"Don't cause any trouble for me tonight, Trae, alright?" I hollered toward the phone.

"You're no fun!" He chuckled, *"Alright babe, I'm leaving work now, you want to meet there in an hour?"*

"Yeah, Jake should be getting the girls from daycare, so let me make sure he didn't forget, and then I'll see you there."

They chatted for a few more minutes while she texted her ex to make sure he had indeed not forgotten their children, and I reapplied some simpler makeup. I shut down my computer, then headed to the closet to grab a leather jacket and a pair of my boots that I'd left behind once. I'd take a night. It seemed like a good solution to the chaos in my head. I'd just take one night away from him being in my house, cooking my food, and sleeping in my bed. I wasn't going to let myself get put under some kind of spell where suddenly I was begging him to claim me and effectively ending my life as a normal woman. If I went to him with these feelings he could just suck them away, but then how would I ever know what I want? What did I want? I wasn't some emotional blood bag - I had plans.

"Ready, Bels?" Shannon called from the front of the suite where she'd begun turning off lights. I quickly checked my phone and saw that my post was already at 2000 likes and it'd only been a few minutes. Perfect.

"Yep, let's get out of here."

20

THOMAS

Something was wrong. That morning when I'd left Annabel she'd been grinning from ear to ear and kissed me passionately before telling me she'd see me later. We'd spent the early hours of the day slowly making love and laughing together and suddenly the only responses I was getting were things like, *"Nah, I'll see you tomorrow."*

I needed to see her. If I could see her, we could talk, and if we could talk, I could fix whatever was bothering her. Maybe it was my fresh wounds from Monique and Yusuf leaving, but not knowing what was wrong was driving me insane. I'd spent the afternoon sitting in my office area tapping my pen against the card table anxiously when my phone notified me that she'd posted a new video, which could have made a man rise from the dead. Her curves had been hugged tightly in serpent-covered mesh and when she rose her leg over her head to land on the ground beside her you got a view of the bottom curve of her ass and the exquisite jiggle of her plush thigh. The same thighs that had been around my head only hours before. Tightly. When the night manager came in for his shift and asked me about my day, I'd almost ripped his face off. Literally.

I'd met her a week ago. I knew I was being insane, but I also knew she was mine. I also knew that *she* knew she was mine. But the smallest fraction of my brain that said she didn't know was trying to break down the walls inside of its cage and go get her.

I'd gone to the house anyway, if for no other reason than to feed Tim and see if she came by before going out, but once the clock rolled over to seven, I knew she'd gone straight from work. I considered staying, but that seemed odd, then I'd considered just going back to the shop, but I didn't feel like being there during store hours while I was so antsy.

I knew I needed to find her - if for no other reason than to keep her safe. She'd agreed to be my primary source for the time being and if anything happened to her, my harvesting could be impacted. I knew how alluring her scent was and she was going to attract every sleazy monster in whatever dive she'd decided to go to.

I walked until I found an empty area and then in a blink of an eye, I'd turned into my raven, spreading my wings wide and taking flight toward the bar she'd been at the week before. On my flight, I could imagine every person pleasuring themselves to her image tonight and her just preening over the boost in sales she'd see over the next few days. She'd told me she did this for her job, but shit, the way that serpent wrapped delicately around her breast... it was too much to see and then not claim her and peel it off her. She hadn't been wearing it when she went in that morning - she'd been wearing a checkered sundress. I knew exactly what she'd been wearing because I'd imagined flipping the damn thing up over her hips as soon as she got home at least fifteen times throughout the day.

I approached the bar district and caught sight of her, her friend, and the tall man sitting at an outdoor table, laughing over a large basket of chips and salsa, a margarita placed in front of her. I landed in a tree across the street, making sure to disguise myself in the thick foliage of the middle branches - the size of a raven was never subtle - and watched. She hadn't changed back into the sundress.

She was immaculate. Her purple hair shone brightly in the setting sun in a large knot on her head with loose strands drawing attention to her perfect smile and green eyes. She threw her head back in laughter, arching her chest out, stretching the snakes over her bust, and I felt lust radiating off the male, while the blonde friend, Sharon? Shannon? She snorted into her drink.

The man leaned onto the table, seemingly the one to tell the hilarious tale, and mimed an animal taking a bite and shaking something, clearly imagining his head in between Bels' breasts. I wanted to peck his eyes out. A few moments later, Shannon raised a finger and headed into the restaurant, leaving Bels and the man alone. He moved into Shannon's seat and put his hand on Bels' leg, making her laugh and she grabbed him by both shoulders and shook him exaggeratedly. He laughed with her and brushed some hair off her face, resting his hand on her neck. I saw red. I wanted to storm over there, shift before his eyes, and rip her away from him. I was just about to plan his murder when the wind picked up and I noticed a scent. I froze, tilting my black head around, trying to figure out where it was coming from.

There was something Other in the area, and I couldn't place it. It didn't smell like any one species. It didn't smell like someone I knew that lived in the area. Then a familiar scent wafted by after the stranger. *Yusuf.*

Where was he? I frantically took flight, soaring over the busy street, searching for him, a hawk, anything. He scented of chai tea and cinnamon - I could place him anywhere. I'd fallen asleep next to him for two centuries, I'd loved him. If every person in the city was stuffed in a room and I were blindfolded, I'd still be able to find him. So why couldn't I see him now? Where was he?

I swooped back over the area, noting that Annabel locked onto my form with a quizzical expression on her face, the jovial one from a few minutes ago was gone and she said something to Shannon and the man before indicating they should leave.

Follow Bels, or find Yusuf? Follow Bels or find Yusuf? Where the fuck was he and why was he would he turn up here now? How did he even know where I was? Did he know I was in Quaker's Wharf or was it some kind of fucked up coincidence?

As quickly as the scent appeared, it was gone, and I desperately continued to circle the area, losing sight of Annabel and her friends. I'd thought I'd lost them both until I saw Annabel's friend wrap his hand around her waist, pulling her tightly against him and pressing a kiss to the top of her head, and then Shannon's.

I had to get home.

21

ANNABEL

A raven had flown through the restaurant patio. Right through it. And if I hadn't known any better, I would have thought it looked directly at me. I pulled out my phone.

ANNABEL: WHAT ARE YOU DOING RIGHT NOW?

He didn't text back right away, which was odd in itself. But... vampires weren't birds, they were bats, right? Then why did it feel like that monster of an animal knew me? Was it an Other? Thomas had said that now that I knew Others existed, that they were more likely to find me, and nothing screamed "Other" like a bird with a wingspan almost as tall as me.

"We should head to the Cauldron, guys, don't you think? I'm catching weird vibes."

"You and your vibes, Bels," Trae chortled, "You think anything bad is going to happen when you're with me?"

"He's basically a giant," Shannon nearly swooned at him, rubbing his short hair as she stood from our table. He'd just gone to get it faded at his Uncle's barber shop and the top was wonderfully fluffy compared to the sides. He stood as well, towering over both of us and wrapping his strong arms around our waists.

"I promise to protect you from the giant bird," he teased.

"Okay, but really, that was a fucking huge bird," Shannon added placing her pale hand over his dark one, "and lots of people are scared of birds. I'm pretty sure that's a thing."

Unease still moved over me, making me bite my lip, "guys, I'm... you know, I'm wondering if I should head home."

"What? Come on, you said you were taking a night off from Thomas and hanging out with us."

"The French guy from last week? The one who looked like an espresso model?"

I scoffed, "says the guy who's literally had life-size cutouts made of him in his basketball uniform."

"College is expensive, babe."

"Never said it wasn't."

Shannon stopped in front of a little store, "I need to run in here real quick, you guys cool waiting for me?"

"Absolutely, babe," Trae leaned down and kissed Shannon on the lips and she beamed, prancing inside.

"So, how's that going?" I asked him, walking to a bench under a tree to sit.

"Really good, she's awesome."

"Good. Hey - she doesn't know about..."

"Oh I know, and I'd like to keep it that way if it's okay?"

I frowned and crossed my leg, "I think you should be honest with her, but it's your relationship so it's your choice. But I know for a fact that if she finds out, and you haven't told her that she will kill you with her own two hands."

His deep laugh resonated through his chest and into the metal bench, "I don't know if we're going to be serious or not, but it's not worth risking fucking everything up over me and you hooking up a few times. I'm not sure how I feel about her having kids, but we are having fun right now and that's all that matters."

"Trae, if you're not comfortable with the girls, that needs to be a conversation that happens sooner rather than later. The girls are her whole life."

"I'm not saying that I won't be into it, I'm just still getting to know her. Don't stress out so much. We don't even have plans for me to meet them anytime soon." He stretched his arm behind me on the bench and smiled, "Now, you *and* Shannon would definitely be something I'd be into."

I laughed and swatted his chest, "you've always been so bad."

"Bad with what?" Shannon asked coming out of the shop.

"He's just a flirt, that's all."

"Are you going to come with us to the Cauldron, Bels?"

I shook my head, "No, I'm suddenly feeling crummy. I'm going to head home. I hope you guys have fun though." I stood and kissed Shannon's cheek and pat Trae's with a little more force than needed.

We waved goodbye and I headed to my Jeep, which was parked about two blocks down. I grabbed my phone to check it, only to see that Thomas hadn't texted me back yet. That was really unlike him.

My shoulder slammed into a shorter man with cropped black hair and olive skin. "Oh shit, I'm so sorry." I said, putting my hands on his shoulders to steady us, "They always say you shouldn't walk around with your nose in your phone - I'm sorry."

"Not a problem at all," The man had a warm smile and dark eyes. Too dark of eyes, I noted when his hands came up to wrap around my wrists.

At the skin-to-skin contact I felt a tap at my mind, almost like someone knocking at a door, wanting to poke their head around inside. I instantly dropped my hands, severing the connection. "Have a good night," I quickly hurried to my car, getting in and closing the door, still able to see the man that clearly wasn't *just* a man.

How many of these fucking things were there in Quaker's Wharf?

I walked into my house, leaning against the door in a sudden state of exhaustion after my nerves had been on high alert walking the four blocks from where I'd parked. "What a clusterfuck," I muttered, dropping my bag and lifting my legs to unzip my boots.

"Tim?" I called for him, reminding myself to feed him - he tended to be a bastard if he got hungry and would try to step on my face while I slept.

I plopped my jacket up onto a hook and headed into the kitchen, making kissy noises for him. As I walked, I took off my accessories to place on the island and had just twisted to remove the chain from my skirt when, yet again, a fucking vampire made me jump out of my skin.

"Jesus Fucking Christ. Again?! What are you doing here? I thought you were coming over tomorrow?" I gasped, grabbing my heart.

Thomas moved to me at an alarming speed and I stepped back, pressing myself into the butcher block while his hands cradled my cheeks and he kissed me, "Are you okay? Are you hurt?"

I blinked at him in confusion, "What? What are you talking about?"

He kissed me again and reached for my hand to place on his face, but his eyes widened and he dropped it suddenly, before grabbing it again and placing my wrist directly under his nose, inhaling deeply.

"What in the actual hell are you doing, Thomas?"

"Where were you?"

"Not that it matters," I started, "but I went out for dinner with Trae and Shannon."

"*Non, ma chérie,* after. After dinner where were you?"

"Uh..." I thought back, "I just walked to my car."

He kissed me again before I pulled back to continue, "Hey, I bumped into a guy - do you know how many vamps there are here? Like, what is the vamp to mortal per diem in Quaker's Wharf? I swore I felt this dude try to harvest from me. It was so weird."

"Where, Annabel?" His eyes were wide and he hadn't released my wrist, slightly tightening his grip.

"Ouch, Tommy you're hurting me, let go," I grimaced.

He dropped my hand like it was covered in acid, "the man, Bels, did you get a good look at him? What did he look like?"

I shrugged and rubbed my wrist, "I dunno, short, tan, dark hair, and eyes. Creepy Other vibes."

He clawed his hand over his face, swallowing, "I need you to text me if you see him again, okay, Bels?"

I pressed my hand over his, making him draw his brows together. "Hey, you're freaking me out. What is going on?"

"You ran into Yusuf. I can smell him on you."

Flinching, my nose scrunched, "You can smell people on me?"

"*Oui.* I know that tall boy had his hands on you tonight too, but we need to focus on one thing at a-"

"The tall boy? Trae? You mean how I hugged my friend goodbye?"

He pressed on, "You need to tell me-"

"Thomas, you're not acting right."

"Bels," He shook me slightly, "Did you even hear me? You ran into Yusuf. My Yusuf."

"Wait," I dug through our previous conversations and pulled the name from my mind, "Yusuf, like Monique and Yusuf? Like soulmates for hundreds of years and disappeared off the face of the planet, Yusuf?"

"Yusuf," he nodded, "was a woman with him?"

I furrowed my brow and thought back, "I...I don't know. I'm sorry, Tommy, I wasn't looking. I knew he was an Other and he was giving me the heebie-jeebies so I left as fast as I could. If I'd known-"

"*Non, chérie,* you did exactly right. You did exactly what I want you to do if you find an Other and I'm proud of you. Besides, there's no way you could have known it was him or to look for her. But you're okay? You're safe? He's the only one you sensed?"

Scoffing, my voice raised unintentionally from his fussing, "I have no idea! I'm just a boutique owner; I'm not Buffy the fucking Vampire Slayer!"

His expression dropped and his eyes darted about absently like he was trying to solve the puzzle, "I sensed another, but I didn't recognize the scent - I don't know-"

"You *sensed*? Or you can currently smell?"

"*Quoi?*"

I frowned, my anger boiling over, "I knew it! You followed me. You were there! You couldn't let me have one night out with my friends, could you?"

"Bels," he raked his hands through his hair, tugging his scalp slightly, "there was something else out there - if Yusuf beelined to you, who is to say something else won't?"

I shrugged, "Maybe he beelined to me because he smelled *you* on me. Ever think of that?" I could see his wheels spinning, "Thomas - you followed me. You can't do that."

"I needed to see you -"

"Are you a bird?" I spat.

He froze for a moment before reaching for me, but I swatted his hand away.

"You're a fucking bird! I thought vampires were bats! You followed me as a giant fucking bird and scared the shit out of me you asshat!"

"You were out with him, looking like that, and I knew Others would be there, and I needed to know you were safe, *mon coeur*, it is my job to protect you - you're mine."

"You are not clothes shaming me, bird boy. I can wear whatever the fuck I want whenever the fuck I want to, and I'm not yours - I belong to myself. Got it?" I gestured to my body with a sweeping motion, "Property of Annabel." I started to walk out of the kitchen but he grabbed my arm again, this time spinning me and pinning my body against the fridge.

He spoke clearly, his voice low, possessive and unyielding. "You are *mine*, Annabel. You are mine until November - those were your terms, remember? This means that you do not put yourself in harm's way, you do not shove me aside to try to make me jealous, and you never, ever stop me from touching you any fucking way I want to. Mine." His lips slammed into me, and his hands cupped my breasts, rubbing my nipples through the thin singlet with his thumbs, "you haven't even let me have a good look at you in this - all I saw was what everyone else saw online, but I get to see it all, don't I, Bels? I get every. Single. Inch of you. I get to see the parts of you that no one else ever will," he kissed his way down my neck and I melted at the sensation of his lips against my skin, temporarily giving in to the heat blossoming inside me.

"Stop, Thomas, I'm mad at you, remember?" I gasped, arching into his touch, "you followed me and watched me - that's stalking. You should leave. This isn't normal."

He chuckled, "You're worried about this being normal? Look at us, *chérie*." He slid his hand up to my throat, stroking the side of it and growling, "*Non*. I'm not leaving." He pulled his face back so he could lock his eyes with mine, "tell me you want me to leave. To my face, chérie." I narrowed my gaze and he slowly smiled, "I feel nothing coming from you but desire. Desire for me. Now do you want to be difficult or do you want me to show you just how much I own you?"

I swallowed, "you can't follow me."

"Answer. Do you genuinely want me to leave? Anything else isn't up for discussion right now." He leaned in, dragging his teeth over the place he held my throat and my body became heavy with desire. He moved to hold one side of my head while the other held a bruising grip on my hip. "I should put you over my knee for even suggesting us being apart. You are my everything, Bels." His menacing growl melted into a deep, low, sensual timbre, "I would cease to exist without you. I need you."

The brattiness bubbled up in my throat and slipped out, unable to be contained, "Oh yeah? You say that to all your food or am I just lucky?"

He slowly dropped to the floor, never breaking eye contact, and placed my knee over his shoulder and ran his hands up under my skirt, rumbling in approval when he felt my soft skin above my thigh-highs.

"I'm the lucky one, *mon coeur*." He placed a kiss on my inner thigh, "You know you're everything. You want to only be my food? You want to water this down and pretend that that is all this is? I will eat your pussy again and again and again until you admit that you are mine. I could consume you until there is nothing left of you but the sliver you are willing to admit belongs to me. But I don't want a sliver, I want all of you, do you understand me?"

I leaned my head back against the fridge, taking a shaky breath and running my hand through his soft hair, "it's only until November."

"Mmmmm," he hummed skeptically and reached up to pull down my skirt slowly, dancing his feather-light fingers across my skin, leaving me in my snake singlet and thigh-high tights. His fingers dug into the strip of naked flesh and he leaned in, running his nose along my crease through the fabric. He inhaled and groaned before placing tortuous kisses on and around my center. I dampened and knew it wouldn't be long before he would taste me despite my pussy being covered. I wanted to take the damn thing off. I wanted to be bare and push his bossy, clingy, possessive mouth right on my clit and take back the power. I belonged to myself. He was meant to service me. Help me. I tightened my grip on his hair and tried to press him into me.

"I thought you wanted me to leave, Bels,"

"Shut up."

He chuckled against my skin, vibrations reverberating through me and taking my breath away. "Tell me what you really want. You don't want me to leave, so what is it you want?" He brought his hand inside my legs and began running his finger under the elastic, snapping it once making me gasp.

"No."

"No what?" He nipped the tender flesh of my thigh with his teeth.

"No, I don't want you to leave."

"So what do you want, *bébé*?"

My core clenched around nothing, demanding his attention. "I want you to make me come. Please," I whimpered, his hot breath came through the fabric and teased at my dampness.

"I've been waiting to see you all night since you posted that fucking video," He kissed me again, slipping his finger under the fabric and to my opening, "do you have any idea how fucking beautiful you are? And so fucking wet."

"Thomas, please. Just do it."

"Just do it? That's all you want? For me to just do it?"

I nodded, "Please. Please make me come. Just fucking do it. If you're going to be here you're going to make me feel good."

He frowned slightly and thrust two fingers inside of me, immediately curling and pumping it brutally against my gspot. He went from 0 to 100 in a moment and my leg shook with the intensity.

"Shit." I grabbed his head again, though this time when I tried to press him against me he complied and latched on to my naked clit, sucking and lavishing it relentlessly. "Shit, Tommy. Fuck," I moaned, "You're going to make me come already. It's too much. It's too much, slow down." I was being slammed by meteors of pleasure, leaving craters in my mind and body that I needed to fill. I needed to be full. I needed him inside of me. I squealed, curling my stocking-covered toes and slipping slightly on the faux brick floor. He wasn't giving me an orgasm, he was taking it, ripping it from me piece by fucking piece as if he was methodically removing my bones. I was running from the onslaught of feelings, trying to hold off and slow him down, to make the moment last, but as soon as I forfeited to the violent need to tip over the other side, he froze. I trembled in panic, "no, no, no, no, no."

"Say you're mine, Annabel."

I tried to push my hips to his face, "This is coercion." I gasped, in desperation to finish I moved my hand, deciding to save myself from the torment, but he grabbed it, halting me. I whimpered, knowing it would only take two seconds more and that it was painful to float in this in between. "You're fucking awful. I hate you."

He frowned, then blew a stream of air at me, making my body concave from sensation and my eyes close tightly. My need was so great that I thought maybe I'd cum just from the thought of it - like maybe I could will my orgasm into existence.

Thomas rose from the ground, "Look at me," he demanded and I snapped my green eyes back open. He growled one more word, "Mine," and slapped my pussy hard. The prickles of pain threw me head first down the mountain, and it wasn't a joyful, tender orgasm, it was a brutal burning completion that I screamed and shook through. My scream turned to a whimper as I tried to find solid ground, only for Thomas to slap me again, pushing his fingers into me, and began slamming them into my soft tissue. I screamed again, throwing my head back forcefully enough that a box of cereal fell off the top of the fridge. I navigated my way through the explosion of feelings, unsure if it was a second climax or a neverending fall from the first, and I desperately tried to find my way back to my tender lover. The one who'd spent the last week slowly waking me up with heartbreakingly soft kisses, and slow, easy sex. I gently scratched my nails against the back of his head, pulling him to me, needing him to hold me - to give me aftercare after such an intense session.

He got close enough to my lips that I could hear how affected he was from watching me come apart like that. His breath was ragged with need and I could feel the length of his erection pushing into my leg. My mind filled with the desire for his more passionate side, I wanted to listen to him say the beautiful things he whispered while we joined together in my bed. I wanted to feel his skin on mine and him rock deep inside of me, moving us as one body. I moaned, pulling him in again, "Thomas, kiss me," I whispered. But instead of his lips touching mine, he rested his forehead against me and sighed, removing his hand gently from my core and squeezing my waist with the other. He brought his fingers to his mouth and licked them clean of me, then sadly shook his head.

"Have a good night, Annabel."

I opened my eyes, confused, and only got my legs to move just in time to watch him scratch Tim's head and walk out my front door. He'd left.

22

THOMAS

I wandered the streets of Quaker's Wharf, feeling too much and too deeply. How had I gone from desire to jealousy, to worry, to possession, to...alone so quickly? She'd asked me to leave then begged me to service her. She'd begged me.

"You're fucking awful. I hate you."

Her words reverberated through my mind.

"It's only until November."

I sighed, pinching the bridge of my nose. How could we go from making love that morning to her not being able to stand my presence? I couldn't manage the ebbs and flows of her affection. I'd told her that I needed her words, I needed communication after what had happened and the words she'd chosen had been to tell me that I was awful. *Fucking awful*, actually. And she said it with so much venom it was as if my presence pained her.

I'd never felt the need for someone the way I felt it with Annabel. I needed her and I had her. She'd agreed that she was mine, only to turn and refuse me and push me away. Her energy danced with mine, creating veritable music between us. I could spend eternity with that woman. I would agree to never see Yusuf and Monique again if it meant I could keep her and I'd barely had a taste of her.

"Hey, Thomas!" I looked up to see Bels' friend Shannon wrapped around the tall man.

"Good evening," I tried to put a smile on my face, but I knew it didn't reach my eyes.

"You okay?" Shannon stopped an arms-length from me, confusion and worry radiating from her.

"*Oui*, just a long day." Shaking off the cloud that loomed over me, I extended a hand to Trae, "Hello, Trae."

He took my hand, shaking it roughly and his anger seeped through to me. I quickly dropped contact with him - I'd told Annabel I wouldn't feed from others and this man wouldn't be the reason I failed.

"Hey, Bels was acting weird this afternoon. You got anything to do with that?" He asked gruffly.

"I just left her place, she's fine."

Shannon tilted her head, "We are going out for a few more drinks, want to go with us? I don't have my kids tonight and I'm not wasting the night off! We could text Bels and see if she wants to come back out now that you're here."

I warmed at the idea of doing something as simple as a double date with my beautiful girl but knew that it wasn't the time. "Thank you, Shannon, but you and Trae should enjoy your evening. I am just walking off my thoughts."

"Okay, well here, give me your phone." I took it out and handed it to her and she quickly typed out a text to herself so I'd have her number, "Figure if you're with Bels you should have some way to get a hold of me if you need me. Especially while we are at work - she is absolutely terrible about leaving her cell on airplane mode."

I couldn't hide the small smile remembering the night we'd watched a cake competition and she'd gone on a full rant about my vampire magic somehow kicking her phone off of airplane mode and stopping her filming multiple times - as if such a thing was even possible.

"Thank you, Shannon. I appreciate it. Don't hesitate to reach out to me either, I'm sure if I have problems reaching her at work that you must have the same when she's at home. We can work as each other's answering service."

She laughed. Her laugh was higher than Annabel's. Where Annabel had a lower and rhythmic way of speaking, Shannon's voice was much more stereotypically feminine and her laugh almost sounded like chirping. "Sounds good, Tommy. We'll see you later, yeah?"

Nodding, I gestured for them to pass me, "Of course. Have a good night."

Trae guided Shannon past him, possessively placing his hand on her bottom which was noticeably flatter than Bels' despite her pear like shape and he glared at me for even following him with my gaze.

Quaker's Wharf in the Fall was so different than when we lived in Boston. It was amazing how a half-hour car ride could make all the difference. In Boston, our haunted tour business would be exploding with drunken college kids and vloggers, and I'd be filled to the brim off happy Red Sox fans. The buzz of living in a city, no matter which city, was so different than a small coastal town whose whole tourism industry was based on the fact that they'd murdered a bunch of women hundreds of years ago over toxic bread.

This small town loved witches now. It was because of the town's sordid history that many people made their livelihoods. It made you wonder how the Puritans would react to a bunch of young girls celebrating a birthday by heading down to a local shop to make their own broomsticks, or that you could get magic wands for chopsticks at the sushi place.

I wandered well into the night, unwilling to return to my air mattress, and resigned myself to a night flight to see some lights and exhaust myself. I'd been sitting on an empty patch of beach, removing my shoes and socks when the crunching footsteps sounded and the scent of chai tea and cinnamon wafted to me.

"Ah, there you are. You have been quite busy, my friend. Your scent is all over this town."

I froze, recognizing the voice. When I turned, I saw him leaning against a tree with the same kind smile he'd greeted me with for 200 years. He had been there through so much, we had been together longer than mortals and their grandchildren's lives, but not for the past year. I'd been alone for a year and had lost everything. I opened my mouth, gaping like a fish, trying to sort through the questions my mind was screaming. Was I happy to see him? Where was Monique? Why now? Were they okay? Did they need help?

"It is good to see you, Thomas." He pushed off the tree and walked toward me but my hand shot up to indicate he should keep his distance.

"Yusuf," my mind and body fought between falling into old habits and hugging and kissing him hello, or if I wanted to punch him in the face for scaring me into chasing them around the world. "Yusuf...it's-"

"I know, my love, it's been a while."

"Yusuf, where the fuck have you been?"

23
ANNABEL

I'd spent the night curled up on the couch with Tim. I kept telling myself Thomas would come back, but he never did. It wasn't until the sun rose the following morning that my heart sank. Maybe I'd freaked out and pushed him too hard, but for him to just leave after what we did? To leave me feeling insecure and vulnerable especially after announcing his ex was back? I pulled the blanket up closer to my face and checked my phone. Not a single text. Not a single call. Did he find Yusuf? Were they working it out? Thomas had said he wouldn't open himself up to that again, but that was before he'd left me. He'd walked away like he hadn't just shattered me from the inside out without as much as looking back.

Sitting up, I held my head in my hands and sniffled. I couldn't let myself fall apart over a guy I'd been fucking for a week. Seven days! I was a strong, confident, independent woman and didn't need anyone else to make my life have value. I made my own and created my own joy. Using the side of my pointer fingers, I swiped beneath my eyes to clean off any mascara flakes and blew a raspberry. Fucking men.

I couldn't even remember what I'd said to him in the heat of the moment. I was out of my mind with lust and anger - I'm sure I would have apologized if he'd stuck around if I'd known he was upset. A loud meow echoed through the room when Tim jumped up onto my lap, purring and coiling himself in the hole of my crossed legs. "I know, he isn't here, so you're starving aren't you?" I spoke softly, scratching his ears and looking out the front window to the street through the lace curtains. My house suddenly felt hollow. There weren't French curses spewing from my kitchen or the sound of gentle kisses trailing up my back to wake me up. He wasn't humming to my plants or feeding my cat.

I shook myself repeating over and over that he'd followed me. He'd stalked me. He'd scared me and then he walked away. Also, he was a fucking raven! What kind of vampire is a raven? At least if he got so mad he left, he wouldn't make me pay for his move or give him a stake in my company. We'd never discussed if this failed because of him - I don't think he ever thought that was a possibility, so he'd never said anything about it.

He had said that I was everything. His everything.

Scoffing, I placed Tim on the floor and got up, straightening the robe I'd passed out in, and grabbed the empty wine bottle and glass from the coffee table before heading into the kitchen. My late-night bowl of cereal was still in the sink and rainbows projected throughout the room through the crystal that my mom had hung in my window when I moved in. Shit, I'd been so drowned in dick town that hadn't even checked in on my moms for days. So much for being a helpful daughter.

I resolved that I'd call them on my way to work and quickly fed Tim, hitting the brew button on my coffee pot. The room felt beautiful and peaceful, but devoid of energy until the machine made a horrible dry grinding noise and I remembered that Thomas had been making the coffee all week and I hadn't set it up last night. How the hell had he dug his claws in so much in such a short amount of time? I slapped the button off, cussing at it and threatening to replace it, then walked from plant to plant, sticking my finger in their soil to ensure everyone would make it through the odd vibes.

With a frown, and partly because I missed the smells of his cooking in my kitchen, I decided to pull out the cheesecloth bag that my mom had bought from the farmer's market earlier that summer. The bag was full of herb bundles and dried fruit rinds and claimed to be a "cleansing simmer pot" brew. The woo-woo lady at the stand had said that doing these simmer pots were another way to cleanse the house without doing a smudging, and my mom jokingly suggested doing it before I moved into my historic row house to get rid of any spirits. I'd just rolled my eyes at the time, allowing her to support the local woman with no intention of it ever resurfacing from the depth of my spice cupboard, but now decided that I'd cleanse the space from top to bottom to rescind whatever welcome that vampy asshole thought he had to my space. He'd have to grovel - outright beg me to let him back in once he realized what an asshole move that last night had been. I smirked at the idea of him slamming into an invisible barrier when he tried to break in next, smashing his face into it like the funny pictures online where people captured their cats on glass tables from underneath.

I read the card tied to the bag and filled my slow cooker with water. The directions said to submerge the bag while thinking about the "brewing intention" or what you want to cleanse from negative spirits, so I grabbed a wooden spoon and held that thing under the water like I was drowning it, the whole time thinking about Thomas and removing the invitation, and didn't remove the spoon until every little air bubble had surfaced and popped. I turned the machine on fully knowing that I was supposed to do it on the stove, but I wanted this space cleansed to death and I wasn't about to go to work with a simmer pot going. With the help of the slow cooker, it could go all day long and I, hopefully, would come home to a delicious-smelling and vampire-free home.

Within fifteen minutes I was out the door dressed in my favorite black flared jeans, a hair metal cropped tee, and space buns atop my head. When I locked up behind me, I could still feel an unsettling silence on my street as I had the night before, like the world had covered me in a cloche, muffling the neighborhood around me. It was past eight, but it seemed that no one else was rushing off to work. Still finding the quiet creepy, I grabbed my phone and called my Mama while hoping that that simmer pot could solve my life's problems and that I'd magically appear in my life from a week ago. Unfortunately, I didn't think one could get refunds on witchcraft, and I didn't brew the damn thing with the intention of time travel.

"Hello?" She answered, her aging voice cracking a bit from a lack of diaphragm support.

"Hey, Mama. Just checking in - how are you and Mom?"

"Just fine love. The kegger ended an hour ago once the strippers left, and we were just about to head to bed to sleep off the ecstasy."

I laughed, "Mama I don't think people who use ecstasy actually call it that. It'd be like a pothead declaring that they were going to go smoke a marijuana plant."

"Well...how was I supposed to know that?"

I smirked and unlocked my car, climbing in and connecting the call to Bluetooth. "I know, not everyone was lucky enough to take fifth-grade drug education. What have you guys been up to? Do you need anything?"

"A visit would be nice."

Scoffing, I pulled away from the curb, "how'd we go from you saying goodnight to the strippers to your horrible daughter never visiting?"

She huffed on the other end of the line, *"Did you see that moon last night? It was insanely bright. Mom damn near couldn't sleep it was shining so brightly into our room."*

"Oh, it was a full moon? That would explain it then."

"Explain what, darling?"

"Everyone had a stick up their ass yesterday. And, when I was downtown, there was a freaking raven flying overhead. Like a real one - not a crow that looked like a raven, but like a giant black bird." He also was a vampire who pissed me off yesterday, but that was neither here nor there.

"That's not unusual, it's Autumn, he was probably just looking for a new nest for his wife. Did you know that ravens mate for life? Smart birds."

"Oh, so they're super clingy in relationships? What a shocker."

"What in the devil are you talking about, Annabel?"

"Eh, nothing, don't worry about it. Just an observation." I turned onto the street where my office was, "I'm just headed into work, Mama, I'm hoping to finish up the launch stuff today, maybe we can do dinner next week?"

"That would be lovely - we have plenty of things we need help harvesting in the garden and Mom mentioned canning. I'm sure she'd love your help processing all that. She worked so hard on the garden this year."

I laughed, "Mama you know the extent of my food processing is turning the dehydrator on and drinking whatever tea you put in front of me."

"That's just fine. Someone has to turn the machine on. Have a wonderful day at work, I love you. Don't let that super moon get to you."

"You too, party animal. Love you." I shook my head, laughing at the strange dichotomy between my mothers; Mom, being a hippie gardener who only crocheted with local alpaca fiber, and my Mama who taught literature at the college in Salem most of her life, and was happiest under one of Mom's afghans with tea and a leather bound book. They were soft but powerful women who thrived in the life they'd made together. Despite being raised in Mom's house with a full working garden instead of a swing set, the most I'd been able to keep alive was Tim and some succulents and the rogue house plant (which I only fostered before my moms come and rescue it to nurse it back to health), but it took well over a decade for me to not instantaneously kill any plant I brought into the house. Mama had even added a solarium to their house so Mom could continue growing things during the horrible Massachusetts winters. Plants were her thing.

I resolved to work quickly and efficiently so I could get home and get thoroughly wine drunk and watch a 90s rom-com. I just needed to survive the anxiety of the day, then I could get smashed and yell at Meg Ryan or something. That seemed like a good enough plan.

I started the morning by filming thirst traps and sneak peeks for the weekend and then piddled away the rest of the day packing up orders and tagging things while Shannon finished up the website and newsletters. We worked in relative silence most of the day, focused on getting the damn launch ready so we could try to enjoy our weekend, but I was still surprised when Shan popped her head into the room to tell me she was heading out for the night.

As a business owner, I could always find something to do. There was always cleaning or organizing, filing or accounting, something to keep me working 24 hours a day, but I was stressed. I was stressed and tired and my stupid anxiety-eating vampire hadn't texted me all day, which shockingly, only increased my anxiety even more. It was like he was cooking his dinner by ignoring me and that didn't sit well with me.

I spent the evening at home eating take-out curry and repeating every line from the movie to Tim with some surprisingly yummy $3 wine from the discount grocery store. One does not simply waste good wine when trying to get drunk. I'd almost forgotten that Thomas had dropped off the face of the earth when the sky had darkened and it felt like a normal evening at home. It had only been a week, there was no reason to completely forget the life I'd made for myself because I had to feed my own cat.

It wasn't until four glasses of wine in and I was singing a closing credit power ballad into the remote that a gentle knock came from my door. I opened it with a smug grin on my face expecting a groveling vampire to be pressed against my spell bubble, only to come face to face with the most beautiful woman I'd ever seen in my life.

She was long and lean with alarmingly straight shiny platinum hair that was cut into a perfectly sharp bob. I'm pretty sure her well-defined legs were at least nine feet tall and she looked like a walking weapon, clearly owning that she was entirely capable of taking off her stilettos and ramming them through your heart. I, on the other hand, stood dumbfounded in my doorway, braless, and wearing an $8 Wal-Mart stretchy muumuu that had brought me insane amounts of joy when I discovered it had pockets. Her painted-on jeans and tight shirt highlighted the muscles of a runner, whereas my muumuu went down to my mid-calf like a sack and had a low enough neckline that I didn't feel like it was trying to choke me, without being so low that I risked a boob escaping and trying to strangle me overnight. Honestly, it was such a great nightgown that I'd ordered four more. Muumuus were top-notch.

I shook my head trying to focus on the creature in front of me that was somehow wearing an unstained white top (even though it was evening), ignoring how my side boobs were slightly pinched under my armpits or how the wine was giving me heartburn.

"Uh, hello, can I help you?"

The woman slowly assessed me from top to bottom before plastering on an ingenuine smile, "Hello, I am sorry, I may have the wrong house."

I snorted, quickly pulling my hand over my breast to pop the tissue out from under my arm, "yeah I'd think so."

Her eyes narrowed on my jiggling chest, pulling her lip back slightly in disgust and I instinctively shrunk back, leaning against the open door and remaining on my side of the threshold.

"I just... I thought he would be here. I am looking for a dear friend of mine and I... swore he had been in the area. ...Do you know Thomas? Is he inside?"

I stared at her, "Thomas?"

"Yes, do you know him?" She tilted her head slightly, obviously smelling the alcohol on me - maybe even smelling him on me too - and wondering if I held more than three brain cells.

"Um, yes. Are you.... You wouldn't be.... Are you Monique?"

Eyes widening slightly in surprise, she quickly schooled her expression, "I am, yes. You know of me?"

I chuckled, "Oh yeah, I fucking know of you. You're 'Monique'. He's only been looking for you for a fucking year," I slurred slightly while gesturing toward her goddess-like body, "Obviously he'd be looking for you. Jesus, I've had one peek at ya and I'd probably look for you too. *Fuck me!*"

"And just who are you, dear?"

"Oh, hi. Sorry. Bels." I extended my hand to her over the threshold which she hesitantly accepted.

"Bels," she elongated my name as she spoke it like I'd given her one with no vowels and too many digraphs.

The finger guns I shot at her came out of nowhere and I cringed internally, "That's my name, don't wear it out."

She pursed her lips and dropped my hand, "Charmed to meet you, Bels."

"Ditto. So, dude, you're really here? When I ran into Yusuf yesterday I thought he was alone."

"I'm sorry, did you say you saw Yusuf?" She asked, stiffening and tilting her head like she'd suddenly become hard of hearing.

"Yep." I said popping the p, "Looks like the band is getting back together."

Monique took a sharp intake of breath, and then scoffed before saying my name, "Bels, it is very important that I find Thomas as quickly as possible, but I do not have any contact information for him. Do you know how I can reach him?"

"Oh yeah, I've got his cell," I said patting down my body, "shit, my phone is in the kitchen, come on in and I'll get it for you."

"Thank you."

We walked down my foyer together, and I noted that she seemed to stick her nose up like she was scenting the house to make sure he wasn't there. She was pretty absorbed in the smell of my stairs before she screeched at Tim, who'd jumped out from behind a corner and slashed at her with his claws.

"Timmy! Sorry, he's not usually cranky unless he's hungry, though, truthfully, same. Hanger is danger, am I right?"

Monique hummed and lightly shoved Tim away from her leg and

continued to click-clack her stabby heels after me to the kitchen where I pulled a scrap of paper and a pen out of my junk drawer. The whole room smelled amazing from the cleansing pot, and I figured that if she left while it was still on that it would kick her back out too.

I looked up at her to see her sniffing and lowering her brows before rubbing at her nose and sniffing again. I considered that the simmer pot might be making her itchy or trying to kick her out, but it could also be the scent wasn't fully masking the fact that her partner of 200 years ripped an orgasm from me the night before only three feet from where she stood.

"How long have you known Thomas?" she asked me, leaning to tap an immaculate nude-colored manicure against the countertop.

"Like a week," I shrugged.

"And yet you know about me?"

"I thought we established that Mo-mo."

One side of her lip lifted in a sneer, "Mo-mo?"

"Sorry, I'm like... it's been a hell of a week, wine is good, and I have no more fucks to give today. You'll have to indulge me."

"Indeed." She took the paper from me, folding it and sliding it into the pocket of her pants, "Thank you for this. I was hoping to speak to him before Yusuf does, do you know if they've connected already?"

"Uh, I don't know, I haven't seen him today."

"Are you sure about that?"

I scrunched my face, "Yeah, I'd be pretty fucking sure if my Significant Other was here." I snorted at the double meaning, "oh my god, a Significant OTHER."

Pursing her lips, she said coldly, "I shall leave you to your evening, Bels. Thank you for your hospitality."

Flapping a hand at her I scoffed, "no problem. When you talk to him tell him to take that stick out of his ass and apologize, will ya?" I herded her toward the door, waiting until she crossed the threshold before saying, "Wait - I uninvite you, or whatever. You are not welcome here!" I spoke with a giggle, mimicking the motion of a cross in front of me.

"It was...a delight to meet you."

"You too, Mo-Mo. Have an awesome night."

I closed the door in her face and sighed. Mo-Mo was H-O-T hot. How great that they could all reunite right after our fight. That was fucking spectacular timing on their part. Gone for a year, then one argument between us, and *poof*! They magically reappeared.

"Well, excuse-moi for not knowing the conjugation of your silly 'poof' word."

His voice echoed in my mind and I smiled into my hand. Did I want them to work it out? They'd been together 200 years and he and I made it a whole six days before we argued, and logically I knew it was probably smarter to let him go back to them and move on. But hormonally, it had been 25 hours since I'd seen him and I missed him already. If they reunited, they could go back to whatever the hell it was that they did, he would get out of here and I could pretend like none of it had happened with my shares intact.

I went back to the kitchen for my phone and tapped the screen, noting that he still hadn't texted me, and clicked my tongue. He'd said I should text him if I ran into Yusuf again, but he hadn't said anything about Monique. He'd probably enjoy the surprise of her call.

Or it would shock him to death. "Cease his existence" as he'd say.

Regardless, if he wasn't going to bother to text me, I didn't need to text him. Closing up the house for the night, I poured some more water into the cleansing pot and reached into the drawer beneath the slow cooker to grab a head of garlic. It could stay next to my bed just in case - there had been too many vampires around for my liking. I was a simple girl - my preferred number was zero.

24
THOMAS

"I'm sorry, I didn't know what else to do," Yusuf's shoulders slumped in defeat, not having expected my hesitancy.

"You didn't know what to do?" I snapped, "How about talk to me? How about tell me what the fuck was going on instead of just disappearing without a word after everything we'd been through? You disappeared. I woke up and thought something horrible had happened to you two. It terrified me." I hit my chest as if I could rip my heart out and show him the pieces he'd left broken behind.

He came and sat in the sand next to me, giving me a few feet of distance. "Thomas, please."

"Please, what? Try to be understanding after two hundred fucking years, Yus? Are you fucking kidding me?"

He sighed and raked his hands through the sand, "I understand why you're angry. But, she left and I didn't know what to do."

I turned to look at him, "What are you talking about? I woke up that morning and you were both gone. Both of you. You left together."

Yusuf shook his head, "No, we didn't Thomas. I'd overheard her telling one of her friends that she was bored. Tired. It sounded like she'd had something planned for a while, but because we'd been together for so long I didn't think she'd actually leave. Call me naive. I figured it was one of her moods; you know how she got."

I nodded, Monique was prone to outbursts. If she wasn't Queen of the Castle she would feel slighted and act out. I always thought it was because she'd been turned so young, our guess was she was probably 21 or 22 when she was changed, but her need for external validation was a constant point of contention in our relationship. If for any reason she felt like Yus or I had done wrong by her, she'd go off and feed off the lust of mortals seeking their desire and praise in their beds.

"I knew how she was. But that didn't suddenly change overnight. We both knew that she had issues with that."

"Yes, that's why when she walked out that night I thought she was just doing what she always did when she was angry. I figured she'd go down to the club, dance, and feast for a few hours, stumble home drunk on lust and we would talk it out in the morning, but when I went down to the club to join her, she wasn't there. The bouncer said she'd not been there all night. I panicked and immediately began searching for her."

Scoffing, I bit my lip, "And it didn't occur to you to walk the five blocks home to tell me that our wife was missing? You didn't think that was something I needed to know? I didn't deserve to know where my two bonded partners were? I had no idea, Yus. No idea. Where the fuck have you been?"

He dug his hands into his coarse black hair, "I was ashamed, okay? I panicked and I ran after her and it was like I went into a blind rage. I couldn't focus on anything but finding her and then when I realized that I'd never told you what happened I was embarrassed to contact you. Then I came home to tell you face to face, and you'd already left and the house was empty, so I put it up for sale. I figured you'd gone too and we'd all need the money to do whatever we were doing."

"I was gone looking for you, Yusuf. I was trying to figure out where you were. I knew Monique had a temper, I knew she was likely to storm off and come crawling back, but you? You'd never left me like that before. I never questioned us. I thought of us all that you and I were the strongest, and Monique was the goddess you and I worked together to please. I didn't -" I sighed.

Yus reached for my hand and I hesitantly let him take it, and we stared blankly out into the black water, "I'm sorry I caused you pain."

"You did more than causing me pain, Yus. You derailed my entire life. I loved you. You were my spouse, my partner. Do you know how long I spent running around France looking for the two of you trying to make sure you were safe? I went to the fucking Coalition for god's sake. I did everything I could to figure out where you went, and when they said you were up to date on your dues and wouldn't tell me where the two of you were, I assumed that it was done and you didn't want to be found. If you were taking the time to pay dues, you could have just as easily called me."

"I'm sorry."

Looking at our clasped hands, his dark skin against my pale, brought back memories of electricity and passion, but now it just harbored heartbreak. "I can't do this again. I can't. You know that, right?"

"What do you mean?" He asked softly.

"We can't go back to the way we were. And I'm sure by now you realize that I underwent a bond-breaking ceremony with the Coalition."

He slowly let go of my hand, digging his into the sand, and began fidgeting, "I felt it when you did. I didn't know at the time which of you did it, but I knew the bond was broken. Then I realized I could still feel her and I knew that it was the bond with you that was gone."

"What else was I supposed to do?"

"Love, Monique is sick."

My head spun to face him head-on, "*Quoi?*"

"Last I found her she was in Istanbul. I'd almost caught up to her when I found someone she'd fed from. They...they were dead in the street. They were killed transitioning into an Undead, Thomas."

"What the fuck are you talking about? She's with an UnDead?"

"I," He paused, "I think she is becoming one, my love. I think she lost balance when the bond was severed and she was hurt without us and... I don't know if it's too late or not to save her."

"Have you told the Coalition? Are they ready to help her?"

He shook his head, "No, I've told no one. I didn't want to risk losing her if I was wrong. What if she fed and an UnDead just happened to follow her and finished the job?"

"That'd be a pretty huge coincidence, Yus."

"I know."

"So you haven't seen her?"

"I haven't spoken to her since the night she left. I've caught up to her twice, once in London and once in Capri, but I didn't approach her. Capri was after the bond was broken and she was visibly different than she was in London. If she'd chosen to leave I wanted to see why; I wanted to see what she thought she'd find that was better than what we had."

"Yus, you could have stayed with me. We could have gone together. You chose to abandon me just as much as she did."

"I know."

"You sold my home."

"I know."

"You never bothered to so much as call me."

"I know. I know, Thomas. What do you want me to say? I was trying to fix this and I couldn't get her back, so how could I come crawling back alone? Then you just went and severed the bond, and I couldn't feel you, and I felt like I was going mad myself! All I had left after that bond was broken was my mission to find her. The bond with her only intensified."

"I severed the fucking bond because it was better to be alone than it was for me to think that the two of you were off living happily ever after. Or fuck - dead! I couldn't have that nagging instinct raging inside of me to find you anymore. Not when you'd proven you didn't want to be found." My voice rose, shaking, remembering all the nights I woke up as my dreams played all the ways something could have happened to them. I clenched and unclenched my fists, struggling to take a deep breath, "Why are you here? What do you want?"

"We need to find her, Thomas. If she's turning, I - we - have to try, and I need your help. The two of us are better together than apart - this last year only solidified that for me."

"Yeah well, the last year solidified to me that you guys never cared about me. You abandoned me and didn't care about our bond at all and were easily able to walk away from 200 years of our lives and disappear into the abyss." The words came out smaller than I wanted. They weren't spoken with the force or anger that I wanted them to. I wanted to scream at Yusuf, I wanted to shake him and make him realize the hell that I'd been through while they'd been gone, "I'm not going with you. Not now."

He rested his elbows on his bent knees, "is this because of that woman?" I glared at him. "She stunk of you, darling. I smelled you from a great distance and thought I would find you, only to stumble into that mortal."

"She stays out of this," I growled, "you do not talk to her, you do not approach her, you do not put a single finger on her or touch an ounce of her energy, do you understand me? You leave her alone."

Yusuf raised his hands in surrender, "I didn't know when I went there that the scent wasn't you, my love."

"Well, now you do. If she tells me that she sees you again our next conversation will not be a kind one. Oui?" Yus sighed. "Yusuf, look at me. Leave her alone."

"If I found her, what makes you think Monique won't?"

"Because Monique is traipsing about Europe apparently, as you were."

"No, Thomas. I don't think she is. Why do you think I'm here?"

My fangs elongated and the taste of copper filled my mouth when they punctured my bottom lip, "Why are you here, Yusuf? Is it, yet again, because I'm not enough, but you need me to be the fixer? That was what our life was, right? You were the peacekeeper, she was the passion and I was the fixer. The three of us worked together seamlessly. So I'm assuming without her passion in the equation that you're here to tell me that you wouldn't have come back just to be with me? You wouldn't have worked to find me unless somehow you thought Monique had come back? *Merde!* And I thought I knew you." Tension radiated from him - I'd hit the nail on the head. I released an unstable breath, "Just say it, Yus. There's nothing left to salvage anyway."

I felt the facade melt from him, exposing the hopeless male in front of me, he morphed before my eyes from a regretful lover to someone who only needed my help, "There's nothing left to save? That's quite the statement."

"It is the truth, the bond is broken, we owe each other nothing. Now tell me why you're here so you can leave." My mind wandered to my Annabel, and I became desperate to hold her, to have her calm me. To hold me in her arms and let me feel her affection and validate my worth despite the horrible words she'd spoken to me. I needed *her* to fix *me*.

"She and I are still bonded. You may have severed both ties, but you only severed one for the two of us. I can still feel her and everything I have found has indicated that she's coming this way if she isn't already here and that she is sick. I think she is realizing she's unwell and is coming to you to fix it - because, yes, you always fixed everything for her. She needs you. We need to let her come to you to ensure she is healthy and well."

"And if she's not? What if she comes to me and she's too far gone?"

He sniffed and shifted his feet nervously in the sand, "I don't want to think about that."

"Well, it's something that needs to be thought about. If you're asking me to murder our wife then you damn well better have come here to do it yourself. Especially as you are the one here that is a bonded partner to her still."

"You know I can't do that. If for no other reason than I am the one bonded to her. It would destroy me to hurt her." It was true that Yus was the peacekeeper in the relationship. He was the one who did whatever he could to smooth the waters and whatever he could to help keep us going. He would always help. He was the balm between Monique's fire and my ice.

I barked out a razor sharp laugh, "You really went through all the trouble of finding me after a year to sit next to me, pretending that you still loved me-"

"I didn't - "

"Let me finish," I glared at him, "You came here, ready to act like we were going to reconcile enough that when Monique showed up that...what, that we'd go back to being a happy family? Or that she'd show up and be unsavable and you wanted me to take care of it? And what if I killed her? What if I somehow managed to get her to the Coalition to save her, or if I had to kill her, were you planning on staying? Were you going to be with me regardless of if she ever showed up? How long were you going to wait before abandoning me again? How exactly did you see this playing out? Were we just going to play house until you got bored and left again?"

"Thomas that isn't fair. We both know that she was very clear that if she was ever to fall to the Undead that she wanted to be executed. She didn't want to become one of them."

"And you came here to make me deal with it."

"I came here to tell you what was happening, Thomas. I came here because you deserved to know."

"Well, thank you," I spat. "You've told me. I'm done being around you right now. I need time to process this."

Yus sat quietly for a while, looking out at the water, before sighing and patting his knees and standing, "Okay, Thomas. I have a room here in town for the week. Can we meet in a few days and try to have this conversation again?"

I looked up at him, "so you can see if I'll do what you want next time?"

"So we can save our wife, Thomas."

"She isn't my wife anymore, and you're not my husband anymore, Yus. I owe you nothing."

He huffed a shocked laugh at my bluntness, "Okay then. I'll check in before I leave town again. Here's my number. Take a few days to simmer down, Thomas. We do not have to be enemies. Don't throw 200 years away because your feelings got hurt." He handed me a piece of paper with his number and where he was staying on it.

"Goodnight, Yus."

"*Bonsoir, mon amour.*"

25
ANNABEL

The weekend came and went. He didn't call or text. My heart fluctuated between red-hot anger and sadness, surprisingly, both over the idea that the three of them must have worked it out and left. No idiot would throw out 200 years of love with someone for some woman they'd fucked a couple of times. Especially not after the other night when he just...left. He'd just left.

It was Monday afternoon before I'd finally gotten a text from him and my heart plummeted at its simplicity.

TOMMY: I NEED YOU.

Rationally, I knew he must have been starving if he'd been true to his word and not hunting, but if he thought he was going to come by, suck my anxiety, and then walk away without apologizing, he had another thing coming.

So what if he "needed" me? I'd needed him that weekend, and he'd never bothered to apologize. He'd never even bothered to text me! The launch was scheduled for Tuesday at 9 am and he had the balls to text me at 2 in the afternoon on Monday? No fucking way, man. The buffet was closed. The whole agreement was supposed to ensure that I had a stress-free and successful launch and he'd flaked on me. Not only had he flaked, but he'd hurt me. He'd broken our agreement, not me.

At first, I ignored the message, unsure of my feelings, because the feminist daughter of lesbians wanted him to crawl on his knees and beg me for forgiveness and for him to fall over himself for being such an asshole, but I was also a horrible gossip. Not knowing if he'd seen Monique or Yusuf was driving me insane. Did he need to break up with me? Was there anything to break up? Was he leaving? Were the three of them going to ride off into the sunset and go terrorize another town? If he was back with them he was going to need to get the fuck out of Quaker's Wharf. I was not going to share this town with him and his lovers. Nuh-uh, no way. And there was no way I was paying for their grand exit either.

I had intended to ignore him just enough to startle him, but as the weekend passed and he hadn't reached out, my anger turned to fear. Then the fear solidified in my stomach as anxiety, then my anxiety turned into to-do lists, and the to-do lists turned into work.

I knew I had cleansed the house but I wasn't sure I'd have the resolve able to sit inside and listen to him bang on the door when he discovered he was unable to come in. I didn't want to cave, so I went to work and busted my ass. I filmed, and folded, and tagged, and filmed more, and worked until my eyes were going to fall out of my head. When Shannon appeared for work Monday morning we put our heads down and raced toward the finish line with blinders on. It was five when Shannon sighed and turned off her computer.

"I don't know what else we can possibly do, Bels. It's going to be great."

"Mmmhmm," I answered, my leg bouncing enough that my knee was audibly hitting the bottom of my desk, "of course, it will be great. You've done amazing work, thank you, Shannon."

"Yeah..." she said skeptically, "But you also have worked ten times harder than anyone else I know. You are a rockstar. So it's time to turn it off, Bels. Let's grab my girls and go get some dinner to celebrate. Chicken nuggets and hot fudge sundaes for everyone! Or hell, take the rest of the night off, go fuck Thomas until you can't see straight and I will be right back here tomorrow morning at 8:00 to panic alongside you.

I chuckled, knowing she didn't know about the fight, "I'm fine. You go ahead and go get the girls. You've gone above and beyond this past week. It's been so nice to have help doing all of this. Go enjoy the rest of your night."

"Annabel, I'm serious, you need to go home. There is nothing left to do. Turn off the computer."

"There's always something else to do." I could fold boxes, film more content, or take more flat lays, or -

"Go. Home. Go feed Tim. Go get drunk for all I care, but you're leaving when I do, and I've gotta go right now. Come on."

"I can't just -"

"Do I need to call your mothers? You need to leave now. End of conversation."

"Why would you need to call my mothers when you're already acting like one?"

"Oh god. You're in a great mood. Get the fuck up, we're leaving." She stood and came to my chair, spinning it out from under my desk, "I will wheel your fat ass out of here if I have to. It's done. It's ready. We're going home."

"My fat ass could kick your fat ass any day of the week," I muttered, extending my hand to grab my purse that Shan extended out to me. "Fine. But I'm not waiting until eight to come in tomorrow. What if the internet crashes or the computer breaks or -"

"ANNABEL," she groaned, "Everything is going to be perfect. Calm down!" She scratched at the back of her neck before rolling out her shoulders, "You haven't even eaten today. I'm worried about you."

I laughed half-heartedly, tapping my fingers against my lips as I stood and evaluated the office, making sure I wasn't missing something obvious, "You don't need to worry, you have just never seen a launch day before. You have no idea what kind of chaos will be unleashed tomorrow."

I begrudgingly left the office with her when my stomach let out an audible rumble and the smug satisfaction on Shannon's face made me want to punch her. I probably was hangry, but I refused to give my stomach something to vomit up at midnight when my nerves got the better of me.

TOMMY: Bels, I need to see you immediately. Where are you?

I was not getting dumped the night before a launch. He could eat tomorrow when the ball was already rolling and I'd be too busy to process how I felt about him breaking up with me. That seemed like a reasonable plan. I wandered toward downtown, walking aimlessly until I ended up at the beach. It was a lovely evening. With September had come a cold snap, giving Quaker's Wharf a break from the abnormal heat and ambient hum of window air conditioning units. The trees along the beach had begun to change, and the small swells of the bay reflected the distorted seasonal colors. The water called to me, far more than dinner, opening myself up to get dumped, or thinking about the launch. I wanted to stick my toes in the sand, read some smut on my phone, and listen to the water. I'd lived so long relying on myself, that reverting to that version of myself for the night seemed like the safest option for my heart and mind.

I burrowed myself into the sand under a tree out of sight from the parking lot with my blanket from my Jeep and landed on reading a new Gargoyle romance, turning my phone to airplane mode and sunk myself into the Los Angelos cityscape where Gargoyles slept so high in the air that no one knew they were there. I read for hours leaning against that tree, dissociating and hiding from the stress that lurked all around me. It wasn't until the female main character began explaining the amazing ability to turn specific appendages to stone during play-time that I realized that the sun had mostly set. Darkness was encroaching on the beach, and the noise of passersby had quieted to nothing.

I tensed, the hairs on my arms standing on end, and felt the prey-like urge to hide. I knew it was the unease that I'd learned came from being in the presence of an Other and sighed. "Seriously? What are you doing here? If I don't answer your text it's a pretty good indicator that I'm not ready to talk to you. I'll talk to you tomorrow," I snapped before even turning around, but the laugh that greeted me was not from who I was expecting.

"Bels. Just who I wanted to see."

26
THOMAS

Contrary to his word, Yusuf had appeared at the Halloween Shop every day since reconnecting; he did not give me any time to process what had happened. He would stand around awkwardly, hungrily grazing on people's exposed arms or staring slightly too long at someone until I'd snap and go to him and listen, once again, to his plea that I close up early and hunt for Monique with him.

I was drained, emotionally from the mental weight of him putting this burden onto me, and physically I was starving. I hadn't fed from Annabel in days - I hadn't even seen her since that night and the beast inside of me was ready to claw out of my skin to go to her. I needed to harvest and I needed *her*. I hadn't intended on our argument lasting this long, I'd planned on going back to her house the next morning and making her breakfast and trying to communicate my needs and feelings, but Yusuf seemed determined to monopolize all of my time.

Sunday evening I'd finally snapped at him, demanding that he leave me alone, and he agreed to leave if I gave him one last night of help. He claimed that Monique was still in the area, but I was skeptical.

I'd smelled an Other in several places around town, but it didn't smell like *her*.

All I wanted was to be with my Annabel. I wanted to hold her, and kiss her and talk to her. I wanted to plunge my cock so far into her that she apologized for ever staying away from me for this long, for thinking I was only good for sex. I wanted to dance in her energy. I knew she must have been anxious and I wanted to help, but day after day, night after night, my phone stayed empty. She never reached out to apologize for the hurtful things she'd said, and she'd never asked me to come over to feed. It felt like she was carving out pieces of my heart with a rusted spoon. I needed her - she was mine. Instead, I was running all over Massachusetts looking for a woman I had no interest in speaking with.

That last night had, as expected, yielded no results. We were no closer to finding Monique than I'd ever been before, and between my hunger and Yusuf's obviously irritated bond, we were about to snap each others necks or have very angry sex. Once I'd felt his obvious lust permeating through the anger, I made him leave, refusing to add that log to mine and Annabel's dumpster fire.

That was why early Monday morning, before the sun even rose, when I awoke to the very distinct feeling that someone was in my shop that I jumped off the air mattress ready to kill the bastard. He'd promised the night before was the last night. Yus' scent was soft, but it was accompanied by another foreign perfume, the one I recognized as the one that had been floating around town.

"Thomas?" Yusuf shouted carefully.

"Just because it's a shop doesn't mean that you don't need an invitation when the doors are locked you asshole," I grumbled while pulling some sweatpants on.

"Just come out here, Thomas."

I walked shirtless out to the front of the shop, yawning and scratching my chest, considering how difficult it would be to disconnect his head from his body so I could get back to sleep and then back to Annabel.

"Thomas!" I stumbled when a hard body launched itself at me and instinctively wrapped my hands around it to steady us both. I felt the softness of the white blonde hair. The slimness of their waist and the strength of their legs. "My love, I've been looking for you!"

I pulled back, eyes wide, to view the creature that looked correct but smelled all wrong, this one smelled of licorice, whereas the woman I'd known smelled of lavender and honey. When I inhaled her hair deeply, the faintest notes of lavender remained - but the sweetness, the honey, was gone.

"Monique," I fumbled for words, taking inventory of her. Her eyes were pools of black and her hair was dirty, her clothes fit her body perfectly and were pristine like she'd just bought them, but her good looks couldn't hide the fact that this woman was a predator. She had made no illusion of softness as she'd done in the past. This creature was like a razor blade. "What are you doing here?"

Yusuf stood awkwardly by the door, as if he was afraid she'd run and I tilted my head at him when his eyes widened to communicate his concern to me. I'd seen the look many times in our lives.

"I have been looking for you! I went home and you weren't there - someone else was in the house and then I had to find you. I had to know you were okay." She laid her cold hands on my cheeks and I cringed away from her touch. Too firm. She was too hard. She was like stone. "Now that we are all back together, we can go home. I took care of the people in the house - they will not bother us."

My eyes flashed to Yusuf who was looking progressively more anxious, "Monique, are you saying you killed the people Yusuf sold the house to?"

She laughed, slightly too high for her typical laugh, more shrill, and desperate, "Yus would not sell our home. They were breaking and entering. I had every right to protect our property."

"No darling, when you left and we couldn't find you I sold the row house. That home belonged to them," Yusuf paced his words slowly and spoke quietly as if she were a caged lion.

"Why would you do that? I was coming right back. Why would you get rid of our home? Our memories?" She tensed, eyes dialating and skin paling further, before she pulled herself back from the darkness, "No matter. They're gone now, so we can go home."

"Monique," I spoke softly as she ran her hands lovingly through my hair. I dropped her waist and took a step back, "Monique, ma chérie, I'm not going anywhere with you. If you want to return with Yusuf, by all means, please do, but my life is here."

She spat out the shrill laughter again, "oh yes, you are doing so well in your Halloween store, Thomas. Stop this, let us go and start over. The three of us together are perfect, we can fix anything. It is supposed to be the three of us."

Gently, I cupped her cheek and lifted her upper lip with my thumb. My heart dropped at the elongated fangs. "Mo, put your fangs away."

"Why? What does it matter?" She tightly wrapped her hands behind my neck, pulling me into her, and went to kiss my neck, which I quickly ducked away from.

"Monique, I need to see you put your teeth away, darling."

"We aren't going to hurt you, love, just do as Thomas asks," Yusuf added from his guard station.

"No, this is ridiculous. I do not go around demanding to look at your teeth. Now pack your things, we have much to catch up on. I can hardly wait to hear of your adventures while we have been apart."

I took another step away from her, "How long, Mo?"

She froze, her eyes widening, "How long, what, ma chérie?"

I sighed and dug my hands in the pockets of my sweatpants, "how long have you felt sick?"

Her tight, shrill giggle bounced and echoed through the large store, "I am not sick, Thomas. I was just ready for us to get back to life as normal so, here I am. I have you, and Yusuf, and the house, and we will go home and before you know it, it will be like none of this ever happened." She flipped from anxious to lustful as she stepped toward me again, "I can not wait to show you exactly how much I missed you, my love."

Cringing, I put my hand out, gesturing her to stop, "Mo, no. The bond is broken. There is nothing left between us. But, if you tell me how long you've been sick I can try to get you some help. Maybe I can fix this." The last thing I wanted to do was to leave Annabel and take Monique to France to the Coalition to be treated, but after fixing her life for so many years it was difficult to turn off the urge when she was standing before me in obvious distress. "Do you want me to fix this, Mo?"

She grabbed my hand and turned to Yusuf, "He broke the bond? It was him? Did you know this? Are you two still bonded? Is it only me?"

"No, darling, he severed the bond with us both." Yusuf continued using his gentle tone and terms of endearment trying to contain whatever she was within the store, if she'd turned, it would be exceptionally difficult to catch her, especially with me having not eaten in days. "Don't worry, pet. You and I are still bonded. I am still here. I'm right here."

"Monique." I said, more authoritatively, "how long have you been sick? I can not help you if I don't know what's going on."

"Why would you break our bond?" Her eyes were almost entirely black, and though they glistened with tears, her voice became gravelly, like she was growling, "Why would you do this to us?"

"You left first. I am not going to rewrite history to make you feel better."

"Thomas!" Yusuf scolded me, "Now is not the time!"

"That woman. The mortal," She ground out. "I knew it, I knew you were having an affair. I smelled you all over that house. Your scent was practically a second skin on her. How long? How long has that woman been interloping?"

I couldn't hide the laugh, "Annabel isn't the interloper in my life here, you are! Now tell me what I need to know so I can fucking fix it and the two of you can leave me in peace!"

"Yus," Her voice cracked, flicking back into an uncontrollable sadness as she ran to him, pressing herself into his chest. When he cradled her adoringly I shook my head. If she bit him while she was transitioning between stages, she could kill him, just like that mortal that he'd found in the road. "Yus, why is he talking like this?"

"Your mind is fractured, Monique, you're not thinking clearly. We need to get you to Paris. Yus, you need to take her. If she isn't too far gone, she is dangerously close." I spoke frankly. Her ricocheting emotions were all the proof I needed that she needed to get to Paris as quickly as possible.

"Do not talk about me as if I am not here!" She shrieked, "You do not get to ruin our lives to screw some filthy mortal, Thomas! I will not let you!" She turned back to Yusuf and began speaking faster and faster until she was slipping between four languages and no longer forming coherent sentences.

"That's rich coming from you, Monique - if I remember correctly, you were the one who held the most affection for mortals. Yus, you know I'm right." I said, looking at him, acknowledging the heartbreak in his eyes.

"My love, will you go with me to the Doctor? We can make the burning stop. Is it burning yet?"

"The burning! Oh stars, the burning." She sobbed, "No! No, we can not go to Paris, not while that mortal wants to ruin our family. We have to stay together."

"You will not touch Annabel, Monique. I forbid it," I snapped. Part of me seemed to leave my body and look on as an observer. There, twenty feet from me, were the two people I had loved more than anything in my life, so much that I spent a year desperate to find them. Now, seeing them together without the bond for the first time, I felt nothing but a fondness for what we'd had in the past. There was nothing inside of me that wanted to return to that life.

Her teeth flashed at me at lightning speed, and almost instantly, I found myself on my back being crushed into the linoleum floor with her crouched above my body.

"Annabel," she growled, "Bels."

I paled, hearing her call her Bels; I knew I'd only called her Annabel. "How did you-" I struggled to get her off me in my weakened state, "You will not touch Annabel. Do you understand me? You touch her and you are dead."

"No, Thomas. She is. I will fix this, my love. I will fix us this time," She snarled, jumping off and using my torso as leverage. The weight of her left my body, and as I clutched my aching stomach, feeling like a boulder had just been launched into me via trebuchet, I heard a crash and a groan. I knew before I'd looked up that she was gone. She was going to go find Bels.

27
ANNABEL

"Fuck, Monique you scared me. How are you?" I clasped my chest, willing my heart to slow, "Sorry to be so jumpy, it's been a day."

"I am fine, Bels. You were a hard woman to find today."

Sighing, I tucked my phone back in my pocket and stood, sweeping the sand off my bottom, "I know, I was working and then I needed some space - did you ever find Thomas?"

A sneer pulled across her face, "Oh yes, I found him."

She felt cold, colder even than she'd felt on Friday, "Oh good, I'm glad you guys reconnected. Did you get what you needed?"

In the darkness, I could see that she was less put together than she'd been before, as if she hadn't showered. Though her clothes were spotless, her hair was noticeably greasy and her skin was dirty. "You okay, babe? You seem on edge."

She moved closer to me, unnervingly slow as if she was deliberately slowing herself down, and lifted her lip, revealing an elongated fang, which she pressed her tongue against until it bled, the minute amount combining with her saliva to stain her mouth red. "I find myself unhappy with you, Bels. Which is a shame, as I thought after our conversation on Friday that you were an honest woman."

I took a step away, my blood heating and those instincts to hide resurfacing at the sight of her teeth, "Well, I was drunk, if I recall correctly. Also, you were in my house for about five minutes. It isn't like we painted each other's nails and swapped love stories. Listen, I'm really sorry but I lost track of time and I have to get going - if you want to meet up tomorrow you can have Thomas text me." I tried to take a wide berth around her, hearing the voice in my head shouting at me to get out of there.

She followed my steps, "Ah yes, love stories. Let us discuss those, shall we? Because in those five minutes in your home, I scented my husband all over you. I feel as though that is a conversation we need to have."

I flinched in surprise, "Wait, what the fuck, your husband? No, you left, he's not your husband. And if he was why didn't you say anything on Friday? You said he was a dear friend of yours."

"He is mine," she snarled, "he and Yusuf are mine. They belong to me- not some pathetic mortal girl."

I scrunched my face, assessing the unhinged creature before me. This was not the same female I'd seen only days before. Her impossibly straight posture was hunched into a pouncing stance, and she looked gaunt. She looked...sick. "Okay, cool, so take him. Legit girl, I had no idea you were still legally married, if I'd known I would never have-"

"You are a disgusting cow and you will never deserve him!" Her voice became shrill, with an underlying rumble that made my skin break out in goosebumps.

"Whoa, dude, no need to be mean, I just said you can have him. This is clearly a conversation the two of you need to have together. I was just an uninformed third party - I knew nothing about this." *Run, run, run. Get somewhere and call Thomas.* Every part of my body tensed as my anxiety and adrenaline rose. This woman was fucking crazy and if Thomas didn't know it yet he was going to hear it from me. He'd told me he went to their like...tribunal or whatever about her and that they were done. He'd never once called her his ex-wife though. Had I been some kind of home-wrecking mortal hussy? "I...I really didn't know, Monique. If I overstepped I apologize. I'll get out of your hair and head home. Have a good night."

The beach had become shrouded in darkness. The trees hadn't shed many leaves yet so the streetlights were blocked from view, leaving us covered in shadows. I couldn't hear anything past the beating of my heart in my ears. If Thomas sicced his ex-wife on me I was going to re-kill him myself.

In a flash, the outlined figure of Monique was by my side, "You can not have him."

"Dude, I said I don't want him! What the fuck is your problem?" *Get to the Jeep.* I kept moving, glancing sideways to the parking lot, and took off running without warning. Or I would have been running if she hadn't caught me within ten feet of where we'd been standing.

She grabbed my arm roughly, her nails digging in enough to puncture my skin. I felt her ram into my mind, sucking my energy like a vacuum. She didn't feed like Thomas - she felt like she was assaulting my senses, crippling me with my own emotions, not slowly dragging a fishing line through my mind or caressing against my walls.

"Fucking hell, um, ouch, Monique, let me go!"

She growled, a low snarling noise, and dragged her nails down from where they'd implanted into my arm, leaving long streaks of blood welling up on my forearm. Then she grabbed my wrist and forced it to her face, locking her dark eyes with mine, and ran her tongue along the blood, humming appreciatively. The bitch had taken my blood, Thomas had never - would never.

"You can't just do this, Monique. Thomas is going to-" I tried to take my arm back, screaming when she snapped the bone at my elbow with one swipe of her arm. Blinding pain ripped through my body, feeling as though each atom that made up my body was splitting and trying to form back into something that wasn't me.

"Thomas is never going to find you again, you insolent creature.

And if somehow, he does, you will be such a shred of who you are now that he will regret ever even speaking to you."

My blood pounded and my throat closed, anxiety taking over as my fight or flight instincts imploded. I knew I wasn't going to escape and my body froze at it as if roots grew out of the bottom of my feet. My limbs shook as I stood rooted to the spot, my mind screaming at my body to wake up and run, and my breaths stuttered. My stomach churned from the pain and for a brief moment, I considered throwing up all over her perfect clothes in hopes that with her vanity, she'd let me go in disgust.

"Please don't do this. Please," my voice wobbled in desperation as her other hand shot behind my neck, fisting my hair and continuing to lick the wound she'd inflicted at an unnatural angle. "Thomas will never forgive you if something happens to me, if you're doing this for him you're doing this wrong. Please stop. Please. I'll do anything, just stop." Tears soaked my cheeks and I was cursing myself for hiding in the small copse of elm trees, "I'll never talk to him again. I promise. I promise. Please."

"No." Her tone was flat. Dead. And in the darkness, I could see the discoloration on her chin where my blood was dribbling out of her mouth.

"No? What - you can't just say no. Please - Thomas will kill you."

"I said no, mortal. Your begging means nothing to me. You are nothing to us, and you never will be anything to him again," She snarled again, slamming her fangs into the crook of my now limp elbow, sucking deep and injecting fire into my blood.

28

THOMAS

"That went well," Yusuf groaned, pulling himself up off the floor and looking at the broken door behind him, "she's strong."

"Too strong," I replied, staring at the ceiling waiting for the stars to clear, "I haven't eaten in days, Yus, I am going to be of no help to you."

He scoffed and walked to me, extending his hand to help lift me, "Yes, but she is going after your new mate so if anything, I'm helping you."

"If she lays one finger on Bels, I will kill her, and I will not apologize."

"If you hurt Monique while there's still a chance of saving her, I will kill you - so make your moves cautiously, my friend."

"The sun is coming up, if she's changed she will be underground for hours until she feels safe enough to find Annabel. We won't find her until closer to dusk; we need a plan." I stretched and twisted, cracking my back, and nodded at Yusuf to follow me back to my bedroom. I needed blood. He trailed behind me wordlessly and I opened the minifridge to remove a medical bag, waving one at him, "you need one?"

Nodding with a sigh, his shoulders slumped, "Yes, that would be great."

I opened two bags, dumping them into disposable foam cups, and handed him one, "Yus, I don't want to hurt her, you have to know that but-"

"But with the bond broken, you don't feel compelled to save her."

"I feel an overwhelming need to protect Bels, and that outweighs any remaining feelings for Monique. It isn't like I purposely want to hurt you, even though you both purposely hurt me."

He scoffed, "Cut the bullshit, Thomas, if you have bonded with Bels you don't need to defend it."

"We haven't done a ceremony or anything. She isn't claimed yet. She wanted to wait."

He assessed me slowly, moving to sit on my bed, "You know that I'm older than you."

"*Oui.*"

"And you know that we bonded quickly."

"Oh really? I wasn't aware." the sarcasm bled out of me. Our bond had begun to form when we fled France, but we quickly performed the Handfeasting ceremony when we arrived in Boston. The bond allowed us to track and feel each other, making us safer in an unknown place. We had cared for one another, but it was also a logical decision.

He scratched at his cut jawline and blew out an uncertain breath, "Thomas, did you know that sometimes bonds form without handfeasting?"

I shrugged, "*Non*, you and Monique made it sound like that was the only way to achieve the link we needed. Every bonded couple I've met has completed the ceremony." We'd been so interconnected when we fled, the traumatic experience and danger causing us to depend on and trust each other sooner than a normal courting.

"It was," he nodded, "I knew the bond was going to form eventually anyway, but doing a handfeasting early solidifies the bond regardless of magics or feelings. One could handfeast with a rat, for fuck's sake if they were only seeking the connection the magic allows."

Running a hand through his coarse black hair he considered his words carefully, "A handfeasting solidifies a bond, but mates or strong emotional connections can create the bond without the ceremony. Of course, if you'd felt that strongly for someone you'd want to handfeast, but you can achieve almost the same result without exchanging blood. The blood exchange mostly solidifies the magical connection, allowing you to feel the other's wellbeing, and allows the magic to drive you together and share in it."

I drank some of my blood, instantly feeling more alert, "why are you telling me this?"

Yusuf looked unwaveringly into my eyes, "Are you bonded with Annabel, Thomas?"

"I just told you that she wanted to wait."

"And I'm telling you that that doesn't matter if the connection is strong enough. Have you felt unnaturally connected to her? Drawn to her?"

That made me explode in laughter, "Of course. I'm obsessed with her. If any other male was acting the way I am toward her I would skin them alive."

"And it doesn't bother you, knowing that you're overly attached?"

"It drives me insane. The fact I haven't seen her in days is rattling me to my core. I need her. It hasn't even been two weeks since we met and I feel like I'm dying without her."

He arched a bushy brow at me, "Mmmmhmmm. And you haven't considered that maybe you are fated?"

I sighed, needing to get the conversation back on track. I couldn't think about fate giving me an amazing woman only for me to have ruined everything already or to potentially lose her to the Undead. "Yusuf, you need to find Monique and take her to France. Now."

"I'm aware. I wasn't expecting her to have the burning yet. Though, I don't know why I thought that, maybe it was just wishful thinking. But we aren't going to find her while she's underground. Maybe we should just go to your woman. If we stick with her, we'll see Monique eventually."

"Annabel is not speaking to me. I'm not even sure where she is today. I also am expecting my next semi of product to be delivered in...." I looked at my watch, "an hour. They won't leave the inventory if I'm not here to sign for it and my blood will be on that truck."

"How much do you have left?" He asked, drinking the remaining contents of his cup.

"One more bag. I need the delivery."

"Shit."

"You can say that again."

Yusuf drummed his hands against his thighs, solving the puzzle in his head. Yusuf was the one who provided support no matter the issue, he only needed to find out what that support could be before he'd do it. "You stay here, get your order. I will begin searching for Monique's lair - at least we know that scent is her now. When you're able, call me and we will switch from finding Monique to shadowing Annabel. I do not want to frighten her by approaching her alone."

I nodded, "please do not approach Bels, I was very clear with her that I didn't want her around you and I don't want you to make her feel unsafe."

"Gods, you lovesick puppy, she *is* unsafe. Or did you not see the same Monique that I did?"

"Where did you even find her, Yus? I searched for almost a year and you just...poofed with her."

"Poofed?" He arched a brow at me and shook his head, "I found her in a bar last night. She was there to feed and I was in the right place at the right time, that's all. I didn't believe it was her at first...I... I'm... I need her to be okay."

I sat next to him, leaning to place my elbows on my knees, "I need you to promise me that you will take her away from here. I need you to promise me that you will get a plane and get her out of my town and away from Annabel. You can't come back when the Coalition is done with her. You need to leave and not return."

"200 years, just like that, love? All gone? Don't even want to get the casual cup of coffee?"

Looking into his dark eyes heavy with emotion, I shook my head slowly, "Yus...the pain you caused me in one year easily caused irreparable damage to us. I can never bond with you again."

He smirked, arching his brow, "Even if I said I'd bond with you and Annabel?"

I growled instinctively, my insides twisting at the idea of having to share her with the man who admitted he wouldn't have come back for me alone - that I wasn't enough without Monique.

Chuckling, he swept his thumb across his lips, "You are so screwed, Thomas. Fated to a mortal - who would have guessed?"

"If that's true, and that's a big if, if anything happens to her, you are both dead."

"Yes, yes, you are very scary, my love," He smiled rubbing my shoulder playfully, "Yes, Thomas. You help me find her and I will take her to Paris and we will not return."

We spoke for several more minutes, trying to devise some kind of plan that would work in my weakened state and then he was gone - out to try and scent Monique's hiding place while the sun was out. If she wasn't fully changed yet, which I didn't think she was, the sun wouldn't kill her, but it would increase the burning inside of her, making it unlikely that she'd try to find Annabel until this evening.

I thought back to the to-do lists that I had seen Bels make a thousand times last week. She had explained that taking an insurmountable task and breaking it down made her feel like it was suddenly achievable. Like she'd said - anyone can do five things, especially one at a time, so as I drank the remaining contents of my cup, I thought about the day ahead. I broke it down.

1. UNLOAD THE TRUCK TO RESTOCK MY SUPPLY OF BLOOD.

2. CONTACT BELS AND FIND OUT WHERE SHE WAS.

3. TRY TO NOT WORRY AND RUN THE STORE UNTIL THE SUN GOES DOWN.

4. FIND ANNABEL AND WATCH FROM A DISTANCE IF SHE ISN'T READY TO BE WITH ME YET.

5. GROVEL AT HER FEET WHILE YUSUF TAKES MONIQUE AWAY.

29
ANNABEL

The lights had been too bright. They flashed behind my closed eyes and I began to hear a chorus of beeping machines and soft-spoken voices. I tried to push down on my hand to shift in whatever bed I was in, only to realize that I couldn't move my arm. My eyes shot open and took in the stark white room that stunk of lemons and alcohol. Each breath felt like someone was sitting on my chest and made me cough painfully.

"Ow, fucking hell," I muttered, blinking a few times up at the ceiling trying to calm myself.

"Baby, you're awake!" My Mom's concerned green eyes came into my line of sight, "Are you in pain? Do you-"

"Jesus, Deirdre, let her be!" Mama's teacher voice bit at her, laced with worry and concentration, "I need you to help me finish this poultice."

"Annabel, darling, do you know where you are?" Mom swept some unruly hair from my head, ignoring her wife.

"I have no fucking idea. Can I have some water? Can I sit up?" I croaked the words, my throat hoarse from screaming and the fight with Monique on the beach came rushing back to me, "Oh my god!"

"Shhhh...are you remembering?" She asked, holding my cheeks.

"I was dead. I was on the beach and-"

"Not dead, my love. Not from that." Her normally serene voice was tainted with worry, "How did...how..."

"Dee, please!"

I fumbled for the remote attached to the hospital bed, allowing it to lift my wrecked body into a seated position so I could see my mothers who were crouched over a small black bowl with my Mama using a mortar and pestle to grind something up.

"What are you guys doing?"

My Mama's shoulders slumped and my mom looked at me warily, "Bels, do you know what happened to you?"

I did. But how could I tell them that I'd been attacked by my fuck buddy's ex-wife who just happened to be a vampire that was completely off her rocker? "Um... I don't know..."

"For heaven's sake, Dee, she isn't going to admit to getting bit by a vampire. Jesus, this is separating, grab me some more leaf powder will you dear?"

My eyes widened and I looked down at my arm, tucked into a sling with surgical wrappings around it, "What? How would you-"

My mom handed her a vial of powder and returned to the top of the bed to hold my hand, "A teenager found you down on the beach, convulsing, bleeding, and cold to the touch. You lost a lot of blood and...yeah, you have a bite on your cephalic vein... someone took a bite and left you for dead."

"Which doesn't follow the typical attacks in the area," Mama muttered, grinding the paste into the little black bowl.

"That bitch bit me?! You guys need to leave, now. You need to-"

Mom shushed me, grabbing my face again, "You're fine. It's fine."

"No, I'm going to turn if she-"

"No, you're not. You...can't be turned into an Undead."

"She's not Undead, she's just-"

"Honey, that's an Undead bite." My mom moved some of the wrappings to expose a nasty green and purple crescent wound which oozed a gelatinous yellow fluid.

"Then you definitely need to leave - how do you guys even -"

"Here, apply this to the lesion, Dee," Mama handed the bowl up to her and my Mom sat on the mattress next to me and began gently packing the pesto-looking concoction into the wound.

"Ow, what the fuck! What is that?" I felt my elbow throb, the infection trying to break through the layer of paste.

"It's comfrey poultice dear, it will help pull the infection from your system. No one should ever leave home without it."

"Will either of you tell me what the hell is going on?"

They glanced between each other, doing that stupid mother thing where they can talk to each other without talking, and then my mom spoke, "Sybil, I think you should explain this - you can stick to the important details better. I always get distracted by the lore."

Mama sighed and put the items she was using on the chair behind her before sitting on the other side of my bed. It was a tight fit with the three of us but their presence helped me feel safe, "Guys, I don't want to hurt you."

"Bels, you can't be changed to an Undead. No one in our line can."

"Now that's not to say you're invincible, if that kid hadn't found you you likely could have bled out and died from that injury-"

Mama glared at her, "but, you can't be changed."

"What in the actual fuck are you guys talking about?" The monitor next to me showed my heartbeat raising and my mom soothingly ran her hand up and down my leg.

"Sweetie, you come from a blessed line of Green Witches."

I scoffed, "Sure, and I'll go to Hogwarts on Tuesday, come on Mom."

My Mama took a cloth and wiped off the goo, removing a large quantity of vamp slime and reapplying more of the green stuff.

"A very long time ago, our family lived in France, outside of Paris, specifically," She spoke without feeling, as if reciting a bedtime story that she should have told me before, "Our family lands were becoming unsafe. There was a sudden surge of Undead Vampires and Others in the area, sparking a witch hunt. Now, France was kind of a mess then, so most people associated the violence with the revolution, but it was an easy scapegoat to take. Witches were being blamed for the deaths and disappearances of civilians even though Green Witches did no such thing." She looked at her wife and chuckled, "Gods can you imagine? Here, mortal, let me smite you with this succulent."

"Stay on task, darling, it's why I deferred it to you."

My eyes widened, they had never even hinted at a knowledge of Others. My moms weren't even superstitious. I celebrated Halloween every year. I couldn't keep anything other than my Grandmother's cactus alive!

"This is to say that a Coalition of Others formed behind the scenes. Witches of every branch as well as representatives from other magical creatures came together to create structure. Consequences. We couldn't allow a group of rogue vampires to be the death of us all. There needed to be rules. By sheer luck, it was discovered that Green Witch magic was repulsive to the Undead. A common treatment for a vampire bite is that comfrey poultice," she said nodding at the green stuff on my arm, "and apparently much of the magic that allows us to manipulate the plants also lives in our blood. If an undead bites a Green Witch, our bodies instantly try to push it out, and the venom burns their mouths, which is probably why she fled before she..."

"Wait, why would their own venom kill them- that doesn't make sense?" I asked.

"Well... I guess to put it simply, they push venom out. It's not like they're eating it."

"But it's part of them. You just said plants were a part of witches and that's why they repel venom. Wouldn't the venom be in their blood and make them immune to it?"

My mom cringed, "Darling, the blood inside of an undead's body isn't that of the undead. That blood contains no venom..."

"Ew! You're saying-"

"Yeah..."

"Oh, gods." I leaned my head back against the bed and looked at the ceiling, shaking it in disbelief, "And you guys wait until I'm almost 30 to try and get me to believe in fairy tales? Come on!"

"You clearly already knew something, love, we just want to fill in the blanks. Why do you think we wanted you to move home? It was time to teach you before we forgot something important."

I pressed my palms into my eyes, "Jesus the almighty baby in a manger. I don't-"

"Anyway," Mama pressed on, "upon the discovery that Green Witches were immune to the bites of the Undead, the Coalition tasked our line with being the eyes and ears around the world to help protect mortals and to report back when needed. Our family moved to Boston and were tasked with protecting the people and witches here, and honestly, for a long time now, there hasn't been anything to report. No Others were behaving so extraneously that we needed to include the Coalition. I don't even think there's been an Undead in Quaker's Wharf or Salem in... what?"

"At least as long as Bels has been alive. There are Others around, but none that want to draw attention to themselves. In fact, there's a huge Other population here. We often have our hands full just acting as the witch mothers to every little demon and werewolf that needs someone to talk to. The Mother has blessed us to be the mothers and it is a task that we do not take lightly," my mom added.

"But- we wanted you to experience as normal of a life as you could while there was no threat. We wanted you to have friends and experience your childhood. We didn't mean to go so long before starting your training but...there was no reason to and then you were in Chicago and..."

"And now Monique bit me and shit is about to hit the fan." I cringed, and my mom leaned over to press a button attached to my IV.

"Just some morphine, love, it will help the pain in your elbow. We can heal the bone more at home to restore your use of it but they needed to set the pins in it."

"How could I live with you and not know anything? How could I live with witches and not know?"

"Not just live with us, Bels, you are one too. You're a part of us."

Mama squeezed my thigh, "I did many of my meetings at my office at the College, or away from the house. Your mother grew everything we needed to help the Others and frankly...you were such a bookworm and uninterested in the plants that you didn't give a shit what she was doing out in the solarium."

"So what happens now? Monique is sick, she needs help, and Thomas and Yus-"

"Honey, you know all these creatures?"

I blushed, "uh, Thomas and I have an...arrangement. He has been running the Halloween store."

My mom arched her brow, "interesting choice of profession for a... vampire, I'm assuming?"

I nodded, the morphine swirling into my mind and making me feel loose, "I need to tell him Monique is sick - I don't think he knows. He didn't tell me..."

"You focus on healing, love. Let us do our job."

My vision began to blacken as the morphine took hold as sleep beckoned for me, but I didn't miss the concerned look that passed between my mothers as I drifted back into unconsciousness.

30
THOMAS

"Where the fuck is she?!" I raged, my insides a mix of fear and anger. Annabel wasn't answering her phone and we couldn't find Monique. What if something had happened to her? What if Monique wasn't even in the area anymore and Annabel had just decided to abandon our relationship?

"Thomas you need to eat - you'll be no good to me if you go out of balance and fall Undead too." Yusuf lay on my air mattress, tossing a ball into the air as if he didn't have a care in the world. "There is a mall full of people right there, go eat something."

"I can't. I can't do that. I promised Bels-"

"She wouldn't handfeast, right?"

I glared at him.

"She isn't your Untouchable, she isn't claimed, you deny that there's a bond, and frankly if you think she's pissed now, wait until you go all Dracula on her. From what you have told me, I don't think that will go over well."

It had been four days since we'd seen Monique and a week since I'd harvested. I was turning into an angry bastard.

"If she's dead somewhere you're not breaking your word. Go. Eat."

My terror boiled over and before he could have blinked, I leaped onto the bed and landed a punch square in Yusuf's face, and he had the audacity to laugh.

"Get off, you lovesick fool," He chuckled, easily pushing me off. Since he'd been harvesting and feeding his strength was at 100% whereas I was pathetically weak. "I am telling you that Annabel will be angrier if you starve to death than if you feed from some- one. Especially when she hasn't answered your calls in how many days?"

"Shut the fuck up, Yus."

My mind swirled with images of Annabel dead at Monique's hand. The fact that we hadn't found either of them was enough to make me queasy.

"You are going to eat. You're going to kill yourself like this. Just this once, and then we can find her and you can go back to fucking and sucking each other to death, okay?" He rose from the mattress and grabbed my hand, hauling me up and I weakly leaned against his shoulder. Fuck, I was so tired. Even just being angry made me tired. I'd been drinking more blood than usual and I still couldn't keep up my strength.

"You're right. You're right," I sighed, "I don't want to hurt her but I... I can't save her if I'm as weak as a teenage boy either."

"What are you hungry for? Joy? Anger? Love?"

"I don't care," I leaned into him, "but I need a lot." He wrapped his arm around my waist and I missed the feeling of butterflies that the action would have given me while we were bonded. This past week had stayed platonic, and it was clear that to him, Monique was the glue that held us together. We had had many conversations that managed to be relatively civil, and we commiserated as creatures in love with missing women. Strange thing for my ex-husband and I to bond over. I stumbled, pausing our walk to regain my footing. "I'm tired, Yus."

He assessed me, biting his lip, "do you want me to go find someone and bring them back here?"

"Non. Non, let us go. Take me to Witchcraft. There's usually a crowd there this time of night."

"Okay, my love. Let's get some food in you. Can you fly?" He asked as we walked out of the building and locked up behind us.

"I'll try," I muttered, cracking my neck and shifting into my raven, falling face-first into the sidewalk. I heard Yusuf snort before he shook himself out, changing into his beautiful hawk. He immediately took flight and I stumbled after him like a drunken gull. I shouldn't have gone this long without eating, but my every moment was consumed by watching the invisible thread that was fraying between Bels and me.

We landed and changed back in the alley behind the bar, and I blended in seamlessly with the other drunk mortals. Who knew that a starving vampire was just a drunk human? Yus paid the cover charge and dragged me inside, and I easily was able to stumble into people, steadying myself on their forearms and harvest small amounts of energy as we worked our way through the crowd. By the time we got to the bar, I felt legitimately drunk from the hurricane of emotions inside my bloodstream.

I much preferred how Annabel and I could share in the harvest, but I couldn't deny that I felt stronger by the second. It was easy enough to execute, as Yus and I had done this for each other under less extenuating circumstances many times. I'd stumble, catch myself, harvest, and then Yusuf would touch them and me to harvest for himself to excuse my behavior. I used to be better at selecting complimenting emotions, but due to the low levels of energy in me, I didn't give a shit and had sampled lust, anger, depression, claustrophobia, confusion, anxiety, joy, and disgust in less than five minutes.

Yus tapped the bar and ordered two whiskeys to help us blend in, and then immediately began flirting with the thin woman to his left. I thought I was going to be sick. The bar was spinning beneath my elbows and I dug my palms into my eyes to try and balance myself.

"Thomas? Are you okay?" A soft hand ran over my back, rubbing it kindly and when I inhaled créme brûlée and coffee, my head shot up.

"Shannon!" I grabbed her by her shoulders, making sure not to touch her skin.

"Hey bud, what's...wow how drunk are you?" She leaned around my face, assessing me and trying to meet my eyes.

"Where is she? Have you seen her?"

She looked hesitant to answer, but sighed and nodded, "I saw her yesterday, she isn't good, but thankfully the launch went off without a hitch thanks to all the preloading we did on Monday. I was able to go in on Tuesday and hit load and we were rocking and rolling. Terrible week for this shit to happen though. Who gets mugged in Quaker's Wharf anyway?"

"Wait, what? Annabel was mugged? Where is she?"

"You didn't know? Monday night someone assaulted her on the beach, she was in the hospital for a few days, but they released her yesterday. Someone really did a number on her. And of course, being Bels, she won't file a police report. She said she didn't remember anything enough to give the police information anyway, but I feel like she's lying."

Trae walked up next to her and wrapped his arm around her small shoulders, his height making her slender top half appear even more minuscule, "Hey, you're not word vomiting all over Thomas, are you? Tequila always makes you talkative."

She shrugged, "Guilty."

"Shannon, I haven't talked to her in a week. I didn't even know this happened, where is her phone?"

"It got broken in the mugging. I'm sure she's not avoiding you intentionally unless you haven't apologized yet. Then she might be."

I was taken aback, "apologized?"

Sighing she shook her head, "okay, I'll take that as a no. She said you guys had a fight and you left her at home upset and never called to work it out."

Fury roiled in me and I stood up, feeling more energized now that the harvesting had started to settle in me, "I called her. I must have called and texted her five times on Monday. She hasn't reached out at all."

"Well...maybe she isn't ready to talk to you yet," Trae contributed with a helpful yet sarcastic tone.

"Has she told you such?" I glared at him.

"Naw, man, I haven't seen her- only Shannon has."

Shannon pulled herself up onto a barstool, her generous hips spilling over the sides of the seat, and signaled to the bartender to bring her another tequila, "She's staying with her moms while she heals - she hasn't even been into work yet. Whoever it was shattered her fucking elbow to the point she needed surgery. She almost bled out. Not what I was expecting to hear Sybil, that's her Mama, called me about the launch Tuesday morning."

Yusuf spoke up from my other side, "Wait, Sybil Williams is her mother? The literature professor at Salem?"

She nodded and threw her shot back, "Well she was, she retired earlier this year. Her memory is going which is why Bels moved back here."

"But you're sure, Sybil Williams?"

Shannon furrowed her brow, "Yeah..."

"Is she related to Deirdre Williams?"

"Yus, what's going on?" I looked at him, searching his wide eyes for answers but Shannon made a hissing noise around her lime, bringing my attention back to her.

"Yeah, those are her moms. Did you have Sybil at Salem?"

"Uh," Yusuf hesitated, "Yes, I'd just been looking for her regarding a research project but hadn't been able to connect with her." He clawed his nails into my bicep and I glared at him.

"Is she safe? Can I help?" I would get on my knees and beg if it got me back in Bels' good graces. Groveling was on my to-do list after all.

"I think if she wanted to see you she would have found a way to get a hold of you, man. Maybe you should just back off - she said you were coming on really strong," Trae said, running his hands over Shannon's pear-shaped torso.

"Shush, be kind!" Shannon scolded him, "I swear, sometimes I think you are too protective of her." Moving her attention to me, she pulled out her phone and text me an address, "This is her moms' address. She doesn't like flowers. Get her a Raven plant and take her a coffee - pumpkin spice latte. Do. Not. Push. Her. The more you push the more she'll retreat. Got it?"

"A Raven plant?" I asked.

"Yeah they're called a Zz or something like that, just google it. It's a big black houseplant. She loves them and kills them regularly so she always wants another one."

I barked a laugh, "She kills Ravens?"

With a shrug, she looked at me quizically, "Just the plants, not the birds. Oh! Did she tell you we saw a giant Raven over the bar district last week? It was insane. Closest I've ever seen one fly to me."

"No way," Yus drawled, "a Raven? Around here? What are the chances of that?"

"Oh, black sweet potato vines also make her happy."

Trae chuckled, "Why do you know her favorite plants if she can't keep them alive?"

She shrugged, "Girls know this stuff. Jake sent me flowers once and she went on a giant rant about how sending someone flowers was stupid because they'd just whither and die. She said men should be smart enough to only send plants."

A thought occurred to me, "Shannon, what about Tim? Is he at her moms'? Should I go over and take care of him?"

"Do you have a key? I don't know who's taking care of the cat."

"Okay, well at the very least I'll go ask her if I need to check on him...I wouldn't want anything to happen to the little guy."

"You like that stupid cat? Damn thing always hissed and clawed at me," Trae grumbled and Shannon's head whipped in his direction.

"And when have you been around Bels' cat?"

I knocked the bar twice, "On that note, I'm going to head out I've got groveling to do." I nodded toward the exit and bumped Yusuf to have him follow me. I felt infinitely better now that I'd fed, but I knew it was another thing I'd probably have to apologize for when she finally spoke to me.

"Seriously, when have you been in her house in the last three years? Have you gone to Chicago?" I heard Shannon hiss at him as Yusuf and I exited the building and went out onto the walkway.

"You want to tell me what that was all about with Bels' moms?" I asked him, weaving around people to turn back down the alley.

He leaned closer to me and spoke softly, "they're the names I was given by the Coalition on Sunday to check in with if I needed help finding Monique. They wanted me to report her as an Undead to them."

"Wait, what?" I slammed my hand into his chest and stopped him dead in his tracks, "Why would Annabel's mothers even know about the Coalition?"

"You didn't know?"

"Okay, Yus, you're freaking me out, what is going on? Are they hunters?"

"No, no, nothing like that," He looked around the walkway, deciding it was too crowded, and pulled me into the alley with the hand that had been on his chest, "Thomas, what do you know about Green Witches?"

I shrugged, "They like...plants." Chuckling in disbelief I pulled my hands through my hair, "Are you fucking telling me that Bels is a witch? She doesn't even have an alter in her house."

"I don't know a damn thing about your woman, but Sybil and Deirdre Williams are a Green Witch line assigned to the Boston area by the Coalition. That's all I was told."

I drug my hand over my face and put my other on my hip and began pacing up and down the dark corridor. "Then why have I never heard of them? We have lived in Boston forever. Surely we would have been told about the Williams family if that were the case. The Farleys were the Green Witches you met with in Boston, not the Williams."

"They were our witches, yes, but they're not the only ones." Green witches acted as the in-between for Others and the Coalition. Their job was to monitor supernatural and paranormal activity in an area, collect dues, conduct investigations and report back to the main Coalition office in Paris. They were the ones you went to if you were injured and didn't have a personal doctor. They were the ones who could ship you back to Paris for being too reckless. They were... immune to vampire bites.

"Oh my gods." I froze, "Oh my gods. If Bels is a Green Witch, Mo can't hurt her - this is wonderful!"

Yusuf scoffed, "Oh please, we both know that Monique could gut her in a moment. Not being able to turn her is not the same as not being able to kill her, and frankly with her mental state right now, death might be the better of the two choices. You heard her friend say she'd been in the hospital, right? I can almost guarantee you that she wasn't mugged."

"Have you met with them yet? Have you met Sybil and Deirdre?"

"No," he shook his head, "I didn't want to report Monique as a danger to the mortals unless she actually was. I didn't want to put her in the position where they'd shoot first and ask questions later."

"They're not hunters, they wouldn't hurt-"

"They may not be hunters, Thomas, but they have hunters. Don't be dense."

"You always handled the witches. You paid our dues, you handled the meetings... I've never had to meet with a witch! I only know what you've told me!" I shoved him, feeling out of control from a taste of anger that pulled to the surface from the bar. I remembered the quarterly meetings where he insisted that I stay home with Monique, pulling gold out of the safe and disappearing into the city, only to return exhausted hours later after they'd interrogated him regarding suspicious activity. It was a big city - there was often someone misbehaving.

"I was the oldest! Do you think I was going to voluntarily put you and Monique on their radar? It was easier to keep our exposure to them limited. I did it to keep you safe, my friend."

"Well, we're seeing them now. Come on."

"Thomas it's past midnight!"

I didn't hear him as I shook into my wings and took flight going South.

I knew she was an Other. I saw her in my mind, puttering around her kitchen, poking her long black nails into that stupid glittery skull pot and her voice filled me.

"WHY SHOULD THEY LIVE IN BORING TERRA COTTA? I KNOW I WOULDN'T ENJOY THAT."

"I FIND PLANTS PEACEFUL. I'M NOT VERY GOOD AT IT, BUT MY MOM HAS A GREEN THUMB"

"I OFFERED TO MOVE THEM TO CHICAGO TO BE WITH ME AND THEY FLAT-OUT REFUSED. THEY'VE BEEN HERE LONGER THAN I'VE BEEN ALIVE AND I THINK THEY'RE JUST SET IN THEIR WAYS, BUT THEY'RE ALMOST 70 AND GETTING FORGETFUL."

"THEY SAID I NEEDED TO COME HOME TO LEARN ABOUT THE FAMILY BEFORE IT WAS TOO LATE."

My girl, *mon coeur*, she belonged in my world. She was supposed to be with Others. She was supposed to have magic. That fact alone solidified what I'd already felt - she was supposed to be mine.

31
ANNABEL

My moms were witches - fuck, *I* was a witch. That's a lot to put on someone at almost 30. Like, wasn't this a conversation we should have had when I was in puberty? *Oh, you're at the special age where your body is changing, you'll grow boobs, and get your period, and by the way, you're a witch, here's an American Girl book that will tell you everything you need to know.* I didn't think there was an American Girl book on being a Green Witch, but if there was it was going in my cart the second I found it.

I was in the hospital for several days recovering from the injuries sustained by Monique, which left loads of time for my moms to sit in the uncomfortable pleather chairs and tell me our family story while I was high enough to not question a word they said. I came from a long line of Green Witches, descended from a coven in France that specialized in plants or plant products. We were like...crunchy organic witches or something like that, which probably meant I should apologize to all the essential oil ladies I'd yelled at at those home parties. Our family was a part of "The Coalition," which I briefly remembered Thomas talking about, and our job was to make sure that creatures paid dues (what the fuck), followed the rules, and distributed correspondence as needed. My moms swore that the Coalition was pretty hands-off in our area, but with Monique going off the deep end, I was going to learn all about them really quick. So actually, I was totally right when I accused Thomas of having an army of caped vampires hiding in the shadows. There was a fucking United Nations for Others, and I was to be a part of it.

I hadn't spoken to him. My moms brought me to their home to do some kind of Harry Potter potion thing on my elbow to allow the bones to heal quickly, and I hadn't gotten a new phone to replace the one that was ruined at the beach. I was thankful to be out of the sling in less than a week instead of the six weeks the doctors had estimated, but I still didn't have full use of it and wanted to cry whenever I bent the joint. Hiding with my moms and having the distance from the real world was good for healing, but horrible for my mind.

I found that I was torn between missing Tommy desperately, wanting to talk to him and be with him, and being wounded that his exes came back and I hadn't spoken to him since. It felt like he walked away entirely and I was sulking, licking my wounds, knowing in my heart that I wouldn't have walked away. Not from him. I wanted to have him talk to me about all the blank spots in my moms' stories and I wanted his experience alongside me on this journey. We left off on a miscommunication and that alone was pissing me off. If there was one thing that would make me put a romance book down immediately it was the miscommunication trope, and yet here I was, living in one with a fucking vampire who was my...subordinate in a weird way. But the few times I'd found myself standing at my mothers' front door, the idea of leaving the safety of their warded home had completely freaked me out and I had gone back to bothering one of them about some random magic question I'd pulled out of my ass.

My moms seemed to recognize my hesitancy in leaving, so they parked me in the solarium every morning with a stack of books and diaries to read and learn about what it meant to be a Williams. They'd bring me cups of tea they claimed would "open my mind" or "soothe my soul" - like they were fucking witches or something, and I'd drink them without question. Sure, as a result of my hiding, I was learning a lot about the different uses of plants, but I was also dying to get back to work and help Shannon with the fall launch. I was a boutique owner, not a plant whisperer. I was itching to go ship orders, make thirst traps and pretend like none of this had happened.

Within a month I'd gone from planning on flirting with the previous owner of the Halloween store to having been bit and almost murdered by a fucking vampire on my favorite beach, while also somehow wanting desperately to fuck a different vampire, who was also involved with the murderous one. It was...unnerving and confusing to say the least. Somehow, viral fat chick Annabel had been turned into a hot trauma sundae topped in sexual frustration and unused magic, who also peed a lot from my days hooked up to an IV and the consuming of said teas.

The solarium was my Mom's domain, overflowing with plants and flowers that could delight in the sun and grow. Mama had built it for her one year so she could continue growing things over the New England winters and the warm bright space was good for all of us. It was a place you could go any time of the year and inhale the scent of fresh herbs and bask in the three walls and ceiling of glass. It was my favorite place in high school when I was feeling particularly emo as I could lie in there and read shit like *Jane Eyre* and Poe while watching the rain fall. Mom said I was to study among the growing things to grow as a green witch, but I'm pretty sure she just wanted me to bring in some vitamin D to counteract the crippling anxiety I was suffering from without my feelings eating not-boyfriend. What I'd wanted to do was yell 'fuck anxiety', go dance in a black lace bra and get serotonin hits from people liking and following my ass jiggles on social media. Where there's jiggles there will be giggles and where there's giggles there is bound to be at least a singular hit of serotonin. I wasn't picky - storebought would be fine.

Serotonin was what I wanted, but apparently, my mothers' comfrey poultice did such a good job extracting the venom from my bloodstream that I was to study and prepare myself to be on comfrey tending duty. It was decided that "we" - since apparently, I was part of the coven now - needed to make full stores of the comfrey poultice in case Monique couldn't be located quickly and other Others were injured. Terrifyingly enough, Undead could infect anything other than a green witch, but instead of them looking like blood-sucking zombie demons, to mortals it often looked similar to rabies. With Others that weren't already vampires, it was far more terrifying and dangerous. Rabid venomous werewolves were not to be trifled with, so learning about poultices was what I was doing all day, and typically since I wasn't sleeping well, all night.

"Bels?" My mom entered the glass room off the back of the house and I looked up from the book that I hadn't been reading or retaining, "You good?"

"No, I'm not good, Mom." My haven of a town had been stolen away by my lover's ex-wife and I was lost in a sea of emotions. Not knowing what happened to Monique kept me happily smashing comfrey and hiding in the comfort of my mothers' cooking and cliché midnight margaritas, which they'd begun after watching Practical Magic and decided to adopt the practice as their own. I couldn't say that I was mad about the cliché since I was being spoiled by their Jimmy Buffet frozen margarita maker and top-shelf tequila. Like they'd said, if they were going to live their best witch lives, they were going to go all out, and as a new baby witch, I was going to join them.

Mom sighed and plopped onto the white wicker couch beside me and gave me a sympathetic smile, "I know, it's a lot, isn't it?"

I glared over the book at her, "You know, if you guys had told me about this shit years ago I would have been better prepared to handle the whole blood-sucking vampire thing."

"I know, but just because we have gifts from the earth doesn't mean I can see the future, sweetie. I would never have seen this coming. I never would have thought you'd get bit by an Undead in Quaker's Wharf, let alone you falling in love with an Other. Call me naive but I figured we had time for this to come to light by itself."

I hissed, embarrassment coursing through me at the knowledge that I spilled my guts while wasted on said top-shelf tequila and told them everything. Because obviously, every mother wanted to know about their daughter's fridge sexcipades with the supernatural. "I don't know that I'm in love with-"

She interrupted me with an arched brow, "don't lie to me, Bels. Lie to yourself, but don't lie to me. If you're not in love with him, drunk you certainly is." She leaned forward and lifted the tome I was perusing and flinched, "Ugh, I hate that one. Though I suppose I'm not the bookish one in the family. I swear the trees talk to your Mama about what was written on their pages. I would so much rather her just tell me what to do and come out here and get my hands dirty."

"That's why you guys make such a good team, right?"

Mom smiled, "we are best friends. It makes everything easier."

I bit my lip and spat out the question that had been bothering me since they'd told me, "you guys told me I came from a sperm donor and IVF when I was a kid. I'm not actually like a nymph or a changeling or something ridiculous like that where I grew out of the ground like a daisy?"

Snorting, she shook her head, "of course not! You're a perfect test tube baby. Just the way we wanted you. Though you have been horrifically expensive from the moment we thought about having you... you're lucky you're worth it."

"So...Witches. It's a maternal line thing? Is the daughter of a witch guaranteed to be a witch herself? How did you know I'd be a witch if you used some rando off the street? Am I part warlock?"

"No, it's a maternal line," she drank from the giant blue water bottle that was always at her side, "though the amount of power and disposition toward magic depends on the child. As I'm sure you've figured out, your Mama and I are very different witches, but every witch contributes to her coven to make a perfect puzzle. You've always been a missing piece while we waited for you to come into your magic. Everyone was shocked when you didn't manifest in your teens."

Everyone. Like I needed to grasp there was a whole fucking gaggle of witches hanging around. "Wait, you mean I was supposed to have a Sabrina moment and wake up to a talking cat or something?"

"I accidentally grew my mom's bonsai tree into a full-size tree when I was 9. I was so worried she was going to be mad at me, not knowing what we were. It cracked the ceiling. All I'd wanted was to play with the little rake in the sand and there I was, exploding my mother's tree because my Grandma made me mad," She chuckled at the memory.

"Yeah, but the whole green witch thing is so weird. Grandma couldn't even keep a cactus alive." I shriveled my face in disgust, "that awful woman didn't have a nurturing bone in her body."

"Hey. May I remind you that she's your Mama's mother?"

I laughed, "and you fucking hated her too!"

She shuddered, "Yeah, you're right, I did."

"So what were their powers?" I asked, "I don't know what I'll lean towards. Mom has paper, you have plants, I'm assuming your mom had plants too?" She nodded, "What about Grandma?"

"Oh, your Grandma liked poisonous plants. She was a real peach."

That made me chuckle, "What? You mean my dear old Grandma was out there growing nightshade in her window planters or something? Is that why Mama hides in books? So she could identify if that awful woman was trying to poison her?"

She snorted, "No, but there was a reason you were never allowed behind the outbuilding. She wasn't dumb enough to keep nightshade in the house and her whole piece of the woods behind her property was filled with nasty plants that kids had no business being around."

I closed the book, sighing, "This is too much. How am I supposed to reconcile who everyone is with who I thought they were?"

"No one is different, baby. We're just a little...extra. Someone just seasoned our stew better or something."

I shook my head, "Or something." Picking at my cuticles, I continued, "Mom, what if I want to have kids? Are there rules? Is it safe? Am I dooming my kids to be babysitters for the creature from the black lagoon if they're female? Are we all stuck as Coalition minions? What if they identify as female? Is this a body part thing or a gender identity thing and -"

She smiled, "One, Frasier's a nice guy, I have never found that he requires much looking after, and two, don't overthink it. The earth gives us gifts in their own time and way." She paused, shivering, and turned to the front door, assessing it before the doorbell rang, "Speaking of...we have a visitor. They tripped the wards so they aren't mortal."

"At least we know it's not Monique. Thank you, sunshine for stopping the bitey ones from coming out during the day." I groaned as she walked toward the door, "Is it normal?"

"As opposed to..." She laughed, heading toward the entrance.

"Something that wants to kill me? Or eat me? Or lie to me? Does it have wings or fur or anything that a month ago would have bothered me?" I hollered and she opened the door, her laughter stopping immediately.

"*Bonjour gardienne*, my name is Thomas Corbin. I am looking for Annabel, is she at home?"

My heart froze. He found me? He looked for me? Just as I was about to feel the warm fuzzies, my mom slammed the door in his face and yelled, "Am I inviting the rat-with-wings inside, or is this a safe zone?"

I laughed, loving that my Mom had my back. "He's a raven, not a pigeon. And no, don't invite him in, have him walk around the house and I'll talk to him on the patio." Standing from the wicker loveseat, I closed the book and laid it on the cushion, knowing it didn't matter what page I was on since I wasn't understanding any of it anyway. I stepped out into the sun from the back door and sat on one of the chairs surrounding my mothers' fire pit, which I wasn't entirely sure was just for marshmallows anymore, and willed my heart to maintain its rhythm while I heard her give him my instructions.

My mother's backyard had always been peaceful to me. They owned a large historical home and we had a postage stamp of a yard that was lined around the perimeter with an extra tall privacy fence. They'd built a ton of raised garden beds in the yard and created a brick patio and walkway through the plants. While it meant that I didn't have a "yard" per se during my childhood, I was always flooded with memories of stealing blackberries off the tree in the northwest corner, or painting shallow terra cotta pots and making little toad homes for the garden's "tenants" whenever I visited home. I hadn't had a normal upbringing, though that made much more sense now, but it wasn't bad. No, the shriveling plants surrounding me reminded me of all the afternoons picking seeds from sunflowers and reading poetry in the hammock. It wasn't typical, but it was good, and it was mine.

Thomas walked around the back of the house, his shoes crunching against the leaves that had just begun to fall onto the brick pavers, tearing me from my memories, and paused when he saw me. He looked oddly at home in my mother's yard, his dark slim cut jeans and Bowie shirt empha-sized his slim frame while also drawing my attention to his delicious shoulders which were flexed from the large raven plant he held in his arms. His dark eyes widened briefly at the red and angry-looking tissue that was healing on the crook of my elbow and immediately flashed to my side, crouching between my knees and placing the plant at his side.

"Fuck, I forgot how fast you are," I gasped.

His hands were all over my body poking and prodding for physical and emotional damage while muttering under his breath in french, "*Mon coeur*, are you okay, *ma chère*? I-"

I felt him knock against my mind and I leaned back, disconnecting the tie between us, "Hi Tommy."

Fingers flexing, feeling the loss of my touch, he spoke softly, "are you well? Are you whole?"

My anger flared, "Whole? That's an interesting choice of words. Like someone maybe, I dunno, took a fucking bite out of my arm?"

He at least had the grace to flinch, "I tried to find you, I tried to call...I had no idea she would hurt you until I saw her, and by then you'd already stopped speaking to me and -"

"You walked away and didn't come back. You didn't warn me, Tommy. You didn't ever tell me she could be a danger to me. You were all, 'they're gone and there's nothing between us,' which is definitely not the vibe I got from her when she attacked me. Jesus, I wouldn't have chatted with her on a dark beach if I'd thought I could be her dinner."

"I know. I know."

"How did you find me?" I asked, indicating for him to sit, but he continued to hover.

"Shannon."

"Ah. That Benedict Arnold."

"I was so scared, Bels, I didn't know where you were, or if you were okay...I thought you'd just dropped off the planet because you were angry with me. You said you hated me! I wanted to give you space-" His speech accelerated, his panic coming off him in waves so potent I didn't need to be a vampire to feel them.

Part of me enjoyed watching him spiral. Part of me loved that he was so worried about me and uncertain of our future. The other side of the coin wished I'd never walked into that Halloween shop and that my life had remained simple. I sighed and stuck out my hand, "You must be hungry."

He took my hand immediately but I didn't feel a pull, "Fuck that, Bels - I was-"

"It isn't November and I made a promise. I told you you could have me until November as long as you didn't harvest from anyone else. Have you?"

He dropped his hand and shook his head, "You were gone, Bels. I was getting sick." He looked at me imploringly, "If I go without for too long, I could turn too. If I needed to be able to find her and contain her I couldn't go in weak and risk-"

"That sounds like a lot of excuses to me, Thomas. Did you harvest from someone else instead of coming to me?"

"Annabel, please listen to me and know this - I am sorry. I am sorry that I hurt you. I am sorry that *she* hurt you." He kneeled again between my knees and held my chin in his hand, "It killed me to be

241

parted from you. I didn't want anyone but you but I could feel myself slipping. Bels, I... I think we're-"

"Everything okay out here?" My Mama was leaning against the frame of the solarium and looked between the two of us, "You must be Thomas. I'm Sybil Williams. I've been assigned your family's case."

He frowned, "I'm sorry but you are mistaken, they are not my family, not anymore. The Coalition broke the bond earlier this year. I have no trace or attachment to the Rogue."

I looked between them and furrowed my brow, "You knew? You know? You knew about this whole fucking Coalition and witch thing? Are you fucking kidding me?" I snapped and felt a silence fall over us. I turned to Mama in surprise, but she was muttering something into her mug and fluttering her fingers downward sealing us into a bubble of silence.

"I assume you'd like some privacy for this conversation, darling."

"YOU CAN DO THAT?!" I squeaked, "You can just wiggle-wiggle your fingers and suddenly everything goes quiet? What in the actual fu-"

She just grinned at me, "There's a reason you've never heard your mom and I-"

I shouted, "Ah! If you're about to talk about your sex life you can turn around and go right back inside."

The witch cackled and turned around, "Don't invite him in unless we are keeping him, please."

"I already didn't invite him in, Sybil, you don't need to-" I heard my Mom shouting through the house before my Mama closed the sliding door behind her, muffling the conversation.

The silencing bubble was unnerving. We were outside, and yet the sounds of nature and traffic had disappeared, leaving an unsettling hum in their wake.

"She must trust me not to kill you if she's going to silence us and walk away."

"I think she's more worried about me killing you, you French fuck! You knew I was a witch?"

He jumped and shook his head furiously, *"Non, amour,* I swear to you that I knew you were different and that *we* were different but I had no idea. I didn't even know your mothers were the witches in the area until Yusuf brought it up yesterday."

My lips pursed as a fit of unwelcome jealousy ripped through me and an ugly laugh echoed around the bubble, "Right. It's not just two of you, it's three. And how is Yusuf? Are you guys back together? Ready to cart Monique off to your happily ever after and pretend this all didn't happen?"

"You're kidding with me, right?" He asked dryly.

"No, why would I be joking? You have the opportunity to reunite your family and get out of Quaker's Wharf. You can take her back to Paris and you guys can get a cute little french apartment and start over."

"And what makes you think that any part of me wants that?" He bit, "I've been honest with you from the beginning that I do not wish to reopen that part of my life." He gestured to the door, "I just told your mother that I had the bond broken and have no ties to them."

"So you haven't been spending this last week with Yusuf?"

"Quoi? Non, I....*Oui,* but we have been trying to find Monique before she gets us all killed. There's a limited amount of time to heal an Undead; Yus has to get her back before it's too late and-"

"So, the short answer is 'yes.'"

He growled, "Yes. But he needed my help - she's too strong for him to do it alone and it will be quite the struggle to get her to France with how long she's been hiding."

"My moms can't heal her?"

"Non, chérie."

"So you're going to France."

"Non! Why aren't you listening to me? They're going, I'm staying. I belong here with you, Bels."

I laughed, "Why the fuck would you stay? Our agreement is done in November - frankly, it should be done now. No, you know what? It is done now." Resolve slid into place, coating my heart in cement, "Not only did you feed from someone else, but you didn't help me with my anxiety leading up to the launch. None of our deal was adhered to, so there's no reason to drag this out any longer."

His face flashed through multiple emotions, confusion, sadness, and rage contorting his features all in the blink of an eye. "*Non*."

"Too fucking bad, Frenchie. Deals off." I stood to go back in the house, wanting to escape from the conversation and my impending panic attack from formally ending our arrangement, but he quickly grabbed my hand and smashed through my metal barrier, coursing through my emotions. He tapped into the fear and sadness that I'd been grappling with all week, as well as the hurt and heartbreak that he'd left behind.

"Oh, Bels. *Non*. Listen to me. You're mine. You said... *non*. You belong to me. We belong to each other. You agreed to give this a chance. The deal is not off"

"Get out of my head! You didn't hold up your end of the deal. We're officially divorced, mmk? Go to France, rebuild your family, and leave me alone."

He tightened his grip on me and growled, "You're mine. Annabel. There are things bigger than us in play here. You belong to me. Stop fighting it and let me fix this." He gestured between us, "I fucked up. I made a mistake. I let you hurt me when you said I was the fucking worst and that I was coercing you. I wanted you to want me the way I wanted you and you hurt me so I left. I fucked up by walking away instead of talking to you, but you're fucking up now by making the same mistake."

"Well, I guess we're both fuck ups. It doesn't change anything. There is no reason for you to stay here."

"*Non*, of course not, because you clearly know better than I do on what I want or what the fates have decided is waiting for us."

"I'm the witch here!" I shouted, "You can't pull the paranormal shit on me anymore because I'm just as deep in this as you are!"

"I'm almost 500 years old, Annabel! You have no possible comprehension of the depth I'm at."

"All the more reason for you to fuck off to France and leave me alone, Grandpa."

He released me and shouted in frustration, raking his hands through his hair and pulling at the top of his head, pacing back and forth across the brick patio, "Annabel! Gods dammit you little witch, listen to me!"

"Should I be offended by that?"

"I love you."

I scoffed, "What did you just say?"

The tension eased from his shoulders and he spoke softer, "I love you, Bels. I love waking up with you in the morning. I love feeding Tim and cooking you dinner. I love watching you hum to your plants and pet your books like they're sentient. I love that you are a witch and we can do this now without hurting each other. I love how you feel and how I feel when I'm with you. I love you, Bels. And I wouldn't love you this easily if there weren't bigger players involved."

"Oh, so I'm unlovable unless some vampire goddess tells you I'm worthy?"

"Just...FUCK." He shouted and spun on his heel, then turned back to me and slammed his lips into mine.

One touch of his lips. That's all it took. Just one. My soul calmed and my heart soared. My stomach did the ridiculous flipping sensation that I'd get from driving over a hill too quickly and my brain deflated like a discount whoopee cushion. My hard edges softened in his embrace and I felt his gentle caress in my mind. My resolve faltered. I hurt and he soothed, and I kissed him and he kissed me back, losing the pain of the past week within our passion. I melted into him, allowing him to hold my plush body against him with his inhumane strength and for the first time since I was attacked, I felt safe. I felt whole, just like he'd asked me before, only then I didn't realize that I was missing a piece of myself - it was just a little more complicated than a piece of my elbow.

But I *wasn't* safe. Where he would be, the danger would follow. I couldn't compete with the excitement of 500 years of previous lovers and life. I was a simple green witch with a passion for clothes and books and skulls… I was part of my mothers' line. I would need to stay in Quaker's Wharf and learn to be the witch the Coalition needed me to be, and figure out how to balance all of these new plates I had to spin. The easiest plate to break with the least amount of fallout to the community was the one that held my heart.

I withdrew from his embrace and shakily placed my hands on his chest, gripping and smoothing his threadbare shirt, "You need to leave, Tommy."

He rubbed his hands along my spine and touched his forehead to mine, "I love you. I will go, but I am not leaving. You'll find immortals have incredible patience."

"You can't love me," I whispered, shuddering from his touch.

"I can and I do. This is bigger than us, and I want to know what it is, *mon coeur de sorcière*" He shifted to kiss my forehead and embraced me tighter before I moved away.

"What does that mean?"

He gave me a soft smile, "My witch heart."

I took two large steps back, "Has Yusuf found her yet?"

"*Non*. We don't know where she is. I need you to be safe and stay here with your mothers while we search for her. I will tell you when it's safe." His aura dampened, worry etching across his face.

"You can't declare that I should stay in this house like this was your fucking idea. I'm here because *I* came here, not because you told me to."

"Yes, I know. I'm sure you've seen some kind of show with a vampire hunt in it, yes?"

"If she wants to kill me, she'll get me anyway," I said, pursing my lips.

Thomas sighed and kicked at a weed growing between the bricks, "we already know she wants to hurt you, Bels. Please…don't be reckless."

I looked at the creature in front of me. He was a perfect predator disguised in a slender muscular frame with stupidly shiny brown hair and a touch of scruff. He was exquisite, but it was all a trap. They were all made to be traps, and the little goth girl in me died at the idea of being caged, even if it *was* by a beautiful monster.

"I need you to leave now, Tommy."

He nodded quietly, "*Oui*," he turned and began to walk back to the side gate but stopped abruptly and said, "I will find her and I will keep you safe no matter the cost. I will show you that you are more to me than my past and I will earn your love, *mon coeur*. Do you understand me?"

"Goodbye, Tommy. Thank you for the Raven."

"*Je t'aime* Bels. I'll see you soon."

32
THOMAS

T he sun filtered through her sheer curtains, casting a soft warm glow on her otherwise pale skin. Her violet hair shone pink in a certain light, and when it did, her flush was that much more pronounced, making her all too kissable. Her lips parted slightly while she slept and she'd moan softly, embracing every moment of relaxation she could before she had to wake up for the day and put her unfeeling female mask back on. I could lay beside her and watch her eyes flutter with dreams with her body curved under mine for the rest of my existence. This was not just a deal to lessen her anxiety, it was the beginning of something more. The beast inside of me knew it just as well as I did, and neither of us had any interest in ending this arrangement in November.

I tilted my head down and placed a trail of soft kisses down her exquisite back, tracing her shoulders with my finger.

"Amour, it's time to start another day," I spoke into her skin, knowing that being the first sound she heard in the morning was a gift. I wanted to be the first and last thing she heard or saw every day. I wanted to be that constant for her. Fuck, I hardly knew the woman, but she felt like a perfect Autumn day. She was just right - just perfectly right.

She groaned and stretched, uncurling her legs from where they were against mine, and rolled slightly to face me, "hey, you."

"Bonjour," I smiled and leaned in to brush my mouth against hers and was rewarded with her turning fully, her warmth pressing into me and molding to my form. She hummed against my lips and withdrew from me with a smile.

"I think it's kind of a rip-off that I'm dating a vampire and yet you're a morning person. That's dumb on so many levels."

I chuckled, squeezing her closer to me in an embrace that brought my nose into her neck allowing me to inhale her intoxicating ginger and citrus fragrance. My fingers flexed into the soft flesh of her hips, grinding my pelvis against her, "I could do this every morning," I admitted.

"Do what? Cause so far you haven't done anything."

"Oh really?" I laughed, dragging my teeth along the column of her throat, and she elongated herself like a cat stretching in the sun, "should I stop then, mon coeur*?"*

"Fuck you." I felt her grin. I felt the affection in her words, despite their meaning.

"Gladly." I pressed one more kiss to her throat and then rolled over so she sat astride me, my length pressing against her heat. Nothing was separating us in the mornings - we'd lose our clothes throughout the night, worshipping each other's bodies until we collapsed, sleeping in the nude.

She squealed, pressing down into me, "if it's time to start our day, what makes you think I possibly have time to fuck you and make coffee? Don't you think the coffee is more important?"

I scoffed, "Oh, coffee is more important than me? Merde, Bels, that's great for my confidence."

"Shush, Frenchie. Let me enjoy this." she slid down my body, dragging her breasts against my skin with a mischievous grin, and throwing her long hair over her shoulder, "They say it's the best way to wake up in the morning."

"I'm not going to argue with that, amour."

She took my length in her hand, pumping it slowly, before she leaned in and pulled her tongue along the underside, tracing the vein upward with her stunning green eyes locked on mine.

"Fuck, you're beautiful," I groaned, finger-combing her hair into my hand, wrapping it twice around my wrist, "you're perfect."

She flashed me one more smile before she tilted her head and took me between her lips, fluttering her tongue against me, and pressing me along the roof of her mouth. I groaned, moving my other hand to her head as well, and sat up slightly to watch Bels take my cock into her throat. "Merde, just like that." I hissed, feeling the walls of her throat close on me, tightening the channel and forcing me back out. She gasped, a trail of saliva connecting us as she withdrew, and then she dove again, hollowing her cheeks and devouring me in a seemingly effortless way that drove me insane. She drew her hand down, dragging it through her labia, collecting her desire, and began rubbing it into her clit, jumping slightly at the stimulation which only shoved me further into her throat, almost causing her to gag.

"Fuck, more, just like that, beautiful. Look at how good you are taking me, love, look at you."

She moaned at my words sending vibrations through my body, coiling my desire tighter inside of me. "You keep up like that and I'm going to cum in your mouth, Bels." She hummed in approval again and I began to fuck her face slowly, holding her head still, and taking her mouth for my pleasure. I chased it, feeling it tighten, feeling lost in her warmth until a jolt of pleasure came from behind. Her cream-covered finger explored my ass, probing inside of it and making me see stars, curling her digit toward her as if she was beckoning my orgasm to come this way.

She withdrew her mouth, licking it leisurely, "is this okay?" she asked softly, curling her finger inside of me again.

"Fuck, yes it is. Fuck." I groaned, pulling her mouth back onto my length and tilting my hips to allow her better access. She pushed her finger in more before slowly adding a second and scissoring them apart, all while taking me down her throat to the hilt. My body ratcheted up a never ending roller coaster, my mind warning me that when this crested it would be the climax of a lifetime.

She pressed into me once more, firmly milking me with her two fingers before I exploded, holding her face against my pelvis, shooting my cum down her eager throat, pulsing and grunting as if I'd never orgasmed before.

"Fucking hell, Annabel!" I growled and released her and she pulled up my length taking ragged breaths, oh so fucking slow as she withdrew her fingers from my ass. She grinned and kissed the inside of my thigh.

"Now that we've gotten that out of the way, I need to get to work," She patted my hip playfully, "and you get to go make me my coffee."

Groaning, I lay in the bed like I'd melted into it, "anything for you, my love."

"Then you should probably go get me a castle while you're at it, Dracula."

I laughed and chucked a pillow at her naked body causing her to squeal as she ran away to take her shower.

Every morning. I wanted this every morning.

"Evening, love."

My eyes fluttered open from my nap to see black, not green staring back at me, "when are you going to find her and get the fuck out of here?" I growled at Yusuf, closing my eyes and begging the powers that be to bring naked Annabel back to my dreams.

"As soon as you help me do it." He grumbled, rising from my air mattress and throwing a set of clothes at me, "you know if you'd let me stay here we could work later and start earlier."

I huffed, opened my eyes, and glared at him, "Yeah, when hell freezes over Yus. I see Bels handling me sharing a bed with my ex-husband so well, don't you?" Rolling off the mattress I stretched fully, shaking into my raven to fly across the store to the empty bathroom. Some tensions needed to be worked out that were best not suited for company. Every day without Annabel was torture. It was torture in the purely romantic way of missing and craving her at all hours of the day, but it was also torture because I'd never had to exist in a permanent state of unquenchable desire before this. I needed her. I could stroke my cock for three days straight and it still wouldn't free me from the need to get my hands on and inside of Bels.

I knew I was being a cranky bastard, but it felt like every moment I was apart from her someone was tightening a wire slightly more, digging it into my skin. My longing for her was leaving thousands of microscopic cuts on my body that couldn't heal without her near. The pain of our separation only confirmed Yusuf's suspicions that she and I were fated, as he was experiencing the same level of distress being apart from Monique despite them being Handfeasted and us not. Needless to say, he and I were not enjoying each other's company.

He was running me into the ground between operating the shop, looking for Monique, and the time I spent circling the Williams family home. Monique had hurt Bels once, I wasn't going to let her do it again on my watch, regardless of how Annabel had refused to see me again after we spoke in the backyard. I didn't need to talk to her to protect her, and as soon as it was safe, I was bringing her home. We could speak then.

The calendar inched closer to Halloween, and with that came its own set of problems. Not only was the store packed with customers daily, much to Yus' satisfaction - he was quite well fed in my company - but the attention it would garner if Monique was out on such a public night would be catastrophic. Halloween is considered in many circles to be the Other's night off, as everyone keeps off the street to avoid the mayhem of all the mortals' tacky celebrations. However, with Monique going slowly insane, it was a genuine concern that if we couldn't get her to France by then, she would run rampant through the streets of Quaker's Wharf, drinking and murdering her way through town in an attempt to satiate her bloodlust. Such a blatant disregard for the rules would only result in Sybil and Deirdre having to call in the Coalition, and they would divide and relocate all the Others in the area until the mortals' memory of the massacre faded.

I wasn't going anywhere, and I wasn't going to let the Coalition move me away from Annabel. If that meant that as the guardian of the Williams line she was stuck in this region for the rest of her life, I would be there right alongside her. Us, the cat, and our cooking shows. We would read in the rain, take glass-blowing classes, and cook ridiculously extravagant food for only one person to eat. We would go out on Friday nights with her friends and spend Saturday mornings in bed. I would get us back to that even if I had to personally murder every Other in the Boston area to prevent the Coalition from stepping in. No one was taking her away from me. The idea of anyone separating us made the beast within me snarl and slam against the cage it was so tenuously trapped within and frankly, I'd happily unleash him if they tried to touch her.

I took my time walking back to where Yusuf was waiting, not wanting to spend a moment more with him than I had to. If my fated's safety wasn't at risk, I would have washed my hands of them long ago, instead, I was spending every free moment sniffing around Quaker's Wharf for a hint of licorice that was getting less traceable by the day.

"What if she's moved on?" I asked loudly, walking back into my living area.

"Why would she do that? She said she wanted us to be together, if she left she wouldn't have a chance in doing that."

I shrugged, "I don't know Yus, she isn't well. Maybe she went back to the house in Boston? She could hide out there, it would be easier for her to feed and it would give it time for things to cool down here. If she wanted us together, why hasn't she come back to us?"

He leaned into the mini fridge, grabbing two bags of blood and tossing one toward me, "I suppose. Though, if she thought she'd killed or changed your Annabel, wouldn't she have wanted to stay close to watch the drama play out?"

"Unless she's worried I'd kill her for it."

"Which you would."

"I would." I agreed solemnly, ripping a small corner off the bag and drinking directly from the package, "It would be done in a heartbeat, Yusuf. If she hurts Bels my statement still stands."

He groaned, dumping his bag's contents into a foam cup which he attached a lid to and stabbed with a straw, "I'm aware. You've made it very clear that your allegiance isn't with her," He took a sip and paused in thought, "though who knows, maybe at this point that would be the best choice. How long do we let this chase go on until we tell the witches we need help?"

"There's no rule saying she can't be Undead, Yus, she just would need to find a coven and get her shit together. They won't kill her if she can remain in the shadows and follow protocol."

"But, I ...we..."

"Yes. You'd need to break your bond. Unless you're itching to meet the same fate. Is she worth losing yourself for?"

"I always thought I'd answer yes immediately to that question, but now? I don't know. Maybe I should just find myself a nice plump witch and settle down." His grin was teasing, knowing full well that a vampire and a witch were an unusual pairing.

I growled, "find your own witch, friend. I will not share mine."

Tisking playfully, he winked, "and to think, you used to share so well, love." He pulled out his phone and cursed under his breath, "we need to head out, the sun went down an hour ago."

It was a cycle. Hunt all night with Yus, sit in the tree outside of the Williams' home at dawn and dusk, work the shop, and try to find time to eat and sleep. I didn't know how much longer we could keep up the pace we were running at. Frankly, I didn't know how much longer I'd care before I'd turn her in to be added to the Undead rosters and send Yus to Paris to get his bond broken so he could move on with his life. I needed to focus on the important things, the most important being getting back to the point where I could wake up to Annabel's eyes instead of my ex-husband's. The sooner he was gone, the faster my heart could heal.

33
ANNABEL

The fall launch had sold out and I'd had positively nothing to do with it. It should have made me feel successful, but instead, it made me feel inconsequential to my brand. I'd hired some college kids to go help Shannon pack and ship orders while I "convalesced" at my mothers' house, but I was losing my mind from being so absent from work. With some witchy help, I'd been healed for over a week but Mama insisted there was a "rule" for sake of appearances that I had to remain at home to have proper time to heal from my "mugging." Knowing that I was perfectly fine, and yet be stuck hiding and reading plant books at my mommy's was enough to make me climb the walls. I wanted to get back out there. I wanted my life back. The fact that Monique had stolen any semblance of normalcy from me made me want to stake the bitch myself, though, again, know it all Mama had "rules" about that too - this one stating that I would have an absurd amount of paperwork if I killed someone in my jurisdiction without prior authorization or use of an approved hunter. So bossy.

Bossiness must have been genetic because I was annoying myself with how much micromanaging I wanted to do while away from

HalloQueens. I'd gotten Shannon to recycle some of my old videos as well as posting a few explaining that posting would be sporadic as I'd been assaulted, but that orders would be shipping out at a regular pace, but she was hesitant to put her face on the social media pages, even just to release statements, and our pages had gone stagnant as a result. I had tried to convince her on a video call that it was the perfect time for her to step into the role of thirst trap marketer, but she turned white as a ghost and hung up with the excuse that one of her girls needed her. There was apparently a rumor going around that I'd been assaulted by an internet stalker, which resulted in many people reaching out to tell me about how I needed to be safer online and how I needed to practice more discretion when posting about my body. After all, it was the tempting videos of myself that I posted that were tempting stalkers to act out. Cause that was a subtle slut shame if I'd ever heard one.

Despite having to pay a staff to handle to launch for me, I still managed to turn a sizable profit, which had my Mom all excited about how I could step back, maintain my role as "CEO" and divert my attention to the Coalition. I supposed I could, but I wasn't even 30. The idea of going hands-off seemed impossible and irresponsible, so that led me out the second week of October to reclaim my life and my brand.

Bringing in the new staff had already complicated Shannon's life during the launch and she was flustered by having to train the four temps on our shipping procedures while basically running the back end by herself. Apparently mailing packages in an aesthetically pleasing way was a hard thing for a few of them to understand and she wanted to rip her hair out. She needed me back just as badly as I needed to get out of the house.

"You shouldn't be going anywhere until this is taken care of." My mom scolded me like a child while I packed up the things I'd been keeping at her place. I wanted my life back, I wanted to go home and I wasn't about to hide out at my parents' house for the rest of my life. And I missed my cat! Besides, Monique couldn't come out during the day, and I was a motherfucking witch - that should mean something to the supposed flocks of Others that would be seeking me out. The attack of a green witch had drawn some attention and I had no more fucks to give. If anyone had the audacity to touch me again the hammer was going to be laid down.

What I wasn't going to tell my mothers was that from the very moment I left their front door until I got to my office, I could feel eyes drilling holes into the back of my head. I sat in my Jeep for a few moments after parking, assessing the area around my office, seeing if I could sight any danger that I might be in, but I ended up chickening out and texting Shannon and asking if she'd come walk me inside. Thankfully her mother-hen tendencies were perfect for the job.

"Thank you for just admitting you were uncomfortable instead of trying to brave through it," She said, opening my car door and hugging me before I could even exit the vehicle.

"I'm fine. I swear. God, you look great!" Shannon had the world's most impeccable pear-shaped body, which was only exacerbated by her hips widening more during her pregnancies. You could tell that the axe handle across her ass bothered her a bit, but I thought it was the most amazing body shape I'd ever seen. She had slender shoulders and perfect mid-sized breasts with a flat feminine stomach and ass and thighs for days. Seriously, her thighs were so delicious looking I frequently wanted to chew on them like a drumstick. Having the girls totally messed up her confidence and in a last-ditch effort to turn my absence into a positive and for her to reclaim her sexuality, I suggested again that she shake out her frustrations on film while I "healed". She suggested that I kindly go fuck myself. I wished I could just tell her I'd gotten bit by a vampire and she should be proud of her body and show it off everywhere without fear of a stalker. It was a showstopper.

"You look better than I was expecting." She said, assessing me from top to bottom. She looked around my car and got a glint in her eye. "Dude, did you ever actually try this on?" She quickly lifted her loose green crop top to show me the black sheer bra that was covered in small mesh bats and I squealed, not caring that we were in the fucking parking lot.

"Oh my god, that looks so good! Did it-"

"Yep, sold out. But I put one aside for you once I saw it on me, I knew you'd want one too."

"Goddess bless you, dear one. Gosh, I love your boobs. I wish mine were tiny like that."

She cackled, "They're still D cups, it's not like I'm on the itty bitty titty committee."

I gestured at my enormous chest and arched a brow at her, "comparatively? I think if I got a reduction they wouldn't let me go any smaller than where you're at now."

Taking my hand and pulling me out of the Jeep to walk inside she grinned, "well, don't get a reduction. That would be a crime - I'll tell you once your back starts curving and you need to take care of them. Just wait until you're done having kids cause let me tell ya, kids are brutal on the boobies. We opened the door to the suite as she cupped and lifted her chest musing "19" before releasing them and watching them fall and spread, "29." She repeated the process, lifting and dropping her breasts until I thought I was going to pee myself from laughing.

"There. Now you're inside." She stopped fondling herself, smiled softly, and hugged me.

"Did you really just distract me with boobies to help me through the parking lot?"

"It worked, didn't it? Don't question the method if the results are what you needed."

"You're the best friend I could ever ask for."

"Doesn't sexual harassment exist in this place?" A strange male voice muttered and my head shot up. The college kids, Matteo, Nevaeh, June, and David were huddled around a computer that Shannon had set up specifically for printing and viewing orders as she was growing murderous with how often they were looking over her shoulder to have her print out packing slips.

"Not when you're the bosses and you're harassing each other. Guys, this is Annabel, the owner of HalloQueens, and she's in to work with us today. I expect you all to show her just how helpful you've been around here." Shannon's boss voice was stunning. Firm and commanding, yet soft enough that they'd approach her if they needed her - like she managed two small children daily or something. The new staff smiled and waved at me before disappearing into the stock room with stacks of empty buckets to pack up orders.

"How has that been working out?" I asked out the side of my mouth, watching them smile and joke with each other while the printer spits out slip after slip.

"It's been amazing, come look." She led me to the stock room after the staff and I gasped at the amount, or rather the lack of, boxes lining the space.

"Holy shit - we need to order more inventory."

Shannon nodded and beamed, "we've been working very hard to make sure you had the time you needed to heal from your ordeal. I've already talked to them all about staying on for the Christmas rush and two of them are locals and said they'd be happy to help over winter break, the others would be traveling home to see their families."

"Well, I can't be mad at that. If the added bodies are increasing productivity enough to reflect it in sales I'm happy to keep people on." We headed back to our desks and I plopped into my pink chair, turning on my computer for what felt like the first time in ages.

"My moms want me to go more hands-off with the boutique," I grumbled, rotating my chair to look at her.

"How do you feel about that?" She asked, reawakening her screen.

"Well... we'll see, I'm not quite sure how I feel about it right now." I knew rationally that the eventual goal of all business owners was to reach a point of success where they got to step back and let the brand run itself, but it was hard to wrap my head around the idea when it was all balanced precariously on a few seven-second movies of my ass.

"Lose yourself in finding some new product babe, do the stuff that brings you joy and we'll handle the rest until you're ready to decide what you want moving forward."

"I don't deserve you," I sang at her.

"I know," she sang back, "Which is why you're coming out with me on Thursday."

"Ugh, I don't know how I feel about third wheeling with you and Trae."

"What about Thomas? Didn't he-"

"Shannon? Can you help me find this belt?" One of the kids hollered and Shannon gave me an apologetic smile before getting up to head back to them.

I spent the day half beginning the curation of next Spring's collection and half daydreaming about how I would spend time if I didn't have to work so damn hard for everything I had. If I stepped back from HalloQueens and focused on marketing and curating, I would have way more time in my day. Time in which I could learn how to be the best fucking green witch I could be. Mom said she managed to blow up that bonsai tree in elementary school. I had so much to catch up on, so many trees to explode.

Could we travel? Could I go to Paris and meet the Coalition and learn more about my place in this world? Could I learn from other witches and then go back to where we were staying to a perfectly cooked dinner and a sarcastic man in a frilly apron?

Every vision I dreamed up included Thomas by my side. It was infuriating. Yes, he had come to my moms' and apologized but it wasn't safe to be with him. It wasn't smart to be with him. It wasn't logical to be with him. And yet my mind fixated on the magic we created when we streamed energy between us. Now that I knew magic was a thing, I knew that the current of emotions that we could channel between each other was not normal, nor was it something we should take for granted. It was a gift from the goddesses. To imagine a life where I not only had to be dishonest about who I was but also had to live with the weight of the anxiety that I'd been shouldering...maybe he was supposed to be mine so we could work together and make the world a better place for the Others I would be responsible for.

Thomas could help me. He could make me stronger. I could learn from his past and he could, if nothing else, teach me the French I'd need to speak to the coalition. I snorted at the thought of Thomas getting progressively more irate at my butchering of his native tongue. Making the vampire angry didn't scare me; it aroused me - an alarming amount. It was a far more appealing future than marrying Gary from accounting and having to hide my midnight margaritas for the rest of my life. I bet Thomas could learn to make a bitchin' margarita.

"Earth to Bels! You've been staring at your screen for like ten minutes on the same piece of underwear, and frankly, emerald green lace isn't that exciting." Shannon smirked, rotating back and forth on her chair.

"Shit, sorry, I was just thinking-"

"You were thinking about the sexy Frenchman that you've been stupidly ignoring for weeks?"

"Yeah." I groaned, scratching my scalp where my space buns were pulling, "just...do you ever imagine what your happily ever after would look like? Like... does it ever taunt you from behind this curtain, showing you just enough details to desire it but not enough to feel confident in your decision?"

She scoffed, "Bels, I've known you for a decade, you're never sure about anything outside of your work. But, yeah, I think about what it could be, or what I want it to be. It's changed a lot over the years. I had thought that it was Jake. I wouldn't have married the prick and had our girls if I had ever thought he wasn't the endgame. I'd imagined us growing old and watching the water on rocking chairs on a cabin's porch, and having loads more kids and grandkids. I thought we'd be the family that was so huge and full of life that the amount of love we created was enough to power the rest of our lives. Like, if we loved hard enough we could get through any amount of bullshit the day would throw at us as long as we got to tumble into bed together at the end of the night. Now we fight about socks and I feel like I spend all my time undoing the shit he's doing with the girls. I'm on crying kid duty until I'm able to let my hair down when they're gone, and then I feel guilty about going out when I miss them so much."

I frowned at her, "Babe, you don't have to feel guilty for having a life outside of them."

With a shrug and a sigh, she continued, "I know. I'm just saying Happily Ever After can look different in different stages of our lives. Now I'd settle for a burly dude that's an ass man with a soft spot for little girls and a love of nature. That sounds nice to me. But, if my happily ever after doesn't even include a guy, I don't care either. I can have a happy and successful life without one, you know?"

"You just don't want it to," I smiled softly.

"Yeah, I don't want it to." She hit a few more keys on her computer and the screen went blank. "Okay guys, quitting time! Let's get out of here."

The new employees came out of the storeroom laughing and leaning into each other and waved to us on their way to their cars as Shan and I locked up.

"Ugh, it's so dark. When is daylight savings starting?" She grumbled, fiddling with her keys to locate the one for her car.

"Not for a few weeks, but don't worry, Winter will be here soon and then it will be dark at 4 pm every night anyway. Yay for seasonal depression!" I spun around in the damp parking lot, fall showers making the asphalt shimmer under the roadside lights. In a few weeks, Quaker's Wharf had gone from too hot to handle to the perfect setting for a spooky movie with dark streets, a near-constant drizzle, and the leaves falling all around.

"Not helpful, Bels." She leaned against her car door, jumping back and touching her now wet clothes with a grimace, then gave me a concerned look, "I know I'm a mother hen, but are you going to be okay? You can talk to me, you know that, right? I'm here for you."

"I know, and I love you for it, but don't worry about me, my mind is just in a million places at once."

"I don't want to overstep, but you were so much calmer and more at peace when you were seeing Thomas regularly."

"That was like a week, you can't formulate an opinion of my life with a week's worth of evidence," I grumbled.

She put her hands up in surrender and then opened her car door, sitting inside the small sedan, "I'm just saying, time doesn't mean shit when it's your Happily Ever After."

"And you think mine is Thomas?"

She shrugged, turning her engine over, "I'm not saying it's not. I'm saying I think you should go home, drink a couple of glasses of wine and then let the poor guy apologize again while he licks you to at least four orgasms."

I cackled, "You're too much. I love you, I'll see you tomorrow."

I drove to my rental in silence. The rain had started again during the short drive and visibility was low, making me more cautious than usual and I white-knuckled my steering wheel. It may not have been exclusively the rain making me anxious. I hadn't been here since the attack, and while I was itching to take back my normalcy, I was scared. I was scared enough that I circled my block half a dozen times in hopes of finding a parking spot closer to my house than the spot five blocks away that was sitting free. The world was so still. The moon was hidden and the trees were darkened by the autumn rain; it was dark out and even the idea of walking the few blocks home made me pick my cuticles and reach for my phone when I pulled into the spot five blocks away. It was too far to go in the dark. It was too far to go in the rain. It was...it was scary. I should just call him. I could call him and he'd walk me home, no questions asked. Swallow my pride and call the man. My stubbornness wasn't worth dying in the street for. I was scared and he could fix it. The simplistic word, "scared" felt wrong and it was coated with rage that that awful female had ruined my illusion of safety in the world. A film reel of all the different ways I could end up in the hospital again in the distance between my car and house tormented me while I tried to lose myself in the rhythm of the rain-drops hitting my car so I could psyche myself up, messing with the finger support on the back of my case while I tried to grow the balls to call my bodyguard.

My passenger door opening had me screaming and jumping out of my skin and a hand clamped over my mouth. Grabbing my heart, feeling as though it was going to explode out of my chest, I ripped the hand off with my other. Tears immediately began pouring from my eyes, as though my emotions had been waiting for my facade to crack.

"Fucking hell, Thomas, you scared the shit out of me! Don't sneak up on me like that! You almost gave me a heart attack." I took deep, unsteady breaths, trying to soothe myself, when he cupped my cheek, wiping my tears, and I felt his tender caress in my mind, slowing my heart and regulating my breathing. "What are you doing here?"

"I'm sorry, amour, I didn't mean to frighten you. I didn't want you walking to your door alone."

I flopped my head against the headrest, looking sideways at him. "How did you even know where I was?"

"Don't ask me questions you don't want to know the answer to, Bels." I glared at him and he weakly added, wiping another tear from my face, "I've been keeping an eye on you when the sun goes down. I never intended to invade your space, I just wanted to make sure you were safe and I swear I'll stop once we find her but-"

Practically jumping over the center console, I grabbed his shirt and pressed my lips to his. He hesitated at the crazy woman throwing herself at him, but quickly melted, bringing his strong hand behind my head and pulling me into his body.

"Thank you. I was...thank you for keeping me safe. Thank you for knowing what I need without having to ask." My phone had been in my hand about to call him to walk me into my house, and he had been there the whole time. Every time I'd been scared of the world since he'd met me, he'd been there to watch me. I could pretend to be indignant and angry that he was stalking me, but all I felt was relief, and I wasn't going to push him away pretending to be anything but grateful.

He softly kissed the side of my mouth again and smiled, stroking my arm lovingly, "Can I drop you off at your house and park the car?

The rain isn't going to let up. I can take you home and make you some soup."

That made me laugh, "I haven't been home in over a week, I'm sure all the food is bad."

He blushed and reached between his legs to pick up a grocery bag that smelled deliciously of basil, "Tomato soup and grilled cheese? Seemed like something you'd enjoy on a rainy evening. I'm not above earning your forgiveness with food. I'll cook for you forever."

I nodded, "so you never intended to invade my space, but you have groceries?"

Thomas shrugged, "It's just soup, I figured even you would be able to handle reheating a can if you wouldn't let me in. But, *oui*, I did bring a few extravagant things purely out of optimism. One of those being a microwave lava cake that I thought sounded fascinating in the store, and a teenager alarmingly overshared that they were her favorite on her period, so I knew it had to be good. The teenagers nowadays have no filter - it's very odd - but also, period-approved lava cake? That can only be a good thing, *oui*?"

I smiled and nodded, "switch spots with me."

He jumped out of the car and ran around to the driver's side while I climbed into the passenger seat and he pulled us back onto the slippery road to go back to my house.

"Annabel, I am sorry. You know that, right? I am sorry that I didn't communicate and-"

"It's okay. It's okay, Tommy" I repeated, grabbing his hand and drawing circles on it with my thumb, "it's not a coincidence that I feel more comfortable now than I have all week. You're my walking, talking, Xanax and I've missed you. You make me feel better." It was true, my anxiety had all but disappeared. I was aware, I knew that someone out in the world wanted to hurt me, but I trusted that with him by my side he wouldn't let me die. He wouldn't let her bleed me dry. "I sincerely hope that you're not just sucking all my emotions away to make me tolerate you, but I do appreciate your calming effect."

He shook his head, "I can't manipulate our desire for each other,

I've told you this from the beginning. And after reflecting and dealing with this bullshit, I promise you to never take away your anger or manipulate my way out of an argument with you. We will communicate, be it with words or our bodies, but I will not have us shoving shit under the carpet and ignoring it while it grows into something unfixable. I'm not letting miscommunication take you away again."

"That's a very nice, if not unbelievable statement."

"We are a work in progress Bels. Let me cook you dinner while you shower and warm up and then we will talk, *oui*?" He slowed the car to a stop outside of my building.

"*Oui.*"

He arched a brow, "are you speaking french now?"

I shrugged and reached for the door handle, "I am apparently a French guardian of monsters so I should probably try to learn."

Thomas' dark eyes turned molten, "I can teach you all kinds of dirty French things to whisper to me in the dark."

Before he could elaborate more, I grinned and jumped out of the jeep, heading up to my darkened stoop, unlocking the door and darting inside, kicking off my wet shoes and leaning to the wall to turn the chandelier on. My heart warmed seeing my place, even with the boxes in the corners and the new dust bunnies. "Tim?" I called, walking into the living room in my socks, happy to see my trinkets and fuzzy blankets. I couldn't wait to curl up with one and an awful harlequin romances I'd gotten at a garage sale. It felt like I had come home, and it hadn't felt like that before I'd spent time away from it. "Tim!" I called again, walking through the dining area and into the kitchen, plopping down my purse on the island, making kissy noises, and searching for him. His bowl was full, and I thought he would come running at the sound of my voice, but I couldn't find him.

I headed to the stairs, continuing to make noises for him to come find me, thinking maybe he'd fallen asleep or accidentally locked himself in one of the bedrooms. "Where are you, baby? Mommy's home!" Sure enough, at the top of the stairs, the bathroom door was shut and I could hear the sound of his soft paws against the door, asking to be let out. I opened it and smiled, but he immediately sprinted off down the stairs instead of stopping to talk to me, "how long were you locked in there, Timmy?" I poked my head inside and was thankful not to find a giant mess of cat poop I'd have to clean up, but I'd never known him to get locked in somewhere before. Maybe Shannon had put him in there so she'd be able to find him?

The wind blew harder outside, and rain pelted the antique windows. The lights flickered and I frowned, walking toward my room to strip out of the wet clothes so I could get back downstairs so I could find my box of emergency supplies before Thomas got back and needed to be reinvited inside and the power went out.

Peeling the wet clothes off me and tossing them into the hamper, I grabbed my "widow's robe", which was floor-length silk with black fur around the neck and wrists. It was luxurious and I'd paid too much for it, but it did make me feel like I'd gotten away with killing my cheating millionaire husband, so it was worth the expense for the boost in my confidence. I took my space buns down, jumping slightly when a crack of lightning flashed outside the large window in my room.

"Easy, Bels, chill out," I muttered to myself, starting to brush out the wavy mess of purple hair in front of the mirror on my dresser.

"They say that prey instincts exist to help creatures survive. Humans are not the apex predator so you poor things still jump, or feel nervous or get a sick feeling when you know you are unsafe. And you, my darling, are definitely unsafe."

Her voice froze my blood. I could feel each cell solidifying and stopping in their tracks. I saw her then, leaning against my doorframe in my mirror. She was so pale she was almost green. She looked gaunt and the black bags hanging from her crimson eyes amplified the fact that this was a rabid animal. This creature was dangerous, and she, sadly, was my lover's ex-wife.

I spun around, facing her, and assessed her, the only thing that still appeared like Monique was her white hair and ridiculously long legs wrapped in perfect skinny jeans. Even her nails had turned yellow and sharpened.

267

"Well, howdy friend. Uh...you're not supposed to be in here." I reached behind me hoping to reach my phone without drawing too much attention. "I cleansed the space while you were here and I uninvited you....you... you need to leave."

She snarled, exposing red gums and stark white pointed teeth, "You think uninviting me can keep me out of your pathetic excuse of a home? I can do whatever I please!" She took a few steps into my room and assessed it, "Do you have any idea how boring it has been waiting for you to come home, though? You took your time, my sweet. I will admit that I was quite saddened to learn that you were not, in fact, dead, or undead, as it may be."

"Well...life's a bitch. You didn't bring the right weapon to the fight. I'm apparently not susceptible to the bitey-bitey." I glanced around her. Could I get to the stairs before Thomas needed an invitation inside? The cleansing must not have worked on her since she was in the house while I was simmering it. My mind raced trying to do the math and weigh the risks and rewards of running away from a rabid vampire. "I don't know if you've heard," I continued, edging along my wall as she began picking balls off my string of pearls plant, making me see red, "Hey! Hands off the plants, Mo-Mo. You want to kill me, not my plants. Don't hurt them because you sucked at your job."

She looked at me like a sullen cat and knocked the pot off the window ledge, sending it to the ground and smashing the pot.

"Wow! Okay, so that was rude. If I wasn't going to tell the Coalition how crazy you were before this, I definitely am now that you're fucking with a green witch's plants. God, how sick are you? Who hurts succulents?! They're fucking succulents!"

She bared her fangs again and picked up my fiddle fig propagation, tossing it and catching it repeatedly in one hand.

"Dude, not my fiddle! You know how touchy those things are? That one is just a baby and its mom has gone to rehab with my Mom three times already. Put it down and we can talk."

She smirked, then hurled it in my direction in a flash, giving me only a moment to scream and duck before the ceramic pot shattered against the wall behind me.

"Jesus Christ, you crazy bitch! What the fuck is wrong with you?!"

One after another she picked up plants and threw them at me, one of the larger plants hitting me on the hip as I turned to run to the stairs. I was less than ten feet from them, tears in my eyes at the abuse of my poor babies and screamed when a burning sensation clawed into my spine and I was spun and smashed into the solid wood banister. She withdrew her hand from behind my back, licking the flood off her knife-like nails.

"You are positively terrifying, do you know that?"

"And you are a disgusting slutty little bitch, are you not? You have tried to steal my Thomas from me and I need him. I need him and Yusuf to come home so we can fix everything, and so I will get better. I can not get better if they don't return home, and if I must kill you to convince him to do so, I will do it with a smile on my face."

"One, I'm a witch, not a bitch, Two, I'm 99.9% sure that if you kill me, Thomas would be hella pissed. I don't think he'd be ready to play house with you if you murdered his Untouchable."

She hissed and jumped back, "No! You are not bonded! He would not have bonded with a mortal like you!" She tilted her head back slightly, eyes and nostrils widening as she tried to scent me for a bond, a grinch-like grin slipped into place, "You do not smell of his blood - you are not Handfeasted. He is mine, he would never bond with another."

"Yeah, that's not what he said. He said he specifically broke your bond because you walked out on him." I tried to run down the first few steps, I didn't know why I was antagonizing her, but I'd remembered from my crime shows that I needed to keep her talking. The more she talked, the more time I bought myself and the more likely I was to get out of here safely. If superhero movies taught me anything, it was that I just needed to get her monologing.

"He is coming home with me!" She snarled, grabbing for my hair and getting just enough of it to make me fall and slam my back into the top three stairs.

"Fuck! You have totally lost your marbles! Do you know who I am? I am the Coalition Green Witch! If you kill me they are going to come find you and you will die, Monique. No more chances. You kill the only heir to the Williams witch line and they will fuck you up!"

Her eyes widened and she leaned over me, close enough that I could smell the rotting flesh coming from her.

"God you're like the creepy gatekeeper in Mordor! Brush your fucking teeth, bitch." I shoved the heel of my palm upward, smashing it into her nose and causing a spray of greenish-black fluid to hit the wall of the stairwell. She howled in pain and I ran the rest of the way down the stairs, flinging the front door open and screaming, "Thomas!" as I ran back to the kitchen to grab my purse, knowing that my Mama had put some holy water inside of it along with a few other "helpful" things.

Monique jumped clean over the railing, landing without a sound, blood like slime gushing down her face and her snarl exposing the red stain on her fangs. She had turned into a creature too quickly for me to comprehend. She'd looked sick at the beach, but she certainly hadn't been this hunched, growling animal thing - that would have been a dead giveaway to not socialize with her when she appeared that night.

"I will enjoy giving him your neck, little witch." She swiped the top of the credenza in the hallway and ripped the lamp from the socket, smashing the glass against the wall, "And since biting you doesn't seem to do the trick, I think I'll have to remove it entirely."

Lightning flashed again and Thomas appeared in the door, paralyzed as he assessed the chaos and destruction around us.

"Darling! Your ex is here!" I squeaked, "And, uh, she isn't happy with me. Could you please come in and escort her off the premises? Please?"

He sniffed the air, "You're bleeding *amour* - have you been bitten?" He inched into the house like he was approaching a skittish horse.

I shook my head, my body giving into the adrenaline and beginning to tremble as I held onto the butcher block, knowing that she could close the distance between her and me in a moment, regardless of the length of hallway and cabinetry between us. "No, she cut my back, I'm okay. No bites."

He nodded, taking another few steps toward her, "Monique, love, you need to come with me, Yusuf is looking for you."

She snarled at him, "This disgusting mortal claimed herself as your Untouchable! You belong to me."

"*Oui*, my love," he soothed, glancing at me again to ensure that I was intact, "I am yours. You know how ridiculous mortals can be. Let's go find Yusuf and go home, *oui*? Let's go help you get better."

"Kill the witch and I will go with you! You kill her and show me your loyalty, or I will kill her to show you how much it hurts to lose someone you love!"

He was almost within grabbing distance of her, "I know exactly how that feels, Mo. Remember? I am the one that woke up alone in our home one morning. Let's leave the simple witch be and go find Yus. You did well getting the house back, so let's go home." He put his arms out as if to beckon her into his arms.

She glanced between the two of us and even though I knew he was lying, it still hurt. He loved *me*. I could feel it in his gaze, his touch. I knew it, through all the bullshit and all the hurt and all the complicated circumstances. He loved me. The fact that should have been reassuring, broke me as I knew he would give his heart back to her for my safety. I whimpered at the idea he would sacrifice our happiness for my life.

I shifted against the counter and his eyes shifted to me, imploring for me to work with him, "Tommy?" I spoke softly, following his lead, "Tommy, I think you two should go. I can call Yusuf for you and have him meet you at the store."

"That is a great idea. I need you to call Yusuf. Do you hear that Monique? We will go meet Yus and go home. Come on, love, take my hand."

She flinched, some part inside of her fighting against her bloodlust.

Some part of her was still in there and she shook her head as if to clear an argument inside of her that no one else could hear. "Kill her, or I will kill her, Thomas. Show me your love." He looked at me pleadingly, and I nodded, glancing at my back door, wondering if I could get it unlocked and get around the house to the street in the time it would take him to grab her. If I could just get the lock undone... "Thomas!" She screeched, "Kill her!"

"No, my love, let us leave this place and she won't bother us. Let's go home." He was within grabbing distance of her now and flicked his eyes between us over and over again, playing scenarios out in his head.

"No!"

It happened so fast. He reached for her and she hit him with the back of her hand with unnatural force, snarling and screaming at him then she turned to fling herself at me. I screamed too, scrambling for the back door but crashing to the floor as Monique grabbed my ankle. Pain radiated through my shoulder, combining with the ache from the stairs. I moaned, seeing stars, but quickly refocused, kicking at and screaming at the creature trying to crawl its way up my body. We slid along the brick floor as the blood from my back and her face combined in our skirmish.

"Thomas! Thomas please!" I cried out in fear, slamming my forearm into her neck, struggling to keep her away from my face. She knew biting me wouldn't do it. She couldn't change me, she'd have to kill me with her bare hands and she was determined enough to shred me into pieces. I knew as my strength wavered in my arm, adrenaline far past spent, that this was how I died. This was the end.

34
THOMAS

The room exploded in seconds. One moment I thought Bels might get out the back door and I could grab for Monique to contain her until Yusuf arrived, and the next Monique was snarling and snapping at Bels' throat as I held my head, trying to steady myself from the impact of her backhand.

"Thomas! Thomas please!" Annabel screeched, the fear in her voice causing me physical pain.

"Bels!" I roared as I flew across the space to them, grabbing Monique and throwing her, her body smashing into the island, splintering the butcher block as if a boulder had hit it instead of a small female.

I shoved Annabel behind me, her shaking hands clutching at my shirt as I crouched defensively, prepared to lunge at Monique if she dared head back this way.

"Thomas, if she leaves she will just come back. She'll keep coming back - she's sick." Annabel's usual confident tone wobbled with fear while she spoke into my back. "What do we do? What can we do? You can't let her leave."

"She's not going anywhere, *mon coeur*, I swear it." I ran my hand over her leg behind me, attempting to ease her nerves.

Monique unfolded herself from the rubble. Her leg was bent the wrong way and a piece of her forearm had punctured her skin.

"How is she still moving?" Annabel whispered in disbelief and my blood chilled at the site of a corpse slogging its way back to us. If Monique was this far gone, it meant it was too late.

I pushed her back toward the back door, every instinct in me insisting that I remove her from danger, "Bels, you need to get out of here."

Her fingers dug deeper into my shirt, pulling me into her front, "she can't turn me, she can turn you - let me-"

"My love, she is the monster under the bed. I will not-" I roared, Monique's razor-like nails digging into my calf and ripping into my skin with the delicacy of a rusted steak knife. The jagged marks bled profusely and the pain was so blinding that my vision wavered.

"Get off of him!" I could hear Annabel screaming and felt her moving under me like she was kicking in desperation, "Please, leave him alone!"

"He is mine. He is mine!" The creature screeched. She was no longer Monique, no longer the woman I'd loved, not even the woman I'd tolerated for Yusuf's sake. This was the demon depicted in Hollywood and literature. This was death wrapped in festering flesh. She was a virus with the sole mission of destroying any semblance of humanity in hopes of reclaiming it as her own. With inhumane strength, she grabbed my thigh and threw me over her head, smashing me into the floor on her other side.

"Don't touch her!" I spoke weakly, feeling a sharp pain in my side, and ran my hand over it, seeing it covered in my blood when I pulled it away. I hissed, feeling a piece of the butcher block embedded into my side.

"As you wish, Thomas. I will not touch her. I will touch you instead." She lunged on top of me, gnashing her teeth and despite my best efforts to remove her from me, her claws dug into my neck and when I reached up to remove them, I was crushed against her mouth, fangs digging into me and branding my skin. I screamed. The venom of the undead made my blood boil and my eyes rolled back in my head. Somewhere in the distance, I heard Bels. I heard the terror and heartbreak ripping from the depths of her heart. My arms sprawled out as my power left my body, oozing away like my life source.

"I will kill her anyway, you must know this." Monique's words burned against the holes in my neck, "and it will be all your fault. We could have left together. We could have started over."

I gasped, feeling weak in a way I hadn't experienced in hundreds of years, "you started this, Mo. You left me. You...you ended us. You didn't need to come back."

"Of course, I'd come back for you. I will always come back for you, we were promised forever. We were bonded," She planted a soft kiss on the bite, her saliva beginning to close the wound.

My peripherals began to fade into a black vignette and the world went out of focus entirely. I felt her weight leave my body, and I heard her say something, but could not decipher it. I tried to will myself to move, to save the little witch who'd only barely forgiven me. I wasn't ready for it to be done when our story had barely begun. I wasn't ready to go yet.

I allowed my body to fall toward where I heard Annabel screaming and the animalistic snarls in the distance. The pain in my side worsened and I yanked at the embedded wood, hissing in pain as I removed an eight-inch slice of wood that had been shattered off the counter with an edge sharp enough to puncture my skin.

I examined it blearily as if it were a magic wand floating in front of me, beckoning to me to use it. My brain was slow, too slow, and I tried to decipher what my mind was telling me to do.

"Tommy! Tommy, please!" Bels' scream pulled the thread between us tight and my head cleared momentarily to find her. She was on the floor, struggling to keep the beast away from her. I looked between the only two women who had owned my heart and the shard of wood in my hand.

"I'm sorry, *amour*. I'm sorry," I whispered reverently and flung myself with the last bit of strength I had in me, collapsing atop Monique's back, feeling the white blonde hair against my face as I had each night for over 200 years and felt a single tear escape my enflamed body as I slammed the wood into her chest. She froze instantly and I rolled off them exhausted and burning into a puddle of blood.

"Monique! No!" Yusuf appeared out of nowhere, howling at the back door, banging against it, unable to enter without invitation, "Monique! You killed her! You killed her!"

I gasped like a fish out of water before two perfect green eyes floated above my face, "Tommy. Oh my god, Tommy. Where is it, where -"

"ANNABEL LET ME IN!" The desperation in Yusuf's voice must have torn at Annabel's heart because she responded immediately.

"Yusuf please come in!" She shouted at him while patting my face and neck, looking for each and every injury, "Yusuf, please help me! Help!" Warm, wet drops fell against my skin, and somewhere far away, I felt lips touch against mine. "Yus, you have to help me save him!"

My head fell to the side and I saw them, my two life partners, one still in death and the other holding her, wailing at the shattering of their bond. The sobs and howls filled the home, creating a soundtrack to the heartbreak. Monique's eyes were lifeless, seeing nothing even as they looked at me. None of this was supposed to happen.

"Bels," I gasped, "Bels..."

"I'm here! I'm here, Tommy. I'm right here." Her soft hands cupped my face, "I'm here."

"You need to leave. You need to go."

"What? No, no, you're hurt, let me fix it."

"Bels, she bit me. I've been bit. You need to go, you need to run. Yusuf needs to kill me. I won't change. I won't become that monster."

"Yusuf!" She shouted, "Yus, he's been bit! What do I do?!"

He didn't answer her, lost in the grief of rocking his deceased lover.

"I'm not going to let you fucking die, Tommy. I say no, and I'm the fucking boss. You're not just going to turn into a monster in front of my eyes."

I gave her a sad smile, swallowing some of the burning in my throat, "It will be fast. Just a poof and I'll be gone. I love you, Annabel."

"Shut the fuck up, Thomas! You're not going to die. You don't get to poof!"

I reached up with arms heavier than lead, pushing her hair out of her face, "tell me you love me too, amour. Let it be the last thing you tell me. Please don't let you telling me to shut the fuck up be the last words I hear from your beautiful voice."

She laughed while she sobbed. "Wait. Wait. No! Thomas! Thomas hold on."

I felt cold as she climbed away from me, leaving me in a pool of blood, the burning was tapering off. I knew a bite from an undead turned one faster than the slow progression of unbalance as Monique had experienced, but I thought I would have had more time. I thought there could have been more time to say goodbye. My eyes closed slowly and my body turned as still as stone. I could only pray that my beautiful Annabel would be gone when I awoke in the next phase of my life.

35
ANNABEL

My heart broke at the sight of Yusuf sobbing into Monique's straw-textured hair. I couldn't imagine the heartbreak of losing someone that you'd thought would live forever. They had had multiple lifetimes of love and it had all ended on my kitchen floor. Such a story deserved a better ending than that, but I didn't have time to grieve alongside him. I wasn't ready to let my love story end before it'd even begun.

I scrambled across the kitchen, slipping on the blood coating the brick and my uneven footing only drew attention to the wounds I'd acquired. My back burned where her nails had clawed at me, and I had numerous contusions on my shoulders, hips, and legs. She should have bitten me. I would have made it through a bite, and I swore on any magic I had in me, Thomas would too.

I dug through my purse on the counter, pulled out the book and supplies my mothers had sent home with me, and rushed back to his side, laying his head in my lap, knowing I had to act quickly. If he woke up from the stone-like state without healing, it would be too late. I immediately took the knife which had been blessed and cut the bite wound off his skin as if I were skinning an apple, then I packed about

278

four times more comfrey poultice on it as was needed. I held it with my hands, pressing it into the new wound, begging the toxins to pull back out as they had done for me.

"Please, please, Thomas you can't go yet. There are bigger players at work here. You kept saying there are bigger players...They need to make their move," I made an unattractive snort as I tried to reign in my snot and feelings, "Please, love. I forgive you. I won't fight with you. I will accept your apology and I will make this better. Any dangers we face we can do it together - we can be together. Just come back. Someone has to cook for me and I need you to teach me all the naughty french words you promised." I laid my head on his chest, pressing harder against the wound, feeling a slime-like substance ooze between my fingers. I prayed to anything that was listening that this plant could save him. It was so much faith to put in a plant.

"Here. Give me the knife." I jumped, having almost forgotten that Yusuf was here but nodded my head toward the pile, not even caring if he was going to murder me at that point; let him have his pound of flesh if that's what he needed.

I watched with watery eyes as he strategically placed small lacerations in the creases of Thomas' elbows and on the tops of his feet, and packed comfrey into each wound, wrapping each with the roll of gauze I'd gotten from my purse. He sighed, curling in on himself and resigned that he might lose both of his lovers in one night.

"I'm so sorry, Yusuf, but it was too late. There was no bringing her back."

"I know," He sniffled, "that doesn't make breaking the bond hurt any less."

"I'm so sorry."

"Well, you'd know, right? I'm sure your bond is in tatters right now too."

We pressed our hands against all of Thomas' wounds and I breathed slightly easier as each gauze strip began to seep with the same venomous slime.

"I told him there was no bond," I spoke softly, "and yet he still told me he loved me. I don't feel like a bond is breaking - maybe this is all a farce. Maybe we just cared for each other without the bond he swore was there."

"Of course, he loves you, Annabel. He loves you with a ferocity he never showed either of us. You are fated to be together- that is why your heart hurts as bad as it does right now. That's the bond."

My eyes overflowed with tears and a sob escaped while I wiped my face on my sleeve, not removing my hands from his wounds for a moment. "Stupid fucking bond. It's like I don't get a say in my own life when it comes to him. He makes all these awful decisions and I'm just stuck loving him no matter what? Will I be stuck loving him forever even if he's gone? What if he's changed? How will we know if this works? When will he come back? I'm...I'm new to all of this."

He gave me a sad smile, "I know, darling girl. We can only wait. He will either wake up and be okay, or he will kill us both."

"Jesus, you're just about as good at comforting as he is, no wonder you got along for so long," I laughed.

Yusuf leaned against the island cabinets and closed his eyes, keeping his hands pressing into Thomas' feet. "Has he told you about how horrifically he got sick on the ship to America?"

"The ship? Oh god, I forget how old he is sometimes."

He chuckled, "It was horrible. We were supposed to be these big, bad, monsters - or at least that's what the French had painted us as before we fled, and there was the baby of us, only a few decades old, vomiting over the side of the ship for weeks. He claimed the sailors tasted awful and that was why he was losing weight, he has always been a food snob, but it was really because he couldn't handle seasickness. I don't think we ever got him on a boat after that. He didn't even return to Paris until planes were invented."

Thomas groaned beneath my hands and I used a clean towel to dab the slime away from the poultices, hopeful that the response meant it was working. "Until planes were invented...do you have any idea how insane that sounds to me? I'm not even thirty. My life has been made up of thrilling moments like watching terrorist attacks live on TV or being delighted when the MySpace servers were wiped from the internet, and yes I'm aware it's strange those are two defining moments in my life. I didn't flee a revolution and then wait for fucking planes to be invented." I sighed, "I don't know what he could possibly see in me when he's lived through so much and I had my first kiss only fifteen years ago."

"You are a green witch, you are goddess blessed."

"That means nothing to me. I have no idea how any of this works."

"Then how exciting that you'll have him to teach you."

I lifted one hand to sweep a piece of Thomas' perfectly shiny hair off his lifeless face. "Please, please, please, let me keep him." I placed my forehead against his, "I'm not done with him yet."

"I wasn't done with her yet either," He spoke softly, heartbreak lacing every word, "Over 200 years...tens of thousands of nights together, and he told me, he said to my face that if she touched you that he would kill her. He knew how this would end. He knew who he loved more."

"He tried to get her to leave, Yusuf. He offered to leave me and return with her to you. I swear, he didn't want to hurt you like this."

Yusuf scoffed, "No, you'll find he never intentionally hurts anyone, but he's quite good at unintentionally achieving the same result. He has a talent for being quite the dick."

That made me laugh, "It's okay, I do too. Must be why we're made for each other." I grimaced, the pain from my injuries amplifying as the adrenaline began to wane. I laid my head on his chest, keeping pressure on his neck, "there's really nothing I can do but wait?"

Yusuf nodded and smoothed my hair, "yes, Annabel, but you'll find in your life with an immortal that we have incredible patience. We can wait forever for the good moments to come."

I smiled, "he's told me something similar before." I sighed, acknowledging the creature across the kitchen who'd tried to kill me several times, "What do we do with Monique? It's not like I can call the police."

"No. We'll have to call your mothers to lead the ceremony. I guess you're getting a little bit of Green Witch training this evening as well, you'll get to witness how we say goodbye."

I smiled sadly at the handsome man with olive skin and coarse black hair who was now staring down an empty and unfamiliar eternity, "Thank you for sitting with me. Thank you for talking to me."

He rubbed my shoulder, "I don't know what to do next either, Annabel. We'll both just have to do our best to keep the love alive even if we have to do it alone."

"But I don't want to do it alone." The man I knew was the love of my life was still as death. His cold head was heavy in my lap, his normal playfulness trapped within a frozen body. "A life without him would be like a life without the sun. I need him."

"I've told him many times to listen to me, as I am far older and wiser than him, and I will tell you the same. Hear my words and always remember, Annabel, that we Others will always thrive in the darkness the Goddess provides us."

I sniffed, trying to manage the uncontrollable feeling of loss ripping its way through my system, and released the pressure on Thomas' neck to wipe off my hands and call my mothers.

"Hi darling, you didn't come over tonight - you head back home?"

"Mama...I've got a dead vampire in my kitchen," My words came out between sobs, "I need help. I need you to come-"

"Sweetie is Thomas okay? Did he hurt you?"

"No, he saved me but she bit him and he killed her and -"

"Lord, the CIA agent in charge of listening to your phone calls is getting an earful of your Halloween novel, isn't he? Don't give him any spoilers!"

I chuckled painfully at her paranoia and smoothed Thomas' hair, noticing the shine was leaving his perfect wavy locks.

"I need you now, Mama. You and Mom."

"Already on our way sweet girl. We will be there in a moment. Love you."

"Love you too."

It seemed to be only seconds later when my moms came through the front door, nervously calling for me and heading into the kitchen, but it could have been an hour. I'd lost all track of time holding Thomas against me, desperately seeking access to our circuit where our shared emotions lived.

"Oh, Bels!" My mom rushed to me, and quickly assessed Thomas, "how long has he been out for?"

Wiping my nose on the shoulder of my shirt I shook my head, "I don't even know at this point, it all happened so fast."

"Deirdre I think this is the more pressing issue, we need to perform the rights. We need to do it before it's too late and there's none of her left to dedicate back to the balance."

"What? But what about Thomas? I need you to help me and I need - fuck her! Sorry, Yusuf, but fuck her! It's too late for her, what about him?"

Yus had taken up residence right next to Monique, holding her feet in his lap, running his hand up and down the long expanses of her legs.

"You've got him, darling. Just, let us do this. It is our responsibility to restore the balance of the earth" My mom soothed me and headed over to my Mama, the two of them having a soft-spoken conversation, glancing around at the remnants of the night's battle. My landlord was going to kill me.

Together, they sat on either side of Monique's unmoving body, my Mama turning to Yusuf sympathetically, "It's time to say goodbye. We've got to let her go."

He kissed Monique's hand a final time and nodded while whispering to her body in a language I didn't understand. With a heartbroken nod, he slid back to watch my mothers help his beloved move on.

Across her body, they held hands and closed their eyes. "Bels, we are going to seal ourselves into a shield, we won't be able to stop until her body is gone. You're going to be on your own, do you understand? We won't be able to hear you or speak to you during the rights."

"It won't hurt you too, will it?"

"No, Bels, this is our gift. You stay with your love." My mom smiled gently and they began a chant in monotonous, quiet voices. I felt the air change when their voices became muted. They had sealed themselves into their own space, much like they'd done at their house when Thomas came to see me.

"I guess you're not going to get trained after all, eh little witch? Your kind are so secretive about what happens at the end," Yusuf wiped his nose.

"I guess not." I ran my fingers absentmindedly through Thomas' hair, continuing to try and push feelings of love through the stone-like stillness of his body, my heart breaking as they bounced off the place where I used to feel his mind. "There's no way I'd rather be in there than right here though. I'm not leaving him."

I glanced up and saw my moms still kneeling, holding one hand and repeating something together, while my mom began to squeeze singular drops of some kind of liquid over the top half of Monique's body, before passing it to my mama who did the bottom half. The air inside the bubble darkened as the water droplets began to smoke.

I continued to caress Thomas' hair as I leaned against the cabinets and watched the ceremony, which was becoming more and more obscured by the minute. It wasn't long at all before I couldn't see my moms at all through the swirls of smoke and energy encased within.

My sorrow was spiraling the longer Thomas took to open his eyes. Being unable to access his mind like we'd done so freely before was tightening my lungs and throat and drowning me. I felt things too largely, too extremely, and I had nowhere to put them with him unresponsive. It felt like the thread between us was stretching to an uncomfortable tension, as if my soul was tied to a medieval rack, and each minute he was gone tightened the crank a little more.

"Tommy I don't have a list for this," I whispered into the quiet kitchen. It looked like chaos was ensuing inside the shield, but outside of it, my home felt like a graveyard. There was that unsettling stillness to the quiet when a tornado of magic was only a couple of yards away. "I'm not sure how to break this down into the next steps, even if I had my sticky notes, I wouldn't know what to write down first - I don't know how to fix this."

Seemingly out of nowhere, a heaviness overtook me, and my breaths became short, I felt like I was about to be launched into a panic attack while simultaneously being crushed. Searing pain ripped from my chest and I gasped, tears beginning to flow at an alarming rate almost instantaneously compared to the despondent trickle they'd been a moment before.

"Yusuf," My voice was wobbling, but I needed someone and I was alone except for my lover's ex-husband. "Yusuf, I need help." I carefully put Thomas' head down on the floor, feeling my body begin to tremble.

"What is going on, Annabel?" He had appeared by my side without being seen, "Fuck, what is going on?"

"Everything hurts," I sobbed, "Everything-" a scream ripped from my body and my eyes slammed shut.

"Shit - your bond is breaking, Annabel, we're going to lose him. We need to kill him before he turns and enters a frenzy."

"This is - Yusuf! It feels like I'm dying," I whimpered, feeling as though my heart was being ripped in two, half turning to ashes while the other was engulfed in flames, "Yusuf, help me."

Yusuf got up from the floor and banged on the wall of the shield, "You must stop! Annabel needs you!"

"They can't hear you. They said they couldn't stop," I gasped, my limbs beginning to shake and my pulse pounded, "Is he dying Yus? Is he - he can't-"

"I'm so sorry Annabel." He soothed mournfully, "the pain will pass once he's gone. You're just feeling the break. I promise the pain will stop."

"If he's gone then he's Undead and he doesn't want that!" I unsteadily began to unwrap the comfrey poultices, seeing that they were indeed draining the venom out of his bloodstream, "why isn't the comfrey working!"

"I don't know, chérie. I'm so sorry. If I end him now, the pain will stop, do you want the pain to stop now?"

I scrambled to my purse to see if I had any more fresh poultice inside of it, but hissed as a piece of butcherblock slid through the skin of my palm. Hissing I drew it to my mouth to suck on it, trying to soothe the pain, and froze as an idea came to me.

"We are not killing him, Yusuf. Use me. I'm a green witch!"

"Yes..."

"How do we handfeast? How do I... tell me! Now!"

"Bels, if you handfeast with Thomas he may pass on anyway-there's no guarantee that it will fix anything and then you'll just have to feel the bond break all over again, and potentially have to end him when he's awake and dangerous. The first feeding frenzy is terribly dangerous."

"My blood is resistant to venom. My moms said that the blood in his veins is different than the blood that made him. If my blood is in him, maybe it can push the rest of the venom out, please, I need to try."

"Annabel, it's like marriage you can't just-"

"We are bonded without the fucking handfeast anyway! Tell me how to solidify it so I can save him you stupid bird!"

He nodded, resigned, and came to sit with me, picking up and handing me the knife, "He is still as stone, I don't know if it will work as well without him drinking it into his mouth, I've never seen it done like this"

Another flash of burning pain hit me and I wailed, "I don't care! Tell me what to do."

"Cut your wrist and cut his. Usually, it's biting but -"

"I don't care what I'd usually do, tell me what to do now." The pain was almost debilitating as it ate away at my soul.

"Cut the wrists, declare your intentions, drink each other's blood, then press your wrists together for me to tie them as one to bind them."

I slid the knife unsteadily across my wrist, enough to allow a bead of blood to appear but not enough to cause permanent damage, and I tried to cut Thomas' but the knife wouldn't penetrate his skin in his state.

"Yus, I need you to cut him, please. I can't get it, I need your help."

He chuckled, "never thought I'd lose them both and then marry one off..." he spoke more softly, low enough that I couldn't hear exactly what he was saying, and easily slid the knife across Thomas' wrist with his vampire strength. "Now, Bels, declare your feelings and intentions and then draw a mouthful of his blood into you."

Trembling, I held onto his forearm, "Thomas, I need you to come back. It's not November yet and you owe me a CGI baby and a happily ever after."

"Intentions, Bels, not jokes, this is permanent."

I wept, "I don't do serious!"

"Well do it now!" He snapped at me.

"Thomas, I want to love you. I want our bond. I want to live a boring life with you by my side. I want to drive you crazy, I want to live a life that is so combined that no one will be able to tell where I end and you begin. I want to feel what you already knew. I want what you were promising me but my mortal heart was too stubborn to accept. Please come back and live that life with me. I want you." I looked up at Yusuf and he nodded, "I want to look into my eternity and know that you'll be beside me. I want our love to be the never ending cup you said you felt." Lowering my voice and leaning my forehead against his, I whispered, "I love you, Thomas Corbin. I promise I'll be yours if you'll be mine."

I leaned over, unable to move his frozen arm, and prepared myself for what I expected to be the most disgusting moment of my life. I wasn't a vampire, I didn't want to eat blood, fuck, Tommy was a vampire and even he didn't like biting people, but when I leaned down, kissing his wrist and opening my lips to drink in his lifeforce, it felt like the most natural thing in the world.

He tasted like sweet wine and rainy days with gothic books. He tasted like an embrace. He tasted like mine. I easily pulled a mouthful before kissing his wrist again.

"Now try and get some in his mouth," Yusuf guided me. I sat up on my knees and pulled his bottom lip down, thankful that his mouth was relaxed and we wouldn't have to pry his jaw open.

"He can't speak his intentions," I whined, desperation filled me for us both. I was feeling this awake, what if this was torturing him and he couldn't even voice the pain?

"Do you know them?"

"Yes. It all boils down to him loving me and claiming I was his. He knew and he told me freely," I placed my wrist between his lips, squeezing painfully so blood would drip into his mouth and hopefully down his throat.

"Now come place your wrist against his, Annabel." Yusuf grabbed another gauze wrap and after placing our bleeding wrists together he began to wrap them, speaking as he tightened and tied the gauze. "These two beings, Witch, Annabel Williams, and Vampire, Thomas Corbin, vow to share and ease each other's pain. To celebrate and promote each other's joy, and to nurture, cherish, and rejoice in their bond. By the binding of their blood in a knot, so shall these beings tie themselves to each other for as long as their love will carry them in this life. As your hands are now bound together, so shall your lives and minds be bound as one."

'There it is done." He sighed and sat back on his ankles, "You are bound."

"When will the pain stop?" each breath I took was a chore, my head was spinning from hyperventilating for so long.

"When he crosses back to this side. We can only wait." He looked back at the shield which was now encased in solid darkness and a tear slid down his cheek. He sighed, wiping it away, and looked back at me, "do you want me to slip you out of the knot?"

"No," I said hurriedly, "No, I'm going to keep us joined until he wakes up."

Yusuf nodded, "I am going to wait for your mothers to finish and then I'm going to be gone Bels. Take care of him for me?"

"As if our blood is one." I nodded, my breathing shallow and my body out of adrenaline. I situated my body next to Thomas on the ground, our joint hands by his side and my body on his as if I could heal him by touch. I could only hope that my blood would do what the poultice couldn't. Hope was all I had. Hope, and anti-vampire blood. Laying my head on his chest, I tried to slow my breathing to a deliberate pace, already feeling more peaceful just from touching him like that. "I need to rest, Yusuf, I can't keep my eyes open."

"Rest and heal, Annabel, I will not leave you until Monique is gone and your mothers return. I will watch over you."

I kissed Thomas' cheek, still frozen in time, and nuzzled his permanent stubble, "Thank you, Yusuf." My eyes drifted closed, focusing only on pushing my love and life through the bond, and into his body to bring him back. If losing him felt like I was going to die, I had no doubt in my mind that he was mine. He was mine, and I was, as expected, too stubborn for my own good to listen to his heartfelt pleas earlier in the week. I wanted to show him that he was right and that we were one. I wanted him to open his eyes and see our wrists bound together. I wanted him back.

In the darkness, I felt myself sinking, sliding into unconsciousness while my love for him poked and prodded at his mind like a tendril, seeking any weak point in his stone. *Come back, come back, come back.*

Then, suddenly, I was able to take a deep breath. The lungful of air made my mind swim and my body melt against his. It was in the last second before unconsciousness when my tendril of love began to retreat back to me so I could sleep, that I felt it - a chasing feeling after my life force. Then, I felt him grab onto it from the other side and welcome me into a lover's embrace.

"Bels?"

EPILOGUE

“Are you certain *mon coeur*? It's Halloween, I'm not supposed to go out, it's too easy to be exposed.”

I scoffed, popping the overdramatic collar of the Dracula costume I insisted he wear, “Halloween is my favorite holiday, Tommy, you're just going to have to get used to taking the risk. Besides, the whole 'it's too easy to be exposed' thing is stupid, if anything, shouldn't you blend in better on Halloween?”

“Bels, it's not for us and it...how you say, plays into harmful stereotypes.” He gestured at the ridiculous costume, “Look at this. How many vampires have you met that wear this?”

I shrugged and added a small skull pin to his red cravat, “None, but you haven't taken me to Eastern Europe yet.” I grinned up at him and placed a soft kiss against his lips, rubbing my thumb against the ragged silver scar on his neck.

“Why did I have to be fated to such a stubborn mortal?” He grumbled and huffed, but I knew he was excited to go on the Bar Crawl with us. “Also, that dress is too much, that stupid tall man won't be able to keep his eyes off you.”

"Trae," I said firmly, "doesn't matter to me. Besides someone has to be your Mina."

"Trae better not matter. Silly tall man-"

"He's a basketball player. They're tall. Don't feel inferior because you're shorter than him."

"I am not-" I arched a brow at him and he stopped his rant mid-sentence.

"I post myself less dressed than this on the internet on a daily basis. Don't be going all caveman on me now."

He grumbled something in French that I didn't understand as the doorbell rang and I patted his chest, heading to answer it.

"If you let us stay home I will fuck you all night! Straight into the mattress!" He called after me and I laughed.

"You'll do that anyway. Come on, we're living a little." I opened the door to the most voluptuous and slutty Scooby Doo I'd ever seen, and a perfectly lanky Shaggy.

"Slutty Scooby! I love it!" I grinned and pulled Shannon into a hug, holding her close for a moment longer than usual. After almost losing Thomas, I found myself offering affection more freely to those I cared about. I released her and gave Trae a side hug, "Hey Shaggy."

Shannon grinned, "Hi Bels, come on, I need to get hammered and celebrate that Jake has two sugar-high kids tonight while I get to go out and enjoy my evening."

Thomas chuckled, embracing Shannon too, "Did the girls have a good Halloween?"

"Oh yeah, Annie was perfectly at home as a Queen and Emily was a very reasonable Unicorn. Even let Annie pretend to ride her a few times."

I laughed, imagining Annie, who had always been the bossy one, manipulating her little sister into thinking that was somehow a great idea. "Did they get a lot of candy?"

"Oh yeah, we took them to four different neighborhoods. Jake is in for a terrible weekend." Trae beamed alongside her, rubbing her arm, "Should we go? Looks like the car is just around the corner."

We laughed and joked as we headed out onto the street, noting the few straggling kids out after trick-or-treating hours, and proceeded to drink our way through all five witch-themed bars and breweries that Quaker's Wharf had to offer. After far too much booze, dancing, and laughter, Shannon and Trae disappeared into the night, leaving me and my vamp to wander the streets of the town.

"Thank you for coming out tonight. I know you're a million years old and cranky, but you're going to have to start acting like a thirty-year-old." I wrapped my arm around his waist, leaning into him while I dug through my purse for a concoction that removed hangovers that my Mom had casually slipped me the other day.

"And what do thirty-year-olds do that I don't?" His dark eyes sparkled like the night sky and had taken my breath away so many times in the past few weeks after I thought I'd never see them shine again.

"They make stupid drunk decisions with their girlfriends." I grinned up at him and moaned at the touch of his mouth on mine, drawing his tongue into me, playfully teasing each other and stumbling along the sidewalk.

"Ah, you forget, *amour*, that I can't get drunk. Only you get to blame your decisions on alcohol consumption."

I bit my lip and leaned up to grab his face, pulling it back to me and kissing him again before realizing that we had wandered all the way to the graveyard that backed up to a large plot of woods and then the beach beyond.

"So I get to make enough bad decisions for us both?" I cupped him through his pants and he hissed.

"Annabel, what are you planning my troublesome witch?"

I shrugged, stepping backward away from him, "Just wanting to feel alive."

He arched his thick brow, "and how do you propose we do that *chérie?*"

"Chase me."

"What?" He laughed like I was kidding, "Come on, let's go home."

Shaking my head, I took another step back, *"non, mon corbeau,* you are going to have to catch me if you want me to go home with you."

"I can see in the dark better than you and the bond will lead me to you anyway, it's not a fair chase."

"See how much I care, Frenchie. Sing yourself a pretty song and then come and get me."

"Annabel, you're not going to like what happens when I catch you -"

"Says who? Come get me, bird boy!" I squealed, laughing and stumbling through the cemetery gate, weaving my way through the stones as the moon cast ominous shadows behind each one. It had rained that afternoon, like most fall days, and it made the moonlight reflect brightly off the asphalt and rocks, lighting my way enough that I didn't feel entirely like I was running in the dark, but the shadows did make it feel slightly like I was running in that scene in Snow White where the trees are attacking her. If I wasn't careful, I would crack my neck. At least I knew he would find me if I hurt myself.

My breaths were coming hard enough that they created puffs of fog in front of me. It had been getting progressively colder and it was obvious that winter was coming. I could only hope that he'd fuck me against a tree or let me be on top so I wouldn't freeze to death in the wet leaves. He would have to fuck me when he found me - that was the point of the game, right? I reached the trees right as I heard the flap of giant wings behind me and I squealed.

"Shapeshifting is cheating!" I yelled darting deeper into the woods, each stick making horrifically loud snaps as I stepped on them, and they scratched up my calves as I lifted my cheap red velour dress so I wouldn't trip. A shadow passed overhead and he materialized in front of me.

Thomas stood tall and grinned, "You said no such thing. That wasn't in the rules."

I screamed and turned around as fast as I could, slipping against the damp ground and propelling myself off of each tree that I reached. I had to climb hastily over several fallen trunks and I knew he was still too close for me to slow down for the obstacles, it would probably be faster to run around things.

"Annabel," His voice was song-like in the dark, coming from no obvious direction and making goosebumps erupt over my skin. Hell, he could have been in a tree for all I knew, "*Mon coeur*, I will always catch you... if you stop running I might just reward you."

I snorted and made a sharp left, bolting toward what I thought would be the beach, I knew it was a few acres between the cemetery and the beach, so I should have been able to find it easily. Unfortunately, while the moon had lit up the cemetery fairly well, the trees obscured a lot more light making everything look pretty similar and there weren't a lot of identifying land-marks among the dark silhouettes. I paused momentarily, and couldn't hear him behind me at all. I took off again knowing that if he hadn't caught me yet, it was only because he didn't want to yet. I looked over my shoulder again, hoping to see him to gauge our distance, but the moment of distraction cost me, my foot clipping on a root and I went flying through the air, almost landing on my face when a firm pair of hands caught me out of nowhere.

"Careful *chérie*, if you break your face we won't get to play your game."

I squeaked, "Where did you come from?!"

He turned me around and smacked my ass, "Run, little witch." He evaporated into a mass of black bird again, making my heart nearly beat out of my chest.

I booked it in the direction I'd been going, still wanting to get to the beach instead of weaving through the trees. I knew I'd be more in the open, but at least I wouldn't trip on a tree root again. I hauled myself up a hill, feeling my breath getting short and knowing that I would need a break soon. A fat girl break meant that I needed to find some-where to hide.

I took a deep breath before cresting the hill and cursing; I'd been going the wrong way, I was back at the cemetery. I risked a glance around and didn't see the shadow of his raven, so I sprinted to the ancient sycamore tree to rest in its shadow.

I could hear nothing except the pounding of my heart, thudding in my ears. I swore it had to have been loud enough to alert him I was there, as if it were the *Tell-Tale Heart* from Poe's writings, torturing the narrator each night from beneath the floorboards. *Would a madman have been so wise as this?* I was mad. I had to be. I invited a predator to chase me, and deeper in my madness, I couldn't wait for him to catch me. *I smiled - for what had I to fear?*

"Boo," His voice came from above me and I jumped at the sight of him sitting on a tall branch of the tree as if he had landed there as his raven before shifting.

I squeaked and began to run, only for his body slam against my back, making us to slide down the hill in a smear of mud and rolling us in the air so we landed on his back instead of mine.

"I win," he grinned, "what do I get for my prize?"

"Me." I smiled back, my heart still pounding from the adrenaline, and my hair curtaining us, "Always me."

He untied his ridiculous cape, and rolled me onto it, protecting me from the damp ground. "You are the greatest prize in the world, *amour*. But I'm afraid you'll have to pay for your recklessness. Who runs through a cemetery on Halloween night?"

"Someone who isn't afraid of the dark, I suppose."

He raised his brows and hummed in amusement, leaning down to leave a trail of kisses down my neck and onto my bust, nipping the top curve of my chest which was attempting to escape from my costume. He easily ripped it open, the flimsy seam in the front not standing a chance against his strength, and he groaned in appreciation at the black lingerie I'd selected for the evening.

"You are the most beautiful woman I have ever seen." He worshiped me through the lace, kissing, licking, and biting my nipples while rubbing the lace into my sensitive skin.

"He says looking at my boobs and not at me," I teased.

"I could say it to something else if you prefer, Bels." He rucked up my skirt, feeling my bare legs that had been scraped up and covered in mud. When he reached the apex of my thighs he groaned, "you went to five bars with no panties on? You naughty witch."

I shrugged, "My vampire mate would never have let anyone close enough to try anything."

"All the same," he rumbled, lowering his head and pulling the skirt back over his head to keep my legs warm. He dug his fingers into the flesh of my inner thighs, spreading me, and placed kisses toward his goal. I looked above me at the moon, thanking the goddess that this male was still there with me, and moaned when the warmth of his tongue dove into my slit.

He lapped at my cunt, sucking and nibbling at the sensitive nerve endings making me tremble and roll my hips against his face.

"Fuck, Tommy, right there, don't stop." I reached down to press his head into me through my dress, but couldn't get a grip on his hair through the cheap fabric, "Tommy." I groaned, pushing myself up into him since pushing him down wouldn't work.

He took long, lingering licks from ass to clit, worshipping each part of me equally with precision and familiarity. When he placed his hands back on my bare thighs and I felt the gentle caress of him against my mind, I welcomed him in. I poured the love and fear and appreciation I'd felt since the night I thought I lost him, letting it cascade over him. I poured my love into him like the bottomless vessel he considered me to be, but he fed me right back, ensuring that I wouldn't empty, connecting me to his lust and adoration. If there were a lack of words to explain the depth of feeling we'd accepted for each other, they were easily found in the mixing currents of our emotions, creating a circuit between us, charged and ready for whatever was coming.

My core tightened and my chest hollowed as I lost my breath, heading closer to completion, knowing he would never leave me alone on the other side of a scene again. Using my legs on his shoulders, I tried to tighten him against me, my body shook at the sucking sensation in exactly the right place. As I was about to tumble into the darkness we both craved, he froze and I whimpered like a wanton romance character.

"Please," I begged, "I'm so close."

He came out from under my skirt, pulling his cock free from his black trousers, and notched himself at my entrance, "If you'd stopped running you would have gotten to finish in my mouth, letting me lap up every last drop of your desire, however, since you lost the game, you will scream as you cum on my cock."

I chuckled breathlessly, "man, what a lose-lose situation." I gasped as he slammed himself into me fully and stilled, "fuck!"

"Mmmm, I thought I wanted to see your face as you writhed and begged, but I think I want to fuck you so hard that can't move tomorrow. Then I can spend all day fucking you any way I'd like- every way I'd like, while you're trapped in our bed."

"Promises, promises." I groaned, rotating my hips against him, begging him to begin moving. He pulled out leaving me feeling hollow and wanting and quickly flipped me to my hands and knees, throwing my skirt up over my ass, and reentered me, reaching forward to wrap his fist around my hair.

"Hush, *mon couer*, and cum for me." He slammed into me over and over again, rubbing perfectly against the spongey tissue of my g-spot, tightening me with forceful thrusts powerful enough to move me along the slippery grass on his cape, only to be dragged back by the hold he had on my hair.

I felt my inner walls become plump, short circuiting my brain as the tissues engorged until he raked past it one last time, making me release a stream of my cum around his cock with a scream.

"Yes, just like that, my good little witch. No one makes a mess like you do."

I whimpered knowing full well that another orgasm wasn't far off, once I came like that, the slightest breeze could tip me over the edge again. Thomas was unrelenting in his pace and pushed the severity of his lust through the bond. I felt how hard I was making him and how difficult it was for him to keep going and not cum at the sight of my ass jiggling while I greedily took every inch of him.

"Give me another one before I cum in your mouth amour. One more."

He pushed in and froze, my pussy clamping down on him and trying to squeeze him out of my channel. The size of him inside of me could make me cum without him moving when I was this sensitive.

"Oh god, move, fuck me, shit!" I groaned, trembling beneath him.

"No, my witch, you fuck me. Bounce your pretty little cunt on my cock. Let me see you move."

I moaned as I took control, pushing and pulling myself against his length, my insides preparing for another mind blowing orgasm that I was trying to put off. I knew my body, and I knew if I could hold out only a few moments more, the sensation wouldn't be as intense but it would be just as good.

"None of that, Bels. When I tell you to cum for me, you cum for me," He ordered, pushing his hand under our joining and rubbing ferociously at my clitoris. I screamed again, my knees buckling and my ass lifting higher as I pulsated around him, seeing stars behind my closed eyes, hearing just how wet I was from my desire as he continued to claim his prize.

I whimpered at the aftershocks of my orgasms until Thomas slapped my ass, "Up, my love." standing and hauled me to my knees in front of him. I opened my mouth and gratefully took every ounce of pleasure I'd given him back. Sucking him down, cleaning off his cock with my tongue and moaning at the combination of our flavors.

"Fuck, Annabel. So damnsed good," He smoothed my hair lovingly and we looked at each other with his softening length in my mouth. I swallowed once more, releasing him, and opened my mouth to show him that I'd taken every drop.

"Such a filthy little witch." He said, pressing adoration into my mind. He lifted me from the damp ground, laughing quietly at my exposed breasts, "I don't think we can go home with you looking like that."

I leaned into him, drunk off the emotional exchange, and kissed his chest, "No? Not a good look for me?"

"Oh, it is the very best look for you, but it is for my eyes only."

"Yours, and everyone on the internet. Besides, it's Halloween, everyone is out in their underwear" I smirked.

Thomas bent and lifted the cape off the ground, snapping it a few times in attempts of cleaning it off, before tying it around me. It was large enough I was able to close it around my front, covering my exposed bra.

He leaned down once more and kissed me deeply, "I think I could learn to love Halloween."

"Oh yeah, something change your mind?" I grinned into the kiss.

"I got quite the treat."

He wrapped his arm around me, kissing the top of my head and walking us back toward the cemetery entrance. He pulled out his phone to order a car and I leaned against his firm chest, blissed out from sex, and looked into his deep dark eyes, "I love you, Thomas."

He smiled softly, cupping my cheeks and kissing me softly, with an intimacy I never expected when I walked into the Halloween store almost two months ago. "I love you too, Bels. I will always be here to chase you through the darkness."

THE END

ABOUT EMELINE

Emeline Quill is a compulsive consumer and creator of new adult romance. She loves the escapism provided by fiction and has spent the majority of her life avoiding reality by sticking her nose in a book. In fact, she loves books more than she loves pizza - and as a Chicago girl, that's saying something.

When Emeline isn't reading or writing, she is spending time with her family and obnoxious Goldendoodle. Emeline wants to create a world where being the funny fat friend isn't a curse to live in the background, but where the curvy girl gets many happy endings and the happily ever after she deserves.

If you'd like to connect - follow Emeline on various social media platforms or join the mailing list!

ALSO BY EMELINE QUILL

MILLIE CLARE TRILOGY

Amelia Clare was raised to be a chaste young woman of God, but when that is taken from her, Millie must go on a journey of love, loss, self-acceptance and claiming her sexuality. The Millie Clare trilogy follows her from the end of Middle School to Adulthood and is done in a time hop style.

BURNED

ASHES

DIAMONDS - Coming Soon!

QUAKER'S WHARF

Quaker's Wharf is supposed to be the quieter version of Salem and the residents enjoy living just outside of the inflation that the Witch Trial tourists have caused in the neighboring town. Quaker's Wharf has much of the same history and has deep magical roots. Mortals have lived there for hundreds of years, happily raising families and going about their lives - so what happens when the Monsters that go bump in the night come out to play? Quaker's Wharf is a series of interconnected standalone paranormal romances, featuring plus size main characters having spicy relationships with paranormal creatures.

1. The HalloQueen

2. SmashSquatch - Coming Soon!

3. The HellHounds - Coming Soon!

4. The Moth Madam - Coming Soon!